# Dedication

*My Mother's Apprentice* is dedicated to Betty Bergquist, an original Tensie (Darlene) from *Stuck in the Onesies*. She's been such an inspiration to me, not only in writing *My Mother's Apprentice,* but learning how to thrive after losing ones I love and still have a sense of humor. This poem she wrote certainly applies to storing up those memories for when we need them most.

## SUMMER DAY FOUND
### By Betty Bergquist

Gentle breezes, flowing softly
Waft through the leaves of lacy green.
Neighboring gardeners, sleepy insects
Set the stage serene
Sloping lawns with houses perched
Their window boxes glowing
Sun filled laughter, bubbly chatter
Another way of knowing
Days to cherish
Days of feeling, intoxicating, senses reeling
Oh, to store these summer moments
Keep them locked away
And when winter's rains and bareness come
And turn your mood to gray
There you have it, there it is
Your lovely summer day.

# Contents

# Prologue
## 1971

Karen and Ginger were the daughters of Barb and Ellie, ordinary women who lived in extraordinary times. *Stuck in the Onesies* told Barb and Ellie's story. *My Mother's Apprentice* will fill you in on their daughters, Karen and Ginger. If you haven't read *Stuck in the Onesies* or need a quick refresher course, this prologue will give you the inside scoop.

The first thing you need to know is that if you've ever played the game of jacks, you know if you get stuck in the onesies on your first turn, you're forever trying to catch up.

---

"Yeah, you remember Mike?" sixteen-year-old Ginger asked as she sat cross legged on the warm tile floor facing Karen. She pulled her long auburn hair back into a pony tail and tossed the ten metal jacks on the tiles to take her turn in the fivesies. She scooped up five in one swoop and caught the red ball with the same hand. She quickly finished off the other five and threw the jacks back down for the sixies.

"You mean the same guy you climbed out your window to go out with last weekend?" Karen was still in shock at Ginger's nerve. She was too chicken to even think about sneaking out. Avoiding the wrath of her dad was something she worked hard at.

"Yeah, that's the one." Ginger threw the ball up and swooped up six jacks. "Mom and Dad had been fighting for a few hours. They were really going at it, so disappearing was no problem."

"Man, you're braver than me," Karen said. "No way I'd have the nerve."

"It doesn't take much to be braver than you, Kar." Ginger smiled and Karen nodded. She was a self-professed scaredy-cat.

Karen looked up to see Ellie, Ginger's mom, appear in the doorway. She looked hard at Ginger trying to warn her but was too late. Ginger goofed her second swoop as she caught a glimpse of her mom in the corner of her eye. Her heart skipped a beat. "Dang, stuck in the sixies!"

"Whaddya need to be brave about?" Ellie asked Karen whose cheeks flushed as she tried to come up with an answer. Ellie had heard the girls talking about her fight with Will but pretended to have missed it.

"Promise not to tell?" Karen asked trying to stall so she could come up with something. She never was good at thinking on her feet. Ellie nodded. Ginger came to her rescue.

"She's freaked out because she got a D on a history test." Ginger lied. "And doesn't want to tell her dad." Ellie tucked that comment away for later. Evidently, Ginger was good at lying on her feet, when cornered.

"Well, I wouldn't wanna tell him either!" Ellie said and chuckled. "Maybe you can get the grade up with some extra credit work or something before he finds out." She reached down and patted Karen on the head who was now on her threesies but goofed on her third swipe of the jacks.

"Dang!" Karen fussed.

"Here," Ellie sat down between Karen and Ginger, crossed her legs, tucking in her housedress here and there, and gathered up the jacks and ball. "Let me show you girls how it's done." She proceeded to start in the onesies and whooped them clear through to the tensies in just a few minutes. "And that ladies," Ellie sat up straight, "is how it's done." She swiped her hands together to show she was finished. Too bad she couldn't earn money for playing jacks. She'd be rich.

"I don't know how to say this, so I'll just spit it out. You, me, and the boys will be moving to Waldorf the beginning of next month." Karen and Ginger looked from her, to each other, and back to Ellie again. Ginger knew her parents were having problems. Not that it had ever been a walk in the park between those two, but things had escalated lately. Loud fights, slamming doors, and an occasional, "Fix your own damn dinner!" from Ellie when the fighting wouldn't stop. Her mother was crying all the time, even when her dad wasn't home. That's when she knew it was really bad.

"I hate that we're leaving Radiant Valley, but living in chaos isn't good for any of us. I'm sorry I've been such a wreck, Ging." Ginger knelt, reached over for her mother, and hugged her from behind.

"Hey, Mom, I think it's gonna be a change for the good. I'll be happy to get the heck away from here." Ginger squeezed her mom hard.

"Hey, don't forget about me!" Karen pretended to be offended.

Ellie had fretted about telling Ginger they were moving thirty miles away. Will's affair had been enough to drive the final stake into the heart of her marriage. Roberta, the "other woman" was a former mutual friend of her and Barb's, making Will's transgression even more painful for all of them. It had created a more than sticky situation not only between her and Will, but Barb and her husband, Jake, too. Ellie and Will's failed marriage turned out to be more of a damaging force than she'd imagined. The two couples had been best friends for years and had celebrated holidays and milestones together, but this would change that forever.

Her marriage had been over for a long time. She knew now what she had realized years earlier, but the babies had just kept on coming. She found herself starting to look forward to her new beginning and Ginger's support made her heart swell with love for her not-so-little girl.

"No way we'd forget about you, kiddo," Ellie said to Karen. "You and your mom will always be around making new memories with us." Something told Ellie things would never be the same, but she kept that to herself. She reached over and scooped up the ball and jacks and stood up. The girls joined her.

"So, you guys gonna go to the pool or what?" Ellie asked. "We can drive down to Waldorf later this afternoon and check out our new digs, if you want." The girls grabbed their beach towels and headed out the door. Ellie grinned as she heard the screen door slam behind them.

It wasn't every day you get a do-over, but Ellie was getting hers now. While she was worried about leaving their old life behind, she found herself beginning to embrace her new one. Regrets were for when it was too late to change something. This was anything but that. She grinned as she looked at the jacks in her hand and walked out of the room into her future.

## Chapter 1

*"Live for yourself and you will live in vain. Live for others, and you will live again." —Bob Marley*

1973

## "YESTERDAY ONCE MORE"
### The Carpenters

Sometimes living on a hillside in Jamaica with only one electrical outlet and no phone was a plus. This was one of those times.

Ginger wasn't looking forward to her best friend, Karen's reaction, to the letter she mailed to her well over a month ago. It should have arrived by now and Ginger knew within a few hours of reading it, Karen would have crafted her reply. She was sure Karen's response was in the mail on its way to Jamaica by now. Ginger dreaded Karen's handwritten smack upside the head. She knew once Karen was done with that, she'd go on to "Why didn't you call me? You know I'm always in your corner!" Ginger knew what Karen would say before she wrote it. They'd been friends since they were five years old. Their moms, Barb and Ellie, had been the closest of friends and their daughters had followed suit. Karen was Ginger's best and only female friend. She hated to think what life would be like were that to change. Even though they saw most things differently, it didn't matter. Ginger was the artsy type, tall, auburn hair, and slender. Karen was the smart and practical one with dark brown hair and as she liked to call it, "jumbo petite" in size. The one with the "pretty face." The two hardly ever saw eye to eye on just about everything, but it never mattered. Ginger hoped her letter wouldn't change that.

She wondered when Donovan, her live in boyfriend, would get home. She looked at her watch, the only piece of real jewelry she still owned. The rest had gone the way of pawnshops or sticky-fingered friends. It was a gift from her mom for her birthday six months before Ellie died in a car accident in 1971, just two years earlier. A drunk driver hit her car broadside. That was the day they took Ginger's sunshine away.

Ginger loved the watch. It looked like a gold bangle bracelet and had a blue topaz on each side of its face. She'd come close to selling it a time or two when things were tight, but Donovan wouldn't let her. She'd always love him for that.

The plywood walls of their little hut held up the corrugated sheet metal that rippled to double as a roof and gutters. It would have been considered well below standards in the US, but it was the norm here in Jamaica.

The yard made up for whatever the house lacked. Hibiscus, poinsettias, and bougainvillea draped themselves over the little stone wall she and Donovan had built around the edge of their lot. The colors alone were enough to wake her up every day, but she still brewed coffee over an open fire in the mornings, using the sleeping embers in the fire pit from the night before. The Queen Ann palm had grown to twice its size since she planted it right after she arrived, six months earlier. Jamaica was a colorful contrast to the way things looked in the States in the winter and she was okay with that. The dirt floor made it easy to keep clean. No need for a mop and who could complain about that, except when the rains came. All one could do was wait for the sun to shine again and in Jamaica, it always did.

She shook her head to clear the memory of what she was hiding from Donovan, but knew that wouldn't help. She picked up a stub from a joint left over from earlier in the day and lit it up. Sitting on her favorite branch that twisted under the banyan tree, she inhaled and held in the smoke. There it was, that familiar wave of relief. She finished the ganja and picked up her guitar.

She'd been told she had her mother's voice. Some days Ellie's words were echoed in her songwriting. It seemed Ellie's reflection followed her just about everywhere. They both had the auburn hair and olive-toned skin. Their voices were similar and they looked alike, but Ginger thought that was where the likeness ended.

Her newest remake of a song was "You Are My Sunshine," using the reggae style she'd learned to emulate since meeting Donovan. She leaned into the song and lost the negative thoughts for a while. She stopped for a moment when she thought she heard footsteps and listened. She looked up to see Paulie peeking at her through the banana tree leaves.

"Awwk! Sunshine! Awwk!" the green parrot squawked.

"Geez oh flip, Paulie," she repeated one of her mom's favorite phrases and put her hand to her throat to slow her heart that had skipped a beat. "You shouldn't sneak up on a girl like that!" The bird hopped to the ground and waddled over to her, his green feathers glowed in the Jamaican afternoon sunshine. She reached out and stroked his head. She was the only one Paulie would allow to touch him. Donovan never could understand how she'd been able to get the bird to trust her. She assured him Paulie was a good judge of character. Paulie became her trusted friend and proved to be a good confidante, one that didn't require a letter or an explanation.

"So, Paulie," she leaned the guitar against the tree, "I guess she's gotten my letter by now. By the looks of things, I should have another week or two before her reply gets back to me." The bird waddled in a circle in front of her. She walked across the yard and pulled off a bunch of small green bananas. Pulling the ripest one off, she peeled it and broke it in half, part for her and the rest for Paulie.

A trickle of sweat escaped down her face from the afternoon sunshine. She gathered up her hair and twisted it into a knot on the top of her head to cool off.

Her love of rich foods haunted her thighs, but she discovered it was nothing a diet pill or two couldn't handle. The meds helped keep her slim, if not just a little edgy. She reasoned that working on a singing career dictated a good image, and she needed all the help she could get.

She picked up the guitar again and glided back into the song. Sometimes she stared at the sea, but most times she closed her eyes, until memories showed up and then she'd open them again. Her younger brothers, Timmy and William, had become her kids by default when her mom passed away. Her parents had been in the middle of an ugly divorce when Ellie died. Ginger moved back to her dad's to help out. She felt bad leaving them when she moved to Jamaica, but she had to get out of there. They were now alone with Dad and Roberta, his new wife and one of Ginger's mother's ex-best friends. She just couldn't deal with living there anymore. One of them had to go and it was apparent it wasn't going to be Roberta. When Ginger met Donovan and started to fall in love with him and the idea of living in Jamaica, the decision was easier. Jamaica was the perfect escape route.

The beep of a car horn in the distance pushed away her memories. She looked down the hill to see Donovan waving as Kenroy drove away in his taxi. He turned to walk up the path that zigzagged its way up the mountainside dodging banyan trees that had taken up residence long before the path had come along. They were leasing the land from a Jamaican landlord. "Quite a difference from Standish Drive," she had written in an earlier letter to Karen trying to describe her new home. "There's no snow sledding down this hill, but sometimes when it rains, the neighborhood kids slide down on cardboard boxes."

"Ginga!" Donovan hollered in his half English, half French Jamaican accent. He waved up at her and she blinked in the sunshine that peeked through the leaves of the trees. Putting her hand over her eyes so she could see where he was, Donovan's dark skin glistened in the sun and the orange tee shirt was drenched with sweat. His dreadlocks were tucked under his brown knit hat. She stood up and leaned the guitar against the base of a banana tree and walked down the path dodging the ruts from the last hard rain that had dug into the hillside. She lifted her skirt to avoid the branches as she walked past her garden. She always thought it funny that what grew wild along the roads of this island were houseplants back home in the States.

When she moved to Ocho Rios with Donovan, or Ochi as the locals called it, she was surprised. She'd thought Jamaica would be one long beach day, but soon discovered there was a price to be paid for the lush tropical setting. The borrowed clouds from the rain forest down the coast in Port Antonio made rain frequent on the north coast of Jamaica. Then she discovered waterfalls. They were everywhere in Jamaica, from little to large, narrow to wide. The sound was always the same and loud enough to drown out most any bad mood she might have.

Donovan met her halfway up the path. She stood on her toes and kissed him on the cheek. "Hey, how was work?" she asked. She turned and began to walk back up the hill. She looked over her shoulder as they climbed back up the mountainside single file.

"It was work, you know?" Donovan answered. As soon as they got to the top of the hill he reached over and tugged her back to him. He pulled her hair loose, and it fell back down over her shoulders. He ran his hands through her coconut milk-washed hair. He loved running his fingers through the silky strands. He turned her around by the shoulders to face him.

"Guess what?" she asked.

"What, mi lady?" he sat on the wall they'd built together and pulled her down onto his lap. She threw her legs over his and held him around the neck, laying her head on his shoulder.

"Jack Ruby might want me to sing at his tavern regularly!" She felt his back stiffen. He sighed. Jack Ruby was a well-known record producer and sound system entrepreneur.

"You don't have to hang out down der, Ging. I make 'nuf money for us to fix up de house and save some too," he pled his case. She was so weary of male insecurities and wasn't used to Donovan showing his.

"It would only be three nights a week and you can come down and hang out while. It's not a sure thing just yet, but I hope it will be." She jumped up to start filleting the fish she'd bought from their neighbor, Matthew, after he returned from his morning fishing trip.

Donovan walked over and started a fire to cook dinner. He gratefully changed the subject. "You get new charcoal?" he asked.

"Yeah, Matthew finished a new batch in the pit. He promised it's a good batch and will last a while." Matthew was a fisherman and charcoal-making entrepreneur.

"I'm gonna take a shower, Babe," he said as she placed the frying pan on the fire to get it good and hot. He headed over to their makeshift bathroom. The cistern sat on the roof of the bathroom and enabled them to collect water to meet their needs, at least most of the time. It worked great until a drought would come, about every 20 years or so, according to the landlord. The water level had gotten pretty low this year before the rains finally came. And came they did.

She carried the fish to the "kitchen" which consisted of a washbasin, a plank of wood for a counter-cutting board, and a fire pit on the ground. She filleted the fish and heated up the oil in the iron skillet over the wood fire. She sliced an onion and a carrot from their hillside garden and threw them in with the fish to brown. Paulie circled her on the outdoor kitchen dirt floor clucking as a reminder to her that he hadn't eaten enough this afternoon. "Don't worry, boy, you'll get yours," she tossed him a piece of bread to tide him over as she finished preparing dinner. She walked back over to where the old refrigerator was plugged into their only electrical socket in the bedroom, opened the door and pulled out a bowl of leftover callaloo (what Ginger fondly called an upgrade on American spinach) from the night before.

She heard Donovan turn the shower off. He stepped out and wrapped a towel around his waist. "Should I dress for dinner, dear?" he joked, grabbing her hand, and pulling her to the bedroom.

"Only if you lose the towel, my man," she jerked the towel loose and it dropped to the ground. He took the bowl of callaloo out of her hands and sat it on the bedside table. She darted back over to the frying pan on the fire, picked it up, sat it on the ground. There was no need for a hot pad on a dirt floor either. Another plus. She giggled as she ran back to their bedroom brushing the banana tree leaf to the side that acted as a curtain.

The heat of the day waned as they lay in each other's arms until their hunger pains began to get the better of them. "I guess we'd better finish cooking dinner," Ginger said. She stood up and wrapped the sheet around her as she headed back to the fire and put the pan back over the coals.

"Oh yeah," Donovan said as he reached into his work pants pocket and pulled out an envelope. "I stopped at the post office and there was a letter there for you from Karen." He handed the envelope to her and her heart sank. Geez, she didn't waste any time.

—Chapter 2—
1973

## "DARK SIDE OF THE MOON"
### Pink Floyd

Karen pulled the mail from the post office box. She didn't bother checking it too often since more often than not it contained bills that she had to give to Peter who had to rob Paul to pay anyways. However, living all those miles away in West Virginia, letters from Maryland and Jamaica often trumped her desire to avoid the bills. She hurried back to the car that she'd left running while three-year-old Nellie slept in the backseat.

Karen sifted through the ten-day accumulation of advertisements and the cellophane windowed envelopes. Those were her least favorite. They were the ones that reached into their checking account and robbed her of spending money. It seemed she never had enough money for the bills and definitely not for spending. She was a stay-at-home mom and Lee was a bricklayer whose work was weather-dependent. Living in the mountains of West Virginia proved it to be a tough way to make a living, especially in the winter. They did their best to save what they could in the warm weather but were always happy to see spring show up again.

Karen smiled when she spotted a red, white, and blue airmail envelope. She tossed the rest of the mail onto the seat and looked at the return address. St. Ann's Bay, Jamaica, W.I. Sure enough. She ripped it open and pulled out the familiar handwriting written on stenographer paper, dated three weeks earlier. "Gotta send her some nice stationery for her birthday," she said aloud to herself and began to read.

February 12, 1973

Hey Woman?

Greetings from Jamaica. I'm sitting on a tree stump in my yard that overlooks the sea wishing you were here to "sea" it with me. When are you guys coming for that long-promised visit? I've been here six months already? I'm really missing you, girl. Really need my best friend fix right now.

Your last letter said that things were going better for you these days with the hint of a possible move back to Maryland. Any more on that? I know you'd be happy to leave the snow-covered mountains of West Virginia. Ain't no "Almost Heaven" in it for you, I'm thinking.

Donovan's job on the construction site of the new resort, Hyatt Regency in Ochi (it's what the locals call Ocho Rios), is going well. He comes home hot and sweaty every day, takes a shower, and then I make him hot and sweaty all over again. Haha.

Guess what? I got a lead on Jack Ruby's, a nightspot in Ochi. He's also a record producer and it's where Bob Marley got his start. He might hire me to play three nights a week. I talked with the manager and played a few tunes for him. I think he liked me and said he'd let me know within the next couple of weeks. Maybe when you and Lee come for a visit, we can go down and check it out. I hear lots of music people from Kingston hang out there while they're vacationing in Ochi. I'll get all kinds of exposure if I can play there. Cross your fingers or put in a prayer with the Big Guy for me, k?

I also have a lead on maybe being an extra for a James Bond flick they're gonna film here. Yes, you can have my autograph? An "extra" what, I'm not sure, but I'm thinking once they get a load of my extraordinary acting skills, I'll be James Bond's main squeeze. What acting skills, you ask? It's my daydream, so hang with me.

So, I've got something I need to get off my chest and tag, my friend, you're it. You're always "it" it seems, doesn't it? Enough of the drum roll . . . so here goes.

So, I found myself a few weeks late and not for tea. Actually, I wasn't late, but my period was. I was so freaked out, Kar, I tried to call you, but you didn't answer. Not to lay a guilt trip on you or anything, but I gave up and did it anyway.

Karen looked up from the letter and stared at the red brick of the post office wall. "Did it? Did what?" Surely not another one . . . she took a deep breath and looked back at the letter.

Anyway, I've been so busy with working on new songs and trying to set up steady gigs, I just couldn't do it right now, you know? Be a mom, I mean. It just wouldn't work for us at this point (Donovan doesn't know, please keep this just between us). I mean we're living on the side of a hill in something that is little more than a lean-to. I know it's the norm for people here, but I still feel like I'm camping. Don't know how I'd teach a kid to crawl on a dirt floor . . .

Here in Jamaica, they use herbs for just about everything. I'd heard that there was something I could drink to bring on a period. Viveen, an older lady that lives up the path from us gave me a few cups of guinea hen tea. I drank it and by the end of the day, I was bleeding big time. Like a bad period with some cramping. I'm thinking that maybe I wasn't really pregnant, but can't say for sure, so there's no need to alarm Donovan. There, I feel better. Sorry if I put a kink in your day.

Please don't be mad at me, Kar. I know you're disappointed and don't understand. You are the best mom I know. When I think of how you didn't want to be pregnant, but went through it anyway, I know *it was the right thing for you to do. I just couldn't do the same. Not this time.*

Karen leaned her head back on the headrest, her thoughts bumping into each other. *Doesn't Jamaica have birth control? Geez, there's probably some kinda back bush tea for that too. What the heck was she thinking?* But, she knew in her spirit exactly what Ginger was thinking. She knew Ging wanted kids more than anyone else she knew, she just didn't know it yet. Having kids isn't about timing, it's about love. She'd be such an awesome mom, if she'd just give herself the chance to experience it. She took a deep sigh, shook her head as if it would help, and continued reading.

*Sorry to dump this on you. I don't even know why I am, except I had to tell someone. Someone that loves me and will love me in spite of what I've done.*

*It was the weirdest thing. Once I drank the tea, I was sorry and changed my mind for a while. For a bit, I didn't think the tea was working, but as the day went on, it did. It took about 21 hours for the whole thing to be over. I cried like I haven't since Mom died. Felt so bad knowing that she also didn't wanna be pregnant with any of us, but did it anyway. I was glad Donovan was at work when the cramps got bad. He never suspected anything and still doesn't.*

Karen was stunned. Shoot, if weren't for "oops", and their moms having unplanned pregnancies, neither of them would be here. Barb and Ellie had toughed it out each time they found themselves pregnant time after time. Why was Ginger dumping this on her? She thought back to the days not long after Ginger's mom, Ellie, died.

A silent tear slipped down Karen's cheek. Ginger rarely talked about her mom who had been best friends with Karen's mother, Barb. When Ellie died at the hands of a drunk driver two years earlier, the accident yanked Ginger back into a life she'd been very happy to escape. She and her two younger brothers, William and Timmy, moved back in with their dad. Ginger was eighteen and able to live on her own but knew her brothers needed her there. Karen had done her best to keep close to Ginger in the months that followed, but the 400 miles between them made it a challenge.

"I can't believe you're really going back there," Karen said into the phone as she stretched the curly green cord across the kitchen. It had only been a few weeks since Ellie died. She reached over and stirred the spaghetti sauce and added more baking soda to help Lee with his notorious indigestion.

"What else can I do, Kar?" Ginger leaned back onto the sofa of her mom's bachelorette pad that she and her brothers were vacating. "I can't let Timmy and William go back to Radiant Valley alone."

Ginger knew they needed someone other than the soon-to-be wicked stepmother. Roberta just happened to be one of Ellie's former best friends. She'd been the other woman in the not-so-hidden shadows of the divorce.

"It just stinks, is all, but you don't need me to tell you that. You're the one living it," Karen wiped the sweat from her forehead. Cooking steamed up her kitchen and didn't help her disposition. "I just wish he'd let you stay there at your mom's."

"I tried to float that trial balloon, but it wouldn't fly," Ginger answered. "I tried to make him see how easy it would be to just pay off this trailer with Mom's life insurance and the boys and I could just stay here," Ginger scoffed. "But, nooo, we have to be one big happy family . . . just shoot me."

And so it went, Ginger and the boys moved back in with their dad.

It made sense that Roberta wasn't into the "good old days." So, the good old days were no more, not in memory and certainly not reality. There was no reminiscing about their mom. The good old days were shoved into a box somewhere and stored in the attic of Ginger's mind marked, "Never really happened."

The long-distance charges piled up between Maryland and West Virginia for the next few weeks, but Ginger didn't care. "Don't worry about the phone bill this time, I'll be back in Radiant Valley before it comes in the mail. Let Dad worry about it."

"Aren't you worried about his reaction when the bill comes? It's gonna be tough to dodge that bullet with you living in his house."

"Nah, he'll gripe a little and then realize I'm fixing his problems instead of adding to them." Ginger got up from the couch, stretched the phone cord, and grabbed a Pepsi out of the fridge. "Besides, I can only hope he'll take it out on Roberta," she said as she kicked the refrigerator door closed.

"Now *there's* an upside!" Karen laughed.

Karen shook the memories from her mind and pulled herself back into the present. *Okay, enough of Memory Lane, finish the letter.* She flipped over to page three.

> Did I tell you I tried to grow dreadlocks? Turns out, silky red hair isn't the best texture for that hairstyle. Ruth, my neighbor, offered to help me, but after about three hours of trying, we both gave up. Looks like I will just have to settle for a few braided cornrows . . .

Karen shook her head. What's next, tattoos? She'd always felt frumpy when she compared herself to her sidekick. It didn't help that Ginger was a single redhead on the upswing with a potentially glamorous singing career living on a tropical island. Karen was a wife, mom, and part time student. She didn't think juggling carpool responsibilities and term papers were near as glamorous.

It didn't help that Karen had had a love affair with food that started a war with her bathroom scale and self-esteem. She was happy enough in her marriage to Lee. Happy enough. She continued the letter.

> Well, looks like school will let out soon. The neighborhood kids will be heading up the hill and they're expecting a treat from me. I promised them some breadfruit chips (right from a tree in our yard) and lemonade (another tree) when they get home today. Better get it ready before they bombard me. I have such fun with them after school. Most days, I play the guitar and they sing along. You should hear "You are My Sunshine" with a reggae beat?
>
> I love hanging with the kids, but it really makes me miss Timmy and William. I haven't heard much from them in a while. Got a few short letters when I first got here, but not much since. I hope they're okay living with Roberta's tribe. I keep telling myself that they're resilient and will be fine . . .

Karen stopped reading and thought, once again. Ginger would be the best mom ever. She never met a kid she didn't like or one that didn't like her back. What was she thinking? She leaned back on the headrest again and took another deep breath before finishing the letter. Maybe she'd had enough of raising kids from taking care of her brothers so much. She heard Nellie stir in the back seat and looked in the rearview mirror as the three-year-old shifted positions and continued to snooze.

> Please don't hate me, Kar. I know you don't understand any of this and most days, I don't either. I just know that my music is gonna take off soon and I can't wait to take you with me. Just wait.

*Give Lee and Nellie a great big hug from me. Let me know when you think you can make that visit happen?*

*Love ya forever,*
*Ging*

Karen felt as if all the air had been let out of her. Something was wrong and it wasn't *just* the abortion. "Did I say 'just?'" she said out loud. It was time to talk Lee into taking a trip to Jamaica. She knew that wasn't going to be easy. The cost alone would be a challenge, but she was after all, her mother's apprentice. It was time to figure it out how make this his idea. "Time to make Mom proud!" she said aloud. "Let's see how well she trained me." She put the car in gear and pulled out of the parking lot.

Karen talked out loud to herself all the way home, trying to formulate her response to Ginger in her head. Nellie never woke up when she carried her into the house and laid her on the sofa. Karen turned the TV on so that Big Bird would be there to greet Nellie when she woke. She put away the groceries and started dinner before she sat down at the kitchen table and began to craft her response to Ginger. She grabbed a Reese peanut butter cup to curb her appetite. Chocolate had always been her weakness and nemesis. She'd gone up a few sizes since moving to West Virginia and was becoming good at avoiding mirrors.

Writing letters had been a lifeline for her since she lived so far from her family and old friends. After writing one, she felt as if she'd had an hour-long therapeutic conversation, even if it was one-sided.

*Hey, Ging,*
*Got your letter and yeah, you rendered me speechless and we both know that's not an easy thing to do. You know I've got your back and your secret's safe with me. I'm just happy that you're*

okay and didn't get sick or anything. I just want all your dreams to come true. Sounds like they have a tea for just about anything down there. Wonder if I could get one that would make me lose weight . . . that's just a joke, by the way. I'll stick with coffee and donuts and keep the thunder thighs intact.

I don't know when we'll visit but will try to make it happen within the next few months. Have to get Lee to think it's his idea, but ya'll don't call me my "mother's apprentice" for no good reason. I'll get the job done. Give me a few weeks to work my magic. I'll throw in a few prayers while I'm at it.

Nellie is doing well. Three-year-olds are the best. They think you're the greatest and believe everything you tell them. It's nice to be someone's know-it-all and not have to know all that much. Ha ha. I crack me up.

I hope you get the job at Jack Ruby's. Sounds like a good place to do some serious networking and a James Bond film? Now THAT would be cool. I think the first one, Dr. No, was filmed in Jamaica too. How did you find out about it?

Karen sat to think a minute before continuing. "Mommy, look!" Nellie pointed at the television. Mr. Rogers was singing his "It's a beautiful day in the neighborhood" song yet again.

"I see, Honey." Karen walked over and fiddled with the antenna so Nellie could see it better, knowing she had some time thanks to the guy in the red cardigan. She went back to the kitchen table and wrote some more.

I was invited to join the church choir, but I declined at first. Lee overheard me talking to Peggy about it and he started laughing and warned her about my singing voice, or lack thereof. He said it jokingly, but truth be told, he's suffered through more than one of my concerts while on a long drive or unlucky enough to be in the next room as I sing in the shower. Music makes me happy. I guess you know all about that, huh? Too bad those closest to me have to invest in ear plugs. She talked me into going anyway and promised there were enough people there to drown me out. Hope so?

It's crazy cold outside today. No snow, but the wind is blowing up on this blasted hill and makes me wish more than ever that I was outta here. Gotta quit eating so much junk food (I write as I take the last bite of a Reese cup). Why does everything that tastes so good have to be so bad? Gonna have to ask that question when I get to the other side of the rainbow. Self-control and chocolate just don't mix.

It does look like we might be moving back to Maryland (can you see me clicking my heels?). The coal mines are shutting down at a fast clip and when the coal stops, so does the money. We'll see what happens. Can't be quick enough to suit me. I'm not cut out for this cold weather and country music on every station. No amount of Calgon in my bathwater can take me far enough away from this mountain . . . Didn't know I was a city kid, but I guess I am.

Well, I'd better get going. It's time to finish my English paper while I burn Lee's dinner. I've gotten pretty good at that. Another talent handed down from Mom. My apprenticeship is still intact. She and Dad are doing well, by the way. If we're still here in WV, I think Kelly will come down and stay with us for the summer when she gets out of school. That way, Mom won't have to worry about a sitter in the summertime and Nellie will have someone to follow around besides me and Sambo, the cat.

Gotta go. Write back as soon as you can and let me know about the singing and acting gigs? Sounds like a blast and yes, I'm jealous, just so you know.
Love always,
Karen

Karen put down her pen and thought about adding a P.S. to say that one day the timing will be right and that Ginger will make a great mother, but decided against it. She folded the paper, put it in an airmail envelope and sealed it. She and Nellie would go to the post office in the morning. She'd bought ingredients for lasagna, Lee's favorite. A good mood was essential. They had looked at fares before, but just couldn't swing the cost along with him missing work in order to go. Just how to make it his idea, she wasn't sure, but knew that his favorite meal wouldn't hurt.

She'd been saving pocket change for a while and figured it would be a good start towards their Jamaica tickets. As the noodles were boiling on the stove, she pulled out the coffee can, dumped the change, and started separating the coins. By the time the noodles were soft, she was ready to count. She heard Lee's pickup truck pull in the driveway. "Daddy's home!" Nellie stood up and ran to the sliding glass door and looked outside. Lee was about the only thing that would draw her away from Mr. Rogers who was singing his sign-off song. The little girl jumped up and down, her blonde curls bouncing in time.

Lee opened the door, scooped up Nellie, and inhaled her joy. "How's my girl?"

"I good, Daddy! See," she pointed to the television and leaned towards the floor, "Mr. Rogers sing."

"I see that!" Lee put her down and she toddled back to the living room and started swaying her little hips and singing along. He walked over to Karen, kissed her on top of the head, and looked at the table. "And the queen was in her counting house, counting all her money?"

"Yeah, but looks like the queen needs to keep on stealing the change out of your pockets when she does your laundry. I checked on the cost of plane tickets today. Looks like I'm a little short." He knew she was talking about Jamaica and saw the air mail envelope on the table.

"Get a letter from Ginger?" He picked up the envelope and then tossed it back on the table. He knew Karen had been day dreaming again. "Well, I think you're in luck, mi lady." Lee took a bite of the lasagna sauce that simmered on the stove. "Mmm, this is good, Hon."

"Thanks. What's the lucky part?"

"Bob Johnson signed the contract today for five foundations and gave me a nice advance. We don't break ground until May, so we could go to Jamaica in April I'm thinking."

Karen jumped up from the kitchen table, "Seriously?" She wrapped her arms around his neck, hugged him and leaned back to look him in the eyes to make sure he wasn't kidding. His eyes met hers and she knew it was true. He never could look her in the eyes if he was lying or teasing . . . a plus for her and a minus for him. "That's awesome! Guess I need to add a paragraph to my letter." The water for the noodles boiled over the edge of the pot hissing as it hit the burner. She reached over and turned off the gas, grabbed the pot and poured the noodles into the colander in the sink. "We can call the airline in the morning and figure out flights. How long can we stay?"

"Probably a week or so. I'm gonna take a shower and we can figure it out after dinner."

Karen looked in on Nellie as she sang along to the Electric Company before she turned back to layer the lasagna in the pan. She finished and popped it in the oven. It occurred to her that there was no need to unleash her mother's apprentice skills into action this time. She sat back down at the table and ripped open the letter to Ginger. Grabbing her pen, she added the news.

P.S. Well, it must've been the prayer that worked, 'cause I didn't even have time to get the lasagna into the oven before Lee came home and announced some good news and bad news. So, which do you want first? Guess you don't get to choose, so you'll get the bad first.

The <u>bad</u> news is, he got another job here in WV and has five foundations to do in May for a chain of convenience stores, so we won't be moving out of here right away. The <u>good</u> news is, they gave him a nice advance and we'll be coming to Jamaica sometime in April! By the time you get this letter, I should have the details worked out, so give me a call and I'll let you know when we'll be there. Can't wait to see you! Guess I need to find a bathing suit big enough to cover up my bad habits . . .

Karen stared out the kitchen window at the almost leafless tree branch that bent in the winter wind. One leaf hung on as if saying, "No!" to winter. She could relate. She could hear the shower running and Big Bird singing along with Nellie and his friends. Life was good, but about to get better. Warm Caribbean breezes and turquoise water with her best friend held the best promise of spring she could remember.

## "SO VERY HARD TO GO"
### Tower of Power

Karen booked their flight to Montego Bay on Pan Am from National Airport in Washington, D.C. Her parents were excited to meet them at the airport for the hand off of Nellie for the week.

Lee loaded the suitcases into the hatchback of their Chevy Nova. Karen tucked Nellie into the back seat with her pillow, stuffed elephant, stack of coloring books, and bag of Barbie dolls. She was a little disappointed that Nellie didn't seem to care much that they were leaving for a week, but they both agreed that she was too young to understand.

After a seven-hour drive, they pulled into the airport parking lot. Barb and Jake, Karen's dad, got out of their Chevy Vega. Hugs and handshakes were quick. Karen looked around and saw her mom pulling Nellie out of the back seat. "Boy, she doesn't waste any time!"

"She's been driving me nuts, she's so excited," Jake said. He walked away from Karen and Lee and went to hug his granddaughter. Nellie giggled and smiled as her grandparents fawned over her. "Well, I guess she's gonna be okay," Lee said. Karen watched her parents turn into giggling goofs. They were still a handsome couple, her mom as pretty as ever still with black hair (only her hairdresser knew for sure . . . ) and a slender figure. Jake was graying at the temples and Karen noticed a pair of reading glasses in his shirt pocket, a sign that the years were piling up.

"Man, I don't remember getting the princess treatment like that." Her heart dropped just a little. Nellie loved the attention and wasn't worried about saying goodbye to her parents. "Doesn't she know we could die in a plane crash and she'd never see us again?" she asked Lee. She leaned her head on his shoulder.

"Yeah, well we'd better get checked in or we won't stand a chance of falling out of the sky." Lee kissed her on top of her head and picked up their suitcases. Karen sighed and grabbed her purse from the back seat.

Jake held Nellie on his hip as Barb reached over and fixed her ponytail that had shifted during her nap. "We're going to The Enchanted Forest tomorrow," Barb said to Nellie. "I got you a stroller at a yard sale so you won't have to walk so much."

"I hope it's a big one," Jake laughed. "I have a feeling I'll be pushing both of you before the day's over."

"You're a fine one to talk," Barb said while poking him in his belly. Karen was used to the banter between her parents. They had been best friends with Ginger's parents until the O'Reilly's divorce. Neither Barb nor Jake had been willing to give up their best friend allegiances, so it got sticky between them when the O'Reilly marriage fell apart.

"Well, we gotta get checked in," Karen said. She leaned in and kissed Nellie on the cheek. "Be good for Grandmother and Granddaddy." She ran her hand over Nellie's golden curls. "Mommy and Daddy love you."

"Grandmudder give me this!" she held up a new Barbie doll and smiled. Karen took a deep breath to keep the tears locked up.

"That's great, Honey." Karen squeezed her one more time.

"So much for clingy goodbyes with you two around," Karen said and Lee laughed. Karen pulled her camera out of her purse and handed it to Barb. "Here, take a picture in case we do crash. At least she'll know what we looked like." Sometimes Karen's common sense didn't kick in right away.

Barb rolled her eyes and took the camera. "If the film survives the crash, I think you will too." She looked through the lens, snapped the picture, and laughed as she handed the camera back to Karen.

"Okay, it's time to go," Lee took hold of her arm. Karen was surprised at her own maternal feelings that were making it tough to turn and leave. She hugged the oblivious Nellie and walked with Lee to the terminal.

<hr/>

They walked down the steps from the plane onto the tarmac in Montego Bay. The Caribbean heat smacked her upside the head. Karen felt beads of sweat rolling down her forehead before her feet hit the ground. She reached for a bandana that she'd tied to the handle of her purse. "Want one?" she held a kerchief up to Lee.

"Not yet," which she knew meant "Keep it handy till I'm sweating bullets and grumpy," in marriage talk. They rounded up their luggage and sailed through customs. Lee pushed the cart out the door to the open-air lobby of the airport. A tall Jamaican woman in a white blouse and tight blue mini skirt asked where they were going. "We have friends picking us up," Lee explained. She nodded, smiled, and pointed to the waiting area.

Karen could see Ginger's auburn hair lit up by the Jamaican sunshine before she saw anything else. "There she is!" Karen pointed. She ran past Lee as he pushed the cart through the door.

She pushed past the roped off waiting area and made it over toward Ginger. "Karen!" Ginger called and waved. They hugged and their smiles were contagious as onlookers graciously gave them space.

Karen leaned back and looked at her friend. "You look great, Ging."

"You too, Kar! It's so cool that you guys are here!"

Lee pushed the cart up and Ginger turned. "Well, look who made it to Jamaica! And to think we don't have any football to watch or deer to hunt, but you came anyway!" Lee smiled and gave her a bear hug picking her feet up from the pavement.

"I'm thinking some Red Stripes will make up for that!" Lee said. Red Stripe was the beer of choice in Jamaica. "Where's Donovan?" he asked looking over her shoulder. Ginger pointed towards the curb. Lee saw Donovan leaning on a car waiting and headed his way while Karen and Ginger continued their reunion. They followed him holding hands as if they were eight years old again, picking up where they always left off.

Donovan's muscles filled out his white cotton shirt. "Wow, looks like you're staying in shape, Bud," Lee patted his own stomach. "It's been a little tougher for me!" Lee and Donovan met a few years before when Lee traveled to Georgia to work in the winter months when it was too cold for masonry work in West Virginia. Donovan followed Lee back to Beckley that spring to work with him. He met Ginger when she came to visit. It was lust at first sight and the two became a couple instantly.

They did their guy back-slapping hug and when they were done the girls had caught up with them. Karen leaned into Donovan for a hug.

"You ready for this? An entire week of us bunking with you guys?" Lee asked.

"Couldn't be more ready, Mon," Donovan answered. "Gave me the kick in the pants I needed to get some tings done and ready for you."

Karen gawked at the bougainvillea that grew over just about every fence and wall. Mountains jutted up the side of the island, the green reaching for the blue sky. "Boy, you have your share of mountains too, it looks like," Karen said. "But, I guess it doesn't snow here, so it's not so bad." Her aversion to mountains clung to her from being snowed in time after time back in West Virginia. "I can't get over how pretty it is here. We flew in right over the water and it's the most beautiful turquoise ever, and look at all the flowers!" Donovan opened the back door and Karen and Ginger ducked into the back seat.

"Wait till you see Ginga's garden. It's beautiful." Donovan said with his thick Jamaican accent.

"Nice car, Man," Lee said.

"Tanks, but not ours. It's Kenroy's taxi. He took the day off and let us use it to come pick you guys up," Donovan beeped as he passed the car in front of them on the two-lane "highway."

"It's crazy the way you guys drive on the wrong side of the road," Karen said. "Have you done it yet?" She looked at Ginger.

"Nope, and I figure that's a good thing. I wasn't that good at it on the right side of the road!" Laughter broke out and not one argued with her. Ginger's driving abilities had always been questionable at best. She was much like her mom, Ellie, who was crowned the infamous, "Mrs. Wrong Way," when they were kids.

Karen and Lee oohed and aahed at the spectacular views of the sea as they traveled along the north coast of the island. "I can't believe the British let this place go. Look at all this untapped coastline." They rode through the tiny towns of Falmouth and Duncanstown. Children walked with their moms through the markets on crumbling sidewalks and men congregated sitting on a windowsill or porch step. The scent of ganja came and went and the smoky smell of a wood cooking fire was never far away.

"Hey, I packed some Jiffy popcorn, stinky cheese, and Old Bay. I kept meaning to ask you, is your stove gas or electric?" Karen asked. Ginger looked at Donovan's eyes in the rearview mirror. The two broke into laughter. Lee and Karen looked at each other not getting the joke. "What's so funny about that?" she asked.

"Kar, we don't have a grill or a stove," Ginger giggled. "We cook over a wood fire pit on the ground," she cracked the window to get some air flowing. "I guess I left out a few details with regards to our living conditions." Ginger laughed again. "All those years of camping on Assateague helped prepare me for life in Jamaica." Growing up, their families had spent weeks at a time camping on Assateague Island, near Ocean City, Maryland. It was the only way they could afford a week at the beach.

"Well, you *can* make coffee, right?" Karen asked. "Because I am the Queen of Caffeine, you know."

"When did *you* start drinking coffee?"

"When I found out it would wake me up. There's no more "Mr." In my Mr. Coffee pot. He and I are on a first name basis."

"Well to answer you, yep we can make coffee," Donovan said. "Wait till you taste Jamaica's Blue Mountain coffee. The best in the world, they say!" He looked at her in the rearview mirror. "Who's hungry anyway?"

"Are you kidding me?" Lee answered. "Have you seen the tiny rations they serve on planes these days?" He held his hands up showing how small.

"Yeah, there's a tiny plate with tiny food fit for tiny people," Karen chimed in.

"No problem, Mon. We fix dat right now," Donovan said as he slowed the car down and turned off into a gravel parking lot. "Big Daddy's Jerk Pit" was a round open-air building with a thatched roof. Bar stools sat around the perimeter of the circular counter that was made with concrete and soda bottles mixed in for color. The cooking took place off to the side in a makeshift cinder block barbeque pit. The aroma wafted through the air. "Man, this smells awesome!" Lee said as he shut his door and looked around.

"Do you think they have a ladies' room?" Karen asked.

"Well, if they don't I can find you a bush out back and stand guard," Ginger said.

"Must be my lucky day," Karen said and pointed to a rest room sign. "I'll be right back," she said to Ginger.

She was starting to get the idea that life in Jamaica was way more rustic than West Virginia where she had found that she'd had to learn to be flexible for things like frozen pipes in the winter. Not being able to flush a toilet or get a glass of water could really cramp a girl's style.

She walked out of the "ladies' room" that turned out to be little more than a hut with a hole in the ground and saw Ginger talking with a guy with long dreadlocks. The man walked away and Ginger joined her as they walked to where Donovan was leaning on the car with a paper bag full of jerk chicken. Lee walked over carrying four Pepsi bottles.

Ginger handed out the jerk chicken that was wrapped in white paper. They walked over to a picnic table and sat down.

"Wow, this gives a new meaning to 'finger licking good,'" Karen said as she took another bite.

"And it's got a kick to it!" Lee said. "Pepsi tries, but doesn't do much to douse the flames!" He took a long sip of his soda. Karen reached in her purse and handed him a roll of Tums before he could ask.

They finished up their lunch and piled back into the car, heading further east along the coastline. Karen was enamored with the Caribbean and its different shades of blue. "Can we go snorkeling while we're here?" she asked Ginger who deferred to Donovan.

"Yeah, Mon," he said looking at her in the rear-view mirror. "No problem. We have snorkels and fins. You can do it at our beach." He pointed towards the water. "We live right across the road from here."

"See about halfway up the side of the hill? There's a green roof," Ginger pointed. Karen leaned down to see out the window and briefly saw the house as they drove by. It was quite a ways up the side of the mountain.

"That's yours? How do you get up there?" Karen asked.

"Well, the ski lift ain't working these days, so we generally walk and/or climb!" Ginger giggled.

"You can't drive? You get out here on this busy road?" Karen wasn't excited about hiking straight up a hill for a half a mile in this heat and did a poor job of trying to hide it.

"Don't worry, it's not so bad and if you get tired, I have a few strategic points where you can stop and sit for a while."

"It's no wonder everyone around here is skinny," Karen said.

"That and a steady diet of fish and veggies," Ginger added. "When you're broke, you eat what you grow or catch or what your neighbors decide to share."

The view of the coastline as they continued toward Ocho Rios to meet Kenroy, took Karen's mind off the upcoming climb. She gawked out the window to catch the view of the sea. No matter where she was, if there was water around, she was content. The sea went from aqua to royal blue in places.

"There's a waterfall not far from the road here," Donovan pointed. "Dunns River Falls."

"Yeah, and there's Laughing Waters too not far from where we live. Not as big, but just as pretty and doesn't cost to go. Empties right into the Caribbean," Ginger said. They continued down the two-lane road towards Ocho Rios. They could see bits and pieces of the town across the water. Ocho Rios hugged the bay and the sea shone like a gemstone in the sunlight. The resort town was nestled between the foot of the mountains and the sea, giving shelter to boats of every size from those with oars to cruise ships.

People milled around, some with purpose and some not. Despite the heat, many wore long sleeves which Karen thought strange. "They must handle the heat better than I do, long sleeves and pants don't seem to bother anyone." She fanned herself with her boarding pass.

"Here, I got this for you," Ginger handed Karen a straw fan that had "Jamaica" woven on it. "Don't leave home without it."

"Wow, now *that's* a best friend!" Karen started waving the fan back and forth.

The little town consisted of a grocery, a post office, and a few other essential businesses. Craft markets built in makeshift shacks targeted the tourists from the resorts and cruise ships. "Yep, you can get everything from tee shirts to ganja and all at a negotiated price," Donovan chuckled.

"Oh, I already got some of that," Ginger said. She pulled a plastic bag out of her pocket.

"Where did you get that?" Karen said as her eyes opened wide.

"When we stopped at the jerk pit," Ginger said.

Karen remembered seeing Ginger talking to the dreadlocked guy when she came out of the ladies' room.

"Here, smell." Ginger handed the bag to Karen.

"Put that away!" Karen said and looked around for a cop to bust them while everyone else laughed at her scaredy cat ways. She slunk down in her seat and Ginger reached over and patted her hand. "Don't worry. Nobody around here cares."

They pulled up in front of the post office. Donovan beeped the horn when he spotted Kenroy. He looked up and bounded over to the car. Donovan hopped out of the driver's seat and squeezed in the back with Ginger and Karen. Kenroy took the wheel. They made their introductions as they drove away and headed back toward the house on the side of the hill.

The children walking home from school wore clean, crisp uniforms of tan and blue "Strange to see kids wearing uniforms to school," Karen said. "And riding taxis. Where are the school buses?"

"No school buses here. It's on the parents to get them there." Ginger shrugged. "They don't make it easy, that's for sure."

"So, Kenroy, what's shaking in Ochi today?" Ginger tapped him on the shoulder.

He looked in the rearview mirror and made eye contact with her, "Pretty quiet today since no ship in town, but I see Jack Ruby and he ask 'bout you."

"He did? What did he ask?"

"He want to know if you are reliable if he hire you."

"Wow! What did you say?"

"I say you never been on time for anyting in your life, but were worth de wait." The car erupted in laughter.

"This girl never met a microphone she didn't like, believe me, she'll be on time for *that!*" Karen said and looked at Ginger. "So, when do you start?"

"You want we go by der now?" Kenroy asked.

Ginger looked at Karen. "Yes, she does!" Karen answered and patted him on the shoulder.

"What if he wants me to start work right away?" Ginger worried out loud to Karen.

"Are you kidding me? We'd have a party there every night you had to *work*. If you can even call that work!"

They drove through the little seaside resort town of Ocho Rios. Hotels dotted the waterfront and mountains climbed toward the sky in the background behind the city. There were a few shopping centers with grocery stores and clothing shops. A craft market made from makeshift bamboo and tarps sat with hopes of greeting souvenir hungry tourists. Tee shirts and baskets along with wood carvings appeared to be the biggest sellers. "Can we go there one day?" Karen asked.

"Yep, I promised my neighbor, Arlene, we'd come by her booth while you're here," Ginger replied.

"There's where I work," Donovan pointed to a construction site with high fences and a tall structure. "I was able to get off work all week since the concrete pour was delayed."

"Well, we're quite happy for the delay, my friend," Lee said.

They drove through town and passed the clock tower that sat on the town square that wasn't "square" at all, but triangular. People milled around in the steamy Jamaican sunshine. Kenroy turned off the main road and headed towards the sea to Jack Ruby's.

When they pulled up to the curb, it looked to be just like any other bar, apparently much more appealing in the night when lights could shine away some of the dingy.

"I'll jump out and see if he's here. Why don't you guys go on down to the wharf and take a look? I'll catch up with you when I'm done," Ginger said.

"Okay, we'll wait for you there," Donovan said as she closed the door behind her.

"Wish me luck!" Ginger said as she waved and headed towards the door.

Kenroy drove the taxi down to the wharf and they all got out. Karen reached back into the car and grabbed her new fan.

They walked down the pier that led to a few cabin cruisers and a pontoon party boat. There were handmade signs for fishing trips and sunset cruises. A colorful motor boat puttered by as the sun shone on its silvery catch of the day. The fisherman waved and Karen waved back.

They walked over to a low lying branch of an almond tree that offered both shade and a place to sit. Donovan walked back from a little grocery store with four Red Stripe beers. He handed them out and held his up for a toast.

"To a great week of fun and friendship!" They clinked their brown bottles together.

"And Ginger's new gig!" Karen added but not without noticing that Donovan frowned just a little at her comment.

They sat in the shade and talked about their plans for the week. Snorkeling was at the top of Karen's wish list and fishing for Lee. Both would be easy orders to fill according to Donovan and Kenroy.

Karen looked up to see Ginger headed their way. "Hey!" she waved and stood up. Ginger waved back.

They all stood and drained their Red Stripes. "I got the job and start Thursday night!"

"I'm thinking that calls for refills," Lee said as he gathered up the empty bottles. He jogged over to the store and traded them in for five new ones. He returned, handed them out, and raised his bottle. The others did the same. They clinked each other and Karen offered up a toast.

"To Ginger and the launching of her singing career. So grateful to be here to see your debut!" Again, she couldn't help but notice Donovan's silence.

Kenroy's taxi pulled up along the curb of the two-lane highway to let them out at the bottom of their hill. Lee and Donovan pulled out the suitcases and they all said their goodbyes. "I will work on a fishing trip and we will go to the falls on Friday, my day off," Kenroy said. Karen hugged him goodbye and Lee slapped him on the back before Kenroy jumped back in the car and pulled away.

"Boy, I sure am happy to play the girl card today. Glad we don't have to carry these suitcases!" Karen said and they crossed the road and headed up the path that zigzagged up the hill making it less steep than it appeared. Karen put her sweatband on her head and followed Ginger. Lee and Donovan followed behind with the suitcases.

"Yeah, this women's lib stuff is gonna be the death of us, I'm thinking," Ginger answered. "I kinda like having suitcases carried for me among other things," she winked at Karen.

"You guys coming to visit gave us the excuse to build on the second bedroom. It's a little rough and not quite finished, but I think you'll be comfortable," Donovan said to Lee.

"Hey, I know we will be, Mon," Lee had picked up some Jamaican slang with Donovan way back when they worked together.

They walked past a few shacks along the way with their neighbors waving hello as they passed. Karen could see inside some of the homes as they walked up the hill. They were neat and tidy despite their meager belongings. Children began to follow them up the hill. The smell of wood burning came and went, depending on who and what was cooking.

"Hey, it's Auntie Ginger!" a skinny boy came running out of the bushes and fell in line with them as they headed up the hill.

"Hey, Roger," Ginger said. She patted him on the head and pulled him close. His tan school uniform had a crisp crease on the pant legs and sleeves. "How was school today?"

"It good, Mon. Teacher sick and let us play," Roger said. Other kids fell in line behind them and chattered with their updates.

"It's like hanging out with the Pied Piper," Karen said to Ginger. Karen could see the kids flocked to her, much as they had done with Ellie, Ginger's mom. "You're *your* mother's apprentice, you know that?" Ginger smiled and kept walking.

"They love me and I love them right back. Can't have too much love!" The irony of the abortion hit Karen again, but she tucked the thought away. They trudged on up the path. "There we are," Ginger pointed a few more yards up the hill. At the clearing, Karen saw a plywood structure with a corrugated tin roof and cinder blocks on top, presumably, holding it in place. There was a block structure to one side of the property, a fire pit, and small table sitting outside. The four walked up and the guys put the suitcases down.

"Awwk!" A green parrot flew down from a low-lying limb. Karen felt a tickle from his wings as he squawked in her ear on the way down to the pathway in front of them.

"Oh my god!" She jumped back and Lee caught her elbow keeping her from taking a tumble. Her hand landed on her heart as she tried to catch her breath.

"Well, this must be Paulie," Lee said. The parrot squawked again, this time in confirmation.

"It sure is," Ginger said and crouched down to go eye to eye with the bird. "What's the matter, Bud? Bet you're hoping for some supper soon." She reached over and Paulie allowed her to briefly touch his wing before scooting over towards their home.

"So, welcome to our castle," Ginger said with a wave of her arm. "Here's my kitchen," she walked over and pointed to the fire pit, a countertop made out of a leftover piece of green Formica, propped waist high by two stacks of cinder block, and a wrought iron table with three chairs. "It's not much, but it's home."

"It's amazing, Ging," Lee said. Karen looked around speechless, her mouth hanging half open. Lee worked hard to cover her not-so-hidden shock. "What's this?" He walked over to the block structure.

"That's the shower," Donovan answered, opened the curtain, and Lee poked his head in. There were paving brick laid on the outside and inside of the shower stall creating a dressing room on the exterior.

"Great design," Lee said. "Awesome job with the pavers, Mon!" Lee had taught Donovan how to lay the brick when they had worked together.

"Tanks, Mon." Donovan walked over to the open-air kitchen.

Karen breathed it in. "I can see why you love it. You have your own personal paradise as far as I can see," she said.

"Yeah, until it rains and we're confined to the bedroom, but it works." Ginger said.

She wished she didn't envy Ginger so much. Here she was, a mom with the most awesome little girl. She was happy for Ging, but admittedly as green as Paulie. "What's not to like?" Karen threw an old withered pink Hibiscus flower at Ginger and they smiled at each other. No matter how long it had been between their visits, they never missed a beat.

"Well, it appears as though you have the answer to all your prayers, Ging," Karen nudged her with her arm as they sat on the wooden bench that overlooked the hillside. The breeze cooled her off. "Living in a tropical paradise surrounded by all this. Heck, in and outside of your house."

"Well, it ain't much of a house yet, but it will be one day," Ginger grinned at her friend. "It's so good to have you here, Kar." She tossed a leftover piece of mango to Paulie. He squawked.

"Do you think he said 'thanks?" Karen asked.

"Well, he is Jamaican, you know. Probably 'tanks' is more like it!"

"So, have you made any friends here?"

"Yeah, Arlene and I are pretty close. I help her with the kids sometimes when she needs a sitter while she's working at the straw market, but most of the women here shy away from me."

"Why's that"?

"Not sure except I think they feel I took away one of the good men and I suppose I did." Ginger elbowed her in the side. "You know these Jamaican guys got it goin' on, right?" She winked at Karen.

"Hmm . . . I think you mentioned that once or twenty times before."

"Yeah, well I think a few of them have done a voodoo or two on me." She tossed the mango seed into the bushes below.

"Voodoo? Really?"

"Oh yeah, it's everywhere back up in the hills."

"What about this Rastafarian thing? You think that's gonna last?"

"As long as Bob's around, it will," she said, referring to the Bob Marley craze.

"Hey, Ging," Donovan walked up behind them and put his hand on her shoulder. "We gonna go see Matthew about a fishing trip." He kissed the top of her head. "Be back in a few minutes."

"Okay," she looked up at him. "We'll just hang out here and chill till you get back."

"Let's make the best of it, Whadya think?" Ginger handed Karen a joint the size of a small cigar.

"Yikes," Karen took the cigarette. "I think we must be having company if we need all this. Gimme a match!" The girls shared the joint passing it back and forth and laughing in between.

"Well, we don't have to sit in your living room and pretend we're at the beach 'cause we already are," Karen said. She and Ginger had often fantasized about tropical surroundings while looking at Coco, Ginger's palm tree that had been in her living room. She'd planted it from a Florida coconut and it grew so large that when she moved, she'd donated it to the Washington, D.C. Arboretum.

"When did you start smoking cigarettes?" Karen thought she was seeing things. Was this the same person that used to dog her about her former cigarette habit and shamed her into quitting? "You gotta be kidding me," she added before Ginger could answer. "What about your voice?" Karen reached over and punched Ginger in the arm. "I thought you wanted a singing career!"

"Ouch!" Ginger rubbed her arm, sat down on the bench, and lit up.

"But really, Ging, who starts smoking at your age?"

Ginger stood up, "I guess just losers like me," and walked to the edge of the veranda Donovan had built.

"Stop that. Your 'poor me' routine doesn't fool me none."

Ginger smiled and looked at her friend. "You're right, Kar. No need for a pity party. It just calms me sometimes," she sat back down next to Karen. "I picked one up when I first got here and before I knew it, I bought a pack and here I am," she held the burning cigarette up in front of her face. "I'm as baffled as you."

Karen shrugged and let it go. Abortions, cigarettes, what's next?

Ginger stubbed her cigarette out in her makeshift coconut shell ashtray.

"Whew, I'm so sweaty," Karen said as she pulled off her sweatband.

"Why don't you jump in the shower and cool off?"

"I just might do that." Karen stood up and looked toward the "bathroom."

"You're gonna have to give me a lesson on how it all works."

"Let's do it, Princess," Ginger said.

"What's that supposed to mean?" Karen asked.

"Well, princesses aren't used to cold showers, are they?"

"Cold huh? Why does that surprise me? If that's the current situation, then 'Princess' it is." She grabbed the towels Ginger handed her. "It's weird that you would even have running water on the side of a hill."

"We catch the rain water in the cistern." Ginger pointed to a big black plastic basin on the hillside above the shower. "And that's what we use." Karen walked over to the cinder block shower stall.

"When you need to flush," Ginger pointed to the toilet, "just fill this bucket up from the spigot, pour it in the tank and push the handle."

"Just an extra step or two," Karen said. "I think I can handle that." She walked in, pulled the curtain closed behind her, and undressed. She turned on the water, stepping under the shower one leg at a time, letting the chilly water cool her sweaty skin. She was determined to get the grimy sweat washed off, one big goose bump at a time. "Brrr!"

"Here!" Ginger reached her arm inside and offered up a bar of Ivory soap and a bottle of Prell shampoo. "There's a little ledge in the wall you can sit them on."

"Thanks," Karen said and shivered a little, determined not to let Ginger know how cold she was. "Wow, this feels great once you get used to it!" she called over the sound of the water hitting the sides of the shower stall

"Now where have I heard that before?" Ginger answered and Karen smiled to herself. As girls they swam in the waves at Ocean City and it was a frequent response with regards to the question, "How is the water?" before they'd get in. The chilly Atlantic salt water could sometimes take getting used to. "Not bad, once you get used to it." Translation: "Come on in, hypothermia ain't so bad!"

Karen was surprised when she got used to the cool temperature so fast and lathered up her hair. She closed her eyes and leaned back to rinse the suds off her head enjoying the coolness of the water on her back.

She opened her eyes to see a large green lizard on the side of the wall. They went eyeball to eyeball for a split second before the lizard jumped to the other side of the shower stall near the door-jamb. She let out a yelp, slipped and grabbed the side of the stall, almost losing her balance.

Ginger ran to the shower and poked her head inside. "What the heck, Kar? Are you alright?"

Karen stood as far back in the corner as she could, her heart pounding. "There's a . . . lizard?" She tried to cover her body up with her hands, but only looked stupid trying. Karen pointed to the wall next to Ginger's head. Her eyes followed Karen's finger and she saw what looked like a baby alligator, otherwise known as a gecko, hugging the cinder block. Ginger's hair got wet as she reached over, picked him up, and tossed him outside.

"Oh, that's just Bruce," she laughed. "You'll be fine" she closed the curtain. "He won't eat much, Princess." Karen stood in the corner of the shower, leaned her head back on the wall, shook her head, and laughed. She finished rinsing and turned the water valve off, wrapped her hair in one towel and dried off with the other.

"Life with you is just one fun thing after another," Karen said as she slipped on Ginger's robe and her flip-flops. She pulled the shower curtain open and headed to the bedroom. Ginger's back was to her as she stood at the kitchen counter chopping onions. Karen reached over and snapped Ginger with her wet hair towel as she walked across the dirt floor.

"Ouch!" Ginger yelped, her hand involuntarily covering her butt where the towel had landed. "Girl, you forget I just saw you naked. I could tell people!"

Karen stopped, paused for a second, and burst out laughing, knowing it was true and a real possibility. "You, bitch!" The word didn't cross her lips much, but it wasn't every day she came eye to eye with a wall hanging alligator and a best friend that would dime her out.

They could hear Lee and Donovan talking as they headed back up the hillside.

"Hey, Babe!" Donovan called. "Red Snapper!" he held up a string of silvery fish. "Matthew had a good day fishing."

"Great!" She walked over and cut chives and dill from her herb garden pots at the edge of the kitchen floor, put them up on the cutting board and chopped away. Karen came back out from the bedroom dressed in a long blue paisley skirt and flowing blouse.

She had taken Ginger's wardrobe suggestions to heart. Skirts were cooler than pants in the Jamaican heat.

"Hey, can you grab that large frying pan with the lid?" Ginger nodded towards the plastic bin that held their kitchen supplies of pans, utensils, and bowls. Karen reached in the bin and pulled them out.

Lee walked up behind Karen, patted her butt and gave her waist a squeeze. "How you doing, Hon?"

"Pretty good. Had a shower and met our newest friend, Bruce, the alligator, aka lizard." She sat the pan on the counter.

"Uh oh, how did Bruce make out?"

"Well, Bruce was evacuated from the shower and is probably nestling under her pillow by now," Ginger laughed, and Karen shivered. "Can you guys get the fire started?"

Donovan walked over to the pile of firewood he kept wrapped up in a blue tarp and pulled out a stack of logs and kindling. "Here, let me help," Lee said and the two of them huddled over the fire pit.

"Just what a pyromaniac needs," Karen said. "Another pyro to play with and a legit reason to do it."

"Yeah, Don plays with fire and I get to use the sharp knives." Ginger held up a fillet knife. She turned to the fish on the counter and began to work her magic. "I'll take it easy on you and cut off the heads, except for Don's. He likes it." Karen squirmed and helped to cut the limes in half and Ginger squeezed the juice into a bowl of water. She swiftly cleaned the fish and dropped each piece of meat into the water to soak. "They call this 'Escovitch fish.' Very popular here in Jamaica." Once the fish was marinating, she walked over to the refrigerator in her bedroom and pulled out a jar full of a green pasty substance.

"What in the world is that?"

"It's green seasoning. We make it ourselves and lather it on just about whatever we're gonna cook."

"What's in it?"

"Oh, chives, cilantro, garlic, onion, you name it." Ginger opened the jar and held it up for Karen to take a whiff.

She took in a breath, "Whew! I hope it tastes better than it smells!"

"You know me, the more garlic, the better." Ginger put the jar on the counter and started pulling the fish out of the lime marinade. She lathered each piece with the green paste and rolled the fish in flour.

Once the fire was going strong, Ginger took the pan, poured in some oil, and laid it over the coals. She added the fish and the sizzling began. "I'm shocked you can fry anything over a campfire," Karen said. She sat down on a log next to Ginger.

"Yeah, remember when we camped? It was all we could do to get it going long enough to burn a few marshmallows."

"Then they got a Coleman stove," she looked at Lee, eyes wide open, as she realized she'd never told him this story. There weren't too many of those after five years of marriage. "We knew we were uptown then," she squinted to remember more. Then she did. "Oh yeah! You clogged the jets up on the stove roasting marshmallows," she laughed. "Your mom was pissed!"

"Yeah, we almost got sent to our tent."

"She made you clean it up and then my mom taught us how to do it the right way, as I remember," Karen said.

Ginger took a deep breath. She did that a lot when she thought of her mother.

"That's when we crowned her 'Marshmallow Mama,'" Karen added. "She didn't cook much except for spaghetti and burgers. Then we added roasted marshmallows to the dessert menu."

Ginger added another pan of vegetables to the fire and kept watch over it until everything was ready. Karen set the table. "Hey, weren't these your mom's plates?" She held up the square pink Melamine platter.

"Yeah, I was able to find space to bring them back here on my last trip home." Ginger took a plate from Karen and loaded them individually with food. "Don, dinner's ready!" she called. The guys looked up and waved as they finished their conversation with Matthew. The girls finished setting the table with mismatched plastic tumblers. Ginger pulled the lemonade from the fridge.

They each pulled up a chair or tree stump stool and passed around the plates of food. "I think this one has eyes just for you," Karen said as she passed the fish to Donovan, she cocked her head to one side. "But maybe not, I think it just winked at me."

"If he did, he must be duppy, 'cause he's pretty crispy!"

"What the heck's a 'duppy'?" Lee asked as he reached for the bowl of yams.

"Ha! Duppy like a Jamaican ghost, Mon."

"What part of Jamaica did you say you were from, Don?" Karen asked.

"My family is from the Maroon people in Moore Town. It's about a two-hour drive from here."

"What's the 'Maroon people'?" she asked

"We are descendants of escaped slaves that managed to free themselves from the British and have remained separate within Jamaica ever since." He leaned over, reached for a lemon wedge, and squeezed it over his fish and vegetables. Karen could've sworn the fish blinked.

"Was it different growing up there compared to here in Ochi?" Karen asked and took a bite. "Mmm, Ging, this is great," she added before Donovan could answer.

"Well, yeah it was. It's a very close-knit community. I have to take Ginga there soon and show her."

"Whew!" Lee pushed himself back from the table. "That was off-the-hook delicious, Ging!"

"I had a little help from my girl here," she said looking at Karen.

"How about Lee and I clean up and you go get your guitar?" Karen asked. "We haven't heard any of your new stuff yet." Before Ginger could object, Karen and Lee had scooped up the dishes and were headed to the counter that had been strategically placed close to the shower stall for water access. Lee picked up the pan of water that Ginger had placed on the fire to heat up while they ate dinner. He poured it into the metal wash basin that sat on the counter and Karen smiled when she saw the bottle of Ivory Liquid detergent. Her mom had always used that brand. She was happy to see the tradition continued across the sea. Karen washed and Lee dried while Donovan took care of clearing the table and putting away the dried dishes.

Ginger pulled her guitar out of the case and walked over to the tree stump stool that Donovan had made for her to use when she played. He'd carved her name in it and gave it to her for her birthday. It was just the right height and he'd polished it up so it wouldn't snag her clothing. She plucked the guitar strings and adjusted the sound. "You are my sunshine, my only sunshine, you make me happy when skies are gray," she strummed the guitar and slapped its side to add a percussion beat to the song. She sang their childhood favorite with the reggae beat she had written about in her letters.

Donovan walked out of their bedroom with a bongo drum under his arm. He sat down with the bongo in between his knees and joined in the music hitting the reggae beat.

Lee rolled up another tree trunk stool next to Ginger and Donovan. He pulled Karen up from her stool, hid behind her and put his arms around her waist. He knew it was her all-time favorite song which made it his.

They sang along. Karen let it transport her back to when they were kids in the back of old Betsy, the station wagon. More often than not, they were headed to Ocean City or Chesapeake Beach. The tune brought her Aunt Ellie back to life. The days of riding down the highway with their moms and a car full of kids, headed to the beach. Ginger strummed her strings and Donovan joined in on his drum,

> You are my sunshine
> My only sunshine
> You make me happy
> When skies are gray
> You'll never know dear
> How much I love you
> Please don't take my sunshine away

She looked below them to the Caribbean, watching it glisten in the evening sun. It had started to dip below the mountains behind them. Matthew and Arlene walked over and sat down. Before Ginger finished, several neighbors and children had joined them. Karen looked around and smiled, feeling the love that came from every angle. The children danced in the middle as if their bare feet had no choice. Before long, the adults joined in. Karen and Lee found each other on the dirt dance floor. She kicked off her flip flops and hugged his neck. Their bodies swayed to the reggae beat. She was so grateful for this man that married her when he didn't have to. She'd turned up pregnant at the beginning of her senior year of high school. He could have left her alone and afraid, but never flinched at standing by her, even when three weeks after they married, she miscarried. Their high school sweetheart love had beat the odds and seemed to just get better with time.

The Jamaican rum came out from under the bed and drinks were passed around. Ganja lit up the corners of the night. Ginger sang No Woman, No Cry, Bob Marley's latest hit, and the crowd joined in on the chorus "Everyting's gonna be alright . . . " Several songs later, Matthew pulled out his harmonica and the trio found their rhythm.

A taxi pulled up on the road below. A tall thin woman got out of the back seat, slammed the door, and the taxi pulled away. She made it up the hill and Karen looked over at the edge of the crowd to see that she carried a child on her hip. The crowd swayed to the music as the woman elbowed her way to the center of the dance floor and stood in front of Donovan as he beat on the drums. Her hair was braided and she wore ragged cut-off jeans with a not-so-new Bob Marley tee shirt. He looked up at her and his eyes flashed open in recognition. His hands slowed over the bongos and the beat faded. Ginger looked over to see why he'd stopped. Her eyes went from Donovan to the woman and back again. Matthew's harmonica fizzled out on a squeaky note. The crowd looked over to see why their music died.

"Tabitha, Whey uh a do yah?" he responded in patois. *What are you doing here?*

"Yuh come back a Jamaica an don't tell mi?" the woman asked Donovan in patois, Jamaican dialect.

"Weh yuh a do yah?" *Why would I do that?* Donovan responded.

"Me carry me dawta fi see har fada." *I brought my daughter here to see her father.* She walked closer to him.

"Me hab four pickney weh nuh know dem fada." *I have four children and none know their father.* "Her name Donna," the woman said. She jostled the child to her other hip. He frowned, did the math in his head, and then stared at her. His face did little to hide his shock.

"How yuh know seh she a fi mi pickney?" *How do you know she's my daughter?* Donovan asked.

"Cooyah pan har han, she have yuh birthmark." *You can look at her hand, she has your birthmark.*

Donovan's eyes moved to the little girl's hand. Sure enough, it was the same heart shaped birthmark that both he and his father had.

Donovan's face relayed his familiarity. He said nothing for a second and took a deep breath. Ginger understood his deep breaths. They meant, "let me think about my answer for a second."

The crowd began to go home as the confrontation continued. They whispered and looked back over their shoulders as they walked up the lane and down the hill, wondering what drama was unfolding. "Truth soon come," Matthew said to Arlene.

"Why you no tell me you pregnant?" Donovan asked her.

"You were off in the US. I no know how to fine you!" she looked from side to side feeling outnumbered, but relaxed when she saw the crowd was thinning. "Susan said she see you in market, so I knew you come back."

"If she mine, I take care of her," he looked her in the eye. He knew she already had three other kids by two different men and was married to neither. He had met her when he returned to Jamaica after his visa expired in the States. They met during a night of rum flavored dancing as he tried to forget Ginger, thinking she would never come to Jamaica. He woke up next to her with a three-year-old climbing into the bed between them. He didn't remember much from the night before. He looked around at the tidy bedroom with lace doilies on every surface. Bright colored plastic flowers tried unsuccessfully to cheer up the room. A soft breeze blew through the window. He tossed off the blanket, grabbed his clothes and got dressed. Tabitha woke up and pulled her three-year-old over for a hug.

"Where you going?" she looked at him from the bed.

"Home, back to Ochi," he answered.

"You want I make breakfast?"

"No tanks. I go home now." He leaned over and hugged her shoulder. He wasn't sure of the proper protocol for the morning after a one-night stand. All he knew was, it made him feel like crap. He'd never turned his back on someone he'd made love to before.

He got lucky when a taxi headed back to Old Fort Bay, stopped at the corner. He slid in next to two other passengers in the back seat. He stared out the window at the passing coastline. He beat himself up several times. Guilt followed him, but as time went by, he was able to ignore his indiscretion and the guilt lessened. Especially when Ginger agreed to join him in Jamaica. Until tonight.

Karen and Lee didn't understand too much of what went down but managed to figure out that this woman claimed Donovan was her child's father. They picked up dishes from the impromptu party and put them in the sink basin. Donovan and Ginger had walked the woman back to the road to catch a taxi. Their voices rose and fell. "Let's head to bed so they can have some privacy when they come back," Karen suggested.

Lying in bed, they could hear snatches of conversation when Ginger and Donovan returned to their room. "I didn't know!" Donovan hollered. Karen and Lee looked at each other. Karen sighed and lay in Lee's arms. They could hear Ginger throwing hurtful darts.

"Think this will blow over by morning?" Lee asked.

"The only thing strong enough to do that is a hurricane and I don't think there's one on the way." She snuggled under his arm and laid her head on his chest. She ran her fingers through his curls. She always found comfort in touching him that way.

After making love, Karen rolled over on her side to find sleep and thought about the abortion that Ginger talked about in her letter. She'd aborted her baby to pursue her singing and it now appeared she had a ready-made family in spite of herself. Karen knew, even if her friend didn't, what Ginger would do.

## "TOP OF THE WORLD"
### The Carpenters

Rodney, the neighborhood rooster, announced the dawn, not once, not twice, but countless times throughout the first hour of daylight. Karen gave up on trying to sleep while Lee snored. She shook her head as if that would help the cobwebs, slipped on her flip flops, and walked over to the bathroom.

Karen had learned to peek inside to see if Bruce had decided to revisit the scene of his crime. So far, she'd managed to avoid a rematch with the green gecko. She didn't see him, took a deep breath and went inside. Once done, she flushed the way Ginger had told her, slipped out of the bathroom, and headed over to Donovan's handmade bench. She plucked a mango from a low hanging branch along the way. She sat down, stared at the sea, and breathed in its beauty. Better than caffeine. Kinda.

The sun peeked out in between the rain forest clouds that came from the direction of Port Antonio. Donovan had explained that depending on how far the clouds floated their way in the morning, seemed to determine much of their weather for the day. It was normal to have bountiful rainstorms with intense sunshine in between. The pattern allowed just about anything to grow, earning St. Ann's the Garden Parish title in Jamaica.

Karen held the mango in her hand and it caught Paulie's attention. The bird skittered over and stood in front of her. He made a soft cluck.

"Oh, I see you," she whispered, took a bite of the fruit, took it out of her mouth, and tossed it on the floor for Paulie. He scooted over and picked it up, threw his head back and swallowed it whole. He blinked and his eyes got big when the fruit traveled to his tummy and Karen stifled a laugh. "Guess I need to learn to take smaller bites! I'll keep that in mind for next time, bud." She heard someone walking up behind her and turned to see Ginger coming her way wearing a long orange caftan.

"I would've started the coffee, but don't know how to light the stove."

"Yuck, yuck," Ginger grinned. She plopped down next to Karen and together, instead of sipping coffee; they drank in the view. They said nothing for several minutes.

"You okay?" Karen asked. She reached over and touched Ginger's hand.

"Yeah, I'm good. Just shell shocked is all." Ginger blew her breath out between her lips until they puckered. "Guess I'm gonna be a momma by default."

"Yeah, there's always that. Did you have any idea about any of this?"

"I knew he'd had a one-night-stand when he came back to Jamaica. Who was I to judge?" She took a bite of a banana and held it up for Karen to take a bite, but she shook her head. "Besides that, I was waffling between Jimmy and Donovan back then. He thought I wasn't gonna come to Jamaica."

Ginger and her high school sweetheart, Jimmy, had been on and off for a long time. She discovered Jimmy had another girlfriend and they had recently broken up when she met Donovan. When his visa expired and he had to leave, she was torn about what to do. In the end, her fascination with Donovan and the desire to escape her circumstances, outweighed any feelings for Jimmy.

"He's gonna go see her this morning," she said referring to the baby's mother. "He wants Lee to go with him."

Karen raised her eyebrows and leaned back to look at Ginger. "Seriously? Why Lee?"

"Not sure, maybe protection, you never know when things might go sideways around here." Ginger pulled a cigarette out of her pack of Virginia Slims and lit up. She exhaled up into the sky. "He's probably afraid that I might not behave like a lady." She took another drag. "Imagine that."

Ginger stood up. "But here's the upside. You and I get the morning to ourselves. I'm thinking we spell that "B, E, A, C, H." She stood and pulled Karen to her feet.

"I'm thinking you're right," Karen clapped Ginger on the back. "You two will figure this out, Ging."

"Yeah," Ginger answered, but her voice betrayed her lack of confidence. "Did you know the baby's name is Donna? After Donovan."

"Are you kidding me?"

"Nope. He has a namesake, it seems."

"Geez, Ging. How's that make you feel?"

"Like I've been sucker punched. Know what I mean?"

"Yeah, I sure do. But really, how does he know it's his little girl for sure?"

"Evidently, she has his birthmark. A heart on her hand just like his . . . and his father's." Karen had no comeback for that.

They walked back toward the kitchen table. Donovan had started the fire and the coffee pot was going. The liquid inside the glass bubble on the top of the blue speckled pot had just started jumping up and down, a sign the coffee was beginning to per-colate. Ginger sliced up mangoes and pineapple, put out a con-tainer of cottage cheese from the fridge and served everyone at the kitchen table. Karen handed out cups, plates, and forks.

"The coffee will be ready in a minute, so hang in there," Donovan announced as he sat down. The one-year-old pink elephant in the room named Donna hung out for a bit until Donovan broke the ice. "Sorry for the drama last night, guys."

Lee and Karen looked at each other. "No problem. You'll figure it out," Lee said. "Did Ginger tell you I'm going to Golden Grove with Donovan?" Karen nodded.

Ginger changed the subject. "So, I guess we'll be snorkeling if you guys wanna go when you get back. We'll be right down at Old Fort Bay beach," Ginger took a slice of mango, cut it in half and took a bite. "We can pack your swim suits, so no need for you to go home first."

"Yeah, we will leave soon and be back as fast as we can. We'll head down to the beach when we get back," Donovan answered as he pulled the coffee pot off the fire. He poured a cup for each of them. They ate breakfast in silence, each lost in their own thoughts wondering how things would go with the baby's momma.

After the guys left to catch a taxi, the girls packed up for the beach. "I've got two mangoes, pineapple chunks, cheese, and crackers." She put them in the sack along with a thermos of lem-onade. "Here's some stale bread to feed the fish." Ginger handed a bag of leftover crust and heels to Karen.

Each loaded up with a towel and a set of snorkels and fins. They made it to the bottom of the hill and stood by the two-lane high-way, waiting for traffic to clear so they could cross. When the time came, they jogged to the other side and continued heading down the lane of the Old Fort Bay neighborhood toward the sea.

"Nice house," Karen pointed to a new masonry home as they walked toward the sea. Bougainvillea hung over the fences on the few houses that dotted the lane. Most were bordered with wrought iron fences and locked gates. A lawn mower groaned as a groundskeeper pushed it through the grass. "Not too many people out and about." It was definitely an upscale neighborhood compared to the hillside across the street.

"Yeah, one of these days, Alice," Ginger answered quoting Jackie Gleason. The Honeymooners had been one of her parents' favorite shows growing up. "One of these days we'll come off that hillside and live on the sea."

"No doubt you will." Karen spotted the sea. "Oh my, Ging!!" The cobalt blue sea glowed. The sight of salt water never ceased to make her smile, but the colors of the Caribbean in Jamaica left her groping for words.

She followed Ginger through a path in the bushes and came out on a sandy beach. The beach was small but deserted. They threw down their towels, "I don't think there's a need to 'stake our claim' today, but just in case." Ginger said. They'd always put down plenty of towels and blankets when they went to the beach to protect their waterfront view from late arriving beachgoers. "Old habits die hard."

"There's nobody here but us? I don't think I've ever had that luxury." Karen said.

"Okay, let's get you snorkeled up." Ginger showed Karen how to adjust the mask. "Put a little spit on your finger and rub it inside the goggles. It helps keep the lens from clouding up under water." They put their fins on and did the big foot duck waddle backwards into the water.

"There's the reef where you see the little waves," she pointed about 20 yards off shore. Once in waist deep, they put their faces down and started paddling.

Karen laid face down in the water and paddled. She floated easily and could see grass flowing back and forth on the bottom. She swam behind Ginger as they headed toward the reef. After she got used to hearing the sound of her own breath through the snorkel, she was awestruck as fish of every color swam around her and peeked out from the reef. She pointed and talked under water, mostly to herself. Her excitement didn't disappoint either of them. They doggie paddled during a break and waved to a fisherman in a boat just beyond the reef. "Hey, it's Matthew!" Ginger said to Karen. "How's the fishing today?" she hollered.

"Irie, Mon!" He held up a string of large silvery fish. Both waved in approval and he continued down the coast. "I'll get some from you later!" Ginger waved him on and he gave her a thumbs up.

"Looks like fish for dinner. Don't tell these guys." She pointed down toward the fish that circled her fin covered feet. They pulled their snorkels down over their eyes and plopped their faces back in the water.

Once underwater and alone with her thoughts, Ginger's mind wandered back to Donovan, his daughter, and her mother. "The what ifs are gonna drive you nuts, stop it!" she mumbled through her snorkel. She spotted the friendly face of a blue doctor fish that hoped she'd brought the breadcrumbs, and she had. The "what ifs" went away and for a few minutes, all that remained was the world below the sea. She wondered if she could just stay there.

Donovan and Lee squeezed into the back seat of a taxi with another passenger. The car drove further up the mountain dotted with shanties along the roadside twisting one way and then another as the road climbed the mountainside.

Every now and then, a great house sat off in the distance. "Who lives there?" Lee asked.

"Nobody I know, that's for sure. These old British great houses are all over the countryside."

Fifteen minutes later, they climbed out of the car and Donovan handed the driver his fare. The taxi drove away and they looked around for someone to ask directions. He had been to Tabitha's home only once before and had been in a stupor, so memory wasn't an option. Donovan spotted a store and they walked over to the hut. He leaned on the glass countertop that housed cigarettes, lighters, sweeties, and razors. Canned goods lined the back shelf and fresh fruit hung from baskets tied to the ceiling. A woman sat on a stool weaving a little girl's hair into braids.

"Mornin'. Do you know where Tabitha Milford lives?"

The woman looked from Donovan to Lee whose white skin made her radar rise.

"Who want to know?"

"My name is Donovan," and before he could finish his name, her eyes lit up in recognition.

"You baby Donna's fada?"

"Well, yes, or," he stuttered, "I think so."

Lee scratched his head as he tried to understand as Donovan and the woman started talking in patois. It seemed to be a combination of English, and he wasn't sure what. Donovan had explained it was South African and English mixed. It didn't matter that English was involved. Once they started talking, it was just like any other foreign language. Tough to understand. It was like they had a different word for everything.

"Do you know where she lives?"

She put the comb down and turned her daughter around to face her.

"Go tell Aunty Tabitha come down here. There's a man named Donovan that wanna see her." The little girl looked from her mom to Donovan and back again. She turned and ran out the back door of the shop.

"Tanks for your help."

"How much are the bananas?" Lee asked. He pulled out Jamaican dollars before she could answer. "Never mind. Here you go," he plopped the bills on the counter. "Keep the change and thanks for your help." He handed a banana to Donovan who stood there wondering how to fill the awkward silence.

He was spared when the little girl came running back into the shop, half her hair in braids and the other half flying free. "She say she meet you at the school," she pointed down the road.

"Thanks so much for your help." He looked from the daughter to the mother. "Have a good day."

"You be good to Tabitha and Donna. She name her after you, you know." Donovan nodded, the knot in his stomach grew. The two men headed down the street, Lee peeled his banana and finished it by the time they got to the school. Donovan handed his back to Lee. "I can't eat anything right now, you go ahead." The building was concrete and painted a dirty yellow, presumably going for the "Golden Grove" theme. They walked into the courtyard made of dirt and a circle of huge truck tires that created a raised flower bed of sorts. A palm tree rose from the middle yielding a sorry amount of shade. They sat on the rims of the tires. The Jamaican sun brought beads of sweat out on Lee. "Here, Mon, sit in the shade," Donovan pointed. Lee didn't argue.

"So, what happened, Man. Is the baby yours?"

"She could be. I'd just come back from the US and didn't think Ginga was going to join me here. I was staying at my aunt's house. I woke up at midnight from a dream and couldn't get back to sleep. I walked down the street to find the local rum bar." Jamaica's first commercial crop, rum, kept the local economy going. There were rum bars on every corner and sometimes in between. "She came in right after I did and we both started drinking. Next thing I knew, I woke up in her room the next morning."

The words twisted the knot in his stomach even tighter. He was embarrassed in front of Lee as well as himself. He'd known dozens of boys without dads growing up. Donovan's father was a full-blooded Maroon of Jamaica and in their culture, men didn't leave their children wanting for anything.

"I'd never done anything like that before or since, just so you know. Not something I'm proud of . . . " His voice trailed off.

"No need to go there, Man." Lee shook his head. "Would you like me to go for a walk and give you two some privacy?"

Donovan leaned his head back to consider the offer when they both saw Tabitha with Donna on her hip, and a grown Jamaican man walking down the dirt road to meet them.

"No, Mon. Tinking I might need your help after all." They locked eyes.

"Got ya covered," Lee clapped his back as they stood and walked to meet her. He got his first close look at Tabitha and was surprised that Donovan had said she was thirty-four. She looked much younger. Her shorts were the same from the night before and she wore a blue tie-dyed tee shirt that had a smiley face printed on the front. Her face was anything but "smiley." Baby Donna was as chubby as every baby should be and a skin tone similar to Donovan's.

"You soon come," Tabitha said.

"Yes, I wanted to talk more. Who's this?" Donovan asked, looking at the man that stood next to her.

"Dis my son, Roger." The young man's eyes shifted from Donovan to Lee and back again. Donovan put out his hand. Roger hesitated, but took it.

"How old are you?"

Roger's eyes went to his mother who nodded. "Nineteen, sir." Donovan blinked. Tabitha had started young.

"Well, I can see your momma raised you right. You can call me 'Donovan.'" He turned back to Tabitha. "You caught me off guard last night." All the things he'd rehearsed in his head left him. He stumbled through the investigation.

Baby Donna wore a pink sundress that was a little too small. Her bare feet dangled at her momma's side. Her big brown eyes followed whoever was talking. She tried to put her hands in Tabitha's mouth as she spoke, but her mom leaned back and kept talking.

Tabitha didn't mince words. "Do you want be fada to your dawta?"

Donovan plopped back down on the tire wall, stunned by her direct approach.

"Yes, I want to take care of my daughter. I want to be her fada," his voice trailed. Donovan knew he couldn't ignore his little girl as so many Jamaican men might do. Many men left children with no father to support them and all in the name of Rastafarianism. Donovan didn't buy into the lifestyle, but many Jamaicans did. He would be her father in the ways that mattered. He was a proud Maroon.

He gave Tabitha a handful of cash. "I will give you more when I can." She looked down at her fistful of money. "Can I hold her?" He was surprised at his own request.

She handed the little girl over to him. He took her in his hands, sat on the ledge, and put her on his lap facing him. The baby looked back towards her mother and then at Donovan. She patted his cheek and smiled. He looked into the mirror of his daughter's eyes.

***

They ducked into the back of the taxi. Neither spoke for a few minutes when Lee took the plunge.

"I think it went pretty well."

"Yeah, till I tell Ginga I will have Donna every weekend."

"She'll be okay with it, Don," Lee tried to convince them both with his words.

"She want to sing," Donovan said. "She no wanna be a mother."

"You might be surprised, Don."

"No, dis I know," Donovan leaned his head on the back of the seat. The memory of the afternoon he figured out about the abortion came flooding back. He knew Ginger drank the medicine woman's tea. Secrets were hard kept on the hillside. She was sick for a day or so, and that was that. It occurred to him that if she had not, they would be expecting his second child.

***

The guys jumped out of the taxi and headed to the beach to meet Karen and Ginger. They ducked in the bushes and changed into their swim suits.

Karen now considered herself a snorkeling expert and pulled Lee into the water and together they swam out to the reef.

Donovan and Ginger stayed on the beach and he told her about their visit with Tabitha.

"I will be taking care of Donna on the weekends so Tabitha can work."

"Don, I work most weekends."

"I know, I will take care of her. I won't let this affect your singing, Ginga." He pulled her over to him and she leaned her head on his shoulder.

"Could make for some good song lyrics, I'm thinking," she answered. They sat in silence for a while. "Well, we'd better get going or I'm gonna be late for my first gig."

Donovan put his fingers to his mouth and whistled for the snorkelers to come back. They packed up their gear and headed back up the side of the mountain to get ready for Ginger's debut at Jack Ruby's.

A band was playing as they walked into the dance hall. Donovan led them to a table, Lee pulled a chair out for Karen, and she sat down.

Ginger turned and walked toward the bar. She could feel the beat of the drum in her heart as she walked by. The horns sang the tune and toes that weren't on the dance floor dancing, were tapping on the floor under the table. "Do You Remember the Days of Slavery?" she looked up to see Burning Spear (Winston Rodney was his real name) and caught her breath. Everyone said he was the new Bob Marley. She was playing in between *his* sets? Her heart skipped a beat. She remembered what her mom had always said, "Take what God gives ya and use it to go places." She took a deep breath and used the adrenaline to her advantage, as Jack Ruby looked up from counting the piles of cash that laid on the desk behind him. He had a round face and short beard. His eyes were friendly enough.

He'd been sitting in the back of the restaurant when she auditioned, so she wasn't really sure what he looked like. "Mr. Ruby?"

She carefully sat down her guitar case and stuck out her hand across the counter. He cocked his head to one side and took it. He recognized the olive tone of her skin and silky auburn hair from her audition. It wasn't often a red head had such a combination and could sing and play the guitar. "I'm Ginger O'Reilly."

"Yeah, well dats de first ting we fix," he said.

"Excuse me?" Ginger leaned in closer.

"Your name, O'Reilly's not so much Jamaican."

"You don't think they'll figure that out when they see me?" There are those times when you want to rewind and eat the words that just came out of your mouth. For Ginger, this was one of those times.

"Many won't see you because you will be a voice on a record to them, nothing more. Name is what matta."

"Hmm, a new name, huh? I'll get to work on that right after my set." She was excited he was talking about recording already. She tried hard not to do her happy dance in front of him.

"I 'ave it figured out for you by den." He nodded toward Randall, the manager she'd met before. "Randall will introduce you." Randall nodded, letting Jack know that he was on top of things. Jack turned back to his piles of cash and kept on counting.

She looked around to find a spot to get ready. The crowd applauded as Burning Spear finished his set, her queue to get ready to play. She picked up her guitar. "Thanks for the opportunity. I won't disappoint ya," she said to the back of his head and he nodded.

She turned and walked toward Randall who stood next to the steps that led up to backstage. She glanced toward the crowd and saw Karen wave and she smiled back as she stepped behind the curtain. She took her guitar out of its case, pulled the strap over her head, and plucked on the strings lightly to make sure they were still tuned. The crowd's focus had moved from music and dancing to food, drink, and conversation. She walked onto the stage and sat on the stool. Her fingers strummed the guitar strings, but the soothing sound didn't quiet them down.

Randall jumped up on stage and pulled the mike out of the stand. "Hey, everyone! Let's give a big Ochi welcome to Ginger!" The crowd hushed and there was a weak amount of applause, most of which came from Karen's table. She closed her eyes and began to sing, letting the music transport her past their lack of interest. It worked for her every time, if not the crowd.

Richard, the drummer from the Burning Spear band, saw the crowd needed a beat to reel them in. He finished off his Red Stripe and walked to his drums, and picked up his sticks along the way. He picked up on her beat ever so gently and within a minute, the crowd swayed as one.

He played to her song. Richard nodded to his trumpet playing buddy, Clarence, who walked over and picked up his instrument. The Caribbean beat was synonymous with the new reggae sound. The crowd hushed. Her voice carried her over the room and captured every ear. The edge of her soul poured through her words and fingers. The beat of the drums and soft lullaby of the trumpet took a back seat once the crowd caught on. The audience felt her presence. Her songs flowed from one to another. Some were renditions of old and a few were hers alone. Ginger was in her element. Finally.

"I have one more song to share tonight. It's an old one that perhaps you've heard before. It's my reggae rendition, I guess you could say." Her hand ran over the smooth mahogany of her guitar.

"I want to dedicate it to Karen who's in the audience tonight," she shielded her eyes trying to see her through the stage lights. "Raise your hand, Woman!" Karen slipped up her hand. "We used to sing this when we were kids." The crowd applauded, she closed her eyes, and left the room in her mind, stepping onto the make-shift stage of her mom's back porch when they were kids.

"You are my sunshine, my only sunshine," Richard and Clarence adapted to the sound once again. "You make me happy when skies are gray," she slipped into the back porch of her parents' home, singing into a wooden spoon with Karen. A renegade tear slid down her cheek. She shook her head and reminded herself to get a grip. She gave Richard and Clarence a queue to step it up and gave the tune an upbeat turn halfway through. The crowd loved it and followed one another to the dance floor. Men and women sang along as they swayed in each other's arms. Ginger and the band extended the song for another five minutes. When they wound it down, the dance hall erupted with cheers. Ginger stood and acknowledged Richard and Clarence, "Give it up for these guys!" The applause continued for a minute and died down as she left the stage and headed for their table.

Donovan met her halfway and hugged her tight. "Great job, Babe." He smiled and held her head in his hands. He looked into her eyes. "Your dream is coming true." Her eyes welled up, but she held the tears back, too happy to give them space just then.

Karen and Lee stood behind Donovan and took their turns for hugs and kisses. They sat down at their table and ordered a round of drinks. Ginger took a breath and grabbed Karen's hand. "Come on, I need to get outta here for a minute." The two stood, grabbed their drinks, and walked out of the dance hall and into the evening breeze coming off the sea.

"You really hit a homerun tonight, girl."

"Thanks, but Richard and Clarence really bailed me with their back up."

"Yeah, that's true, but 'You are my Sunshine,' was a big hit, Kiddo."

Ginger pulled out a pack of Virginia Slims and a pack of matches. She tried unsuccessfully to light the cigarette in the breeze until Karen moved to block the wind. "Thanks," Ginger said.

"That's what friends are for. Standing in the way of adversity even when they don't wanna endorse bad behavior!"

Ginger grinned, took a long drag, and leaned back on the side of the building. She let the smoke go. "I know." She stared into the night as people walked up and down the dark street. "What am I gonna do, Kar?"

"Only you can answer that one," she reached over and squeezed Ginger's arm. "You guys will figure it out."

"Yesterday, things were much simpler."

"And today they're complicated, but I've never known you to be so crazy in love with anyone like you are with Donovan." Karen knew she was treading on thin ice. Ginger was not good at talking about feelings.

"Yeah, it's way different with him than it was with Jimmy. On many levels." Their relationship had started on a high physical note. Sometimes she felt as if she were mesmerized by his accent, work ethic, and even the cultural differences. She was beginning to think the more different things were, the better. Now the difference had shown itself in the manner of a ready-made family she wasn't sure she wanted right now.

"Some levels are better than others, I'm thinking," Karen grinned at her. "You know I'm with you, no matter, from the basement to the penthouse."

"Yep, even when skies are gray." They both nodded. Ginger took a long drag. "I know I gotta stop this mess." She looked down at the cigarette in her hand. "Tomorrow, I'll think about that tomorrow," she said in her best Scarlett O'Hara imitation.

"Okay, Scarlett," she said with her fake southern accent. "We'd better get back inside before the guys find someone else to dance with," Karen said.

"Yeah, and we both know how much Lee wants to dance," Ginger raised her eyebrows. "Now *that* would be worth the price of admission!"

"Well, maybe he's not into dancing on the dance floor, but I'm sure he's hoping to get a few drinks into me before we head home." Karen winked at Ginger as they turned and walked back inside.

The guys were waiting with refills sitting on the table. "See, what'd I tell ya?" Karen said to Ginger.

"Huh?" Lee asked. Karen shook her head, smiled, and raised her glass for a toast. "To Ginger and staying outta the Onesies, going straight for the Tensies of reggae."

# "TAKING CARE OF BUSINESS"
## Bachman Turner Overdrive

Ginger wondered how it had come to this. Singing at Jack Ruby's five nights a week and playing mom off and on weekends for the past year. It proved to be good for everyone. She looked over at Donovan as he hammered the last of the roof on the house they'd built over the past several years. It was finally finished.

She'd been reluctant to love little Donna, but the vibes the little girl sent her way left her powerless. Donovan's daughter spread smiles everywhere she went.

Ginger's career flourished after a few months of singing at Jack Ruby's. She accompanied many reggae stars such as Burning Spear and Justin Hinds as back up on their records. Their success catapulted hers. She was now quite the anomaly, a white reggae star with the stage name of Ginger Starling. As promised, Jack Ruby had come up with her stage name. It turned out to be just what Jamaica wanted. With the release of her reggae version of "You Are My Sunshine" she was on her way. She wasn't crazy about all the touring that came with success. The guys had been bugging her to go on the road with them. For now, she just wanted to stay on the island and continue her song writing while living on a hillside in the Caribbean.

She and Winston (Burning Spear to his fans) finished their last set, stood and took a semi-bow, and thanked the audience. She headed toward the bar.

"Sounds like they approve!" Ginger said to Jack as she walked up to the counter. He pushed her usual, a vodka martini, dirty with an extra olive, across the bar to her. She picked up the glass and took a sip. "Mmmm . . . just what I needed." She looked at the glass in her hand, pulled out the olive, tossed back the rest and pushed the glass back at him. He poured another. She wondered again why they made martinis in such small glasses. "A couple of olives for dinner is just what I need!" she laughed. Life was fun. She was writing new music and her agent was able to sell a lot of it. Their bank account started to grow. The albums started to sell and so did her songs.

She didn't have time to write many letters but could now afford to call Karen whenever she felt like it. Trouble was, she either wasn't home to make the call or it was too late and she knew Karen would be tucked away sleeping.

"Me tink the last set was just the right flow. You guys need to record it in that order," Jack said and gave Winston a high five.

"Hey? Am I invisible or what?" Ginger held her hand up and both guys hit her up. They laughed.

A distinguished gray-haired white man walked up to the counter. His buttoned up blue shirt was tucked neatly into his jeans. "That was quite a performance!" He held out his hand to shake Ginger's. She took his hand, looked up at him, and shook her head.

"Thanks. I'm sorry, do I know you?" She cocked her head to one side.

"No, you don't," he answered with an American accent and nodded toward a dark-haired middle-aged woman sitting at the table behind him. "My wife and I heard about your singing and decided to come and check you out for ourselves."

"Well, that's quite flattering. I'm happy you enjoyed the show."

"We sure did and were wondering if you perform at private parties."

"Well, I never thought about it. I guess that would depend." Ginger took a sip of her refill.

"We are just outside of town on the east side. It's my wife's birthday next weekend. We'd love to have you come and sing a few songs. We'll make it well worth your while. It's the only thing she's asked for this year." He motioned to the woman at the table to step up and join the conversation. The woman stood, grabbed a cane, and walked slowly to the bar. She had long dark hair swept up on her head and deep brown eyes. She moved slowly, but carried herself with regal ease.

"Ginger, this is my wife, Sylvia, and my name is David." Sylvia held out her left hand to shake as she held onto the cane with her right. Ginger couldn't help but gawk at her huge diamond ring that sparkled despite the darkness of the bar.

"It's a pleasure to meet you, Ginger." The two women looked at each other. Ginger had a strange feeling that she knew Sylvia from somewhere, but shook it off.

"Same here. I heard you're having a party next weekend," Ginger said. Jack Ruby waved goodbye to patrons as they filtered out of the club.

"I am and would so love it if you could come and play a few songs for us," Sylvia said as she looked from Ginger to David.

"It just so happens that I think I can if it's on Saturday." She looked at Jack. "You didn't have me scheduled, right?" He shook his head. "Where exactly do you live?"

"Well, it should be pretty easy for you to remember. The name of the property is Ginger Star," Sylvia said.

Ginger's eyes flew open with recognition. "That's how I know you!" She smiled. "I thought you looked familiar. I overheard a conversation at the post office last week and someone said 'Ginger Star,' and of course, the name caught my attention. I'd heard about the plantation when Jack gave me my stage name."

"Well, yes, that was me." Sylvia smiled. "Ginger Star is just a few miles outside of Ochi. We'd be happy to send a car to pick you up and then take you home."

They talked about the details. The generous amount they offered to pay flattered Ginger. When she told Donovan she was going to Ginger Star and he was invited to come along, he was excited. "We'll have to check with Arlene to see if she can keep Donna for a few hours," he said.

"I've heard a lot about Ginger Star since I was a kid. It was a sugar plantation back in the day." He reached back in his memory bank. "They say there is a duppy that walks the cliff above the sea."

"Well, I ain't into duppies, so it had better steer clear of me."

Saturday came and the two of them waited at the bottom of the hill for David's driver. A white Datsun sedan pulled up, and Donovan leaned in. "Are you from Ginger Star?" The driver nodded, Donovan opened the back door and Ginger climbed in with her guitar case. He slid in beside her.

Donovan talked with the Jamaican driver whose name was Gus. Ginger leaned her head back on the seat and reviewed the songs she planned to sing. She did this every time she performed, ran the melodies over in her head to calm her nerves and help find ways to connect the songs with the audience. They drove through Ocho Rios and headed east out of the city, along the coastline.

She hadn't seen much of this side of town, so she stared out the window and soaked in the view.

"Looks like the shoreline is below cliffs on this side of Ochi," Ginger said looking out the window.

"Yes, that's right. Ginger Star sits high above the sea with a beautiful grotto down below," Gus answered.

"What's a grotto?" she asked.

"It's a cave where the sea meets the rocks." Gus said. "The Arnolds have built a dock to make it accessible to boats," Gus tried to describe it. "You will have to go see."

"How long have you worked for the Arnolds, Gus?" Donovan asked.

"I work for them ten years now. They spend six months here and six months in the States. They manage to escape the cold of the US from November through April each year."

"Is it true that there's a ghost at Ginger Star?" Ginger asked.

Gus laughed. "Well, if you're talking about a duppy, yes, we've heard tales of that more than once, but if there is, I haven't seen her yet." He looked at Ginger in the rear-view mirror. "Might have heard her once or twice," his voice trailed.

"Oh boy," she nudged Donovan. "Just what I need, a real live ghost." As if she didn't have enough of her own.

Gus turned left off the highway through stone pillars onto the driveway. "Ginger Star" was engraved into the stone wall. The stalks of the red and yellow Ginger Star flowers bent and formed an archway over the road. "I've never seen anything so beautiful," Ginger said. They drove down the road lined with palm trees capable of touching the clouds. The shady lane was dotted with rays of sunshine that dared to peek through. The lane opened to the warm Jamaican sunshine where Ginger Star, the old British great house, greeted them.

Gus put the car in park, jumped out and opened Ginger's door. She swung her legs out and stood up, pulling her guitar along.

"Ginger!" David and Sylvia waved from the top of the half-moon steps. David jogged down to greet them. The three of them walked up the steps to the top of the carved wooden open-air foyer to meet Sylvia.

"Happy birthday! Thanks so much for inviting us." Ginger reached over and took Sylvia's hand. The woman wore a simple blue floor length gown. The diamonds hanging from her ears and neck gave it a sparkling affect.

"Thank you so much for coming. I'm so excited for everyone to hear your music!" Sylvia said. "Come, let's show you around."

They walked through the entrance, down the hallway, to the open-air living room that boasted a view of a cliff overlooking the turquoise Caribbean Sea. Ginger's hand flew to her throat when she saw the view. The Caribbean sparkled its welcome and the banana leaves pushed the breeze their way.

"Wow! I never knew it could be this incredibly beautiful. The sea always works its magic on me," Ginger said. "Hey, sounds like a song coming on." She often wrote lyrics on the back of a napkin or envelope and once, in the dust on the back of Kenroy's car. "Excuse me a sec." She pulled an envelope from her purse, made a quick note and stuffed it back in her woven bag.

"She write lyrics whenever they come to her," Donovan said looking at Sylvia. "You'll hear it again one day,"

Sylvia smiled. "When inspiration comes, you have to grab it." She pointed at a swivel stool that sat next to a black baby grand piano. "We thought you could sit here and play."

"That is perfect," Ginger said. A painting on the wall caught her eye. "Wow, this portrait is really something. I don't know who this is, but I feel like I'm looking right into her eyes and she in mine." A woman stood in a flowing blue dress, holding onto her wide brimmed hat, with the Caribbean Sea in the background.

"It was here when we bought Ginger Star. We were told Adria was her name. She was the daughter of the original plantation owner." David touched his wife's shoulder. "This is one that Sylvia painted," he said as he pointed to a seascape of Jamaica's north coast.

"Oh my! I didn't know you were an artist!" Ginger said and walked closer to the painting. "You guys are just full of surprises."

"Thanks. It's something I've loved to do since I was a girl," Sylvia looked hard at Ginger's face thinking she'd like to have her sit for a portrait one day. She could sense that Ginger's spirit would be easy to capture on canvas.

"Don't let her fool you. She studied art in Scotland before I met her," David said. They followed Sylvia as she walked slowly toward a closed door and opened it to reveal a sunlit studio. Ginger followed her inside. Paints, easels, and canvas frames littered the room. The scent of freshly painted canvas hung in the air.

"This is amazing," Ginger said as she walked toward an unfinished landscape painting. "I can't draw a good stick figure!"

"Oh, I'm sure you could learn," Sylvia said. "Maybe one day you can come back and I'll give you a lesson or two."

"I'd love that!"

"We'd better get set up, the guests will start to arrive soon," David said. Ginger headed over to her stool and pulled her guitar out of its case.

David was right. People began to pull up and it turned out to be a who's who in Jamaica. People Ginger had heard of from

Kingston, the country's capital, St. Ann's, and Montego Bay gathered to celebrate Sylvia's birthday. Evidently, the Arnolds were well connected in Jamaican society.

Ginger began to play and eventually sing. People milled around, smiling at her as they walked past. She played and sang for about forty-five minutes and stopped for a break. She picked up the glass of water that sat close by and took a drink. Sylvia heard the break in the music and headed her way. "Your music is just perfect for the evening, Ginger. Thanks again for coming!" Sylvia said as she walked up.

"You're most welcome, but no thanks necessary. I'm enjoying just being here at Ginger Star. I can see why you love it."

Sylvia stepped aside and a dark-haired, fair skinned woman in a flowing orange dress came up beside her. She was taller than Sylvia with green eyes that set off her pretty face. "This is my dear friend, Judy Ann MacMillan," Sylvia said. "We studied art together in Scotland and she now lives in Kingston."

Ginger stood up from her stool, still holding her guitar and extended her hand to Judy. "It's a pleasure to meet you," Ginger said.

"Your music is inspiring!" Judy said. "I've been hearing wonderful things about it and they were all true, it seems."

"Did you see the birthday present Judy gave me?" Sylvia pointed to an oil painting on the wall above the baby grand piano in the alcove. It was a colorful landscape of the front lawn of Ginger Star.

"Oh, wow! You are truly a gifted artist." Ginger marveled at the colors. She had captured the sea's colors off in the distance with amazing skill.

"Why thank you so much. I'm okay with a paint brush, but can't carry a tune or play a note. I think we're even!" Judy said.

"Well, I'd better get to the ladies' room and back to my next set," Ginger said. "The lady that hired me might wonder what I'm up to if I dally much longer." She winked at Sylvia, put her guitar down, and headed down the hallway.

---

Before Ginger could blink, the evening was over. She packed her guitar away in its case. Ginger looked up to see Judy standing in front of her. She stood up to say goodnight.

"I can't tell you how much I enjoy your music," Judy said. Her shawl floated in the air as her arms seemed attached to her every word in a flowing description. "The way you live in your song," her eyes closed and reopened in seeming surprise. "I just couldn't help but draw the memory." She held up a piece of paper. "I hope you don't mind." Judy handed Ginger a pencil sketch on a piece of paper.

"Mind? Not at all!" Ginger took the drawing and looked down at the paper. Judy had captured Ginger in deep song, her eyes staring off at the sea. The palm trees swayed and guests milled around in the background. "This is amazing! Thank you so much, Judy! I'll treasure it." She hugged her as Donovan walked up to help Ginger carry her guitar to the car. "Look what Judy gave me." She handed the drawing to Donovan.

He looked from the sketch to Judy. "You truly captured her. This is beautiful, but then again, any picture of you is lovely, my dear," he said as he looked at Ginger. She blushed.

"It was my pleasure, darling. It was a wonderful night!" Judy waved to them both as she headed toward the driveway.

Ginger and Donovan walked toward Gus and his car. "Well, I'm officially known as the man that accompanied Ginger Starling to the Arnolds' party." Donovan hugged her shoulder as they rode in the back of Gus's taxi. "You were a huge success tonight, Darlin." She leaned her head on his shoulder. Her music had been a hit.

When she closed with "You Are My Sunshine," people were up dancing and swaying.

"There were so many well-known people there, Don." Her mind swirled with memories of conversations and introductions. "I had no idea it was gonna turn out like that." But more than anything, she felt a connection with Sylvia. Ginger could sense the woman's genuine goodness.

The two women's friendship blossomed over the coming months. They met for lunch in town once in a while and often got together at Ginger Star. Ginger played the guitar and wrote songs while Sylvia worked on her latest painting. Ginger found it comforting to have a friend that she could not only confide in, but just be around without having to make conversation or apologize for being reclusive and quiet. Other than Karen, she'd never had a close girlfriend.

Sylvia had confided in Ginger that she had MS and wasn't sure what the future held for her. "I can't stand the thought of hospitals and doctors," Sylvia said. "But I have to go back to the States soon for treatment. I definitely don't want to get stuck in the hospital here in Jamaica."

"I can understand that. I had to go to St. Ann's Hospital to visit a friend. It was way different than hospitals in the States." Ginger had noticed that Sylvia seemed to be moving slower than before. She was worried that her friend's condition was getting worse, but neither of them allowed themselves to say it aloud.

## Summer 1974

Ginger's schedule increased as the demand for her voice backing up soundtracks for Jamaica's ska and reggae stars grew. She'd recorded "You Are My Sunshine" a while back and for the flip side of the single record, she chose "Magic on Me," the new song she'd written as a result of her first visit to Ginger Star.

Summer turned into fall and rumors of Hurricane Carmen heading their way permeated every conversation on the island. Everywhere Ginger went, the post office, bank, or grocery store, there was always chatter. "The storm come in the night," she heard everywhere she went.

There was talk of a direct hit on Jamaica. "Where can we go? We're sitting ducks on this hillside, Don." She helped him to pick up things in the yard that might blow around in the storm. He had finished enclosing their house with cinder block just a few months before. They were much more secure than before, but Ginger was still scared. Hurricane Carmen's unwelcome visit was supposed to happen in a day or so.

The sweltering August heat was intense, but every once in a while, a cool breeze would come. "It's as if someone turned on the air conditioning!" Ginger mused.

"Yeah, but dat mean storm is coming when it cools off dat way," Donovan explained. "We will be okay here," he reached over and patted her shoulder. She sighed and nodded.

He looked up to see Gus, Sylvia and David's taxi driver, walking up the path toward them. "Hey!" Gus called and waved to the couple. Donovan shielded his eyes trying to see who it was.

"Hey, Gus!" Donovan said, and put down the basket he was holding. He waved and they walked down the path to meet him. Donovan shook his hand and Ginger gave him a hug hello.

"What are you doing here, my man?"

"Well, I see you're getting ready for Carmen's visit!"

"Yeah, we're almost done," Donovan looked around the yard.

"David called from the States and asked that I invite you to stay at Ginger Star during the storm." Ginger and Donovan looked at each other.

"That would be great!" Ginger blurted out. Donovan looked at her, sighed and nodded in resignation, knowing better than to argue. While he'd weathered many storms in Jamaica and felt they would be fine here, he didn't want her to be scared. Not to mention the wrath of Hurricane Ginger could be worse than any rain event headed their way.

"Well, I tink Ginga approves of the plan."

"Sorry, Hon." She reached over and hugged his arm. "I guess I got carried away."

Donovan looked around the yard. They were almost finished with their storm preparations. "Okay, yes, we will come to Ginger Star, Gus."

"Great, when would you like for me to come back to get you?"

Donovan and Ginger looked at each other and they both shrugged. "Well, we are just about finished tying things up here. If you'd like to wait a bit, it will save you a trip back," Donovan said.

"I'm happy to do that. Is there anything I can help you do?"

"No, we just need a few minutes to gather what it is we need to bring with us," he said. "Have a seat."        to the stone wall that bordered their yard. "We'll be ready soon."

They gathered their most important things. Ginger reached under the bed and grabbed her songwriting journal, small cedar jewelry box, and photo album. She figured anything else could be replaced. Other than that, a few pieces of clothing, toothbrush, and her guitar would do it. She went to the refrigerator and pulled out the perishable food to take along, putting it all into the tote bag that Karen had given her. She made a mental note to call Karen and let her know their evacuation plan. Karen had already sent a few smoke signals of worry, sending a message through the phone at Jack Ruby's. She'd stop on the way through town and call her from a phone booth.

"What about Paulie?" Ginger whirled around and looked at Donovan. Her heart dropped when she realized they'd have to leave him behind. Donovan had added a "parrot door" to their bedroom so he could come and go as he pleased, but she was still worried.

"Paulie will be fine, my sweet." He pointed to the bird. "He know sometin' coming with de weather. Just watch him." The parrot skittered back and forth, refusing to leave their sides.

Paulie squawked.

"I'm gonna slice up some mangoes and leave them in the bedroom in a dish for him." Ginger said.

Paulie clucked and bobbed his head up and down in approval. He nudged the bowl of fruit with his beak until it wobbled back and forth and the guava fell to the floor. She bent over and picked it up.

"Okay, okay, I get the hint. Guava too."

"Paulie's okay with it," Donovan said and patted her on the back trying to make her feel better. "He's weathered many storms before Carmen."

Gus smiled and pretended he wasn't hearing the conversation. Birds in Jamaica were often pets. Paulie shook his head and ducked inside through his private entrance. He hopped up onto the bed.

"I'll let Matthew know we're leaving," Donovan said. He turned and walked up the lane. Ginger finished slicing the fruit and went out to wait with Gus. Paulie hopped off the bed and followed her, grabbing a slice of guava on his way out. He hopped up to his favorite branch.

Donovan walked back down the lane and joined them in the yard. They picked up their bags and headed down the hillside to Gus's car. Ginger looked over her shoulder and wondered what they would find after Carmen came and went.

# "YOU AND ME AGAINST THE WORLD"
## Helen Reddy

Ginger pulled the accordion style door shut on the phone booth that stood outside the grocery store in Ocho Rios. Donovan went inside the store to see what was left on the shelves.

She dialed the operator and gave her Karen's number for a collect call. It had been over a year since Karen and Lee's visit to Jamaica. She could hear the operator plug in the number and the phone began to ring. After three rings, Ginger worried Karen wasn't home, but then heard her pick up.

"Hello?"

"Yes, this is the overseas operator. I have a collect call for Karen from Ginger in Jamaica. Will you accept the charges?"

"Yes!" Karen answered. "Ging, are you okay?"

"I'm here, Kar. Just wanted to let you know that we're evacuating the hillside and staying at Ginger Star during the hurricane. I knew you'd be worried."

"Well, you were right about that."

"We were planning to ride it out at home, but Sylvia and David sent Gus over to get us, so it just made sense." Her letters had filled Karen in on her new friends, the Arnolds.

"For sure. Sounds like Ginger Star is a safer place. Thinking you will be much better off there. When's Carmen gonna get there?"

"We think sometime tonight. I'll call when it's over."

"Okay, praying she will take a turn out to sea."

"Me too. Love you guys. Give Nellie a hug from me and slap Lee nice and hard, okay?"

"Count on it. Any excuse to knock some sense into him is a good one! Thanks for calling, Ging. Love you and Donovan. Be safe!"

"Oh yeah, Kar, call Dad and let him know, okay?"

"Sure thing."

Ginger hung up the phone and leaned her head on the receiver, closed her eyes, and took a deep breath. She missed Karen and the security of the good old USA. Whenever there was a hurricane headed to their coast, at least people could evacuate. "God, I don't pray much, but I'm gonna give it a try this time. Please keep us safe." She opened her eyes to see her neighbor, Arlene, clearing out her booth at the craft market. "Hey! Arlene!" she shouted and waved hello.

"No customers today! You guys be safe," Arlene hollered back as she continued shoving boxes into the trunk of a car. Matthew opened the door of the taxi and Arlene got inside. They drove away and both waved. Ginger saw Gus in the parking lot and hurried over to meet him. Donovan walked out of the grocery store with his arms wrapped around two paper grocery bags.

"What did you buy?" she asked.

"Well, supplies were dwindling fast, but I managed to get milk, bread, and the last of the eggs along with a few surprises for later," he winked and a devilish grin crossed his face. She couldn't help but smile. He must've found things to feed her insecurities, like Three Musketeers bars and Pepsi. He always knew the right thing to do.

They climbed back in the car and headed to Ginger Star. She imagined that today, it belonged to her. Today, it was her turn to be the lady of the house. A real house. Too bad her first guest was a hurricane. Gus turned down the lane and the Ginger Star flowers bounced hello in the breeze that was beginning to kick up.

He parked the car in front, walked them up the half-moon steps and down the hallway. He opened the door to their room. She walked inside to find a white canopy bed with mosquito netting above, ready to fall down in a cloud of protection when they were tucked in. Open shuttered windows covered each wall revealing the garden of banana leaves that waved a soft greeting. The Jamaican sunshine streamed through the green leaves and filtered into the room. A striped brown tabby cat rubbed up against her ankles in a welcome dance, but scampered away when Ginger reached down to pet her. "That's Miss Kitty," Gus made the introduction. "She's shy at first, but will soon be your best friend if you let her."

"I love cats," Ginger said and smiled. "We get each other, don't we?" She bent down and stroked Miss Kitty's head behind her ears and looked her in her big green eyes. "I have a lot in common with my feline friends. I like to stretch my claws and love to eat fish." She raised her hands in claw-like fashion. No cat could resist her. She dragged herself away from the cat to follow Gus and Donovan.

Miss Kitty ran in front of them and pushed a door open. She curled her tail around its edge and slipped inside the room. The sea breeze caught the door and it slammed against the wall before Ginger could catch the handle. She grabbed and steadied it and looked up to see an easel. Her own face stared back at her as the woman in the portrait held a guitar. It was her hands that held her guitar and her eyes that captured her. Chills ran up her spine.

"What?" She stepped closer. "Is that?" She looked at Gus. "Me?"

Gus stood still, drew in a breath, let it out, and said, "Well, yes, that tis you, mi lady." He took off his hat and ran his hand through his hair. "But Miss Sylvia don't want you to know. She plan to surprise you." He looked over at Miss Kitty. "And you, you, gonna have some splainin to do," he nodded at the cat, "when Miss Sylvia come home and find you done spoiled her surprise!"

Ginger looked from Gus to Donovan. She didn't know what to think. She was overwhelmed how, by looking at the canvas, it was like reading her own mind. "I had no idea she did portraits," she said.

Donovan walked up behind her to look closer. "Wow, that's incredible." He looked at Ginger and they both nodded. She took a deep breath.

"Well, if Miss Sylvia doesn't want me to know, then I won't know!" She looked at Miss Kitty. "You're gonna owe me big for this one, girl."

"It would make her very happy to surprise you," Gus winked at her. She backed out of the room, waited for Miss Kitty, and closed the door behind them. Gus continued with the tour.

"This is the kitchen area," he pointed down a hallway with a swinging door that more often than not was moving as a staff member went about his or her business at Ginger Star.

"When the storm gets strong, we should all go inside here." Gus led them down a hallway past the kitchen and opened a door that led to a windowless room. He flipped on the overhead light to reveal a room lined with canned goods, candles, and necessities. Cots lined the walls and a chamber pot sat in the corner.

"This is normally the kitchen pantry, but was also created to be a safe room during a storm," he explained. "We will all gather here

when it's time. Until then, I suggest you relax and enjoy yourselves for a while." They headed back toward the living room.

Gus flipped on the TV and they paused to watch news about Carmen. The wind blew the antenna making the news broadcast come and go with loud crackling and a snowy picture. They soon gave up and walked to the front of the house.

Today, the furniture and wall décor was put away and the halls and walls were empty giving it an eerie feeling. The golden sunshine and sea breeze on the green gardens betrayed what would come with the change of the sky. Dark ominous clouds beckoned on the horizon.

"Looks like the storm is on its way," Donovan said and they all looked at the sky.

"It's a strange feeling when you know it's coming and you can't get out of the way," Ginger said. She grabbed Donovan's hand and squeezed.

"If its anything like Hurricane Ginga, I can relate," he teased. She stepped back but he pulled her closer and slid his arm around her shoulder. She was the first to admit that she could fly off the handle when things didn't go her way.

"It's those spin off tornadoes you gotta watch out for!" she teased. "And once a month, all bets are off, Reggae Man!" She nudged him with her hip and ran into the bedroom. He chased after her and closed the door behind them.

***

She slipped her legs over his hips and tucked her head on his shoulder as they laid in bed.

"I hope Donna's okay," Ginger said and nuzzled her face into the crook of his neck. His warm skin always made her feel safe and protected. Jamaica was so primitive compared to where

she had always lived. She began to feel vulnerable knowing that Carmen would barrel down on them in just a few hours. She was grateful to be at Ginger Star, but she found herself imagining awful things that could happen. Since she'd arrived in Jamaica, she'd been caught in two flash floods. After long periods of rain on the island, the water needed to find its way off the mountains and eventually, the rivers and waterfalls would overflow before they could deliver the excess water to the sea.

"Tabitha is many things, but she is a good mother," Donovan said. He had gone to Golden Grove to check on them the day before, but found that Tabitha had taken Donna to her mother's home further up in the mountains to a higher elevation and stronger house.

"I know, I guess I just can't help but worry." She sighed. "How did I get so attached to her so fast?"

Donovan smiled. "Once you realized that God multiplies love and doesn't divide it, you couldn't help yourself." He pulled her closer. "That's why I love you, Ging. You offer your love with no conditions." There was a knock on the bedroom door. Ginger pulled up the covers and Donovan jumped out of bed and headed to the door.

"The breeze has turned into wind," Gus said when Donovan answered his knock. "We had better get ready to go into the hurricane room within the hour." The bedroom shutter blew open and the raindrops flew in sideways across the room. Ginger jumped up wrapped in the sheet and tried to close the shutter. They both got drenched before they latched the shutter again.

They took Gus's advice and while Miss Kitty supervised, dried, got dressed, and gathered their stuff. The breeze outside picked up as they listened to weather updates on their crackly sounding transistor radio.

They looked out the bedroom window. The afternoon light faded into a shadowy darkness as the black clouds rolled in. Rain dotted the sea and a few clouds seemed to reach down and touch it. The voice on the radio said that Carmen should reach Jamaica in the wee hours of the morning. She turned it off and tucked it back in their bag. They closed the rest of the bedroom shutters and locked them the way Gus had shown them.

She opened the door and Donovan and Miss Kitty followed her down the hallway to the hurricane room. Gus was already there, tuning in his radio. He looked up and smiled. "Welcome!"

"Where is everyone?" Ginger asked. She had assumed the rest of the staff would join them here.

"Oh, they all go home and hunker down with their families," Gus said.

They could hear the wind roar and blow the rain up against the house. A few candles illuminated the darkness. She pulled out the ones she had brought from home and lined them up on the shelf that held the canned goods. "We can save these for later," she said. She held onto the white pillar candle Karen had given her during her visit for a few extra seconds.

"I set up some beds for us," Gus pointed to the sides of the room. "Assuming we'll be able to sleep," he added.

"Thanks so much, Gus," she said. "I brought my pillow." Ginger held it up for him to see. "So I'm counting on it."

The wind's song went from a high pitch to a low rumble. Thunder boomed in the not so far away distance and the shuttered windows of Ginger Star chattered. Shadows danced in the hallway.

"We can wait a bit to close the door. As long as you can stand the noises," Gus said. A clap of thunder hit as if it were right above them. The sound shook her body and she jumped.

"Geez oh flip!" Ginger gasped. "That's gonna take some getting used to!"

"We will close the door when the wind reaches us," Gus said.

"Yeah, she gets jumpy when a dog barks. We might be peeling her off the ceiling yet!" Donovan said with a smile.

They sat at the small table in the middle of the room and played a few hands of rummy. "So, Gus, where did you grow up?" Ginger asked as she picked up a card from the stack. The wind was loud and they had to almost holler to be heard at times.

"I am from Moneague," he answered. "It take about an hour to get der from Ochi."

"Is that up through Fern Gully?" Donovan asked.

"Yes, straight up that road past Perrytown. Mi mada still live der."

Thunder clapped overhead making them all jump. They felt the sound in their bones. The wind found its way into the room, blew some of the cards off the table, and the candles flickered. Gus got up and closed the door.

"How long do you think this will last?" Ginger asked. Gus and Donovan looked at each other, shrugged, and smiled.

"You never know," Donovan said. "They say Carmen is gonna hit the southern coast harder, but the rain and wind still come," he explained. "It could take a long time if Carmen decides to park herself over the mountains. Ginger's thoughts turned to Donna, but she kept quiet.

"Yeah, and the flash floods can be a problem later on when the water come off de mountains to de sea," Gus said.

"Do you think there will be any more hurricanes this year?"

Donovan shrugged. "We never know, but wives tales say that if it rain a lot, we don't get them, and this summer we had a drought.

"The saying goes, 'July stand by, August watch out, September remember, October all over!'" Gus recited the local saying. They played a few more hands of cards. Ginger yawned and stretched her arms toward the ceiling. "Let's try and get some sleep before it's too loud to try." Gus said.

"Where is Miss Kitty?" Ginger asked.

"Oh, she find a good hiding place. No need to worry about her," Gus said.

Ginger laid on her cot and pulled the blanket up to her neck. No matter how warm it might be, she always needed a cover. The sounds of Carmen were fickle, going from hard rain blowing on and off the shutters to banana leaves flapping back and forth against the walls. Lightning flashed through the slats, hail bounced off the roof, and the howling wind stopped for nothing. She tossed and turned until she finally drifted into sleep.

"I'm coming!" She opened her eyes to darkness and stood to follow the sound. She could hear the knock and the sound of the little voice. Her feet shuffled and she held her hands out to feel for the door. The wind howled and the shutters clattered, muffling the sound of the voice, but she could still hear her.

There it is . . . Her hands moved along the cool wood of the door and found the cold metal of the door knob. She turned the knob. The door flew open, and banged against the wall, pushing her back to the middle of the room. Donovan jumped up and pushed his body up against the door and shut with it with a thud.

"Where is she?" Ginger asked. She turned and Donovan pulled her to him. Tears fell down her cheeks. She tried to pull away from him and head back to the door, but he pulled her back.

"Where is who?" Donovan asked and tilted her chin up to look at him. Gus picked up a candle that was still lit and brought it over.

"You got up and opened the door!" Gus said. He looked at her in disbelief.

"I did?" She looked from Gus to Donovan sure that he was wrong.

"Yes, you kept asking where 'she' was." He stroked her hair. "You thought she was knocking at the door. Who was 'she'?"

Ginger shook her head. It started to come back to her. "I, I must have been dreaming," Ginger remembered seeing *her* baby, the one she'd sent back, in the dream. The baby she'd never had. It had all seemed so real . . . she looked toward the door. Where did she go?

"Was it Donna?" Donovan sat her down next to him on her cot. He knew she'd been worried about her.

She knew it wasn't Donna in her dream, but let him think so. "Yes, I think it might have been." She looked up to the ceiling and saw nothing. Why was she so real?

Crack! They looked toward the door and then back to each other. Crrraaack! The sound came again, this time longer. Before anyone could speak, a louder CRACK! reverberated and something smacked the house so hard they all jumped.

Donovan jumped up and headed for the door.

"No, don't!" Gus shouted. Donovan wheeled around and looked at him. "Sorry, I know it's tempting," he reached out and touched Donovan's arm. "But we have to wait until the storm is over before we go look," Donovan looked at him, nodded, and went back to sit next to Ginger.

"Can you just lay here with me?" she asked. He kissed the top of her head, laid down behind her, and pulled her close.

They drifted back and were able to sleep in short spurts. When they woke, daylight was pushing through the bottom of the door. Birds chirped again letting them know the coast was clear. Miss

Kitty meowed in the hallway making sure they knew she'd missed breakfast. Ginger rubbed her eyes as Gus moved the sandbags and opened the door. Miss Kitty scooted in and jumped up onto the bed, nudging Ginger's hand.

Ginger stroked Miss Kitty's back. "Oh my, you got wet! Where did you go?" she asked as if she expected an answer. She attempted to dry her fur with her blanket, but the cat jumped back to the floor. "Guess you like it that way. Let's go then." They stood up and followed Gus and Miss Kitty down the hallway. The open-air living room was now home to the huge tree that had cracked and fallen during the night. Limbs reached toward them and Miss Kitty jumped onto the trunk.

Gus and Donovan inspected the damage. "Looks like the roof took a hit when the tree fell." Donovan said as he looked toward the now open sky.

"Yeah, if that's as bad as it get, that's okay," Gus said and stepped over the tree, heading to the yard for further inspection.

"You want me to take you home now?" Gus looked back at them. They looked at each other and Ginger spoke up.

"Not just yet, let's get what we can done here at Ginger Star and then we'll go back." The men nodded in approval. She really didn't want to go back to see what was left of their hillside home. Not just yet. If Ginger Star could lose half her roof, one could only imagine what must have happened to their little home on the hillside.

Ginger walked back toward her bedroom and found all to be secure and fairly dry. She spent the day mopping and sweeping up the debris that had found its way inside Ginger Star's open hallways. The house was built so that you had to walk in an outdoor corridor to get to the other side. It was wonderful most of the time, but not conducive to keeping a hurricane at bay. Gus and Donovan pulled out chain saws from the garage and began to chop up the tree. She pulled the smaller pieces away as they cut and stacked them in the yard.

Ginger picked up the telephone receiver, but the line was still dead. "The phone's still not working," she said when she brought out tea with peanut butter and guava jelly sandwiches. The guys were happy to take a break. They sat on the tree trunk and ate in silence. Miss Kitty wove between their legs. "Don't let her fool ya, she just had a can of tuna," Ginger said as she poured Miss Kitty some milk.

"I will take you home whenever you guys want to go," Gus said as he finished his sandwich.

"How about we finish getting the tree trunk out of the living room first?" Donovan asked and looked at Ginger.

"Sure thing." Ginger answered as she headed back toward the kitchen with the tray and glasses. "I'll bring you more tea." Just then, the lights blinked and the electricity was back on.

"Progress!" Gus said and stood up.

"That's great. I think the stuff in your freezer is going to be just fine." Ginger called back over her shoulder.

They finished up with the tree trunk a few hours later and climbed back into Gus's car. They had to stop here and there down Ginger Star Lane and move limbs that had fallen into the road. They stopped at the phone booth outside the grocery store to call Karen with an update, but the line was dead.

People were everywhere putting their homes back together. When traffic stalled, folks got out of their cars and pitched in to help remove whatever debris was blocking their way. Men reached into the trunks of their cars and pulled out machetes to chop up limbs to making it easier to pull them to the side. The drive that would normally take 15 minutes, took almost two-hours.

"The rivers are swollen," Ginger said as she looked out the window facing the mountains.

"Yeah, and they will get worse before better," Donovan said. "The water from the hills will come down and we always have to watch for flash floods in the days to come after a hurricane."

"Wow, we might not get snow, but we sure get our share of Mother Nature showing us who's boss," Ginger said. She watched out the window and let out a big sigh as she wondered what she would find on their hillside.

Gus parked his car and insisted he come up the hill with them to see how they made out. "Well, I see the roof!" Donovan pointed. They could see the galvanized tin roof. Donovan had laid extra cinder blocks on top for reinforcement and it had worked, keeping it in place.

They climbed up the slippery mud filled pathway and held hands to keep each other from falling. Ginger's skirt was practically dragging the ground from the mud it picked up along the way. "I gotta learn to plan ahead and throw on some jeans for mudslides!" The hot Jamaican sun peeked through the large clouds, bringing with it rivers of sweat.

Their neighbors waved as they moved about, putting their homes back together. A few trees had fallen but managed to dodge the houses. They walked into their yard and looked around.

"Wow, everything except for a few branches looks pretty much the same," Donovan said.

"Yeah, I'm thinking Carmen took it easy on us," Ginger stood behind him as he opened the door to the bedroom where they had stacked the outside furniture. Piece-by-piece, they put their yard back together. The sunshine aided in the drying process and Ginger hoped that in just a day or two, things would be pretty much back to normal. She silently acknowledged and thanked God for the answered prayers.

Rain had leaked in and dampened their mattress. Together, the three of them pulled it out and leaned it against a tree. Their home began to take shape.

Matthew and Arlene came over to welcome them back as they waved goodbye to Gus who was headed back down the hill.

"How did you make out?" Ginger asked them as they walked up and exchanged hugs.

"We were fine. The wind seemed to have its way with the trees though," Arlene said. "Except that one." She pointed to the tall palm that stood between their lots.

"She go down and she come up." Matthew's hands showed how the tree bent in the wind. "She bend down and come up like a young girl!"

"Well, my back feels anything but like a young girl's today." Ginger's hand reached around to her back. It was sore from all the bending and stretching getting Ginger Star back together.

"Squawwwk!" She could see Paulie's green wings gliding her way. He flew in from a distant tree where he'd been spying on their return. The parrot landed at Ginger's feet and walked in circles to welcome her.

"Hey, bud, I missed you!" She squatted down to look him in the eye. "Did you eat all your guava and mango?" Another bird squawked from a distance. She looked up into the trees to see a green and yellow parrot perched on a limb. Paulie flapped his wings and flew back into the woods towards the bird.

Donovan walked up. "Well, it looks like someone found a friend." He pointed to the birds. "It took a while, but maybe Carmen brought them together." Paulie had been a bachelor for a while when his first mate died earlier in the year. Donovan slid his arm around Ginger's waist. "She even look like Paulie."

"Well, birds of a feather and all . . . Should we call a preacher to do the ceremony?" Ginger asked.

"I'm thinking they already took care of that."

"Well, that's what we get for leaving him behind. I think he's ditching us."

"They mate for life, so I think she'll stick around," Donovan said. He wished he could say the same for Ginger.

—Chapter 7—

Winter 1980

## "BOOGIE ON, REGGAE WOMAN"

### Stevie Wonder

Karen finally made what she considered to be her great escape from the mountains back to the Virginia side of the D.C. Beltway. The small community of Centreville, 20 miles outside D.C., was the perfect fit.

She finished up her college classes for the semester in the Spring of 1981 at Northern Virginia Community College and had accumulated enough credits for her Associate's Degree.

"We had to change up and rent that house in Centreville instead," Karen winced when she explained the decision to her mom over the phone while Lee and his buddies piled their belongings into the U- Haul truck. They would be on their way in the morning.

She was getting ready to put on a spread for the moving crew. She slid the pizza pan into the oven. "Lee's job is going to be in Fairfax. It's just too long of a commute to live in Maryland." She squinted as she said it, halfway expecting her mom to reach through the phone and tweak her ear.

"Well, it sure as heck beats 400 miles," Barb replied. Karen breathed a sigh of relief and grinned. She knew her mom would come around, she just didn't expect it quite so fast.

Letters flowed back and forth between Karen and Ginger, but they were superficial at best. Karen noticed that she didn't get answers to most of the questions she asked. Questions like, how were things with Donovan now that Donna was a regular part of their lives? She knew Ginger well enough to know that ignoring the elephant in the letter meant the answer wasn't one she wanted to share.

The last several letters, Ginger talked a lot about her new friends who owned Ginger Star, the plantation that bore her name. Karen had to admit that she had pangs of jealousy every now and then at the thought of Ginger finding a new best friend, but figured it was only fair as she had done the same with Sue back in the States. It sounded like Ginger Star offered a place of solace for songwriting in an otherwise noisy existence between Jack Ruby's and living on the hillside.

<hr>

## 1982

Ginger sat in the back of the seven-passenger van that held her and twelve band members. She gripped her guitar case on her lap. It tapped the van's roof whenever Bart failed to dodge a pot hole and that was often. A joint made the rounds and reached her in the back seat, but she waved them off and leaned her head on her guitar case. She closed her eyes, wanting to be clear headed for the concert. It could be the biggest break she would ever get and she didn't want to mess it up. She reviewed the set in her mind and talked a little to her mom. She always did that when something big was happening. Real or imagined, Ellie always made her feel better. This time, she said this was going to be Ginger's big break.

She cracked her window to let the smoke escape. The van hit another bump and they all bounced around, heads bobbing in all directions.

Getting the gig at Reggae Sunsplash was an honor, even if she was just a backup. The concert was receiving worldwide attention. Tourists were flying in for the event even though it was summertime. Jamaica had been successful touting the event as revolutionary. It was drawing the off season crowd they'd hoped for.

Ginger was nervous, but confident. She'd practiced and was familiar with all the songs. She'd be singing back up for Winston, aka, Burning Spear, and Toots and the Maytals, a popular reggae band. With a little luck, she might be able to do a quick performance of "You Are My Sunshine," for the crowd in between sets. "Sometimes you gotta make your own breaks." She remembered her mom's words and made a vow to turn that possibility into a reality.

Ginger climbed out of the back of the van into the intense Jamaican sunshine. "Get dat suitcase out da way!" the parking lot attendant hollered. She dodged another bag as the driver threw them toward the curb from the back of the van. She jumped up onto the sidewalk and scurried away.

She managed to find the ladies dressing room and dropped her purse on an empty chair. Six other women sat on the chairs and couch in front of the garishly lit counters that doubled as a vanity. A few nodded in her direction, but for the most part, they ignored her which suited her just fine. She didn't like to chit chat before a performance and definitely not tonight.

A hard knock on the door to the dressing room hushed the women. Ginger turned and opened the door. Jack Ruby rushed in. He was in a breathless panic. "We need a backup singer for Marcia Griffiths tonight." He ran his hand through his curly hair and looked at Ginger. "Trudy is sick. Can you do it?" Beads of perspiration dotted his forehead.

"Are you kidding me? I know most of her stuff by heart. I'd love to!" Ginger was thrilled at being on the same stage as this woman who personified the female reggae star. She had class, poise, and talent. Reggae with a little gospel thrown in. Her silky-smooth voice was synonymous with Jamaica. She'd made the transition from ska to reggae, not something all artists had been able to do.

"Well, come on den. I introduce you to her." Ginger followed him down the hall to Marcia's private room. He knocked. They could hear footsteps and the door opened. A tall woman in a rainbow-colored long gown and head dress stood in the doorway. Her Maroon bloodline claimed her regal presence. "I have the answer to your problem. Marcia." He nodded toward Ginger. "Dis is Ginger Starling. She can step in for Trudy." He turned aside and Ginger stepped up. The two women shook hands.

"Winston tell me about you. Tanks for helping me out!" The two women looked into the other's eyes, both grateful.

"It's my pleasure. Jack said he'd give me a list of the songs." Ginger looked back at Jack and back to Marcia. "Since I'm a huge fan of yours, it shouldn't be hard to figure out the backups."

"Yeah, Nancy can help you too." She pointed to a woman sitting on the couch of the dressing room. The woman stood and walked over. She was shorter than Marcia and wore a long flowered skirt. "She's got everyting printed out and an extra set of clothes so you look da same." Ginger smiled. Her mom was right. This was the break she'd hoped for.

***

"I got the job!" Karen hugged Lee when he walked in the door of their new home. He kicked off his muddy construction boots in the foyer on the "mud rug," as Karen called it. She had applied for a receptionist position with a property management firm. "It doesn't pay much, but they have benefits and it's great experience. I'll be able to get my real estate license while working for them."

"Way to go, Kar," he took a deep breath and blinked hard, polishing his reaction. He had mixed feelings about her going to work, but had learned that sometimes it was best to let things ride. Like now. "Proud of you, Hon." He walked over and gave her his usual bear hug and she buried her face in his neck, her favorite thing to do.

"I know you're worried I won't have much time, but it will all work out, you'll see."

He stroked her hair, tilted her head back, and kissed her forehead. "You're gonna be running the place before they know what hit them." Of that, he was sure.

She held up Ginger's letter. "Oh yeah, I heard from Ging. You're not gonna believe what she did!"

"There's not much Ginger could do to surprise me." He picked up the stack of bills on the table. "What?"

"She bought Ginger Star!"

He looked up from the mail in his hand, eyebrows raised. "That plantation place? No kidding? How'd that happen?"

"Well, I guess Sylvia's health has declined and they decided to sell it to her for a song. I think the thought of another hurricane might have scared them off. Not sure."

"Man, I'll bet that set them back a bunch."

"She said they gave her a sweetheart deal. That's the weird part."

"Whaddya mean?"

"*She* bought it. Donovan isn't on the deed."

"Hmmm . . . yeah that is kinda strange."

"Oh well, she's never made much sense before and even less lately."

"'Movin' on up' like the Jeffersons TV show, huh?" He broke out into the hit show's theme song, "Well, we're moving on up." He grabbed her hand and pulled her close as they danced across the kitchen.

Karen joined in, "To the east side, a deluxe plantation on the sea!" They laughed and hugged. "I guess we'll have somewhat better accommodations for our next visit."

"Yep, let's just call them George and Weezie!" And so they did.

Ginger woke up to the sunlight filtering through the curtain-less window. She rolled over and opened her eyes again and wondered where she was. She propped herself up on one elbow and pushed her hair out of her face. There was a dresser with various hair products and a blow dryer.

Then, slowly it came back to her. The night before had started out innocently enough, but quickly escalated. Her first thoughts were of Donovan. "Oh my god, he's gotta be worried sick," she thought. "I think it's Monday and Donna needs to get to school and he's gotta go to work. Geez."

She threw the covers back and sat on the edge of the bed. Her head felt woozy and she struggled to see through the blurriness. What in the world? All she remembered was having a few drinks with Andrew, her manager, after the recording studio. He suggested she come to his place. Since her bus didn't leave for another hour, she thought it made sense. She remembered yawning in the kitchen. She got sleepy, laid down on the bed, and the next thing she knew, here she was. She looked at her watch. 9 AM. She'd slept for at least 11 hours. She couldn't understand how.

She walked to the kitchen to the black phone on the wall. She picked up the receiver, grateful that they had endured the expense of installing a phone. She dialed the operator. "Yes, collect call from Ginger to 555-0980, please." The lady on the other end of the line dialed the number and the phone rang, once, twice, and on the third ring, she heard Donovan pick up.

"Hello?" Donovan answered.

"Yes, I have a collect call from Ginger," the operator said. "Will you accept the charges?"

"Yes!" Donovan answered. "Ginga? Where are you? Are you okay?"

"I'm in Kingston. I came over to Andrew's to wait to catch the bus and the next thing I knew, I woke up here." Donovan bristled. Andrew was almost always a common denominator when they had an argument these days.

"I don't know how I slept so long! I'll be home as soon as I can . . . " He didn't respond. "I'm so sorry, Don."

"Be careful, Ging."

"I'm on my way."

She hung up the phone and looked around. Beer bottles and pizza boxes littered the living room. Ash trays overflowed. A pipe with residue that wasn't ganja. What in the world?

She walked over to the sink and filled a glass with water. She blinked as she drank and remembered something from the night before. She was standing at this same sink when Andrew slipped his hands around her waist. She'd struggled to make him let go, but that's the last thing she remembered.

She shook her head, went back to the bedroom, and grabbed her guitar and purse. Her reflection stopped her in mid step. She stared at the mirror, not sure she wanted to look closer, but she stepped up to the wall anyway. Her hand reached up and touched her hair. There was dried blood and when she looked closer, she had a small cut on her hairline. *What happened?* A chill ran up her spine. She had a sudden desire to get out.

She gathered up her things and rushed toward door, but before she get there, it opened. Andrew walked in.

A few weeks later, Donovan stopped and looked again when he thought he saw Ginger walk into a doctor's office on James Avenue. What would she be doing in Ochi? She'd told him she would be recording in Kingston this afternoon. He turned and walked down the street and looked through the window. It was a doctor's office. He watched Ginger follow the nurse and the door closed.

Birthdays, anniversaries, and Christmases, all tapped Karen on the shoulder to reminder her that the years were flying by. Nellie was now twelve years old and almost a teenager. It didn't escape her that Nellie was only five years younger than Karen was when she married Lee.

She was thrilled to be back and a part of the Redskin hype that only living around the D.C. beltway could bring. She'd turned into a football fan when she married Lee. Her parents were big Redskins fans and raised her to be one too. She decided to find out what all the hoopla was all about. It didn't take long before she was hooked on the sport and the Redskins were her team. Moving back to the D.C. area gave her lots to cheer about now that Joe Gibbs was the coach.

Karen's job in the property management field was challenging, but she wanted something different. Her first love was writing and she decided to pursue a position as a staff reporter when a friend told her about an opening at the Beltway Beat. Working with words made her happy and what better way to make money than to do something she loved? The new position took her all over the D.C. metro area doing interviews and attending school board and local government meetings. She was elated when she was asked to cover the Redskins practices for the week while Bud, the sports reporter, was on vacation. She squeezed in a page or two here and there on her novel when she could.

Every once in a while, she was asked to substitute and write a column for Candy Marsh, their gossip columnist. She loved the creative writing challenge and learned to look forward to Candy's vacations. She kept notes for the next opportunity, so when it came, she had ideas to use for the article.

She took pride in never missing a deadline and after only a year, was now the senior reporter at the Beltway Beat—basically more responsibility for the same money.

She hadn't heard from Ginger for a few months now, but started a new letter anyway. It was a quiet winter Sunday afternoon. She needed to chat.

> Hey there. Hope all is well in sunny Jamaica. It's a balmy 30 degrees with snow falling like crazy here. Lee's working on an inside job in D.C., so at least he's not missing any work because of the weather.
>
> Since the weather's so crappy, I'm working from home today. One of the perks of being a writer. When it snows around here, these people freak out. Either traffic stands still or some yoyo is hitting his brakes and heading for a ditch, trying to take you with him.
>
> Last week, it took me two-hours to get home from Annandale, normally a twenty-five-minute ride in good weather. One thing that West Virginia taught me was how to drive in the snow and it is much easier here, not dealing with steep mountain roads, but when you're playing bumper cars on the beltway, it can make you crazy.

> *I love my job as a reporter. The newspaper business is definitely a man's world. I still have to fight hard to get the good assignments. I love writing the advice and sports columns (I've clipped a few and put in with this letter), but I only get to do that when Candy and Don go on vacation.*
>
> *I love my job, even with the challenges, and thanks to a new crock pot (do you have one yet?) we manage to eat dinner most nights which keeps Lee happy. Once in a while, McDonald's wins out. I have to make sure I save up enough energy for night time activities with him, but what else is new? Haha.*

She put her pen down and thought for a minute. It was all she could do not to ask about Donovan. It had been almost a year since Ginger called to say they'd broken up, but Karen still held out hope they'd get back together. Ginger would never offer up any details, so Karen had tried to let it go, but it wasn't easy.

> *So, how's it going getting Ginger Star all set up the way you dreamed? I loved the pictures you sent when you first moved in. Send more? I'll bet you've really made some wonderful changes. You always had a flair for decorating.*
>
> *They're playing Bob Marley's song, "No Woman, No Cry" a lot on the radio these days. I think you told me about it when he was working on it. Lee said Marley knows what he's talking about in this song and he hasn't even met me yet.*

She put her pen down to take a break. The silent snow fell faster and faster. She pulled on her boots and threw on her coat. She was taking care of her neighbor's cat while she was out of town. Nellie had the day off school due to the bad weather. "I'm going down to Jeannie's to check on Tippy. I'll be right back," she called into the next room. Nellie was glued to the TV afterschool special.

Karen pulled her hat and gloves on as she walked down the street. She could hear an airplane flying toward Dulles Airport that was only fifteen miles away. She looked up to see nothing but snowflakes falling from the gray sky. "How in the world do they fly planes in this mess?" she said out loud to herself. The snow fell so fast it seemed even deeper on her way back from Jeannie's house just a few minutes later.

She looked at her watch—4:10 p.m., and wondered what time Lee would manage to get home driving in this mess. He had been happy they had some inside work in D.C. so that the weather wouldn't hamper his paycheck this week, but it was a bear of a commute, even in good weather. She stomped her boots outside to try and get the snow off, stepped inside the door and pulled them off. She heard the television program winding down.

"We interrupt this program to bring you a special report," the TV reporter said. Video clips of people clinging to pieces of an aircraft in the freezing water of the Potomac filled the screen.

Karen walked over to the living room. "Oh darn! They cut in just as my show was ending!" Nellie fussed. Karen held up her hand asking her to quiet down.

Jim Vance, the nightly news anchor for Channel 4, talked to the camera. "At approximately 4:05 PM, an Air Florida plane fell from the sky and hit the 14th Street Bridge in Washington, D.C." Karen watched the video of the plane's carnage and survivors reaching for ropes that hung down from helicopters. Snow continued to fall as if it couldn't hit the ground fast enough. Her wonder at their ability to run an airport in this weather now felt like a premonition. Where was Lee? Could he have been on the bridge when this happened? It was right on his way home. Her thoughts fed her fears.

She continued her letter but could only focus on the crash. Writing was always therapeutic for her when something was on her mind.

*Evidently, a plane crashed in this snowy mess and hit the 14th Street Bridge in DC. Lee's not home yet and was working in the city today. Praying that he's okay. The pictures on TV are awful. Those poor people . . .*

She finished up the letter, folded the paper, and slid it into the airmail envelope. "Please, God, please let him be okay," she whispered.

She pulled the chicken from the crockpot and started making dinner. She resisted the urge to pick up the phone to chat with Sue while she cooked wanting to leave the line open in case Lee tried to call. Minutes turned into hours. Darkness fell early in January and she knew it would take him forever to get home even though the snowfall had slowed. *Please, God, let him be okay.*

After she and Nellie ate dinner, she washed the dishes while Nellie took a bath. She changed the channel on the TV, but couldn't resist the updates on the crash and flipped back now and then. Jim Vance was the news anchor and Washington icon that she preferred. He kept her posted.

Nellie came out to say goodnight and Karen gave her a longer than usual hug. "Dad's not home yet?" Why couldn't he just work in an office with a phone? It wasn't the first time she'd made that wish. She didn't share her angst with Nellie.

"No, but I'm sure he worked late since it's an inside job." She could only hope . . . and pray. "I'm sure traffic is awful with this weather."

Nellie nodded. "He'll be okay." Her little girl always knew what she was thinking, it seemed. "Love you, Mom," and gave Karen a needed hug. "Don't freak out if you see my light on. I'm thinking there won't be any school tomorrow, so I'm gonna read in bed for a while." She headed toward her room.

The clock ticked the seconds off slowly and 10 PM came and went. She bit her fingernails trying to ward off the worry, but only ended up with a bleeding hangnail. *He's never been this late before.* She saw headlights shine through the window. She popped up off the couch and hurried to the door. She could hear the storm door open as she opened the door from her side. Lee stood there, weary but intact.

"Are you okay? Did you get caught near the bridge?" She fired off questions before he could answer.

"Yes and yes, but I'm fine . . . just exhausted. What a mess." He shook his head, stomped the snow off his boots and for once, she didn't fuss when he missed the doormat. She gave him a big hug once he had his coat off.

"I was so scared. It was an awful plane crash." She headed toward the kitchen. "I'll heat up your dinner." He looked at the TV to the news for an update on the crash.

"It was the strangest thing. I walked down to Jeannie's to feed the cat and wondered how they could run an airport in this mess when I heard but couldn't see a plane flying overhead." She dished up his dinner and put it in the microwave to heat. Karen looked over to see him leaning back on the door jamb. His forehead was beaded with sweat. She dropped the spoon and went to him. "Are you okay? Here," she pulled the dining room chair closer, "sit down!" He plopped into the chair.

"I'm not so hungry. I think I should just go to bed." He slumped over onto the table instead.

---

"Ginga!" Donovan waved and jogged toward her. She saw him coming from two doors away and felt herself take a quick breath. The sight of him always did that to her. Made her remember just how attractive he was to her, physically and emotionally. He looked much the same, shining dark brown skin, eyes that could melt her in an instant, and a smile that lit up the air between them.

Except that he didn't want to light her up any more. She'd toyed with him enough by breaking promises not only to him, but Donna too. Right after they moved to Ginger Star, he'd packed up and left. She'd woke up from a drunken binge to find them both gone with only a short note on her bedside table. She never chased after him. Remembering that she had let him go made her want to cry if she thought about it too long. So she didn't.

Her busy recording schedule and parties at Ginger Star kept her from dwelling on losing him. The vodka and ganja did a good job of helping her to think about other things. She refused to use any stronger drugs. Cocaine floated in and out of the recording studio and parties, but she didn't like it. She told herself that as long as what she used was "natural," it was okay.

She tried to convince herself she didn't care that Donovan belonged to someone else now. He wasn't married, but may as well be. She told herself he had just been holding her and her career back. It turned out that line of thinking had only created the space in time for him to meet a woman that loved him and Donna the way they deserved to be loved. She had no one to blame but herself.

She'd thrown herself into her work, writing songs by day and singing at Jack Ruby's at night with recording sessions in between. The hard work had paid off and her bank account showed it, but her heart was overdrawn.

She found ganja helped to take her mind off her problems. She had affairs with a few guys in the band and a politician from Wyoming on vacation in Jamaica. Andrew was always there, ready and willing.

Their mutual friend, Arlene, had filled Ginger in on Donovan's life. Donna's mother, Tabitha, had taken a job on a cruise ship and left Donna with Donovan full time at least nine months a year. It was a common thing for Jamaicans to seek employment on ships and leave their children with relatives. Donovan didn't hesitate to take on his daughter full time. Ginger hadn't been surprised.

She took a deep breath as Donovan hugged her hello. His scent was the same and the feelings came flooding back. He leaned back and looked at her. "What's wrong?"

She'd gone over how she would deliver the news, but forgot everything she'd rehearsed. "Lee had a heart attack." Donovan stared at her as the words registered in his mind. He frowned and shook his head.

"No, when?" he asked. "How?"

She gave him the details that Barb had shared with her and what little else she had been able to find out. Lee was scheduled for open heart surgery the next day.

"How are Karen and Nellie?"

"I guess as good as they can be. I talked with her once, but she was pretty much out of it." Ginger wished she had a joint handy. "I feel so helpless. I want to jump on a plane and go up, but we're recording this week, so I can't. "

She could see the memories of Lee slipping down his cheeks in the form of tears. He sat down on a bench and she joined him. He put his head in his hands and wept. She slipped her arm over his shoulder and tried her best to comfort him, but instead, they cried together.

"Daddy! What's wrong?" They looked up to see Donna reaching over to console him. Ginger stared at the young girl. She was surprised at how grown up she was. She'd grown tall and was now a ten-year-old girl instead of a baby. She was no longer a little kid, but a tall bronze young lady with shoulder length braided hair. He pulled her close. "Did Ginga make you cry again?" she asked him. Ginger's heart sank when Donna looked at her with a frown from the corner of her eye.

"No, baby. She just bring bad news. Daddy's friend, Lee is sick and Ginga come tell me." He wiped his tears on his sleeve. "Sorry," he said to Ginger through the tears. Donna walked a short distance away when she was sure he was okay. It was obvious she wasn't going to let him out of her sight as long as Ginger was around.

"Nothing less than I deserved," Ginger said.

Ginger stood and smoothed her skirt. She took a deep breath. "I'm so sorry, Don. I know you love him like a brother." She could see his new lady walking toward them. Donna walked over and talked softly to her and explained what was happening. "I'd better get going." He nodded, stood, and hugged her goodbye. She breathed him in one more time.

Ginger turned away. The familiar sadness returned as she walked toward her car. "Nothing a shopping trip to Kingston won't cure," she told herself. The tears slid down her cheeks as if to mock her resolve. She dropped onto the front seat, opened the glove box, and pulled out a cigarette pack she had loaded with joints. She cranked up the radio, rolled down the window, and took a drag.

"You got nobody to blame but yourself."

Seeing Donovan brought back the pain of the note he'd left on his pillow that morning.

"One abortion was too many," he'd ended the brief letter. She was never sure exactly what he meant. Did he know there was more than one? She felt awful about the second one, but when she turned up pregnant after the encounter at Andrew's, and the tea didn't work, what choice did she have? She'd found a doctor in Ocho Rios to perform the abortion. How could she have a baby and not know who the father was? She couldn't live that lie. Maybe a few others, but not that one.

She shook her head to shake the thoughts loose, put the car in drive, and headed toward Kingston. Tonight she would crash at Andrew's and tomorrow she would put the new credit card into play. Maybe they'd go dancing at Epiphany. She hadn't been there in a while and it was one of her favorite spots.

She pulled into the parking lot and turned off the car. She could see the living room light was on. She lit up another joint and finished half before getting out of the car. She walked up to the door and knocked. Andrew opened the door. "Hey, Mon! What's going on, Ging?" He held a drink in one hand and a cigarette in the other. His eyes were glassy. She could hear the music playing in the background and walked in as he stepped aside.

"Going shopping in Kingston tomorrow and wanted to crash here if that's okay." She walked over to the bar and pulled out the vodka. He always kept a bottle there just for her. The apartment was its perpetual mess with take-out containers and empty beer cans everywhere.

"Sure," he said as he walked up behind her and wrapped his arms around her waist. She shut her eyes and took a long drink until she felt its familiar warmth that helped to calm her. They swayed back and forth to the music and she melted into him.

He twirled her around, "Let's go to Epiphany. I hear Winston is playing." He knew she loved Burning Spear's music.

She grinned. "Yeah, why not?"

Fall 1982

She woke with a start as she heard Andrew close the door behind him. She'd passed out on the couch again. Even though they slept together on her sleepovers, she wouldn't stay all night in his bed. She knew this meant many things, but wasn't interested in analyzing herself this morning.

She showered and changed into the clothes she kept in his closet for days just like this. She grabbed a cigarette from her purse and lit up while she put on her makeup.

Even though she'd had two abortions, there was nothing she wanted more than to have a kid of her own one day. Just not today. So, she enjoyed other people's kids as if they were her own. She bought shoes and school uniforms for Andrew's neighbor's children and provided taxi fare so they could get to school. Matthew and Arlene, her former neighbors from the hillside, had moved to Kingston to find work, but had found more troubles than solutions. She decided to drive over to see them on her way out of town.

Ginger rolled down her car door window as she pulled up to their house. "Arlene, what's wrong?" she asked her friend when she pulled up in front of the run-down house they had rented. Arlene sat on the curb crying. She looked up with tears streaming down her face. Why were there so many tears on this island?

"She run away again!" Ginger knew immediately that her four-teen-year-old daughter, Pinky, had taken flight with her friends again. Ginger always thought the girl was runway model material—too pretty for her own good. The streets of Kingston were crawling with men trying to lure girls like her into prostitution. Ginger often wished they had stayed in Ochi.

Ginger turned off the car, got out, and walked over to Arlene. "How long has she been gone?"

"Oh, they find her. She gone six days," Arlene stood up and straightened her skirt. "She in Windsor now." Ginger cringed. She had been there briefly once, dropping off something for a friend. Windsor was a government run girls home near Ochi. Some girls were orphans, but oftentimes, the parent would turn their kids over when they could no longer control or afford to keep them. Sometimes the department of child services stepped in and insisted. Pinky was now classified as a habitual runaway. Ginger knew Arlene and Matthew would never have sent Pinky there voluntarily.

"How about I go visit her later this week?" Ginger asked. Windsor was on the other side of the island, not far from Ginger Star. It might as well have been a million miles away for Arlene since she had no car or money for bus fare.

Arlene's eyes widened with hope. Ginger reached in her purse, pulled out some tissues, and a wad of cash. "Here, get some groceries and put some aside for bus fare so you can go visit her when you can."

"May God bless you, Ginga," her tears flowed again. "You are angel sent from heaven."

"Well, I don't know about that," Ginger pulled her friend close and hugged her. "I don't think I've been there yet and doubt that I will have the price of admission when the time comes!" She held Arlene at arms' length. "Don't worry about Pinky." She wiped the tears from Arlene's cheeks and handed the tissues over. "She's smart and strong. I'll make sure she's okay."

Ginger left Arlene standing on the curb. She walked over to her car, opened the door, and slid inside. Her heart dropped as she thought of Pinky living in Windsor. Ginger had only been there once before and had been haunted for days afterwards. The facility was old and run down with chipping paint and busted windows reflective of the broken lives that lived there. The girls' ages ranged from eight to eighteen. It was obvious that unless one was strong, she would be dominated by the bullies. She hoped Pinky was able to survive it, but then again, being strong in that place meant being tough. She wasn't so sure Pinky was as resilient as she wanted everyone to think.

Ginger drove into the city and went from store to store until she found exactly what she wanted. The store managers ordered what they didn't have in stock. By the end of the day, Ginger Star had new living and dining room furniture on its way. Not that there was anything wrong with Sylvia's furniture, but she wanted to make it her own. Besides, their styles were totally different. Ginger preferred bamboo with lots of color. Sylvia's style was more Mediterranean and statuesque. "Yeah, I can't do the statue thing," she said referring to the Mediterranean style. Ginger picked up a book of fabric samples as the salesperson looked on. "Somebody's eyes following me everywhere I go. Creeps me out!" Her fear of ghosts seemed to follow her just about everywhere.

She already had bedroom furniture she didn't use, so she made sure the new sofa was good for sleeping. She knew the salesman thought she was nuts and she secretly agreed that she probably was. She smiled when he knocked ten percent off because he realized she was Ginger Starling, the reggae star.

"Thanks, but do me a favor and give the discount to the first family on a tight budget that comes in to buy furniture instead of me." She was flattered but never did understand getting freebies when she had more money than she knew how to spend.

She got back in her car and headed down the crowded streets of Kingston. She had a tough time turning down the beggars that were at every corner of the city. After a while, the guys that cleaned windshields at the Halfway Tree intersection without asking knew her vehicle and that she was likely to tip. She kept cash in the glove box just for them and enjoyed knowing their names. She had the cleanest windshield in town.

She headed back over the mountains to Ocho Rios. The drive was steep and the roads twisted and hugged the side of the hills. Once at the top, she could see mountain peaks from every direction.

She was excited to get back to Ginger Star. They were installing her new Jack Ruby stereo system today. Normally, the systems were portable, but she had them custom make the sound system for her music and that of her friends.

Jam sessions were almost weekly now. Every local musician assumed there would be jamming at Ginger Star on Sunday nights. All one needed was an instrument under their arm to get in. After a while, musicians linked up from all over the Caribbean at Ginger Star. The busier she was, the happier she was. She filled every minute with "to do's." Crossing things off her list was only satisfying when she had two more to add. Her jamming sessions and parties helped her to become the consummate hostess and before long, Ginger Star was a sought-after connection in the Jamaican music scene.

She pulled into Ginger Star and parked out front. She could hear them testing the sound system. "Sounds great!" she hollered to the crew that was gathered around the turntable. She put the shopping bags down next to the piano and walked back to her bedroom. The room she once shared with Donovan.

She told herself she'd get used to being alone. First her mom, then her brothers Now Sylvia had left and gone back to the States, and then Donovan had left her alone. She told herself it wasn't that bad, after all, she liked her own company better than most people she knew. She was also convinced most men, except Donovan, just wanted to use her to further their careers or to just forget about having one of their own.

"There's always Kar," she said to herself while she picked up the pink princess style phone to dial. The phone rang several times before she heard Lee answer, "Hello?"

"Hey, Mon, it's Ging!"

"What's happening? Karen just left to pick Nellie up."

"Not much going on here," she frowned when she realized she'd missed Karen. "How you feeling, Lee?"

"I'm better all the time. Got the new job." Lee had been offered a job teaching masonry to inmates in a state prison. It was an answer to their prayers after the heart attack. His doctor told him he'd have to find another, less physical type of job. The new position was on the Eastern Shore of Maryland, near Ocean City. Moving meant they could live within minutes of the beach, but Karen had to quit her job at the Beat.

"Yeah, just got that news flash in her letter. Congrats, Mon!"

"Is everything okay, Ging?" He recognized the edge in her voice.

"Everything's great." "Just missing you guys. Getting island fever, I think."

"Well, you just need to hop a plane and come on home."

"Yeah, well with my recording schedule and a concert that's coming up, I can hardly go to the bathroom, let alone the States."

"Well, how about I send Karen down there to you?"

"What? Are you kidding me?" Ginger's spirit took an immediate leap.

"No, I'm serious. She's been working, taking care of Nellie and me for six months. There's no better time. She's in between jobs. She needs to take some time for herself and we all know, the best thing she can do when she feels like that is to write."

"That'd be great, Lee. When I'm working in Kingston, she'd be alone at Ginger Star with nothing but time." The thought of Karen writing her novel at Ginger Star made her smile and her heart sing. She hadn't felt hope in a long time.

He gave her a quick update on Nellie. Before they hung up Lee said, "I'll get it all set on this end. Sit tight and don't say anything." She took a deep breath. The thought that Karen would be writing in Jamaica made her smile for the first time in months. She knew she'd have to cross the Donovan Bridge with her.

She hung up the phone and sat down on the edge of the bed. Miss Kitty rubbed up against her feet. They'd become inseparable when Ginger was home. "Come on girl, we got some work to do," she said to Miss Kitty.

The cat followed her as she walked into the living room and cranked up the new stereo system now that the crew had left. Bob Marley music floated through every room from the speakers that were mounted in the corners. "Sounds great," she said aloud to herself.

She turned and walked to the front guest bedroom and opened the door. She remembered staying here with Donovan during the hurricane. She pushed the memory aside and envisioned a wicker desk and typewriter in front of the window with a few other "Karen" touches. "Guess I'm headed back to Kingston for more shopping."

<hr>

"You have done nothing but work and then come home and take care of Nellie and me for six months." He handed her an airline ticket.

"What?" She looked at the plane ticket in her hand and back at him. "I can't."

"Yes, you can. You're gonna stay as long as you want. You have no job to worry about and can start looking for one when you get back. Maybe look for a publisher instead of a job. How about that?"

Karen looked again at the ticket in her hand. "It's been a long time since I did nothing but write."

"I want you to take all those notes you've been writing in your journals and do nothing but that."

He pulled her into him. She laid her head on his chest. And he buried his nose in her hair. She had been sad to quit her job, but consoled herself thinking that fate and God (who were mostly interchangeable in her mind) must have other plans. Evidently, He did. Her dream of writing without the worry of the day job was really happening.

—Chapter 8—
1980

## "HURT SO BAD"
### Linda Ronstadt

$G$inger drove up the rain-rutted road, driving from side to side, trying to hold onto her muffler. She pulled up to the ten-foot tall chain link fence with barbed wire strung on top. It looked more like a prison than any kind of home. There were men sitting on the wall just outside the gate. A few catcalls came her way when she rolled down the window.

She ignored them and told the guard she wanted to see Pinky. He opened the gate and pointed her to a grassy area to park. Ginger waited in the open area while the guard went to fetch Pinky.

Ginger looked around. Not much had changed since she had been there a few years earlier. The buildings needed paint and updating. Picnic tables were lined up in rows in an apparent attempt to create a dining hall when meals were served. A dog wandered over to check her out. She put her hand down for him to sniff.

"Do you manage to get any leftovers here, fella?" She stroked his head thinking his lot wasn't as bad as many dogs she knew.

She looked down toward the dorms where the guard disappeared. It was a dismal place with a million-dollar view of the Caribbean. The buildings had rusted metal roofs and looked like it had once been a hotel. There were rickety clotheslines holding the girls' wet clothing. A few girls were at the bottom of the steps hand washing their clothes. They used the outdoor spigot to fill up their basins. She could hear their muffled conversation and while she couldn't understand the words, their tone was clear. They were arguing about something, but she couldn't tell what.

"Go figure," she said out loud to herself and shook her head. She looked back toward the gate when she heard more voices. When one of the girls would walk near the gate, the men would try to talk to her. Some responded to them and others went on their way.

The sadness of this place was palpable. She heard footsteps, the guard opened the gate. Pinky followed behind him.

Pinky was light skinned with large almond eyes. While Arlene was her mom, Matthew was her stepfather. Her biological father had been an Indian shopkeeper who had returned to his homeland before Arlene knew she was pregnant. Pinky was a striking combination of her parents, but one that in Jamaican culture, earned her the nickname of "Coolie." Despite her surroundings, she was still a beautiful girl.

Pinky's eyes opened wide when she saw Ginger and the girl ran into her arms. She buried her head in Ginger's chest. "Miss Ginga! I so happy you come!" Ginger pushed Pinky back and held her at arm's length.

"Are you okay?" Pinky's eyes looked to the side to see if anyone could hear her, and then back to Ginger's. Pinky's eyes filled with tears which fell down her cheeks when she blinked.

"They try to do lesbian things to me, but I won't let them!" she wailed. Ginger had heard there were gangs within the walls of Windsor.

"Oh, my God!" Ginger pulled her close and stroked her hair. "Did you tell the house mother?"

"She no care. Nobody believe it anyway," Pinky wiped her tears on her sleeve. Ginger dug an old napkin out of her purse and handed it to her, wishing she'd stocked up on tissues for the visit. They sat at a picnic table when girls started to walk in to line up for dinner.

The kids gathered in small groups and waited in line for their food. It wasn't hard for Ginger to pick out the bullies. They poked and prodded one another and snatched things away from the younger girls who shrank back. Many stared at Ginger and a few reached out to touch her auburn hair, so different from theirs.

"You should get in line so you don't miss dinner," Ginger said.

The housemother came up and introduced herself. "Good afternoon, I'm Miss Campbell," she extended her hand. She wore a blue flowered housedress and her hair was wrapped in a kerchief. "Are you Pinky's mother?"

"Oh no, just a friend of the family's," Ginger replied.

"Why don't you join the girls for supper?" She smiled with her hand in front of her mouth as she tried to mask a few missing teeth.

"Thanks so much, I'd like that," she said. What she really wanted was to grab Pinky, stuff her into her car, and flee back to Ginger Star. This place gave her the creeps, but she knew she couldn't rescue Pinky, not just yet. They stood at the end of the line and more girls lined up behind them.

Ginger pulled the kids into conversation asking their names and where they were from. Some answered and others just ignored her looking through suspicious eyes. The few that did engage with her, reached over to touch her red hair. "It so soft!" one of the girls said as she stroked her hair.

They took their trays of food consisting of rice, a piece of what looked to be fish, greens, and a piece of festival, a cornbread like muffin that Ginger had grown to love.

"Looks like you guys are getting some pretty good grub here." No one replied. They started eating like it was a race. "What's the hurry?"

Pinky looked up from her plate. "You eat slow and someone take your food." She kept eating. Ginger watched the girls as they gobbled down their dinners. She pushed hers over to Pinky. She smiled and shared it with her friends. Smart kid.

Ginger pulled out a pack of Juicy Fruit gum from her pocket and handed a piece to each girl at the table. Out of the five, only Pinky and one other said thank you. Not that it mattered, but she could see how much these kids needed love. Love breeds respect and there was very little of either going around in this place.

She asked each one how she ended up at Windsor. A few girls at the table were orphans, but most were runaways like Pinky. Only God really knew what they were running from. What was there to go back to? The slums of Kingston or an abusive situation that promised nothing but more of the same? Who deserved that?

She stayed for a few hours after supper when the dining hall became the recreational area. The girls broke off into groups and combed each other's hair, played dominoes, cards, or just talked. Ginger jumped up and searched her car. She came up with a bottle of nail polish. The girls were thrilled at the prospect of a mini manicure and lined up at her table. Ginger recognized the fear in their eyes that disguised itself as anger. She saw the same thing when she looked in the mirror some days.

When it came time for lights out, Ginger hugged Pinky. "We'll get you out of here. Hang in there and once your court date comes around, you should be able to go home." Because she had run away more than once, she'd landed in a system that could tangle up the accused for a long time. "You have a great mom and a good home to go to." Ginger looked her in the eye. "We'll get you home."

"I know, I wish I never left," she said as she buried her head on Ginger's shoulder once more. The guard hollered for the stragglers to hurry up. She stepped back and Ginger reached over to wipe the tear from her cheek.

"We'll get you back home. Just be good and stay out of trouble. Don't let the bullies goad you into anything. Be strong and feel the prayers." She blew her a kiss.

Sadness sat on her heart as she drove down the rutted road. Thoughts ran through her head. Never had she seen such a hopeless place. Children locked up with no one to love or love them back. Sleep eluded her that night and she promised herself she would do what she could to help.

Ginger found herself going back to Windsor every chance she got. She tried to encourage Pinky as much as she could and after a few visits, there was a circle of girls who would hang out when she visited.

Over the next few weeks, Ginger cleared it with the staff and Jamaica's Child Protection Agency to create a library in one of the empty rooms and a recreational area with ping pong tables. Ginger couldn't sleep. After tossing around in bed, she got up and wrote a letter to Karen.

> I'm gonna head up a fundraiser to help refurbish Windsor Girls Home.

She'd filled her in about Pinky and Windsor.

> It's gonna be the last Friday you're here. I hope that's okay.
> There's nothing to do but make a few phone calls for food and booze, so don't even think about

*spending any time getting ready for it. Once it starts, it's up to the artists to sell their stuff?*

*When I saw Pinky in that place, all I could do was think about getting her out of there. Once we finally got her sprung and back home, Windsor still haunted me. I can't imagine having to live there not having done anything to deserve it. I have to make it better somehow.*

She finished up the letter and sealed the air mail envelope. She hoped she could make a difference at Windsor, where it seemed hope turned into hostility and dreams took a back seat.

## "STRANGER IN MY HOUSE"
### Ronnie Milsap

Karen was thrilled when her mom offered to come stay with Lee and Nellie on weekends while she was in Jamaica. "I'm tickled to have time with Nellie alone," Barb said on the other end of the line. "And it's always fun to subject Lee to my cooking. You know, watch his face as he pretends to like it." They both laughed. Barb's small repertoire when it came to cooking was legendary. Spaghetti or pot roast, that about covered it.

Karen called her mom with last minute instructions while she was gone. "I can't believe this is really happening!" Karen said into the phone.

"Honey, you're not a magician, but you're sure looking like one right now. Definitely my apprentice!" Barb said. "Being able to go away to write is what you were made to do. I'm thrilled to live close enough to pitch in and love it that Ginger is finally reaching out."

Karen wasn't sure what Ashton, Ginger's driver, looked like, but he wasn't hard to spot. He stood outside the airport exit in a white shirt and black pants just like the rest of the drivers, but he held a sign that said, "QUEEN OF THE TENSIES." She laughed out loud and waved to the stranger with the dreads that would have hung to his shoulders if he hadn't had it pulled back with a piece of leather string. He walked over and shook her hand.

"Hello, mi lady," he said in his thick Jamaican accent. "I take it you would be da 'queen.'"

"I'm thinking I must be!"

"Welcome to Jamaica! Let me put your tings in the car." He reached over and grabbed her bags and she followed him to the white Toyota sedan that was pulled up to the curb. "Would mi lady like to sit in the front wit me?" Karen looked at him.

"Sure, I'd love to," he jumped in front of her to open the door. "I don't know how I'll handle it riding on the wrong side of the road though," she laughed and he smiled.

"Well, maybe it turn out we drive on the right side and the States is wrong!"

She'd forgotten the part about no air-conditioning. The wind whipped through the car with the windows down. Ashton offered her a leather string for her hair and she didn't hesitate. She reached in her bag and pulled out her signature bandana for a sweatband. She sometimes wondered why she loved it here so much. The heat and humidity made her look like a sweaty mess most of the time.

"Is it alright if I make a quick stop, mi lady?" Ashton invaded her thoughts as the scenery mesmerized her.

"Why, sure," Karen said looking around at the town. Children in uniforms walked down the crumbling sidewalks of the small town of Falmouth as Ashton pulled into a parking space in front of what appeared to be a grocery store. "Is it okay if I get out too?"

"But of course, mi lady," he answered as he turned off the ignition of the non-air-conditioned car. "Jus' stay wit me." He jumped out and ran around to open her door.

Karen followed Ashton down the crumbled sidewalk past a woman sitting next to what appeared to be her handmade baskets into the grocery store. She wondered why they didn't fix the sidewalks. An Asian man sat behind the cash register on the wooden countertop as a woman that Karen assumed to be his wife was stocking the shelves. Karen walked through the small shop looking at the shelves that were crammed full of merchandise. Many items were familiar to her, but three times the price compared to back home. "Geez, two bucks for a bottle of ketchup!" Karen held up the small glass bottle of Heinz ketchup.

"Yeah, Mon, not cheap in Jamaica," Ashton answered her.

"How do you afford this?"

"Mi lady, she make her own," Ashton answered.

"And so would I," Karen answered as she put the bottle of ketchup back on the shelf.

Ashton paid for his cigarettes and Karen bought them each a bottle of Ting. "This tastes like a Jamaican version of Fresca," she thought out loud to herself as she took a drink.

"What tis 'Fresca' mi lady?" but Karen didn't hear him. She continued to look at the colorful flip flops and hats at a sidewalk stand. A Jamaican woman sat on the sidewalk next to her wares and leaned up against the wall. Her legs were stretched out and with her little one balanced on her lap. "Go ya ya!" she called out to a ten-year-old youngster. The kid grinned and ran with an apple in his hand. It was obvious to Karen that the lady was not all that angry.

The woman looked up at Karen surprised to have an audience. She shrugged. "Dey all da same, no matta where dey from." Karen stopped and nodded at the woman's wisdom. She grinned and stooped down to look at the fruit on her stand.

"What's this?" Karen asked.

"That June Plum," the young woman answered and stood to shift the baby to her hip. "Mi mummy she grow it in de hills," her head nodded towards the mountainside.

"Really?" Karen picked one up and sniffed the green and yellow baseball size fruit. "It smells really good."

"Here, you try," the young mom put the baby down on the sidewalk and pulled out a small pocket knife. She swiftly peeled it, carved a piece off, and offered it to her. Karen put the fruit in her mouth and was pleasantly surprised. Ashton watched from a few steps behind Karen admiring her full yet womanly figure. Tendrils fell from the pony tail like brown curly springs. Her brown eyes were deep set and she'd learned to use mascara to bring out her all but missing eyelashes. Her high cheekbones gave her a regal look that Ashton noticed, but she did not. She saw Ashton looking at her out of the corner of her eye a few times. She wasn't used to having men sneak glances of her. It felt strange, but kind of nice.

"Do you take U.S. money?" Karen asked.

"Yes!" the woman said. Karen picked up four June plums, paid the lady more than she should have, and headed back to the car with Ashton. He held onto her arm, steering her back down the broken sidewalk to the car. Ashton closed her door behind her and rushed around to his side with three quick strides around the car.

They continued their trek along the north coast to Ocho Rios. Goats grazed on the roadside like it was normal. The shacks along the sea were just that with an occasional conch shell stand or fruit consisting of bananas, ackee, and oranges. Small colorful boats dotted the shoreline. Fishermen strung their catch up on the shacks for passersby to see and purchase.

"I can't get over the goats and cows just roaming the sides of the roads," Karen pointed to a mother goat and baby. "Look, how cute!" She felt like she was six years old gawking at a petting zoo.

Ginger's letters had mentioned Andrew Phillips who was now her manager. Karen had met him briefly during her first trip to Jamaica and back then, something had checked in her spirit. Ginger had explained on the phone and in letters that she and Andrew were nothing more than "partners in my career." Karen suspected it wasn't necessarily so, but she knew she'd figure it all out once she and Ginger were together again, breathing the same air. Once they shared the same space, she was sure there would be no more secrets.

Karen and Ashton chatted as he navigated his way through the two-lane seaside road they called a "highway." Occasional glimpses of the sea mixed with the livestock wandering the sides of the highway, kept Karen gawking. The sights and scents of Jamaica captivated her again. She drank in the color of the Caribbean combined with the green of the banana and palm trees.

"Wow, look out!" Karen's hand reached for the dashboard to steady herself, as if it would help. She reached down and found her previously unworn seat belt. Ashton laughed and flashed his handsome smile at Karen. A car was passing and coming right at them in their lane. Ashton slowed down and let him over.

"Oh, I'm sorry mi lady," Ashton touched her shoulder lightly before pulling away, surprised at his own boldness. He had figured her to be another spoiled American, but quickly realized that wasn't the case. "I know Jamaican drivers can be crazy. I always look out for dem."

"This is Brownstown coming up," Ashton pointed to the countryside trying to get her mind off the road. "It's where your

American actor, Harry Belafonte, lived with his grandmother when he was young."

They rode along the coastline and the colorful Rasta men caught her attention. "Geez," she exclaimed. "They're smoking ganja right out in the open!" She'd forgotten how up front they were with the weed, even though it was technically illegal.

Ashton laughed. "Ya, dey do dat,"

"See the field over there on the side of the mountain?" Ashton pointed up the hillside. "That tis a ganja field."

"How do you know?"

"Mi brodda help to grow it. Ganja big business in Jamaica."

Ashton turned on the radio. He thought maybe it would calm her down a bit. He was used to Americans getting jumpy in his car. Evidently, the driving style in Jamaica was foreign to most of them. The radio filled the air with the sounds of Bob Marley and the Wailers singing the Redemption Song. . . . "But my hands was made strong, by the hands of the Almighty."

"Hey, I think Ginger used to live on this hillside," Karen said as she pointed to the mountain.

"Yes, mi lady, this is Steer Town, near where she lived."

Karen saw the green roof from the road and enjoyed spotting familiar places as they drove through Ocho Rios to the other side of town. Not much had changed since she and Lee were there. There were a few more hotels and a new tourist trap shopping center. Other than that, things were pretty much the same. They kept going past Ocho Rios and headed a few miles east of town along the coastline.

"What happened to Gus?" Karen remembered Ginger talking about the Ginger Star driver when they went there for Hurricane Carmen.

"He went back to the States with the Arnolds." Ashton answered. "He take his wife and daughter wid him."

"Good for him and good for you, getting his job."

"Yes, he my cousin and get me in at Ginger Star."

Before she knew it, the two-hour drive was over and Ashton turned onto Ginger Star's driveway. The archway of flowers cooled them off in their shade as they drove down the lane.

"Wow," she answered before Ashton could. She remembered the Polaroid picture Ginger had sent of herself standing next to the sign that bore her name.

"Yes, mi lady, this is Ginger Star," Ashton announced as they drove past the sign to the beautiful hibiscus garden in front of them. They drove under the floral archway and semi-circle around the garden to find the magnificent former British great house. A young black woman wearing a maid's uniform was sweeping the circular stone steps. She looked up, reached over, and pulled a rope that rang a bell softly to announce their arrival. Ginger appeared on the balcony above, her hair tucked up under a straw hat that shaded but didn't hide the curve of her neckline.

"Karen! Great timing. I just got back from Kingston!" she waved. "I'll be right down." She turned and disappeared back into the house before Karen could do more than wave back as she stepped out of the car. Ashton opened the trunk and pulled out her suitcase as Karen reached into her purse and pulled out some bills for a tip.

"I hope you don't mind American money, Ashton," Karen said as she held the cash out for him.

"No mind at all, mi lady," Ashton said as he backed up. "But no need for dat, Miss Ginga take good care of me all de time." He waved her off, picked up her luggage, and headed to the house.

She stood with the cash in her hand and tossed it onto the drivers seat for him to find later.

Ginger appeared at the top of the steps where the maid had finished sweeping. She ran down the halfmoon steps holding up her trademark green skirt to keep from tripping. Karen greeted her at the bottom, pulling off her bandana and the leather strap Ashton had given her for the ride allowing her curly brown shoulder length hair to fall. The women hugged and Ginger leaned back to look at Karen.

"I love your hair," she touched Karen's hair and admired the curls. "Did you get a perm?" Karen nodded.

"Sure did." She reached up to try and tame her mane.

"It looks great!" Ginger stepped back and looked at her friend. "I can't believe you're finally here, Kar."

"Me too, Ging" Karen stared at her friend and noticed something different, but she didn't yet know what it was. "I know now why you can't leave this place. Ginger Star is amazing," Karen walked over to a Bird of Paradise flower growing wild in the middle of the yard. "It's incredible."

"I can't wait to show you the rest," Ginger said.

"I can see why you love it." Karen looked up at the house. The former British great house looked like a resort to her. "Not stuck in the onesies any more for sure!"

Ginger smiled remembering all of their conversations on the phone making excuses why she couldn't come home for Christmas or for a week in the summer. It had been years since the two had spent an afternoon hanging on a raft or laying on a towel in the sun. Their best talks had been floating and staring at the clouds. "Making skies," as Ginger's mom, Ellie, had called it.

"I know, Kar. Words just can't describe it, can they?" Paulie hopped up the step, waiting to be acknowledged. Ginger purposely made him wait, grinning to herself while the bird trotted back and forth between them. "Making skies here is incredible too."

"Looks like you made it to the Tensies, girl! This place is amazing."

The parrot squawked. "You remember Paulie?" Ginger asked.

"Of course I do!" she walked toward the bird, but he took flight to a low branch of the almond tree. There was another bird in the same tree just behind him. "Who's that?" Karen pointed to the second bird.

"Oh, that's Carmen, Paulie's main squeeze." Ginger reached into a bowl of nuts and tossed some in the grass between her and the birds. They both jumped off their branches and headed for the lawn to scoop up their snack. "They hooked up during Hurricane Carmen. Hence the name."

"He's the best pet bird I've ever known!" Karen said. "And now you have two!"

Paulie fluttered his wings and squawked in frustration. Ginger laughed.

"What's so funny?" Karen asked.

"Paulie doesn't like it when someone calls him a 'pet,' Kar."

Karen stooped down to Paulie's eye level on the branch, keeping a respectable distance. "Well, I'm so sorry, Paulie. I surely don't wanna hurt your feelings, Bud." The bird stopped squawking and cocked his head toward Karen. "And you too, Carmen." The female bird headed back to the tree, more skittish than Paulie.

"Don't move and he might let you pet him," Ginger said.

Before she could try, Paulie decided to join Carmen back on the branch. "Oh well, I'll work on him later." They turned and walked up the stairs into the open-air veranda that doubled as a living room.

"Wow, Ging, this place is incredible," Karen looked up at the vaulted ceiling. There was carved wood paneling throughout. She ran her hand over it. "Can't get this at Home Depot!"

"Let's sit for a minute," Ginger said. She sat down in a wicker chair, picked up a fan, and handed it to Karen. "Use this. It'll be your new best friend." She'd placed handheld fans strategically throughout the house, knowing that Karen would use them to keep cool.

Karen sat down in a chair next to Ginger and gave it a try. "Thanks for remembering. You've thought of everything." She fanned herself. "I went to pack the one you gave me last time I was here but couldn't find it." She leaned her head back on the chair. "So, you have to commute back and forth to Kingston during the week?"

"Kinda. Andrew wanted me to move to Kingston, but I couldn't bear the thought, so, after I bought this, I rented a flat there to be close to the studio when we're recording." Ginger felt bad for the lie that just rolled off her tongue. She always stayed at Andrew's when she was in Kingston, but didn't feel like admitting that just now. She could sense Karen didn't like him. She decided it was better to wait to drop that nugget a little later.

"Come on," she motioned for Karen to follow. "Let me show you the rest of the place." They walked through the veranda to the side of the great house. A sparkling blue pool the size of a small house glistened in the Jamaican sunshine. A fountain in the shape of three dolphins jumping in a circle spouted water in the middle. On the other side of the pool was a view of the Caribbean Sea that took Karen's breath.

"Oh, Ging, this is amazing!" Karen covered her mouth with her hand. "Look at the view!"

"I told you you'd love it. I couldn't wait for you to get here, Kar." She walked over to the bar next to the kitchen and poured them each a glass of wine and handed one to Karen. Ginger took a long sip and swept her hand across the pool area. "The pool was designed by an architect from Trinidad. I told him I had a love of dolphins and he created that fountain without even telling me."

They walked across the ceramic tile floors past tropical floral arrangements that made Karen's jaw drop. She reached out to see if the flowers were real. They were. The hallway displayed many photos of them as girls dressed up on Easter Sunday as they strolled the Smithsonian and then there was the life-sized framed poster of the Tensies themselves.

"Oh my! Look at this!" Karen stopped to stare at Barb, Ellie, and Darlene in action. It was a black and white photo of them at a Tom Jones concert. They were dressed to the nines, sitting at dinner before the concert.

"Guess if they were eating dinner, they still had their panties on!" Ginger said. They both laughed. Women were famous for throwing their undergarments at Tom during his concerts. The Tensies tried to go to his performance any time he was within driving distance.

"Hey, wasn't Roberta in this picture too?" Karen asked.

"Originally, yes. Just couldn't bring myself to have her beady little eyes follow me around my living room," Ginger said about her stepmother. "So, I had her cut out. If it had only been that easy in real life!" Karen laughed at the thought and nodded in agreement.

The same woman that had greeted her on the front steps walked into the living room and announced, "Miss Ginga, lunch is served on veranda."

"Thanks, Willie," Ginger looked at Karen and made the introductions. "We'll be along in a few minutes."

Willie was in her early 20s and according to Ginger, already had three children. "Not unusual around here. I'm not sure, but I think there are three dads too."

"Geez, dealing with one baby's father is bad enough, I can't imagine three of 'em!" Karen said as she sat down at the edge of the pool and put her feet in the water. She let the cool water and wine do their thing.

"Yeah, well, I don't think she has to 'deal' with them much as they're mostly the absent kind," Ginger joined Karen at poolside. She hiked up her skirt and sat down, kicking her foot in the water making a splash that flew back at Karen.

"Well, that's how it is, huh?" Karen laughed and grabbed Ginger's shoulder pushing her towards the water.

"Nope, just kidding!" Ginger leaned away from her knowing all too well Karen would toss her in without warning.

"But really, she called you, 'Miss Ginga'?" Karen giggled, "I feel like I'm in *Gone with the Wind*."

Ginger laughed. "I've been called far worse, that's for sure!" She refilled her glass out of the bottle that sat at her side and took another drink. "Come on, there's something I want to show you before we eat."

She pulled Karen up by her hand. Karen grabbed onto Ginger's shoulder as she teetered to one side. "Hmm, light weight, huh?" Ginger teased. You used to be able to down one and a half bottles of Boones Farm without taking a nap," she grabbed Karen's hand and led her back into the house.

"Yeah, that seems like a lifetime ago. This is gonna take some practice!"

They walked down an Italian tiled hallway. Ginger reached out and turned the doorknob at the end. "This, my dear, is your room." Ginger swung the door open and stood back swooping her arm making way for Karen to enter.

Karen stopped and gaped at the mahogany four poster canopy bed that sat so high there was a step stool next to it. The room was at the corner of the house with floor to ceiling windows on three of the four walls. Banana and palm trees waved at them through the open shuttered windows and the Caribbean peeked through where the green leaves didn't hide the view.

Karen turned and looked at Ginger. "Wow, this is gorgeous! Quite a difference from the guest room at my house."

"This isn't the 'guest room,' woman." Ginger walked around the bed to the other side of the room. "It's your room. Only yours, my friend. Look at this." Ginger drew a curtain back that opened to a floor to ceiling bay window view purely of the sea. Positioned in front of the open shuttered window was a wicker desk with a glass top. An IBM Selectric typewriter sat in front of the white leather high back office chair that glided back when Ginger pulled it away from the desk. "Have a seat, Kar," Ginger smiled. "It's the writing perch you always talked about."

Karen's hand covered her mouth in disbelief. She walked slowly toward the desk and ran her hand over the back of the chair. "Where in the world? Why, how did you do this?" the non-stop questions poured out of Karen's mouth. She sank down into the leather chair.

Ginger smiled and laughed. "You've always talked about having the perfect place to write since you were a teenager and I figured this just might be it."

"Ging, this is just too much." She looked from the desk to Ginger and then back to the view of the sea.

"I talked to Lee and he agreed that you need to get away to write at least a couple times a year, so now you're all set." Karen stared at the desk and typewriter. "As long as we behave," Ginger laughed. "That's for us to know and him to find out! What happens in Jamaica, stays in Jamaica, right?"

"Just how much did you talk to Lee?" Karen looked back at Ginger.

"Why? Jealous? I hardly think that's becoming, Kar." Ginger giggled at the thought.

Karen had convinced herself that she didn't regret the decision to have a family and be a mother first before she invested full time in a writing career. Some days she had to work harder to believe it than others. Finding time to work on her great American novel was a challenge and she berated herself regularly for not being more disciplined. New Year's resolutions were made annually only to be swept aside amidst her job, PTA meetings, and horseback riding lessons by spring of every year.

She never could understand how her fellow writers could stay up late to write after everyone had gone to bed. Besides, her nightly routine consisted of putting a smile on Lee's face after Nellie went to bed. She was just too tired to get up after that to put any fresh ideas on paper. She would often sit in bed and write notes in a spiral notebook she kept at her bedside. These were notes that would one day jump through her fingers and onto the typewritten page, she had promised herself.

"Lee said I could come back?"

"Yep, he's committed to you getting your time to write and so am I."

Ginger had been in touch with Lee many times before Karen's visit. She had always promised herself that these were notes that would one day jump through her fingers and onto the typewritten page.

"Actually, this was all Lee's idea," Ginger said. "He really wants you to write that book."

"He never seemed to care that much before," Karen said. "But since the heart attack, he's been kind of different about it." She and Ginger could always just about read each other's mind since they were five years old. All these years later, not much had changed. She walked over to the desk and touched the new machine. "Oh, my god!" she reached down and picked up a flowered spiral notebook. The notebook she'd filled with notes and tucked away in her nightstand six months earlier when its pages were full. She opened the book to be sure it was hers. The curled up pages and coffee stains were easy to recognize. "How?" she turned and looked at Ginger. "I looked all over for this when I was packing!"

"I had Lee mail it to me. He said you'd started a new one." Seeing Karen so excited gave Ginger a rush of happiness she hadn't felt in years. She sat down on the edge of the bed and ran her hand over the white eyelet lace comforter. Ginger had remembered that Karen always loved eyelet lace. She'd had to track down the fabric in the States and had Willie's mother create the bedspread and canopy curtains. "Now here's the deal," Ginger patted the bed and Karen sat down beside her. "You have to commit to writing a certain amount each day you're here or the deal's off for Lee." She ran her fingers through her auburn hair to push it away from her face. "I promised Lee we'd keep our shenanigans to a minimum. So, it's business as usual during the week in Kingston for me and you dive into writing every day here at Ginger Star."

"Not a problem. I just can't believe it, that's all." Karen stood up and walked over to the white leather office chair and sat down. She turned around to face the desk and ran her hand over the IBM

Selectric. She opened the desk drawers to find paper and type-writer ribbons, two bottles of White Out, and a box of Papermate pens. "I can't believe you copped my notebook without me realizing it. You're too much, Ging."

"Ha! I know!" Ginger stood up and nodded her head towards the door. "Let's go eat. Willie's probably having a fit trying to keep the lettuce from wilting."

"That's about the only thing that would lure me away from here and you know it." Karen's love of food had always surpassed her love for pretty much just about anything else, with the exception of her family. She didn't try to hide it and neither did her waistline.

Karen followed Ginger to the other side of the house to the open air dining room that was surrounded by palm and banana trees swaying in the afternoon breeze. A few wooden sculptures sat here and there and some colorful artwork lined the walls. Ceiling fans whirred quietly keeping the air moving.

"Man, you've come a long way since the hillside of Steer Town," Karen picked up a wooden parrot that was painted in pastels. "We saw it from the road on the way here." She wondered if she should bring up Donovan's name or not. She decided not. At least not yet.

"Who's that?" Karen pointed to a portrait of a woman standing in a royal blue floor length dress with the wind in her hair.

"I think she lived here a long time ago. It was here when Sylvia bought Ginger Star. I just left her there."

"Well, I definitely know who this is!" Karen pointed to another portrait. This one was unmistakably Ginger. Her hazel eyes looked right into her. "Where did this come from?"

"Sylvia painted that and gave it to me before I bought Ginger Star from her. She's an incredible artist."

"She sure is. How's her health?"

"She doesn't talk about it much, but I get the feeling, not that great." Ginger changed the subject as she often did when unpleasant things came up. She was afraid Sylvia wouldn't be around much longer but didn't want to say it out loud. Not even to Karen.

They spent the next hour and a half eating salad, Mahi, and callaloo with fresh pineapple salsa. They opened a second bottle of wine. Karen caught Ginger up on the latest comings and goings of their high school friends and what she knew of Ginger's dad, Will. "I only know what my dad tells me since Mom's not exactly close with Roberta anymore," Karen said.

Ginger filled Karen in on the plans for the Windsor fundraiser. She held her hand up, "And don't even think about any of it. Arrangements are already made and we'll worry about the party when the time comes."

"Can you take me over to Windsor?" Karen asked.

"Sure, but don't forget your tissues. It's awful."

Ginger asked about Lee and Nellie. Karen filled in the blanks letting her know the highlights. By the time the second bottle of wine was empty, Karen had gathered up her liquid courage.

"So, what do you hear from Donovan?"

"Well, what took you so long?" Ginger smiled her little half a grin as only she could do.

"Had to pop the second cork to let my courage loose, I guess," Karen leaned back and laced her fingers together behind her head. Ginger's eyes wandered behind Karen and focused on the sea in the distance before she looked down at her hands in her lap.

"Nothing. It's like he dropped off the face of the earth." The two sat in their all-familiar quiet understanding that they'd known since they were five. "Ever since," her voice trailed.

"The abortion," Karen finished the sentence for Ginger, a habit they'd had since they were five.

"Yeah." Ginger nodded and cleared her throat. "I think maybe he saw me go into the doctor's office for the D&C."

"I thought you wanted kids though," Karen probed.

"The timing wasn't right. My singing was just getting launched and I couldn't afford to stall it right then. You know, we've been over this in my letters." She'd left out the part about not being sure whose baby it was, Donovan's or Andrew's. Even she couldn't say that out loud.

"Yeah, I know. I get to read all the bad news and then listen to the good on the phone. You think I don't know that?" Karen asked. She was convinced Ginger sent bad news in writing so she'd have to cool off before she had a chance to respond. Even in person, she still felt that Ginger wasn't telling her everything. Karen knew she needed to let it go. She figured Ginger would give up the truth later if not sooner.

"I knew you'd figure it out," Ginger poured the last of the wine into both their glasses. "Come on, let's light one up," she stood up and walked over to the sideboard and opened the wooden box with the swan carved on the top. She had pre-made joints ready to light. She'd thought of everything.

---

"Okay, Ashton took your luggage to your room and Willie's probably unpacked it all for you by now, so I'll go down to the studio to practice and you get busy writing. I'll see you at dinnertime."

"Willie unpacked for me?" Karen asked eyebrows raised. "Man, I could get used to this."

Back in her room, Karen marveled at the furnishings, dark mahogany and white eyelet lace everywhere. The pillows on the bed were varying shades of soft pinks and aquas, giving the room just enough color. She grabbed the notebook and lay across the bed to read and refresh her memory of what she had written. The Caribbean breeze flowed through the room and the ceiling fan pushed it down on her. She was flushed from the wine and ganja, but never felt better. She laid on her stomach and propped herself up on her forearms and read. The story that had lived in her head for years appeared before her in the scrawled notes she'd written in the middle of both the days and nights, whenever her imaginary characters decided to take another turn in their lives.

Lee had given her the journal for her birthday when they were still dating, encouraging her to follow her dream of writing. Once she'd started the novel, she realized just how much research would be required and was overwhelmed. She'd decided to take the notes as the storyline appeared to her. The research would have to wait until Nellie was older and didn't need her around as much. A historical novel was going to require days and days of research at the National Archives.

She'd attended writers' conferences and heard how others got up at 5 a.m. to write in solitude, but the only thing she could do that early in the day was capture another hour's sleep before the shuffling of pajama covered feet rocked her world for the day. Now she had the opportunity to actually make her story come to life.

"Kar, ready for dinner?" Ginger nudged Karen's shoulder. She opened her eyes and tried to focus before realizing she'd fallen asleep on top of the bed's coverlet.

"Wow, how long did I sleep?"

"Hmm, about three hours. It's almost 7," Ginger walked over and pulled the sheer curtains closed and set up the mosquito netting around the bed. "Gotta close these in the evenings to keep the 'skeeters out."

Karen got up and ran her comb through her hair. Her curly perm perked up in the Jamaican heat. She pulled on her signature sweatband and grabbed the fan from the desk. They headed back down to the dining room. Willie had candles lit everywhere to keep the mosquitoes away. The palm trees swayed in the evening breeze. Karen picked up her glass of ice water from the table and walked to the top of the steps that led down to the lawn. She'd known that Ginger's career was going well but had no idea she was as successful as this.

"Do you ever miss the States?"

Ginger picked up her glass of wine and joined Karen, sitting down on the top step. "Yeah, but mostly when I get stuck in the onesies and want a Mighty Mo and some onion rings from Hot Shoppes."

"Well, that ain't gonna happen. They tore it down last year to make a bigger parking lot for the mall," Karen said.

"That stinks." Ginger let out a chuckle. "Remember when we were sitting in the car at Hot Shoppes and the server on the loud speaker scared us half to death?"

Karen giggled. "Yeah, Mom about peed her pants! I thought we'd never stop laughing."

"The waitress came out on her roller skates to see if we were alright and she about lost her mind falling down and laughing too." Karen sat down next to Ginger on the step. "Nobody could laugh like your Mom," her hand reached over and covered Ginger's. She remembered the lilt of Ellie's voice when she giggled. Ginger leaned her head on Karen's shoulder.

"I'm afraid I'm forgetting her, Kar," Ginger whispered.

"She'll never let you," Karen said and with that, they both smiled and nodded.

"More than you know. You know she's here, right?" Ginger stared at the swaying palm that stood at the bottom of the steps. Karen lifted her head and looked at her friend with raised eyebrows. "I hear her almost every night. It's like she's a duppy and swooshes from room to room with the breeze." Ginger had always been one to believe in ghosts, but Karen didn't buy it. She remembered Donovan had explained to them the duppy was the Jamaican version of a ghost. She didn't like scary stuff ever since they'd seen "Night of the Living Dead" at a drive-in theater when they were teens. She'd sworn off horror flicks and science fiction ever since.

"We can just breeze on past that one, my friend. Pun intended," Karen stood up and reached down to pull Ginger up, but she didn't respond. She just stared out towards the sea.

"It's like I can see her sometimes. Like I could reach out and touch her, but she slips away every time I try. I'm so scared I'm gonna forget her."

Karen wasn't sure what to say. A bird landed at the bottom step and took a sip of water from a puddle on the tile stoop.

"I came all the way here to get away from the reminders. I thought it would dull the ache with some distance, but she came with me." Ginger stood up and walked to the bottom of the steps and stared at a white egret flying up the mountain towards home. The surf was rough and the whitecaps dotted the blue sea. A large white egret landed at the edge of the lawn. Ginger walked over to a ceramic bowl and opened the lid. She reached in and grabbed a fig.

"What are you doing?" Karen asked.

"Willie pulls figs off the fig tree over there." She pointed across the yard. "And I give them to him," Ginger flipped the bird a fig.

"This is Carlton, he stops by just about every night. Typically, egrets don't eat fruit, but he likes figs."

"How do you know it's a boy?"

Ginger shrugged and tossed another piece to Carlton. "Acts just like a guy. Only comes around when he's hungry or horny."

Karen laughed. Carlton fluffed his wings and gratefully took his snack in his beak. He jumped over and gobbled up the fig. Paulie always showed up when he saw fruit flying. He gobbled up the fig before Carlton could get to it.

Ginger nodded at Paulie. "He thinks if he finishes it fast, I'll feel sorry for him and give him more," and she did. "Just like a guy," Ginger laughed and brushed her hands together.

"Just like a woman, you caved in and gave him what he wanted," Karen said. "Speaking of which, I wonder where Carmen is."

"Probably home cooking dinner and man will she be ticked off when he's not hungry when he walks in the door," Ginger said.

The two laughed and Karen was reminded of when they were girls on the Ocean City boardwalk tossing Thrashers French fries to the seagulls much to their mothers' chagrin. "Remember when my mom fussed for us to stop feeding the seagulls? She no sooner got the words outta her mouth when one crapped on her head!" Karen said.

Ginger laughed. "Yeah. Mom laughed till she wet her pants rolling around in the sand until your mom jumped her with Big Blue, her water gun," she plopped down on the step.

They giggled and gasped for air in between remember-when flashes of the scene on the Ocean City beach. Karen's arms flailed as she imitated her mom's reaction. "You're gonna stay in the Onesies this time, Ellie!"

That night, Ginger laid in bed and remembered all the reasons she loved being around Karen, but with the sweet memories came the painful ones. Ginger knew that Karen would want to talk about what happened with Donovan. She'd told her in the letters when they had broken up and cried to her over the phone, but never really answered Karen's questions. She also knew the memories of her mom came packed in her best friend's suitcase. That part she welcomed. Living in parts of her past had become what she liked to do. Her song writing gave her the chance to give her memory an escape hatch from her mind.

This time though, it didn't hurt quite so bad. Ginger found the memories brought her unexpected comfort. She smiled in the dark. She didn't get to talk about her mom when she had moved back in with her dad to take care of her brothers. "Girlfriend certainly didn't like the mention of Mom much," Ginger said to herself as she pulled the mosquito netting around the edge of the bed. But she'd discovered the mention of Ellie was a good way to get Roberta to make her exit. She and the boys had figured that out after a few months. Roberta would get all huffy and make her dad take her to a movie or shopping. Never once did he turn her down.

Karen spent at least eight hours each day transcribing her notes onto the blank pages on the typewriter. Her characters came alive as she pounded on the keyboard. She found herself greeting them in her dreams. When the dreams woke her up, she crawled out of the mosquito netting, walked over to the typewriter, and pulled the cord on the pink desk lamp. The beads that hung from the lampshade created a dancing shadow over the page as she typed. She sometimes stayed up for several hours at a time before crawling back into bed. Having the ability to sleep in, partly thanks to an eye mask to keep the sunlight at bay, until she woke gave her the chance to let her caged creativity escape onto the pages. She hadn't felt this alive in, well, forever.

They both followed their writing and recording schedules all week. Ginger returned on Thursday afternoon. After dinner, Karen popped an eight track of Seals and Croft and the song, "Unborn Child" started playing. "What in the world are you listening to?" Ginger looked at her as she filled up her wine glass.

Karen looked at her surprised. "What are you talking about? It's Seals and Croft? You used to love their music."

"Yeah, well that was before this song came out," Ginger pushed the button to stop it from playing. Karen remembered the article she'd seen about the Planned Parenthood boycott of the group with the song talking about the rights of an unborn child. She didn't mean to play that particular song. Maybe it was time to cross the no longer invisible bridge.

"I know you think I shouldn't have done it," Ginger said as she sat down on the step to the front living room that overlooked the sea. Karen walked over and joined her.

"I just can't imagine. Our moms never even had a choice." Karen said and immediately wished she had kept her mouth shut.

"Come on, Kar, things were different back then. Women were expected to marry young and have babies. It's what they did."

Karen flipped the visiting Carlton a fig. Paulie murmured in protest and flew off to the branch of the cotton tree at the edge of the yard. "Yeah, I know," she hugged her friend. "Were you scared?"

"Oh man, I sure was. I didn't know what to expect. I bled for days and days. I think I almost checked out, but Donovan took care of me," Ginger blinked hard to keep the tears where they belonged. She took a deep breath. "I'll never forget the sound."

"Sound of what?" Karen took hold of Ginger's hand and looked at their intertwined fingers.

"The sound of the machine in the doctor's office," Ginger let out a half laugh, half gulp. "Though I'm hard pressed to really call it a 'doctor's office'." She poured out a description of the day she'd stood in line to get rid of the cells that grew in her belly.

"Well, it's behind you now and look what you've done with your life. You're doing great as a singer and songwriter. You live in such a beautiful place. It doesn't get much better than this, Ging," Karen stood up and pulled her friend up alongside her. They looked out at the crystal blue sea. "You'll have lots more chances to have a baby."

"I did it again," Ginger said in a low voice. Karen stood and stared at Ginger, not sure she had heard her correctly.

"What do you mean?"

"I've had three abortions, Kar," Ginger walked over to the garden of hibiscus blooms. Karen stood staring at her.

"*Three?*"

"Yeah, I got pregnant again right after Donovan and I broke up. Don't ask me whose it was, 'cause I'm not sure." She picked off spent blooms from the bushes as she talked.

Karen didn't move as she tried to process the confession. She looked around at this place called "Ginger Star" where paradise appeared to mock Ginger's sadness.

"Wow," was all Karen could manage. "Now I know why you weren't calling for such long periods of time." Karen knew Ginger needed to let things out and when she couldn't deal with something, she wouldn't call, but resorted to letters that she could control.

Karen had managed to stay busy with Lee and Nellie and convinced herself that Ginger was just too busy with her career and new-found friends to call any more than she did. But she always knew deep down that there was more and here it was, staring both of them in the face. She wanted to say how great a mom Ginger would've been because out of all the people she knew, Ginger loved kids more than anyone. She could get down on their level much more than Karen ever could. It just didn't make sense. Stating the obvious would only hurt Ginger.

Karen looked from the sea to her friend and saw her bowed head and heaving shoulders. She stood and walked quickly to her side sliding her arm around her shoulder. Karen kept her opinions to herself this time. Ginger turned and buried her head into Karen's shoulder. She cried and the words "demon seed" eeked out between the sobs.

Karen consoled her not knowing what to say other than "I know, I know" over and over again. There wasn't much else she could offer. She knew Ginger slept around a lot and had since they were young teens. Karen figured it was something to do with having a dad that never hugged or kissed her and losing her mom that was everything he wasn't when she was only eighteen. But to abort three babies? Ginger lifted her head off Karen's soggy shoulder her auburn hair clung to her face. She took a deep breath.

"Sorry, I don't know why I did that," Ginger said. She took a deep breath. "But I love you for listening and loving me anyway."

Nothing else needed to be said. The gorilla named "Abortion" was out of his cage running loose. Karen had known long before she arrived in Jamaica there was something wrong and now she knew what it was. At least she thought she did.

—Chapter 10—
1983

## "ONE STEP UP, TWO STEPS BACK"
### Bruce Springsteen

The next morning, Karen heard the rustle of the palm leaves outside the window of her bedroom. She'd forgotten just how tranquil the sound was. Rolling over to see the sunshine peeking through the lush tropical garden, doctor birds flitted from bush to bush as the new day peeked through the leaves into her room. She spotted another Jamaican hummingbird on the back patio next to the little piece of waterfall that gurgled its way down the hillside to the sea where Ginger Star had been built some two hundred-plus years before.

Karen stretched in the bed and spotted the hummingbird again. He was drinking the nectar from a cluster of red hibiscus blooms. She walked to the window slowly and stopped at the shutter to stare at the bush. There he was, his long flowing tail glistened with the colors of the rainbow in the morning sun.

She helped herself to the breakfast Willie left for her just outside her bedroom door. She ate and typed feverishly, using her notes and dreams as fodder. She let out a sigh as she ended a chapter and looked at her watch. It was already 2 p.m. She pushed herself back from the desk and stretched.

She stood up, grabbed her hat and fan, and headed out to explore. She walked through the gardens that were scattered throughout Ginger Star. Karen followed an overgrown path down the hillside and thought it strange that it wasn't manicured like the rest of the grounds. She navigated her way using the stones that someone had laid down as steps years before, to keep her footing. "Hmm," she murmured to Paulie as he flitted from tree to tree following her. "Why did she plant a garden so far from the house? And on a hillside no less." Paulie squawked and Karen chuckled.

She walked up to what she had thought was a garden, but it didn't take long for her to recognize the spiky leaves of the ganja plant. "Man, will you look at this?" she said to herself. She reached out and touched a leaf of a plant on the edge of the field that was taller than she. "No wonder she never runs out!" Hearing footsteps, she turned and let out a little yelp of surprise. An old Jamaican man in tattered clothes using a walking stick hobbled towards her out of the ganja bushes. It occurred to her that he held the stick more for defense than walking.

"What you doin' here, Miss?"

"I, uh, I was just taking a walk around," Karen stammered, "around Ginger Star." She wasn't sure if she should stay and talk or turn and run. Paulie landed at her feet giving her a strength-in-numbers boldness. "I thought this was another of Ginger's gardens," she looked back to the ganja. "Well, I guess it kinda is," she looked back at the man.

"You Miss Ginga's friend from 'merica?" He cocked his head to the left and squinted his eyes with an attempt to shield them from the sun with his hand. Karen could see the cloudiness in his dark eyes that hinted of cataracts.

"Yes, I'm Karen," she said as she extended her hand. He switched the walking stick to his left hand and wrapped her hand in his and shook it up and down.

"Me name is Byron. I look afta the garden here for Ms. Ginga," he explained. Ginger had mentioned a groundskeeper. Karen thought this must be him.

"Do you live here?"

"Yes, mam," Byron pointed to the cottage further down the path. "I been here long time now."

"Well, I'm pleased to make your acquaintance, Byron. I should probably head back."

"Come, sit under the banyan tree and have some tea." He walked toward the end of the field, "Get out da heat. I don't often get a visitor." She followed wondering whether she should or not. Paulie's silence gave her unexpected comfort, so she figured all was good. She thought for sure she must be nuts, relying on a bird for reassurance.

They walked towards the little hut that sat to the right of a huge banyan tree with its massive twisted roots. Bryon pointed to a bench made from a tree trunk for the seat and back. It was sanded and curved just so. Karen sat down and leaned back grateful for the rest. "Wow, this is nice. Have you lived here long?" Paulie landed on a banyan branch above them.

"Been here since before me wife died, near ten years now," he answered. "You take it easy and I get the tea." He turned and walked to the house. She looked around as she sat in the soothing shade. She could see evidence of where he sat and whittled wood. The carvings were in shapes of birds and turtles like the ones she'd seen at the craft market in Ochi the last time she was in Jamaica. There was a large stack of wood that he used for carving and another that appeared to be for cooking over an open fire pit. Bryon walked to the black pot that sat on top of the hot embers. He poured the water into a kettle and lowered a metal ball filled with tea leaves to steep. She stood up to help, but he waved her off. "You sit, mi lady. It not often I get to serve a pretty lady!" She smiled and ducked back. She walked over to the vegetable garden beside the cottage.

Byron carried a tray holding two cups of tea, a bowl of sugar, and a small pitcher of milk. "You don't need your walking stick?"

"Nah, that jes for protection."

"I thought it might be." She grinned as he handed her one of the cups. The unbleached sugar had larger granules and was beige in color. He held the bowl out to her. She scooped up a teaspoon, put it in her cup, stirred it in, and leaned back to take a sip. The black tea tasted good. "Mmmm, this is awesome, Byron. Thanks so much."

"I have some June plum. Would you like one?"

"No thanks. I just ate before I wandered off, but thank you just the same." She scooted over on the bench. "Sit down and rest. That's a very pretty sugar bowl," she was surprised at the teacups, saucers, and matching bowl.

"Me wife, she make them and many others," his fingers traced the side of his mug.

"Really?" Karen was surprised. "Is it pottery or ceramic?" Karen was familiar with ceramic art. Her great aunt had owned a shop in D.C. when she was growing up.

"It tis pottery. I 'ave her wheel in mi shed out der," he pointed to an outbuilding with a thatched roof near the edge of the forest.

"What was your wife's name?" Karen asked.

"Lydisha her name. She buried there." He pointed to the edge of the woods near the shed. Karen could see a small wooden cross with a bougainvillea vine growing over it shedding its pink leaves and soaking up the afternoon sunlight. The heat was still there, but the evening coolness could be felt sneaking over the mountaintops as the sun began to dip behind them.

"How did she cook the pottery?" Karen asked and Bryon answered talking swiftly half of it in patois. She had to ask him to slow down or repeat himself more than once. He went on to explain how he had a big hole dug in the ground and would get the coals good and hot so that Lydisha could place her bowls, pots, and cups in the earth to cook. Byron would cover the ware with a light layer of compost to let it bake. "Lydisha, she sell dem at de craft market." He took a drink of his tea. "You live at Ginga Star, mi lady?"

"No, I'm only visiting for a few weeks, but I'm excited to be here and can't wait to come back already."

"Perhaps you come back one day and I'll show you how to use the pottery wheel." Bryon looked towards the headstone. "Lydisha, she would like dat."

"That'd be great, Byron. I would love that!" His smile made her smile back. They sat and talked about Byron's marriage. While he and Lydisha weren't legally married, they'd been together for forty years when she died of what sounded like some kind of cancer. They had six children, the only girl died when she was three in an accident that Byron didn't care to describe and Karen didn't ask. Their boys had grown and moved to various parts of the country. In a country the size of Connecticut, a fifty-mile distance could be like 500 to someone without their own vehicle. Most Jamaicans didn't own a car, so hitching rides, hiring taxis, or riding the country bus was the norm. It didn't sound like he had many visitors.

"I'm thinking Ginger's going to be looking for me soon. I'd better head back to the house."

Byron stood and took his hat off, "Well, it sure was nice meetin' you mi lady." Karen sat her cup and saucer on the tray.

He walked her back up the path toward the great house. The large cistern that collected water for Ginger Star stood between them and the manor house. She could see the old man was getting winded. "Byron, I can find my way." She turned and looked at him. "You need to go back and wash your dishes!" He smiled, leaned on one knee, and nodded.

"Yes, mi lady."

"Thanks so much for your hospitality. I'll be back and I want to see Lydisha's pottery wheel."

"I get it all cleaned up for you."

She waved him on and trudged further up the hill. As she walked closer to the front of the house. She could hear voices. At first, she thought it was the kitchen help bickering, but she soon could tell the raised voices included Ginger. She could see her fussing with a man and recognized Andrew from her last visit. He'd always given her the creeps and Karen had assumed he was no longer in the picture, but evidently not. She stole back to her bedroom to avoid him and being caught up in what appeared to be an ugly fight.

Ginger sat on the edge of the bed as Andrew snored softly. The rustling banana leaves outside the window waved in the moonlight that lit the room with dancing shadows. She wrapped the sheet around her body and padded out the door onto the veranda. The moon coated the lawn with light. She could see everything. The sex had been great and provided the release she'd hoped for, but knew it would never be as it had been with Donovan. She thought perhaps that's the difference between making love and having sex.

"Ging?" she jumped and swirled around, her sheet nearly dropping to her feet as she swooped down and picked it up.

"Geez oh, flip! You scared me half to death, Karen!"

Karen stood up from the chaise on the lawn. "Sorry, I thought you saw me," she picked up her journal. "I couldn't sleep so I came out here to make some notes."

"In the dark?"

"Well, it's not exactly dark with this full moon," Karen reminded her.

"That's for sure," the two walked over to the steps to the living room and sat down. Paulie woke from his perch and joined them, hopping down to the step below.

"When I came back from my walk, I heard you guys arguing, I just headed back to my room. I guess I fell asleep," Karen said. "So, this guy Andrew is your manager and boyfriend?"

"Yeah, I guess you could say that. It's nothing serious though. I don't advertise it."

"Don't worry, your secret is safe with me," Karen said. "Although "Rolling Stone" magazine would probably pay a pretty penny for the scoop. 'Ginger Starling Involved with her Manager' for a headline."

"Guess I'm glad you don't need the money," Ginger said leaning into Karen.

"Well, everyone has their price, you know!"

"Well, what's yours?"

She ignored Ginger's question. "What's he like?"

"Quiet, intense." Ginger looked at her friend. "Hey wait, you know I don't kiss and tell."

"Only to your monogamous tied to the kitchen stove best friend," Karen nudged her.

"You don't look like you're tied to anything at the moment!" Ginger stood up and pulled Karen up by the hand. "Come on, there are Oreos in the cupboard." With that, they landed in the kitchen with a bag of cookies and a glass of milk each.

"Ashton offered to take you snorkeling later today, if you want," Ginger said.

"That would be great! I was hoping to go." They worked their magic on the Oreos, took one more drink of milk each and headed for bed.

She was always amazed there was another world just beneath the surface of the sea. Green flowing plants, purple fans swaying with the sea's current, amazing shells, and fish of every color of the rainbow still captured her whenever she put her face down in the water. She pulled her snorkel up to the top of her head and looked at the conch shell she'd found on the sandy bottom. "Wow, this is too much," she said to herself. Ashton sat on a low-lying tree limb of a bread fruit tree. He stood up when he heard Karen talk.

"You okay, mi lady?" he hollered through his hands from the shoreline where he sat watching over her.

Karen waved at him to let him know all was good. She looked at the shell in her hand and marveled at the soft shiny pink inside and ripply sides. She trudged back to the shoreline picking up yet another conch along the way. "I've never found anything so beautiful before!" She handed the shells to Ashton as he stood up from his branch. She pulled the snorkel mask off her head and her hair fell around her shoulders. She reached for her pink towel that Ginger had given her to use. She wrapped the towel around her shoulders in an effort to hide her chubby self. No matter if she was ten or a hundred pounds overweight, she always thought of herself as fat. The self-conscious part of her had moved in when she was a child and never left.

"I've never found so many shells so fast!" Karen held up the net bag that held her treasures.

"Ya, ya, de hurricane, she leave her mark on de' beach," Ashton answered and took the bag from her hands motioning for her to sit on his spot on the branch. Karen took him up on his offer and sat down.

"There were some beautiful bright blue fish just on the outside of the shallow reef. It was awesome."

"You see barracuda?" Ashton asked.

"No . . . why?"

"Fishermon, he say there were some out der dis morning," Ashton put the bag of shells on the sand.

"Why didn't you tell me?"

"No wanna scare you, mi lady."

"But what if I'd seen one?"

"You come a'runnin," Ashton smiled. Karen punched him in the arm.

"Ouch!" He reached up and grabbed his arm pretending to be hurt.

The sun was beginning to dip behind the mountaintops. "We best go. We'd betta get back to Ginger Star soon. Miss Ginga will be back from Kingston by 7." They picked up the bag and the rest of the towels and headed back to the car. Karen slid in the passenger side of the front seat. They wound through the streets of St. Ann's Bay to stop at the outdoor market for fruits and vegetables. The goats and dogs wandered the streets causing Ashton to slow down in between the curves and potholes that threatened to swallow up the little car.

When they were back on the highway, Karen leaned her head on the window trying to rest. Ashton hit a bump in the road and her head bounced off the glass. "Here, mi lady, put your head over here," Ashton pointed to the side of his arm. Karen was just sleepy enough that she leaned over and snuggled up to his side. Ashton looked down and wondered what it would be like to really get to know a woman like her. He was taken with her ladylike manner and kindness. He'd known Ginger for several years, but she was different from Karen. She didn't seem to have the soft side of her friend, making him realize that not all Americans were as troubled as his boss lady. He wasn't quite sure why Ginger always seemed unsettled in spirit. While Ginger could be thoughtful and generous, he'd seen a side of her that he knew he didn't want to cross.

He looked down at the curly brown hair of his passenger and found her attractive in a girlish type of way. But it was more than that, she had a worldly edge to her that intrigued him. He shook his head and reminded himself of his reality. Karen woke when he turned off the road and headed down the lane to Ginger Star.

She sat up startled that she'd been leaning on him. "Oh my, I'm sorry, I didn't mean to."

"No worry, mi lady, chasing the fish wear you out today." He pulled up to the steps in the middle of the circular driveway. Paulie paced back and forth on the top step. Karen reached down for her bag of shells, opened her door, and got out. "Have a good evening."

"You too, Ashton. Thanks for watching over me!" She bounded up the steps to greet Paulie. Ashton drove to the garage at the other end of the driveway. She turned and watched him go and it dawned on her that she didn't know what the rest of his day would bring to him and, at the same time, she wondered why she cared.

She walked into the breezeway that led to the pool. She could hear voices from the living room and Ginger's silhouette. "What do you mean you don't have more than that?"

"I told you, we have to be able to hook up Monty," Andrew's voice boomed. Karen stopped and stepped back as she could tell this wasn't a conversation to interrupt.

"Screw Monty! He didn't deliver like he said he would anyway." Ginger turned to walk away but Andrew grabbed her arm and twirled her around to face him.

"I told you if you want this album, we have to do it his way." Ginger jerked away from him.

"The album can wait. The load's just not ready yet."

"If the album waits, so will the bank payments, dutty gyal!"

The ugly patois words made her flush with anger. "I told you never to call me that again you . . ." Ginger swung to smack his face, but he caught her arm. They stared each other down for a few seconds when Ginger turned and walked down the step. Karen stepped further back in the shadow of the banana leaves.

Andrew turned shaking his head and swearing under his breath. He slammed his hand on the piano keys as he stormed through the living room and headed to his car. "Vrriiinggg!" the piano chimed and the echo lingered.

Karen stood not knowing what do. She knew if she left, he would know she was there. She stayed where she was.

Ginger called for Paulie and he appeared out of what seemed to be nowhere. The bird whirred and landed at her feet. Ginger stooped down to meet him. "You're the only one I trust. The only one that really knows me." She walked towards the cliff that overlooked the sea and the bird followed her every step flying every ten feet or so to catch up with her.

As soon as Karen could see Ginger was out of sight, she tiptoed out from behind the tree and headed back to her room. She sat on the side of the bed and reached over to turn on the bedside lamp as she made notes in her journal. "I'm not sure what to think.

What did Andrew want for Monty? Why was Ginger so adamant that it not happen? What will happen now? Maybe I should leave, maybe not."

She stayed. She called Lee and Nellie to hear what was happening back home . . . baseball games and horseback riding lessons.

The next morning Karen acted as if nothing happened and Ginger talked as if the day had dawned like any other. But it didn't dawn like the others. It dawned with a cloud that only Karen knew existed, but found that with a few totes of ganja, it went away. Far away.

She wrote as if her life depended on it. As if she'd never have another chance and she knew in her heart, she may never have this kind of time to devote to her book for a long time to come. She shoved the thoughts of Ginger's fight with Andrew into the back of her mind and knew that if she confronted Ginger, her private time of writing and relating to her work could stop without warning. She loved her best friend, but also knew that she was capable of turning people away for a long, long time.

She thought about how every time she brought up Ginger's mom, Ellie, Ginger's demeanor would change. A softness would come over her. The wistfulness of memories flooded the two of them as they recounted the crazy times they'd had as kids. The visit to the White House, the riots in D.C., the many money-making schemes their moms had dragged them into, giving Lucy and Ethel a run for their money. But then reality would set back in and Ginger would change back to the harder tougher almost rock star that she was. She was changing and it was evident their lives weren't so connected any more.

She'd never understood writers block but had hit a part in her story that had her stumped as to which way to go. She stood up next to her desk, stretched, and decided to take a walk. Karen took the path towards Byron's place at the bottom of the hill and thought maybe a change of scenery would help. She didn't see him at first. She walked down the rocky path through the ganja plants to an opening where his little house stood. Pink bougain-villea hung over the roof from the top and canna lilies grew up from the ground providing a beautiful cover to an otherwise run-down shack. She was beginning to realize just how beautiful what most considered poverty could be. Jamaica had a way of forgiving a million sins of neglect with her outpouring of color everywhere. Karen walked over to a hibiscus bush and plucked a yellow bloom. "Dat fits fine over da ear," Byron said as he walked up behind her.

"Oh!" she jumped a little. "There you are," she said as she wheeled around. "I hope you don't mind that I picked your flower."

"Dat's what dey for, mi lady," Byron took the flower from her and tucked it behind her ear. "Dey for making beautiful ladies even more so." Karen found herself blushing in front of the half toothless man. "Mi lady ready for her pottery lesson?" he reminded her. She paused for a second.

"You know what? I sure am," she decided in that instant that her writing could wait. She followed Byron into the shed. He opened the door and brushed back the cobwebs with a broom made of a stick with cornstalks on the end. It was obvious that it had been that long since he'd gone inside.

"Wait der and I bring da wheel outside." He disappeared into the darkness of the shed. A kitten caught her eye. The black kitty peeked out from under the shed so that only her green eyes showed. She bent down and tried to lure him towards her, but he retreated underneath.

"You have kittens!" She stooped to look under the wooden platform.

"Yep, six of dem," he said as he pulled the pottery wheel over to the bench that sat under the banyan tree. Karen followed him over. She ran her hand over the wheel and turned it with her finger. Bryon went back in the shed and brought out an old five-gallon paint bucket full of supplies and sat it next to the wheel.

Karen helped him carry a few pitchers of water over while Byron made the clay as it went around and around on the wheel. "Here, you sit," he held up a little stool that he brought from the shed and sat it down next to the wheel. Karen sat, pulling her skirt up enough to keep it out of the way. She scooted up closer to the table that held the wheel that looked like a dish spinning around and around on the tabletop. Bryon plopped down two handfuls of clay. "Jes pump the pedal wid your foot and work da clay with your fingers." She moved her foot up and down and felt the wet clay spin between her hands.

"It's easier said than done!" she laughed as the clay fell from side to side.

"Jes keep goin', you get it soon," he smiled. "It took Lydisha a while to learn it." He sat down on the bench next to her. Karen worked at coordinating her foot and hand motions.

"It gets harder as it goes around more. I guess that makes sense," Karen thought out loud, not waiting for Byron to answer. When her foot grew tired, she stopped. She looked at Byron staring at her hands around the clay. She knew right away that he was lost in memories of his Lydisha. She sat still not wanting to steal the moment and started pedaling again. Neither of them spoke, the up and down chirp of a bob white clipped the silence. She managed to get the clay to have some resemblance of a bowl and Byron threw more water on to make it more pliable. She was beginning to realize the therapeutic exercise the wheel provided for both of them. She found herself lost in trying to get the bowl shaped just right, allowing her mind the respite needed to free her thoughts.

Before she knew it, the sun was going down and a flock of egrets headed back up the mountainside, a sure sign that the day was winding down. "Wow, I had no idea it was so late!" Karen stopped pedaling and looked at her creation, a somewhat lopsided rendition of a mixing bowl. She stood up and stretched her hands up towards the sky. "Ginger should be back from Kingston soon."

Byron picked up the pottery bowl and walked it over to the shed. "We let dat dry a day or two. Den we bake it." He shut the door to the shed, pushing the bougainvillea vine to the side and out of the way of the door.

"How do you bake it?" Karen looked around not seeing anywhere to plug in a kiln.

"Me dig a hole over der long time ago." He pointed to the edge of the steep decline that led to the cattle field. He went on to explain that once Lydisha had many pieces ready, they would lay them carefully in the hole and cover with sand and let it bake in the hand dug oven of the earth. "She be happy to know someone want to use it again." He smiled his friendly jack-o-lantern smile that warmed her heart every time.

"Well, we'll work on getting more done so we can make it worth the effort to fire it up again," Karen smiled. "Come on up to the house and have some supper with us." She placed the leftover clay on the wooden shelf, pushing the cobwebs aside with her straw hat. She flopped the hat against her leg hoping that no spiders came along with them.

—Chapter 11—
1983

## "SHAME ON THE MOON"
### Bob Seger and the Silver Bullet Band

Put the easels over there," Ginger said and pointed toward the alcove in the living room. "The light's good there and if the weather gets crummy, they'll stay dry." Ashton carried in the boxes containing the individual paintings. He pulled them out and sat them on the display easels.

Karen wondered who the striking woman was walking down the hallway. Her dark brown hair flounced to her shoulders. Her skin was creamy white and her hazel green eyes danced when she smiled. She wore a royal blue shawl over a long flowering skirt. Karen assumed this was the artist that Ginger had mentioned from Sylvia's party so many years ago.

As she walked toward Karen the woman's eyes opened wide. "You must be Karen!" She extended her right hand and held her shawl closed with her left. "I'm Judy Ann MacMillan." Her charm was undeniable, just as Ginger had described, and when Karen saw her art, she knew her talent was for real.

"Oh my, Judy! I thought that must be you. You're just as lovely as Ginger described." Karen gushed with compliments, but couldn't help it. "Your paintings are amazing. I can't decide which one is my favorite." Karen reminded herself not to overdo the compliments, but it didn't help much. "I really have to help Ginger greet the guests, but let's catch up later." Karen gave her a hug.

"Yes, darling, we will do just that. Now go see to your guests," Judy waved her on. Another craftsman carried in a box of Wassi ceramics and Karen pointed him towards his gallery area.

Karen's head swam as she tried to remember names and faces. Among the most recognizable artists were Aaron Matalon and Colin Garland, both artists, and Gene Pearson, a sculptor. They were all displaying their talents to help the Windsor Girls Home. Ginger had done well sharing the girls' stories. "It could have been any one of us at some point in our lives," was her pitch and had everyone believing it was true, even if it wasn't.

Ginger Star took on a glow as the sun dipped behind the mountains and the moon came out. Torches lined the perimeter of the lawn to keep the insects at bay and provided soft flickering light for the activities. "Ging, this place looks enchanted. I didn't think it could be prettier than it is during the day, but I was wrong. You've done an awesome job!" Ginger smiled at her, took her hand, and led her up to the microphone in front of the band.

"What are you doing?" Karen asked.

"Come on, I need to introduce you." Ginger waved her hand at the band that was playing and they wound up their song. People on the lawn and in the living room turned to see what was happening.

"Ladies and gentlemen," Ginger tapped a spoon against her wine glass. The crowd of over a hundred turned their attention to her. "Thank you so much for coming to Ginger Star tonight. I hope you're enjoying the food and drink." They applauded their approval. "Judy, have I given them enough wine? Are they buying any art work?" Judy laughed and waved from the alcove assuring Ginger that sales were booming.

"Yes, but give them a little more. It's all relative, you know!" Judy said. The crowd laughed.

"Okay, everyone. Just a reminder, all the proceeds from tonight's sales will go directly to creating a recreational area for the girls at the Windsor Home in Saint Ann's Bay." The crowd applauded again. "If you've never been there, I encourage you to visit. I promise it will change you. It certainly did me." Ginger looked at Karen. "I'd also like to introduce my dearest friend tonight. Karen Murphy. We've been friends since we were five years old, although I'll spare you the number of years that would be." The crowd chuckled. "Karen is writing the next great American novel and Ginger Star will be able to boast that most of it was written right here. Just like Ian Fleming and the 007 novels, there's no better place to write than Jamaica."

Andrew walked up to the front of the crowd. Karen wondered where he had been. She'd secretly been relieved when she thought he wasn't coming. "Let's welcome Karen!" They burst into applause. Ginger handed her the microphone. Karen waited for the applause to die down.

"Thanks, Ging. I really don't know what to say except that I'm truly grateful for you and our friendship and so very proud of what it is you are working to accomplish this evening. I'm in awe of you, the artists, and your guests." Karen looked out at the crowd and her eyes met with Ashton's. She immediately blushed and could feel the color rise in her cheeks. She pressed on. "I want to thank all of you that have been so kind to me—Ashton, Byron, and Willie. I know I've made friends for life, so this is not goodbye, but so long and soon come." "Soon come" was a common Jamaican phrase that meant one would return or be there soon. Karen had adopted the saying as her own. The crowd responded and Byron's toothless smile radiated from the shadows of the hallway. Ashton and Willie waved to her in thanks. She handed the microphone to Ginger and stepped back as the crowd applauded in approval. Burning Spear began to sing again and the night swayed with the palms.

———

Karen walked over to help Judy pull down her easels for the ride home. "I think the evening was a huge success," Karen said.

"Indeed it was!" Judy's hazel eyes glowed with excitement. "I have very little to take home." Karen bent down and helped her carry a few paintings to the driveway. Ashton had pulled Judy's car up to the steps. He opened the door and reached in to help them put the easels away. His hand brushed hers as she gave him the last one, but not without both of them noticing the connection. Their eyes met and her heart skipped a beat. She shook it off and turned back to Judy.

"Thanks again for helping Ginger raise money for Windsor. She said you were instrumental getting the other artists to join in."

"My pleasure, darling." Judy hugged her, got in the car, and drove away.

"Thanks for your help with everything, Ashton." She could feel the blood rush to her cheeks.

"No need for tanks, mi lady." He tipped his imaginary hat and left to retrieve the next departing guest's vehicle. She watched him and realized just how much she was going to miss him. But she missed Lee more.

She walked back to the party and shook hands with those she'd never met and hugged those she had. As guests began to leave, some with paintings in tow, others with Wassi art or jewelry, Karen ducked down the hallway to use the bathroom. She was excited and sure the night had been a really successful fundraiser.

She was certain that Ginger had raised enough to do what she wanted for Windsor and possibly more.

The door to Ginger's bedroom opened and Andrew walked out in mid-conversation with a guest she'd met earlier. He ignored her gaze and kept walking. Nothing new there, he was always trying to dodge her. That much she knew.

When she returned from the bathroom, a tall black woman she recognized from the party, but didn't know, walked out of Ginger's room and continued down the hallway. She knew Ginger was saying goodbye to her guests and was not in her bedroom. What was going on?

Curiosity got the better of her and she tapped on the bedroom door. When no one answered, she opened the door and walked in. Everything seemed fine until her eyes landed on the dresser where a pile of white powder sat on top of a mirror. She stood there stunned. She stared at the drugs. So that's why people are hanging out in her room. Surely Ginger doesn't . . .

Karen turned and slipped out of the room. She headed back to the living room to find Ginger. When she didn't see her, she walked to the driveway thinking she was saying goodbye to guests. Ashton stood there counting his tips for his valet service. "Have you seen Ginger?"

"Yes, mi lady. She head back to the house," he pointed back from where Karen had come.

"Thanks." She turned and hurried back into the house. She walked down the hallway toward the front of the house again. Ginger walked out of her bedroom and closed the door behind her.

"Hey! I was wondering where you were," Karen said.

"Yeah, just about everyone's cleared out," Ginger said, as she sniffed and rubbed her nose. "Come on, let's relax a while."

Ginger draped her arm over Karen's shoulders as they walked. "I'm so excited that you got so much writing done while you were here, Kar." They sat down on the steps leading to the lawn. Karen knew what the sniffing meant as well as the upturn in Ginger's energy level but said nothing.

"I owe it all to you," Karen said as she took a deep breath trying to decide what to say or do. In the end, she let her non-confrontational-self take hold and said nothing. Sometimes you gotta let loyalty take over for good sense. This was one of those times.

"Well, you've worked hard, Kiddo. We both have and this is gonna be our year!" She sniffed again.

Karen yawned and stretched. "I'm gonna have to get some sleep."

"Yeah, but sometimes sleep can be overrated."

"Not when you don't get enough!" Karen stood up and pulled Ginger to her feet. She hugged her friend, leaned back and looked her in the eyes. "But, I see the rules have changed," Karen said.

"Whadya mean?"

"You said you'd never do anything stronger than ganja." — So much for not saying anything . . .

Ginger took a deep breath, looked away, and then back to Karen. "Yeah, I did say that, didn't I?" She walked toward the sea. The early morning breeze blew big puffy clouds their way, hiding the sunrise for now. "I guess I got carried away with all the partying that was going on."

Karen decided not to push too hard. She could see the emotional tight rope her friend walked and didn't want to get on the wrong side of it. "Just be careful, Ging."

"I will, Kiddo. Don't you worry."

They talked into the dawn about new and old memories and found themselves laughing as the rooster crowed. "Yeah, then she backed it off the sidewalk and managed to park it before Dad came out. 'Damn clutch!' she fussed," Karen laughed. In her story, her mom had overshot her parking place and came up over the curb in front of their house. "He asked about the black tire marks on the sidewalk, but she played dumb." Karen yawned. "She was good at that."

"She had plenty of practice!" Ginger laughed. Just then, the sun peeked out from behind the sunrise clouds.

"Man, sunrises are worth staying up for around here," Karen said.

"Yeah, look at that cloud," Ginger pointed. A large cloud parted to allow the sun's rays through. There was a circular cloud that imitated a halo. "I think it's a halo."

"Wow, it looks like it's glowing." The halo cloud shimmered as it floated by.

"Yeah, maybe it's Mom's," Ginger said. She grabbed a napkin and pen and wrote:

> Halo glowing in the dawn
> Makings skies with everyone
> Shines its love in my direction
> Never mind my never mention

Karen reached for the napkin and Ginger handed it over. "Wow, Ging, this is great. Are you gonna turn it into a song?"

"Yeah, maybe."

"Can I use it in my novel?"

"Absolutely."

So she did.

Karen went to bed, but even with an eye mask and ear plugs, she couldn't drift off right away. She woke with a start realizing that she must have fallen asleep. She checked her watch. "Wow! It's already 1:30!" Her time on the island was running short. She shook off the cobwebs in her head and reached in her closet for a brown and gold cotton skirt with a ruffle that stopped at her ankles. She chose a white button up blouse with flowing sleeves. She grabbed a sweatband and wide brimmed hat and headed toward the kitchen. Oh, how she'd fallen in love with Jamaican coffee. It had a nutty, almost chocolatey hue. She was hooked. So much so, she'd packed an entire suitcase full to take home.

There were several people she wanted to see before she left, especially Byron. They'd spent many afternoons together and he'd come to mean a lot to her. The old man had shown her kindness and love sharing his Lydisha's passion for pottery, giving her lessons on the different types of flowers and plants, and just plain listening to her talk about ideas for her novel. She'd discovered that by running her thoughts past the old bushman, she could gain perspective which made it easier to decide which way her character was going. Sometimes they took on lives of their own and she loved it when that happened. Byron had become her go-to guy for a sounding board.

She heard Ginger and Andrew's angry voices behind the kitchen door. Karen shook her head and wondered why Ginger kept this guy around. She stopped, turned on her heel and decided against the coffee. She headed toward Byron's house instead. She'd heard enough of their arguments and didn't want to hear any more.

She walked down to Byron's cottage, but he wasn't there. She poked around, peeked in the window, and called his name, but no answer. She decided to head down the steps to the grotto and its caves. She held onto the railing made from tree limbs and walked slowly down the steps.

The sound of the sea splashing up against the coral shoreline was hypnotic. She hadn't been down here much. Ginger had shown her the grotto when she first arrived, but they hadn't spent that much time there. The water swirled as it wove its way around the rocks and into the cave at the bottom of the cliff. She walked down the steps carefully, not sure of her footing. She got dizzy if she stared at the gushing water too much. She could see how sharp the coral rocks were. It looked like one wrong step and she could get hurt were she not careful.

The sea foam swirled in and out of the cave and welcomed her like a not-so-silent partner. The sound drowned out most of her memory of yet another fight between Ginger and Andrew. She couldn't understand why Ginger wanted him around. Weren't there other managers even more qualified than him? Andrew scared her and gave her reason to wonder what Ginger was really into. She decided wondering was better than knowing for sure. "Just keep her safe, please," she pled with God. "Keep her from her own undoing." She closed her eyes and sighed, her signature agreement between her and God that she was giving it to Him.

She watched the water come in and swirl around before going back the same way it came into the cave. Shards of sunlight broke through the green leaves and shined down on the water creating a clear aqua color that was magical on its own. She remembered her first trip to Jamaica with Lee when Ginger and Donovan lived on the hillside. Things were easier and simpler then. Part of her wished they could go back to that time. She missed Donovan and his easy ways. She thought it a shame that Ginger had let him get away.

Karen stood on the small deck that had recently been built to create a landing at the bottom of the steps. She heard voices, and, looked around but saw no one. She wondered where the voices were coming from since there was no one headed down the steps behind her. She looked out toward the water and saw a sea plane motoring in her direction. The motor stopped and the plane bobbed up and down in the water. The pilot launched a small boat from the plane and jumped in. Karen stood there staring. The boat sputtered once before the motor started up and began to turn and head her way. Instinctively, she backed up and stood behind the branches of a sea grape tree. It occurred to her that she had spent a lot of time hiding over the past few weeks.

A voice called out that sounded familiar yet close. She craned her neck and saw Byron on the shoreline directing the boat into the grotto. The small boat cut its motor and glided into the cove. Byron used an oar to keep the boat from hitting the coral too hard. The guy in the boat threw him a rope and Byron tied it to the rocks. They talked back and forth in patois so she hadn't a clue what they were saying. Bryon's hands flew up in frustration and he shook his head. He turned and started handing over bundles of something wrapped in burlap. She was pretty sure she knew what was going on. This is what Andrew had talked about, and yes, it was 2 p.m. straight up.

———

Ginger sat on her bedroom balcony overlooking the sea. She watched the sea plane bobbing up and down in the waves. She could see Sanchez steer the small boat into the grotto and heard muffled voices she assumed were Sanchez and Byron. She hated that she was caught up in this mess, but Andrew was right, the bank wouldn't wait.

She continued to strum her guitar and make notes on the page of the song she'd written. She looked at her watch, it was 2:15 p.m. She leaned back and continued playing the notes until she got them right. She wrote them down in her song book. She looked up to see Karen walking up the steps from the grotto. "Oh no!" Ginger said.

—Chapter 12—
1983-1998

## "CANDLE IN THE WIND"
### Elton John

Karen buckled her seat belt as the stewardess mimed the safety instructions for the flight. She cried half the way back home. Leaving Ginger behind made her realize how different things were between them now. No longer girls making skies from the clouds that floated by on the beach or chasing boys in high school, but adults following their own dreams choosing different ways to get there. She shook the tears away halfway through the flight.

She'd always love Ginger like a sister. But this trip had helped her to realize people change and move in different directions. Sometimes they make decisions that take them far away from you. She'd come to the realization that she had to quit beating herself up for Ginger's choices.

She never told Ginger she had seen the sea plane. Truth be told, she was afraid of Andrew and what he might do if he knew he was exposed. The fact that he had been a policeman made it even scarier. She knew he had friends in high and low places. She'd just wanted to go home.

She had finished the first draft of her novel, which gave her a terrific sense of accomplishment. She would always be grateful to Ginger and Lee for the chance to get so much done.

She was happy that they'd reconnected like they had, but sad because she knew in her heart that Ginger was in trouble, emotionally and physically. Karen was depressed because she knew she had closed a chapter in their relationship and didn't know if either of them was ready for the next one. Karen finally faced reality in knowing that Ginger's choices were hers and hers alone.

Karen wiped the last of her tears away and pulled out her manuscript. She took a red pen and began to make notes in the margins. Before she knew it, the plane began its descent to Charlotte, North Carolina. She changed planes and hopped on a prop jet headed to Salisbury, Maryland, the closest airport to Ocean Pines.

The sight of Lee and Nellie as she stepped off the tarmac and into the airport lobby wiped away her sadness and trepidation, replacing it with joy.

"It's so good to be home!" Karen had never meant those words more.

"Mom!" Twelve-year-old Nellie ran to meet her when she stepped off the plane. She wrapped her daughter in her arms and smelled her long blonde hair. The familiar scent of coconut oil never let her down.

She held Nellie back and arms' length. "My gracious, I think you turned into a teenager since I left!" Nellie had filled out and developed more of a bustline in the past month. She looked over Nellie's shoulder to see Lee. She let go of Nellie as he stepped up and hugged her. Karen buried her head in his chest.

"I love you," she said. "I'm so happy to be back home."

"And we're happy you're back." He held her at arm's length, frowned, and took a hard look. "You okay?"

"Yeah, I am now," she said and winked indicating she'd fill him in when they were alone. She couldn't wait to unload her fears and let him sooth her torn spirit like he always did. They gathered her luggage and chattered in the car on the drive home.

Once they were back home, Karen filled Lee in on her trip.

"Sounds to me like she's in some heavy drug trafficking," Lee said. He propped himself up on his elbow facing her as she sat down on the bed next to him. "I'm glad you're out of there."

"Yeah, me too." She apologized for not telling him while she was still there, but knew he would have insisted she leave early. She was enough of her mother's apprentice to know how much to leave in and what to leave out.

A few weeks later, they moved from their rental home and purchased a house in Ocean Pines, not far from Lee's job. The move turned out to be just what they needed. It was only a three-hour drive from Karen's parents, and twenty minutes from the beach in a peaceful, wooded community. Stephen Decatur High School, where Nellie was now enrolled, had half as many students as the one in Northern Virginia and was a Blue Ribbon school.

Now that Lee was established in his new job and they were settled into their house, it was time for Karen to roll up her sleeves, edit the manuscript, and query some agents who might want to sell it to a publisher. It was a long and drawn out process and not a promising one from what she'd read in her writer's magazines.

She also sent out resumes to local newspapers to try and land a day job. Before long, she was hired as a staff reporter for the Ocean City Sand Dollar. "You'll be editor in no time!" Lee said when she gave him the news.

Months went by and finally, she began to hear back from the ten agents she'd queried. Her heart would drop when she'd pull the mail out of the box only to see one of her self-addressed stamped envelopes filled with the copy of her manuscript. Another "thanks, but no thanks," staring up at her.

She'd received a piece of advice at a writers' conference. The speaker said to allow yourself ten minutes of sadness or frustration when you see that rejection in the mailbox. You can cry, fuss, or stomp your feet, but only for ten minutes. Then, find another agent to query, and send it off again. Karen took the advice.

She cried a bit, talked out loud to herself and questioned her ability as a writer. She sat in the driveway for a few minutes to finish up her pity party. She grabbed the mail, her purse, and the bag of groceries and headed into the house.

She heard the phone ringing and she rushed to get it before it was too late, dropping half the mail in the process. She picked up the receiver, "Hello?" she answered. She didn't hear anything on the other end. "Hello?" She hung up the phone. "Must've been a wrong number," she said to herself. A few minutes later, the same thing happened. She shrugged it off and continued putting away the groceries. A chill ran up her spine when it occurred to her it could be Andrew that called and hung up. She decided to shake off the paranoia.

Karen checked for loose change in the pockets of Lee's jeans as she put a load of laundry together. She pulled a handful receipts out of his pocket. She was always bugging him to give her receipts so she could organize them for their taxes. She sifted through the papers, one for gas, one for groceries, and one from a florist. "What the heck?" She stood and stared at the receipt from Kitty's Florist in Salisbury, a town about twenty-five miles from where they lived and close to where Lee worked. It was dated six days earlier and she had not been the recipient of any bouquets. A sick feeling planted itself in the middle of her.

In a knee jerk reaction, Karen picked up the phone and dialed the international operator to call Ginger. She needed to talk to someone that would understand her fear and tell her she was way off base. Ginger picked up on the fifth ring, just as Karen was ready to hang up.

"Aloha!" Ginger said in her normal greeting to whoever was on the other end of the line.

"Ging, how are things going?"

"Karen! I was just thinking about you, Woman."

"Yeah, thought I'd check in on you. How's the record business?"

"Great! We start recording Spear's new album this week." Karen could hear people in the background.

"Wow, that's cool. What's going on? I hear lots of voices."

"Oh, that's just Winston and his buddies in the living room. Did I tell you that I might be an extra on another movie?"

"No, you didn't." Karen stood up and walked as far as the kitchen phone cord would let her and reached into the cabinet for a glass. "What's it called?"

"Club Paradise. I'm told Robin Williams and Peter O'Toole are the main stars." Ginger was slurring her words.

"That's pretty cool," Karen said and looked at the clock. 12:30 p.m. A little early to be drinking already, or maybe it wasn't alcohol...She knew Ginger was too distracted to get into any kind of "I think my husband is cheating on me," conversation. They talked for a few more minutes, mostly about Ginger, and hung up when things got too noisy to hear.

"I guess I'd better get going. Sounds like things are getting ready to jam in there. Spear's got his guitar tuned up," Ginger said.

"Okay, keep in touch when you can." The kicked in the gut feeling was almost taking the wind out of her. Tears slid down her cheeks. She hung up the phone with a kick-in-the-gut feeling. Her best friend was gone to her as well as her marriage.

She waited for Lee to come home, going through a dozen possible scenarios where she would confront him about the florist receipt. In the end, she couldn't bring it up. She left the receipts on the kitchen counter to see if he would offer up any explanation. He didn't. When she went back to see, he had taken the florist receipt and left the others. Case closed. Husband convicted. Girlfriend must be hiding in the closet.

Karen never asked him about the flowers and she refused to be one of those women that followed their husbands or hired a private eye. But what was worse, ignoring the obvious or refusing to investigate? Was she being naïve by leaving it alone?

She noticed that he came home later than usual from work, but always had what seemed to have a good reason. When he would work late, he could call her and let her know, but she couldn't call him since the switchboard was closed for the day. Convenient.

Karen decided the best way to fix her marriage was to work on it. She read books and bought a copy of Cosmopolitan to see how to spice things up. Most of the ideas were ludicrous and many were just common sense. He continued his late schedule and in turn, she took up her old habit, eating for comfort. Cookies, cake, sodas. It didn't matter. At least her overgrown waistline wouldn't abandon her.

She threw herself into her job more than normal to try and survive the long evenings. Nellie was always off at a friend's house or at an after school event. The rejections for her novel still showed up from time to time, but even that denial failed to rival the heartache of the possibility of losing Lee.

She thought about confiding in her mom, but she knew deep down that Barb wished she hadn't married Lee when they were so young. She didn't want to give her any reason to not love him.

The telephone hang-ups continued and it seemed she was the only one they happened to. "Have you guys noticed someone calling and hanging up a lot?" Karen asked Nellie and Lee at the dinner table.

"Nope," Nellie said and Lee shook his head and took another bite of his burger. She shrugged. If there were any clues, Lee wasn't giving them up. They finished eating and Nellie washed the dishes. A definite perk, having a teenager that wants an allowance.

"Hey, have you seen a receipt for flowers?" Lee asked. She looked up from her latest Cosmopolitan magazine. Was he really asking her *that*?

"No, not since you took it off the kitchen counter last week. Why?"

"I need it to turn in at work. I bought the flowers for Greta on Secretary's Day and I want to get reimbursed, but need the receipt and don't know what I did with it." Relief flooded her from top to bottom. She jumped up from her chair and hugged him. "What's that for?"

"For being the kind of guy that would do that," she said and planted a kiss on his cheek. She was so thrilled she'd kept her mouth shut. "I'll keep an eye out for it when I'm doing laundry tomorrow."

She found the receipt in the pocket of one of his work shirts and gave it to him. A week or so later, he brought a reimbursement check back from the office and gave it to her to put in the bank. She was never so happy she'd kept her mouth shut.

1988

Years ticked by measured by holidays and Nellie's school events. The contact between Karen and Ginger had dwindled to a Christmas card exchange. Her father relayed occasional details about Ginger. He was still friends with Will, Ginger's dad. According to Will, she had been in and out of rehab a time or two. Her songwriting was still in high demand, even if her singing was not. She refused to do the traveling required of a successful singing career.

Karen had been raised a Redskin football fan as far back as she could remember. She was surprised to find that living on the Eastern Shore of Maryland; most folks were Philadelphia Eagle fans. As if that wasn't bad enough, the TV stations followed suit.

"Who knew? Maybe we should've thought this move through a little better!" Karen said as she flipped the channel hoping for some Redskin hype. After all, they were soon-to-be Super Bowl contenders. Lee laughed.

"Who would've believed it?" He pulled her down onto his lap. "You being such a football fan." She'd given in and allowed Lee to teach her the finer points of the game on Sunday afternoons shortly after they married.

"You and Dad raised me right." As the playoffs continued, the Redskins rose to the occasion, and were headed to the Super Bowl.

"We live just as close to D.C. as Philly. These TV stations need to figure that out!" she complained to her mom over the phone. Before they left Northern Virginia, she and Lee would go to dinner almost every Friday night at Doc Walker's Scoreboard restaurant in Herndon. "Doc" Rick Walker was a Redskin and Karen's favorite player was Clint Didier, number 86, a tight end. "Never met a tight end I didn't like!" she'd tease Lee as she pinched his butt.

In Northern Virginia, she had had been able to listen to the morning radio shows where coach, Joe Gibbs, talked strategy, and players like John Riggins and Dexter Manley made jokes and talked football. Now, living on the Eastern Shore, all she could get was whatever the Washington Post printed and the six o'clock news decided to talk about with regards to the Super Bowl.

"I'm getting pretty tired of hearing about Elway and the Three Amigos all the time. They act like the Redskins might as well stay home." John Elway was the Broncos veteran quarterback and the Three Amigos was their famed wide receiver trio, Johnson, Jackson, and Nattiel.

"Funny you mentioned that. You wanna go to the Super Bowl? I'll pay if you go with me," her mom asked over the phone.

"Are you serious? What about Dad?"

"He doesn't want to go."

"Heck yeah! Count me in!"

———⬩———

Barb contacted a travel agent and booked their trip across the country to Los Angeles. Leave it to her to find a Super Bowl *cruise*. From LA, they would catch the ship to Mexico and then back up to San Diego for the Super Bowl.

"Whew, I'm exhausted," Barb said as she plopped down on the lobby sofa of the cruise ship. They had flown to Los Angeles that morning and just finished dinner on the ship.

The ship began to pull out of the dock when a voice came over the PA system. "Ladies and Gentlemen, we have pulled away from the dock . . . the casino is now open."

Barb's eyes flashed opened, she sat up, grabbed her purse, and stood. "Let's go!"

"Are you kidding me?" Karen asked. "I thought you were tired!" She rushed to catch up with her mom, who with one artificial knee, could be hard to keep up with when there were slot machines in sight. They sat on stools in front of the one-armed bandits.

She fed the machine some tokens. "Where does the money come out?" Karen asked.

"Mostly your wallet," Barb laughed. "But down there if you win." She pointed to the tray at the bottom of the machine. "If you win a bunch, they'll come over and help you out."

"I should be so lucky."

"That's why we're here!" Barb reached for her cup full of slot machine tokens and pulled out a handful.

She continued to feed the machine. Karen had reached her limit of losing money and sleep. "I'm gonna head back to our cabin. Do you have your key?"

Barb pulled the handle again. Bells and lights flashed. The sound of coins falling grabbed everyone's attention. The casino attendant showed up seemingly out of nowhere. *Ding, ding, ding,* went the bell. "How much did I win?" Barb asked the attendant.

"Looks like a thousand bucks," he replied.

"I'm thinking my work here is done!" Barb said. Karen shook her head and laughed.

"I'm thinking it's not. You'll be back." Karen said. And she was.

The next day, they pulled into dock in Ensenada, Mexico. Barb and Karen stood on the deck of the ship and watched the coastline glide by as the boat navigated its way into port. They spent the day shopping, buying souvenirs for everyone.

"Winning a thousand bucks should work out well for those back home looking for a souvenir," Karen said.

That night, they cruised north to San Diego and got up early to get off the boat first and head to Jack Murphy Stadium.

"We don't wanna waste a minute of this!" Barb said. She was decked out in a burgundy and gold Redskin tee shirt hog nose baseball cap, and jacket. Karen wore her Redskin Clint Didier jersey and jeans.

When they arrived at Jack Murphy Stadium, there were parties in huge tents all around the perimeter. The air was charged with excitement. Barb's Redskins hog hat looked tame next to the costumes most were wearing.

"I told the travel agent I have an artificial knee and bad arthritis and not to give us nosebleed seats!" Her instructions must have been heeded. They had seats in row 8 near the end zone. They were impressed.

"She must've paid attention, Mom. Great job!" The pomp and circumstance of the pregame festivities was amazing. There was an American flag half the size of the football field made up with red, white, and blue balloons all over the field. The Blue Angels flew over the stadium just as the Herb Alpert hit the last note of the Star Spangled Banner on his trumpet and the balloons were released into the sky.

The game began and the Broncos jumped ahead of the Redskins ten to zero in the first quarter. "Oh no, not only are we not gonna score any points again, but she spent all this money too . . . " Karen silently remembered the year before when she and Barb had taken a bus to the Meadowlands in New York to watch the Giants beat the Redskins 17 to 0 in the NFC championship game. "Don't think she's gonna handle it all that well this time around," Karen thought to herself.

The Redskins came roaring back in the second quarter. Quarterback, Doug Williams, led the team to a score of 28 to 10.

Karen headed for the ladies' room thinking she'd beat the crowd before halftime. She took her Walkman radio and earphones with her so she could listen to Sonny Jurgenson and Sam Huff give the play by play and she wouldn't miss anything. Just as she sat down, Doug Williams threw a touchdown pass to Clint Didier, her favorite player, right in front of their end zone seats.

"I can't believe you missed that!" Barb said as she sat back down.

"I know, did you hear me screaming from the toilet?"

"Was that you?" Barb laughed. "Thought maybe you were constipated again!" They settled down and watched the halftime show with The Rockettes and Chubby Checker's "The Super Bowl Twist" with a football field full of baby grand pianos. The Redskins went on to win the game 42-10. Jake never said no to a trip with Barb again. Barb's apprentice took note.

### Summer 1990

"Okay, okay, I'll go," Barb said.

"Oh, Ma, you're gonna love it. Camping on Assateague again and this time, not in a tent!" Karen was excited that her mom had finally agreed to go camping with them in their RV. They'd spent many weekends over the past two years enjoying their new home-away-from-home.

"Yeah, your father knows when to get the heck outta Dodge." Jake would be away on a business trip that weekend. "I did the camping thing years ago, not because I wanted to, but because it was do that or don't go to the beach," Barb whined. "Sharing the beach with two-thousand-pound ponies is always a crap shoot."

"I know, but this is RV camping. It's different. You'll see," Karen said.

The weatherman promised a sunny beach weekend. Karen made sure she had Barb's dark chocolate nonpareils, Pepsi, and plenty of Old Bay on hand for the crabs they were bound to catch. Barb drove down on Thursday evening. Lee and Karen had taken off Friday and were off Monday for Labor Day weekend. They already had the campsite set up with a screened-in tent that housed a picnic table when Barb arrived. The mosquitoes on Assateague Island were legendary. Only fools thought they could stay a step ahead of what locals liked to call their "state bird." Fending off the little buggers along with a steady dose of Off was the best way to keep them biting someone else.

"Looks like a storm brewing over there," Barb said as they took turns hitting the stupid little golf ball around the stupid little mini golf course. They'd all had too much sun the day before and decided to spend time on the Ocean City boardwalk and somehow ended up playing miniature golf.

"Who's idea was this anyway?" asked Karen as she once again, lost the game. She wiped the sweat from her forehead and pulled out a sweatband. Lee ducked his head. He knew things were going south if she was hot and sweaty.

"Not mine, that's for sure," Barb answered. They both gave Lee the evil eye.

"Only a man actually suggests playing anything that entails hitting a ball into a hole, but you must first hit it through the belly of a shark."

"Look out, you never know what you might find in there," Karen said as Lee bent over to retrieve Nellie's ball from the corner of the shark's mouth. She poked him in the butt with her putter.

"Hey, you'd have more fun if you were just a little more competitive!" Lee said.

"I'm competitive," Karen said. "I just don't care if I win or not!"

"Hey, that dark cloud is getting closer," Nellie said as she craned her neck around to get a better look at the sky. Large raindrops started to fall and the wind picked up.

"I'm thinking we'd better head back to Assateague. You never know what these pop-up storms might do," Lee said.

"Oh darn, and I was just starting to learn to putt," Barb said. She let out a heavy sigh, her signature sound. "Just like you to wanna quit when I was gonna win." She gave Lee the evil eye.

"Barb, I was gonna let you win," Lee said. "Just so you know."

"Yeah, when donkeys fly," Karen chimed in. Lee never "let" anyone win.

They turned in their golf clubs and balls and by the time they got back to the car, the wind had picked up and the rain pelted them. They drove back toward Assateague and before they got there, the sun had come out and there was a rainbow over the bay as they crossed the bridge onto the island.

"Uh oh," Karen said as she saw the tents that had been leveled by the storm. Campers were everywhere trying to put things back together. "I hope we're okay."

"Might have to put the screened-in tent back up, but we should be good," Lee said. He turned into their section of the campground. He was right, the screened in tent was on the ground, but that was just the beginning. The door to the RV had swung open and an Assateague pony stood with his head inside, his hind end and tail were the only things visible.

Lee barely stopped the car before he jumped out and ran toward the pony. "Hey! Get outta there!" He picked up a wet beach towel and slapped the pony's hind end. He backed his front legs down and out of the camper, turned and sauntered toward the next campsite. The pony let out a snort of irritation, but kept on going.

They climbed up the steps into the camper. Cheetos were strewn everywhere. "Oh well, looks like I need to crank up the generator so you can vacuum," he said to Nellie.

"Uh oh," Karen said as she held up the wrapper to Barb's giant Hershey bar. "Guess he found your stash!"

"Stinking horse," Barb said. "Guess I'll have to raid yours." Karen looked toward the cabinet above the dashboard. "You never were any good at hiding things." She followed Karen's eyes and opened up the cabinet. A bag of Hershey Kisses stared back at them.

"Hey!" Karen laughed and reached for the candy but was too slow for her mom.

Lee cranked up the generator and Nellie ran the vacuum cleaner. "I'm outta here. Gonna go play bingo at the Berlin fire hall," Barb yelled over the noise. Berlin was a small town just a few miles west of Ocean City.

"Ma, you can't do that!" Karen yelled back.

"Why not?" Barb hollered as she grabbed her sweater.

Karen rolled her eyes. "You're too young to hang out and be one of the blue hairs." Barb was younger than most grandmothers. Both Barb and Karen had gotten an early start in their child rearing careers.

"Well, like the commercial says, 'You gotta play to win!'" she laughed. "Let's go!" Barb yelled back just as Lee turned off the generator. She headed out the door.

"Okay, that does it. I've officially become my mother." Karen grabbed her purse. "Wanna go?" she asked Lee. He rolled his eyes. She kissed him on the forehead and headed out the door.

Karen ducked into the ladies' room after they checked in and got their bingo cards. "I'll find a table and get us set up," Barb said. When Karen found her mom, she was seated with two other blue hairs.

Blue Haired Sweater Lady sat with a man that appeared to be her husband. She pulled out three rubber troll dolls with hot pink, green, and yellow hair and she lined them up in front of her bingo cards. Evidently, bingo players could be pretty superstitious.

Barb leaned over and whispered in Karen's ear, "I'll pay you ten bucks to knock over one of those dolls."

Karen looked at the trolls and Blue Haired Sweater Lady and giggled. "I'm afraid she might turn into a life-sized troll if I do." The vision threw them into a giggling fit.

"Oh my gosh! You have B14!" Karen pointed to Barb's card.

"Bingo!" Barb hollered and threw her hands in the air. "We just made it to the Tensies, Kiddo. How much did I win?"

Blue Haired Sweater Lady with the troll patrol was annoyed. She only needed one more number, but Barb had a good bingo. Blue Haired Sweater Lady reached over and straightened the line of dolls. "Must've fallen asleep on the job. Poor trolls, better be careful or it will be back into the bingo bag until next week," Barb whispered into Karen's ear.

"The problem with bingo is," Karen said, "you win and everyone hates you. You lose and you just wanna spray them with cold water. The negative karma hunts you down no matter which way it goes!"

"Yeah, well they can send all the negative thoughts they want as long as it comes with cash!" She held up $200 in twenty dollar bills that Bingo Man had just handed over.

Karen picked up a bingo card and started to fan herself. Sweat beaded up on her forehead. "What's wrong, you hot?" Barb asked.

"I am. Could I be having a hot flash?"

"Could be, you're forty-four now, you know."

"How did you know when you were going through the change? What were your symptoms?

"Mostly hot flashes. We were out at a gun club dance on New Year's Eve and I started stripping at the dinner table. Your father thought it was a wonderful New Year's resolution, but the fact was, I was really sweating for the first time ever!" Barb checked her cards for the next called number. "I went to the doctor, he gave me some hormones, and it all went away."

"What about mood swings?" Karen asked.

"Never had 'em," Barb answered.

Pausing for a second, Karen asked, "How could you tell?" Barb looked up at her. "Or are you just mean all the time?" Barb reached over and lightly punched Karen on the shoulder.

"Careful, kid. I brought ya into this world, and I send ya straight back to the Onesies if I feel like it!"

❦

## 1998

"I think I'm gonna look into scheduling the gastric bypass surgery," Karen said to Lee. She had a friend that had the weight loss surgery done and was several sizes down. Karen had had a scare with a blood clot in her leg a few months before. She could have died and knew there was a good chance it was a weight related health issue. She was over forty and wasn't getting any younger. It was getting harder and harder to lose weight with her litany of diets and seldom used exercise programs.

"Are you sure you wanna do that?"

"Yeah. After the blood clot, I know that if I don't do something, I could really have some health problems, or worse yet, wake up dead from it." He didn't argue with her.

"Will insurance cover it?" he asked.

"Yep, I called them this afternoon. I told the lady that if I needed to gain a few pounds to qualify, I could make that happen." Karen plopped down on the sofa next to him. "She called back this afternoon to say I had enough co-morbidities to qualify. Nice word, huh? 'Co-morbidity'?" With her blood pressure, arthritis, weight, and the blood clot issue, the insurance company was convinced the surgery would not only help Karen with her weight, but save them money in the long run by getting her down to a healthy weight.

Karen attended a support group for patients that were getting ready to have the surgery and those who already had. It was enlightening. Her doctor stressed the need for exercise and diet modifications before and after the surgery. She started drinking protein shakes which took some getting used to. "Protein in a liquid form doesn't taste anything like a steak!"

The surgery would shrink her stomach to the size of an egg. Afterwards, she would have to learn to eat all over again, beginning with liquids, then soft foods, and so on. Vitamins and protein shakes would become her everyday lifetime regimen. She was up for it.

Karen had the surgery and embraced her new lifestyle. It took about six weeks before she was eating anything with substance and the weight started to fall away. It was six months after the surgery before she had her first hunger pain. She joined a gym and actually went this time. She was determined to be successful and felt like she'd been given a tremendous gift . . . a new lifestyle that would help keep her healthy.

But, just because her stomach was the size of an egg, didn't mean her other senses didn't still respond to the lure of food. The smell of hot sauce on chicken wings was evidently one that did just that. Lee ordered the hot wings and before the server could write it down, her mouth watered. "I can't believe you like hot wings now." Lee's indigestion plagued him less as he got older.

He wiped his mouth with a napkin and licked his fingers. "I know. All of a sudden, I can't get enough of them."

The server dropped off the wings. She reached over and took one. "May I?" she asked knowing his answer.

"But I thought you couldn't eat anything but soup or mashed potatoes," Lee said. He didn't need to remind her.

"Yeah, but I can suck off the sauce!" So she did. It was pure delight to have that taste in her mouth again. She learned she didn't have to have that much food in order to kill a craving. This "learning to eat" thing could be a real plus for her.

"It's kinda like 'waking up slowly' to food for the first time," she said to Lee. "And the smell of these wings just puts me over the edge! Watching TV commercials has shown me what my favorite foods really are." Pizza, marinara sauce, and hot dogs made her mouth water. Now it was hot wings too.

There was a time when she would have been pouring her thoughts into a letter to Ginger, but they hadn't had any contact in a few years now. She'd learned to let her go.

As Karen lost the weight, it seemed to melt away from every part of her, but mostly, her boobs. "Who knew they were deflate-able?"

"These thunder thighs seem to hang on for dear life," she said to her mom as they shopped in thrift stores for new clothes as she lost weight. "No sense buying new if I'm not gonna wear them for long." Within a year, she had lost over one hundred pounds. Almost half of her was gone. Her doctor was happy about the way she'd exercised and gained muscle mass. "Who knew that muscle mass was tied to my ability to consume calories? I should've become a body builder years ago."

She went down a size every month or two. All of a sudden, she realized that her wardrobe didn't have to consist of mostly basic black. She'd discovered that black was a favorite color of lots of folks that were overweight. Karen now found herself buying pastels and brightly decorated clothes. All of a sudden, she could wear her favorite color, Caribbean blue. She was thrilled and thanked God every day.

Going to the doctor to step on his scale was for the first time in her life, a happy experience. She reveled in her success at seeing the number go down each month. She looked forward to the support group meetings to glean more tips and give a few herself. Her energy level increased along with her confidence with every pound that melted away.

Eventually, her appetite came back, but she was able to follow the guidelines her doctor suggested. A protein shake for breakfast, eat protein first when eating a meal, and don't drink your calories. She was at the gym at least three times a week, enjoying it more and more as her body got smaller and smaller.

She loved being able to do normal things like buckle the seat belt on an airplane without praying it would fit, or getting on a ride at an amusement park and the bar squeezing her stomach so hard it left a bruise behind. It took about a year for her to lose one hundred pounds. Almost half of her was gone, but her desires and cravings weren't. "I want my money back," she told her doctor.

"Huh? What do you mean?" Doctor Samson asked.

"You didn't take my sweet tooth out when you were in there!"

"I'm a surgeon, not a magician," he laughed.

Her friends were very encouraging. Sue started handing down clothes to her when she got down to her size. "Here, try this on," Sue said. "I just don't wanna hear about it when it's too big!"

Lee encouraged her, but never said much about her weight loss or how she good she looked. It surprised her that he never complimented her. She gave it a mental shrug.

—Chapter 13—

1994

## "I CAN SEE CLEARLY NOW"

### Jimmy Cliff

Ginger walked down the crumbling steps of the rehab, got into the taxi, and headed to the Kingston airport. She wore her signature green skirt that she always wore to her concerts. She stared out the window of the cab and was reminded why she preferred Jamaica's north coast to the city of Kingston. Here, people were jammed one on top of the other in ghettos throughout the city. Quite the opposite from Ocho Rios, her sleepy resort town that only swelled when a cruise ship was in port for a few hours.

This was her third exit from a completed rehab in Jamaica, but this time she knew something was different. Something had clicked. For one, she'd been scared straight when she got arrested. She knew that landing in a Jamaican jail could make one only wish they were dead. Windsor wasn't a jail, but it may as well have been. Stories of the women's prison were horrific and best left untested.

She'd promised God that if she got out of this without going to jail, she'd never touch cocaine again. And she meant it. Her attorney was able to work a deal for the rehab, but not without costing a small fortune. There were lots of folks to pay off before they'd let the American reggae star off the hook. The attorney also managed to strike a deal with the US government so she could immigrate back to the States. Her bank account was dwindling, but she was going home.

Heading back to the States had been her idea. She knew she had to get off this island. She stared out the window for one last look at Kingston. It wasn't her favorite part of Jamaica and maybe it was better she left from here instead of Montego Bay. The North Coast held most of her memories.

During conversations with her counselor, it had become clear to her that she had never fully mourned her mom. Having to move back in with her dad and his new girlfriend (and eventual wife) to help take care of her brothers, gave her no opportunity to grieve Ellie.

For the past twenty-six years, she had tried to cover it up with drugs, music, and sex. No more. She knew she had to look her losses in the eye.

The taxi pulled up to the airport curb. She handed the driver his fare, grabbed her duffle bag and climbed out of the car. She was leaving Jamaica with a lot less than she'd come with. Ginger Star was gone to her. Donovan had been kind enough to put her belongings on a ship to the States while she was in rehab. He sent them to her dad's house. The first thing she was going to have to do was find a place to live so she could get the stuff out of his garage.

She walked toward the Air Jamaica ticket counter and reached into her purse for her passport, panicking for a second when she couldn't find it at first. She crouched down to dig through her bag. "Whew!" she said when she fished it out.

"You never could find anything in that purse of yours," he said.

She looked up to see Donovan standing above her.

Ginger was scheduled to meet with a probation officer once a month in the States. She wasn't "legally" required to go. It was more of a way for her to check in with the authorities without raising any eyebrows. She assured them she would let them know if Andrew contacted her. They wanted to know the minute he had plans to re-enter the States.

Ginger went through immigration and customs without a hitch. She grabbed her suitcase from the carousel and walked to the curb outside Baltimore Washington International Airport. Her dad stood waiting with the trunk open. She'd seen pictures of him with his gray hair, but was still stunned when she saw him. Despite his age, he was as handsome as ever. "Dad!" He hugged her longer than he ever had before. She looked into his tear swelled brown eyes. She wasn't used to so much affection from him. She soaked it up.

They drove away from the airport. She was amazed at the highways and hotels that had sprouted since she left. The size of everything was overwhelming.

"It was such a shock when Uncle Jake died. I'm so sorry," she said.

"Yeah, he was the brother I never had. It's so weird without him around."

"How's Aunt Barb doing?"

"Okay, I guess. Have you talked to Karen?" He knew she hadn't. Barb had asked him why Ginger didn't keep in touch, but he had no answers.

"No, not yet, but I will." She changed the subject. "This place has grown so much, I'm gonna have to learn to drive and find my way around all over again."

"Yeah, there's construction just about everywhere these days," Will turned onto Route 97 south.

"I don't think this highway was here before," Ginger pointed to the sign as they merged onto the freeway.

"Yeah, it's fairly new. A good connector between Route 50 and the Baltimore Beltway. Lots of new shortcuts for you to learn." They both laughed.

"Just what I need, more roads to get lost on!"

"I hope your sense of direction has improved. You were just like your mom when it came to that." Hearing him mention her mother surprised her. She could count on one hand the number of times that had happened since Ellie died many years before.

"Yep, Mrs. Wrong Way lives on in me, for sure." Ginger pointed at the green exit sign to head north towards Baltimore. He lived in Mt. Airy, about 30 minutes away. "It's been a long time, but aren't we supposed to go that way to your house?" She pointed to their left.

"Yeah, but we're not going there just yet. I have something I want to show you." They drove south towards the Chesapeake Bay Bridge on Route 97 and turned off on Route 3 toward Crofton. They traveled a few miles and he turned off the highway and into a townhouse development.

He steered the car into a parking space facing a brick townhome. "Who lives here?" she asked.

"You do, if you want." He grinned, opened the car door, and got out. She sat there stunned for a second while he opened her door. She swung her legs around and stood up.

"Looks nice. How much is the rent?" she asked.

"No rent, just move in." He handed her a set of keys. "I invested the money you sent me to save for you over the years." Ginger had never trusted the Jamaican banks and had funds automatically transferred to her dad to put aside for her. It turned out to be the smartest thing she'd ever done. The Jamaican government had confiscated most everything she owned in Jamaica when she got busted. "I bought it with your money and it's been a rental for years. It paid for itself and belongs to you now." He handed her a set of keys.

"Oh my God, Dad!" She covered her mouth with her hand and stood at the bottom of the steps overwhelmed. "Well, let's go see!" She ran up the steps, unlocked, and opened the door.

"Sorry about the boxes. I had them sent over just came a few days ago." Large boxes with the contents of Ginger Star and all her worldly possessions of the past twenty-six years stood stacked throughout the rooms. She could see Donovan's handwriting on the labels and ran her hand over the letters, pausing for just a second.

"Dad, this place is awesome, there's even a fireplace!"

"You can still stay with us as long as you want if you wanna unpack all of this first."

"Thanks, but I'll be fine here." She walked over to him. She was thrilled she wouldn't have to stay with Roberta. "I'm sorry I was gone so long."

"I'm sorry you ever felt the need to leave." He'd stocked the refrigerator with Pepsi and other essentials. He grabbed two bottles, opened them, and handed her one. They raised them for a toast. "Here's to new beginnings."

They sat on the living room sofa and talked for hours, more than they ever had in her entire life combined. They talked about her new job that was already lined up at Galore, a local grocery store chain.

"Roberta wants to have a welcome home party for you." He looked at her from the corner of his eye and raised an eyebrow in question. He knew she'd resist. "William and Timmy's families and a few others."

"Aw, Dad, I really don't want a bunch of fuss."

"Yeah, well, you have to see everyone at some point. Might help to get it over with all at once."

"Let me know when." She shook her head and sighed. He'd just given her the keys to her own home, how could she say no?

Will called Roberta and let her know he was on his way home. He hung up the phone and looked at Ginger. "You sure you don't want to come over for dinner?"

"Nah, I can't wait to start digging through this stuff and setting up house," she walked over and hugged him.

"Oh, one more thing." He handed her another key. "See that silver Honda in the parking lot?" He pointed out the kitchen window. "It's yours to use as long as you need till you get your own car." She looked out the window.

"What? Are you kidding me?"

"Roberta just got a new car, so we hung onto this one knowing you'd need something till you got on your feet and bought a new one."

"This is just too much." Ginger shook her head, but he ignored the rebuttal.

"You're gonna have to take the driver test again. The book to study is on the dining room table. I'll take you to practice next week and we'll go to the MVA so you can take the test when you're ready." Ginger was overwhelmed.

"Thanks so much, Dad." He patted the top of her head, hugged her tight, and walked out the door. She watched from the kitchen window as he got in his car and drove away.

"When did he get so old?" she asked herself. She felt as if she'd gone to sleep and woke up twenty years later. She pretty much had.

Ginger sat in her new living room and looked at the boxes Donovan had packed and sent from Ginger Star. Her heart still hurt whenever she thought about him. She remembered their reunion at the airport. "Oh well, quit reaching for the past and put your hand out to the future," she reminded herself. "Hmm . . . could be a song lyric there."

She reached over and found an envelope on the dining room table that was piled high with mail addressed to "Resident", more boxes, and things she didn't have the time to decide whether they should be thrown away or not. She jotted down the thought and stuffed the envelope into her pocket.

Ginger thought about calling Karen. She reached for the phone many times, but never finished dialing her number. She didn't feel like she even knew Karen any more. It had been fifteen years since Karen had been to Ginger Star. They had lost touch over the years and from what she remembered, it was definitely Ginger's fault. She wasn't sure if it was embarrassment or what, but she just didn't have the gumption to call her just yet. She would, she promised herself. Eventually. Just not today.

When she thought about how people had changed, it over-whelmed her. Her dad's hair was totally white and her nieces and nephews were graduating high school. Nellie had graduated college and was married with children. How did that happen?

Moving back to the States was culture shock. Like twenty-six years ago in reverse. Had she really been gone that long? She couldn't remember much of the past five years, that's for sure . . . but that still left twenty-one to be accounted for.

She couldn't get over how much faster paced everything was compared to when she'd left. The roads were bigger and cars went in every direction. Shopping malls, huge movie theaters, and restaurants were everywhere. It seemed as if there were new houses going up on every corner. Where did all the people come from?

Her dad returned a few days later and they spent time driving around parking lots. Parallel parking was as much a challenge as ever. "Why do we have to parallel park anyway? Nobody does it anymore!"

"You'll have to ask the MVA that question. Just keep doing it till you get it right." They were there all afternoon. "It's a good thing my hair's already white," he said.

"Much more of this and you'll start pulling it out!" Ginger laughed. They decided to go ahead to the MVA and get the test over with. She ran up on the curb when she tried to parallel park. Thanks to some timely flirting with the officer, she passed anyway and walked out with her new license in hand.

Spring was showing up everywhere. It was an amazing thing to watch after so many years of perpetual summertime in Jamaica. Ginger missed the colors of the Caribbean and Jamaica's hillsides, but watching the earth come back to life was never a snooze. She made a deal with herself to embrace the four seasons. "Accept the things you cannot change . . . "

She shied away from making friends at work. Who was gonna believe her when she told them that she was Ginger Starling, the reggae singer? She didn't want to deal with the questions and certainly not the raised eyebrows.

She met her first neighbor while she sat on her steps enjoying the sunset. The woman from next door walked her dog on a leash. Ginger got up and squatted down to be eye level with the furry poodle. She was hooked.

The next day, she headed to the animal shelter. She walked past a dozen cages with dogs looking for a home. Then she spotted Spanky. She fell in love with the small black and white short haired dog. He jumped into her arms when the attendant opened the cage and licked her face. She laughed with genuine joy for the first time since she could remember.

Then she made the mistake of checking out the kittens. A striped tabby about four months old reminded her of Miss Kitty at Ginger Star. Ginger had an instant family. "I mean, what husband wags his tail when I come in the door anyway?" Ginger joked with her dad over the phone when she got home. The irony of her dad being her best friend didn't get past her.

"Well, we're a motley crew, aren't we?" Ginger tossed Spanky a new rawhide bone. She sat in the backyard and played her guitar while the two explored. Tiger wove back and forth against her legs, reminding her of Miss Kitty yet again.

Most nights, she would pull out her guitar and work on a new song. Her songwriting proved to be a lifesaver for her. She wrote them in a composition book, numbered chronologically. It was as much a journal as a book of songs. Anyone that read it would see that. She poured her heart out on the strings of her guitar.

Spring turned into summer and summer into fall. At first, she wasn't happy to see Spanky chasing the leaves as they began to fall off the oak tree in the back yard. She cringed at the thought of being cold from winter's chill.

She stopped at a nursery and bought a load of firewood and put it in the back of her new Toyota Highlander. Her brother, Timmy, had helped her to negotiate a good deal on the new car. She brought an armful of wood in the house and stacked it on the hearth. She built a fire and smoke started to fill the room, "What the heck?" and it dawned on her that she hadn't opened the flue.

She reached up into the fireplace, found the chain, and pulled it. The smoke took off up the chimney. "Whew, that could've been ugly!" she said to Spanky and Tiger who circled trying to figure out what was going on.

Her dad's 70th birthday was coming next month. Her brothers wanted to have a party and she was in charge of inviting the guests. "I guess that's smarter than putting me in charge of the food," she said as she agreed to make the phone calls. The only problem was, Aunt Barb and Karen were on that list. "I guess I'll have to make that phone call sooner than later," she said to Spanky. Like he understood.

She arranged a day off from fish filleting at Galore and started making the phone calls. She ran through Roberta's guest list one at a time. She took a deep breath and dialed Aunt Barb's number. She figured Karen was at work and too busy to talk.

Aunt Barb kept telling her she sounded just like her mom.

"I just wish I was more LIKE my mom was."

"Oh, Hon, you're more like her than you know." Barb said. "You can count on us being there." Ginger was relieved.

"What can we bring? How about macaroni salad? I can make your mom's old recipe."

"Nope, Roberta's having it catered, so let's spend her money for a change."

"Just make sure she's got all the bases covered. It's all about the three Cs, you know."

"What's that?"

"Chocolate, Crab, and Cola as in "Pepsi, of course."

"Why did I even feel the need to ask? I'll make sure she's got it covered!"

She hung up the phone and breathed a sigh of relief. She didn't have to call Karen after all. Since when did she become such a coward?

"Well, I did it," she said to herself. She put a checkmark next to Barb and Karen's names. She hoped Karen wouldn't hold her silence over the past years against her.

She took a day and drove to the old neighborhood in Radiant Valley where she grew up. It seemed that everywhere she went; she saw reminders of her mom. Next to every reminder was a memory that tickled her. Memories brought a smile to her face and tugged on her heart. The tugs became easier to take as the day slipped by. Laughter crept in and helped her heart to heal a little instead of always hurting when she thought of Ellie.

She spent time with her younger brothers, William and Timmy. They tried to pick up where they left off, but they both had a wife and two kids a piece. Life had other ideas and demands on everyone's time. She went to ballet recitals and baseball games when she wasn't working nights and hung out with them every chance she got.

Ginger was more of a mother to them than a sister. She and Timmy lived only a few miles apart and they were able to spend time getting got to know each other as adults. They reminisced about their mom. Timmy was only nine when Ellie died, so Ginger ended up telling him story after story. They laughed as she told him about cooking the crabs they caught after midnight, catching the boat on fire, and camping at Assateague.

"Yeah, I remember tormenting Kelly with the frog she found at Assateague," Timmy laughed. He posed his fork as he had years ago, pretending to eat the frog's legs.

"It was a good time till you put him on Mom's breakfast plate."

"Yep. She came up off that picnic table bench like she'd seen a ghost!" They laughed every time they tripped over a memory of Ellie.

Timmy helped when she had something that required a tool to fix. She dragged him car shopping with her when the first one she bought on her own turned out to be a lemon. He helped her hook up her first computer although she rarely touched it.

She felt bad about not calling Karen. She wasn't even sure Karen would take her call. She'd come to realize that Karen did indeed know about the sea plane and ganja business, if only because of the lack of phone calls and letters once she'd returned to the States. Ginger had fallen deeper and deeper into the drug scene until she managed to quit thinking about the loss of her best friend.

Now Ginger was back and she just needed time to put her life back together. Heck, was it ever together? She didn't think so. This was her chance to do it right.

She sometimes felt bad that she didn't just pick up the phone and call Karen. She knew if her friend would even talk to her, she would try and "fix" her. She had learned that she needed to gain confidence on her own first. She loved Karen, but also knew that she would want Ginger to fit into the old mold of who they used to be. Ginger knew she would never be who she was before and trying to help Karen see that right now, seemed daunting and exhausting.

She attended some Narcotics Anonymous meetings, but found the "sharing" to be too much like rehab. She'd done enough sharing to last a lifetime.

She missed singing for a crowd and sinking deep into her music. Giving up on her career as a singer made her sad, but she resisted the urge to give in and feel sorry for herself. She knew that songwriting was a better therapy for her than anything else.

She kept her guitar handy and continued writing new songs, performing mostly for Spanky and Tiger.

She started drinking again. Just a little.

—Chapter 14—
1999

## "ANGEL OF MINE"
### Monica

Barb took care of Jake for over a year before esophageal cancer claimed him. When he died, she felt as though he was just beyond the thin curtain of air in front of her. They'd shared everything since she was 15 years old and now she couldn't get over that he was gone and couldn't tell her what heaven was like. They'd been married since they were kids and it was now forty-six years later. They told each other everything. Well almost. How do you get used to losing *that?*

When Jake was gone, she tried to enjoy the solitude, but the house seemed so empty. It was once filled with grandchildren and friends. While he was sick, it was mostly the two of them sprinkled with visits from the kids. Now, he was gone. Just gone.

All her life, she wondered what it would be like to be on her own. Now she knew. She took the time to rework her will and cleaned out closets. "What are you gonna do when you're done with this mess?" she asked herself as she looked at the piles she'd made all over the room.

She consoled herself knowing Ginger and Karen were friends again. It made Barb smile to think she and Ellie might live on in their daughters after all.

Will's 70th birthday party had been quite the reunion. Karen and Ginger didn't seem to need much prompting from her. The missing years seemed to melt away and if the laughs were any indication, the two fell right back into their friendship.

"You look great, Ging," Karen said as she released her friend from a hug. She leaned back and looked at her. "Your hair is as pretty as ever." The auburn hair had stayed with Ginger with only just a tinge of gray at the temples.

"Me? Look at you! Where's the other half?" Ginger asked referring to her weight loss. "And I'm not talking about Lee!"

Karen still wasn't used to being a "normal" size. Before she could answer, Ginger said, "And your hair! When did you go blonde?"

"Yep, 'only my hairdresser knows for sure,'" Karen quoted the TV commercial. "I decided blonde was the best way to cover the gray." She'd started highlighting her hair and eventually, the blonde took over.

"Save the blonde jokes for Sue!"

"Hey!" Sue chimed in. "Take it easy, you two. I've earned the dumb blonde title fair and square."

"Nobody's arguing that one," Karen said.

The three of them got to know each other that night. They sat at a table swapping stories. Sue was the added buffer Karen and Ginger needed to avoid questions that Ginger had no desire to answer or better yet, dodge.

"So, how's the book publishing going?" Ginger asked.

"Not as well as the weight loss. It took me several years to edit the manuscript, dealing with the day job and everything else." Karen sighed. "But I'm sending out query letters to agents every weekend, hoping for something good to happen."

"It will. Just wait," Ginger said.

"What do you think of this Y2K stuff?" Sue asked. Ginger and Karen just looked at her.

"What do you mean?" Ginger asked.

"You know, when we go from 1999 to 2000 on January 1st. Computers and all are supposed to crash."

"Well, I've got my book backed up on some floppy discs. That's all I care about," Karen said.

"Yeah, if computers crap out, it just might be a good thing," Ginger said.

"Says the woman who's never touched one!" Karen said and they busted out in laughter.

Since Will's party, they'd had a few home movie get-togethers at Barb's house, laughing and crying through the memories of Ellie and the Tensies. A quick toilet papering of Ginger's brother, William's, house in the middle of the night bonded them all even more. The Tensies were back in business.

Barb hadn't felt so great for a few weeks and went in for a checkup. Karen drove down for a long weekend and went to the doctor with her for the follow up results. Barb suspected the verdict and didn't flinch when the doctor said she had cancer that had metastasized on her liver. That's why her back had been hurting.

"I'd rather have a slipped disc," she said and then thought twice of her own dark humor when she saw the look on Karen's face. "It's okay, Hon, we'll head this thing off at the pass this time." She reached over and squeezed Karen's hand that dug its nails into the leather of the chair arm.

"Do you smoke?" the doctor asked.

She cleared her throat and shifted in her chair. "Well, kinda." She and Karen locked eyes. Karen raised her eyebrows waiting for her answer. She'd been trying to quit and thought she'd had her daughter fooled, but from the look on Karen's face, she knew she'd only been fooling herself.

"Well, let's start with a CAT scan of your lungs and take it from there." The doctor closed his file and they checked out of the office. They walked to the parking lot and Karen got in behind the wheel of Barb's white Taurus station wagon.

"Let's stop at Boston Market on the way home and get some meat loaf for dinner," Barb said.

"Okay," Karen said thinking that for once it wasn't her thinking about her next meal, but her mother. Go figure. "She gets a cancer diagnosis and all she can think about is meat loaf?" Karen thought to herself. She pulled into the restaurant parking lot.

"Make sure they give you red gravy with it. I don't want it if they don't have any red gravy." Barb reminded Karen for the third time.

"Are you kidding me?" Karen asked.

"Hey, I'm revoking your 'Mother's Apprentice' status if you come back empty handed!" Barb nudged her as she took off her seatbelt.

Karen laughed and got out of the car. She shook her head on the way in. "I pity the fools if they don't have red gravy," she said out loud to herself. Luckily, they had red gravy and her apprenticeship remained intact.

When they got back to Barb's, Karen called her boss, Clarke, at the Sun Dollar newspaper office to say that she would be working from her mother's house until they figured out the game plan for her recovery. "Take all the time you need," Clarke said. "You can handle whatever needs your attention from there. You only get one mom. Take good care of her." She promised she would.

They sat eating their Boston Market meatloaf. "Your appetite is pretty good for someone that's sick."

"Yeah, gotta keep my strength up," Barb took another bite. "I was thinking though, if I end up checking out, I wonder what Ellie's gonna be like."

Karen almost choked on her green beans. Even in a crisis, Barb was optimistic. Karen was amazed at her mom's ability to talk about dying. "Well, do you think she'll be younger than you?"

"Probably, but I can color my hair to head that off at the pass, but what I'm most worried about is that she's gonna be an expert on everything." She reached for a biscuit. "She's been there a long time now. It's gonna take some getting used to, letting her be in charge."

Karen shook her head. Her mom had just been given a death sentence and here she was making jokes.

A few days later, Barb seemed to be declining and was in lots of pain. Karen checked her into the hospital. The nurse pulled Karen into the hallway outside of Barb's hospital room. "Do you want us to honor her DNR (do not resuscitate) order?" Karen knew she was asking if Barb were in distress, should she just let her die. When Barb had told Karen about the DNR, she joked saying Kelly was second in line for the power of attorney in case Karen didn't have the nerve to pull the plug, she wasn't ready for the question. Not yet.

"Let me talk to her first." Karen said. She turned and walked into the hospital room. Barb sat up in the bed fidgeting with the TV remote.

"These damn things," Barb held up the remote. If it weren't connected to an idiot cord, I'd throw it across the room!"

"Mom, they're asking me if you wanna honor the DNR." Barb looked up from the remote. Their eyes met.

"But we don't even know what we're up against yet." Barb said.

"I know. We need to figure out our game plan."

"Tell them 'no.'"

"That's what I thought, but figured I'd better check with you first." Karen turned and headed back to the nurses' station.

She relayed Barb's decision to the nurse. "Has she seen an oncologist yet?" the nurse asked.

"No, we've seen a few doctors just to rule out a few things, but not an oncologist. She had a CAT scan on her lungs, but it checked out okay."

The nurse set up a meeting with a doctor that evening. Karen, Kelly, and their brother, Jay, joined him in a conference room. Karen had noticed how young the doctors were these days, but this one not only wore the white lab coat, but had enough gray hair to look old enough to legally buy alcohol. "The cancer is all over your mother's liver although we don't know where it started," he said.

"Well, I guess that's what we have to determine . . . to know what we're dealing with, right?" Karen asked.

The doctor pulled the CAT scan films out of a large envelope and held them up to the light. "See the spots here on the liver?" They all nodded. "Normally, I might see a few, but these are all over. It has spread so much; it doesn't really matter where it started at this point."

"So you're saying there's nothing we can do?" The doctor nodded. Evidently, he was used to delivering bad news. "How long does she have?" Karen felt her breath leave her body and that old familiar feeling of dread hit her stomach.

"A week, maybe two."

Karen was making a quick round trip home to Ocean Pines to collect more clothes, etc. Barb was home from the hospital. Kelly and her kids came over to stay while Karen made the quick round trip home. Karen took the opportunity to call Sue and give her an update as she drove on Route 50 West towards the Chesapeake Bay Bridge.

"How's your mom doing?" Sue asked. Having a cell phone helped Karen to keep connected while she traveled the highways. She was grateful for the communication and thought about how tough it would have been just a few years before when cell phones weren't so common.

"Pretty good, just got out of the hospital. I'm headed back to her house in the morning. I went home to pick up some things."

"I sent her a letter."

"Who? Mom?"

"Yeah."

"That was nice of you."

"Well . . . it was a little on the evangelistic side," Sue said.

"No, you didn't," Karen said. She knew how her mom shunned anything "religious." She'd been praying for a way to talk to her, to make sure she was ready for heaven, but hadn't figured it out how to do that yet. "Oh well, we'll see." She cringed.

Karen called her mom to let her know what time she would get back to her house. "Kelly brought in the mail. I got a nice letter from Sue," Barb said.

***

A few days after Karen returned to her mom's house, she had to check her back into the hospital. Barb's pain level had become too high to manage at home. After getting her settled, Karen walked out of the hospital room to ask the nurse a question and buy a round of coffee for her and Lee in the cafeteria. She turned around and headed back to the hospital room when she realized she'd left her purse there.

"You know, she would've really been something if it hadn't been for you," Barb said to Lee. The morphine drip was kicking in and loosening up her typically tight lips.

"Mom!" Karen stood at the doorway.

"Geez oh flip! I didn't know you were there," Barb said. She took a sip of her hospital cup full of Pepsi. "But you know it's true."

Karen sighed and looked at Lee with an apology in her eyes.

"Yep, she would've been a rock star for sure," Lee agreed, trying to lighten the mood.

"Well, given what happened to Ginger, I don't know that I would've wanted her to do that!" Barb said. She tried to sit up straighter in the hospital bed, but laid back down, and pushed her hair from her eyes. Lee and Karen looked at each other.

Later that day in another loose-lipped episode, Barb confided in Karen about her dream journals. "I wrote to Ellie over and over again in those diaries. Talked to her about arguments your dad and I had, yadda yadda."

"Sure you want me to read those?"

"Yeah, why not?

"I guess writing it down was therapeutic. Maybe that's why I'm so nuts. Tried to treat myself. Ha!"

"I don't think there's anyone that's not at least a little nuts, Ma."

"Yeah, I know. Just some more than others. Maybe you can use some of it in your next book. They're in the living room cabinet next to the TV."

Tears welled up in Karen's eyes.

Barb looked at her, reached over and touched her hand. "Don't worry about me, Kar," she squeezed what little she could. "I'm a tough old bird."

"It's not that, Ma," Karen looked into her mother's brown eyes. "You never talk about your faith. I just need to know . . . " she grabbed some tissues from the box on Barb's table. "I want to know that when I get to heaven, you'll be waiting for me." Her evangelical roots were showing.

Barb answered quickly, "Oh yeah, Hon, I'll be there." She squeezed her daughter's hand hard. Karen leaned over the rail and hugged her mom, laying her head on her shoulder as best she could. "Crooked halo and all."

"I have one big concern about when I get to the other side though," Barb said.

"Yeah, what's that?"

"Will Ellie be twenty years younger than me? Maybe I should get my hair dyed one more time . . . " her hand reached up and touched her hair. Karen smiled through her tears and giggled at something her mother said yet again. She was gonna miss laughing and crying at the same time. She did a lot of that when her mom was around.

"Oh yeah, Darlene came by," Barb said. "She dropped in this morning. She gave me this." Barb held up a little gold butterfly on a stand with a crystal shining in the middle of it.

"Oh, that's beautiful!" Karen took it in her hands. It shined in the sunlight streaming in through the window. "She's such a good friend. Loves you so much." Karen made a mental note to make the butterfly her own when Barb was gone.

Tears welled up in Barb's eyes at the thought of leaving Darlene on this side of the rainbow. Karen choked up. She wasn't used to seeing her mother so emotional. Barb was always the strong one, the matriarch that made everything better. The one she laughed and cried with. How was she ever going to say goodbye? She'd always been her "mother's apprentice." What would she be now?

"Hey there, how'd your day go?" Karen asked Lee over the phone when she got back to her mom's house. She let her mom's dog, Sugar, out to roam the back yard and kept an eye on her from the kitchen window.

"It was fine," Lee said. "I picked up the mail and I think there's something here you might want me to open for you. It's from Blackstone and Curtis."

"Really? Is it one of my return envelopes?"

"Nope, looks like something they wrote to you. Want me to open it?

"Yes!"

"Okay, hold on a sec." He held the phone between his neck and shoulder and ripped open the envelope. "Here's what it says,"

> Dear Mrs. Murphy:
>
> I received your query about "Lost Cause." I found the style of writing to be indeed engaging and what I've read so far left me wanting to know more about the fate of the characters.
>
> Please contact me at 555-231-4509 at your earliest convenience to talk about the future of "Lost Cause."
>
> Sincerely,
> Gretchen Blackstone
> Literary Agent
> Blackstone and Curtis

Karen walked off the elevator and stopped at the nurses' station and was told her mom was doing okay. She headed down the hospital hallway and opened the door to her mom's room. Barb laid on her side in what seemed to be a drug induced sleep. "Mom?" No answer. "You awake? Evidently not." Barb's shoulders moved up and down, a good sign that she was still there.

Karen pulled the covers aside and slipped into bed with her mom. She laid her arm lightly around her, careful not to touch her sore side. She whispered, "Hey, Ma. I got an agent today." No sound. No response. "Yep. A real live agent." A renegade tear slid down her face and landed on the pillow. She'd wanted so bad to share the good news with her mom. She wiped the tear away knowing Barb wouldn't approve of her tears. Even at forty-five, her mom always could make her feel like she was ten.

"I don't want anyone feeling sorry for me," Barb had told Karen when she was diagnosed. She wasn't feeling sorry for her mother, but for herself. She couldn't imagine Barb not being there. No phone calls, no one to make fun of, no one to eat chocolate with in the middle of the night. Who was she going to play bingo with now? She grinned through her tears. Maybe she'd now have an excuse never to play bingo again.

Karen laid next to the one person that had taught her every-thing. Like how to put her family first. Like how love meant never having to say it out loud. Like how to extend grace to those that didn't deserve it. Barb might not have been a churchgoer, but she set an example that many tried, but couldn't match. She was the epitome of Karen's favorite saying by St. Francis of Assisi, "Preach the Gospel at all times and when necessary, use words."

She smelled her mother's hair one more time. "I love you, Momma." Every time she left, she knew it could be the last time. She slipped out of the bed, picked up her purse and closed the door quietly behind her.

"Yep, you really are something," Barb whispered loud enough for no one to hear. She closed her eyes one last time.

## "I WILL REMEMBER YOU"
### Sarah McLachlan

Karen sat in the hard, green chair. The wind sent a shiver up her spine. For once, she didn't want to be sitting in the front row. Sitting in one of the green chairs in the front row meant that you were among the closest to the dearly departed. Lee and Nellie sat next to her, both in their own corner of grief over losing Barb and Grandmother.

"It sure is cold for November" Karen thought. She felt someone place a coat over her shoulders.

"You need it more than me right now." Ginger said. "I'll make Sue share hers with me." Translation: I'm gonna pull Sue's off her and put it on me.

Karen thought it odd, but very right, to see them together. Ginger with her auburn hair falling from the stocking cap and Sue wrapped up like a mummy to stave off the wind. "Good luck unwrapping her. You'd have to spin her like a top to get her outta that coat," Karen thought to herself.

"Thanks," Karen said to Ginger and pulled the coat around her shoulders.

Ginger still had the auburn hair and olive complexion. The years had added a few crow's feet here and there, but she still turned heads.

And then there was Sue. She and Karen had only known each other a few years, but shared close bonds. Karen realized that even with the loss of both her mother and father, she was blessed with a family and circle of friends most people only wish they had.

The purple urn sat on the pedestal. Karen knew Barb would have preferred red, but this was as good as they could do on such short notice. It was Kelly's choice, of course. She was the Queen of Purple.

Her mom would have hated a cold day like this. Karen leaned over and whispered in Lee's ear, "At least Mom doesn't have to shiver through this." When her parents had picked out the plots, it was summertime and the view was great, but November's leafless trees and wind, offered a stark reality to her grief.

Barb and Jake weren't churchgoers, but when they passed, Karen knew whom to call. Tim had been a close friend of Lee and Karen's and their pastor for the past ten years in Ocean Pines. He'd handled her dad's funeral just six months earlier. Tim began the gravesite service with a prayer as the wind continued to remind everyone that Old Man Winter was showing up early this year. As he began to read the 23rd Psalm, she noticed that snow flurries began to swirl in the breeze.

Lee leaned over and whispered in Karen's ear, "Geez, he's getting good at this." She nodded in agreement and bowed her head. Too many funerals, too much shock and sadness.

***

Karen tried, but was having a hard time paying attention. She grinned when she remembered Ginger teasing her about taking a step up on the family hierarchy ladder just the day before. "So, I guess you're the matriarch now, huh?" Ginger had asked Karen as they drove to the grocery store to stock up on stuff for the wake.

"Matriarch?" Karen looked up at Ginger.

"Yeah, you know, the head of the family," Ginger said. "Guess that 'apprentice' role is behind you."

"Well, what choice do I have? My only option is to check out in a purple box of my own." It hadn't escaped her that she had taken another rung up the ladder to "matriarch." Just the word itself sounded old.

"Yeah, Matriarch. Sounds like a great nick name to me."

"I doubt you wanna do that," she said, pointing her finger at Ginger, "unless you wanna find yourself stuck back in the onesies."

She reeled her thoughts back in and tried to listen to Pastor Tim. "Yea, though I walk through the valley of the shadow of death, I will fear not." The snow danced to its own tune swirling down around them. She stared at the purple marble box with snowflakes sticking on the top. Pastor Tim finished reading the 23rd Psalm and the snow stopped as if on cue.

Tim addressed the crowd. "When I first met Barb, I was just a little intimidated, but knew better than to let her know that." The crowd chuckled. "We live just up the street from Karen and Lee and are always hanging out at their house or ours. Karen had warned me that Barb was not your traditional 'Christian.'" Karen grinned. Tim was the best at telling a story. She knew he didn't know her mom that well, but that wouldn't stop him from finding something relevant. She wondered what it could be . . .

Tim continued. "Karen and Lee came up for a crab feast while Barb and Jake were visiting. Anyone that knows Barb, knows she could eat some crabs." The crowd giggled in acknowledgment. "I sat down across from her on purpose. Sometimes folks have a hard time knowing how to behave in front of a pastor, but not Barb. She didn't miss a chance to mess with me.

"She told me, 'This is my kinda church. Crabs and hammers that are good for Bible banging.' Tim pulled a wooden crab hammer out of his pocket and held it up. Lee shook his head and laughed again at his mother-in-law's humor. 'Old Bay, a knife, and a good-looking preacher. What more could a girl want?' I told her if she wouldn't come to church, then I would bring it to her. She let me know in no uncertain terms that it was the crabs and not me that got her there." The crowd chuckled. "I warned her that there were a few crabs that escaped the pot and were probably still running loose. She didn't miss a beat by congratulating me on learning how to keep the congregation engaged during my sermon, having to keep one eye open to keep the crabs away from their toes.

"I told her that instead of amens, the crowd would easily come up with a few 'oh craps!' or worse, if Lee was around." The crowd laughed again. Tim continued.

"When she was leaving, Barb came over to me and slipped a crisp $100 bill in my hand. 'For the mission trip,' she told me. He looked at Karen. 'But don't tell my daughter,' she said. 'Don't want her to think I've gone soft in the head or anything.' I kept that secret until today. I think she's okay with it and if she's not, I just might be hearing about it, one way or another."

The mourners nodded and laughed. It made Karen realize that laughing on a sad day was a reminder that this life still offered hope. She could feel it and was grateful for the reminder. She bowed her head as Tim led them in a closing prayer.

Karen opened her eyes, stood, and started to walk back toward the limousine with Lee and Nellie. Lee reached over to the gravesite and pulled a rose from a flower arrangement and handed it to her. A sweet gesture, but she wondered if they weren't supposed to leave the flowers there. She took Lee's hand and since he'd already robbed the grave, she reached down and took the gold ribbon that said, "Mom." She grabbed Lee's hand and walked back to the limo. After all, not only was she the matriarch, she was now Queen of the Tensies.

The ride back to the funeral home in the rented limo to pick up their cars was quiet as Kelly and her husband, Don, Jay, Lee, Nellie and Karen sat staring out of the windows. The not so green hills with the trace of autumn barely still on the trees, rolled by as they traveled in silence.

The limo rode through the hills of Howard County. They passed by Day Road where her parents had lived. It was where they'd spent so many summers eating crabs, swimming in the pool, and just hanging out. A few minutes later they pulled into the funeral home parking lot and piled out of the limo. They walked back into the red brick building to gather up the gift baskets of flowers and plants.

"The folks here at the funeral home have been great. They sure know the right things to say," Kelly said as they walked out of the building one last time.

Karen took the plant from Kelly and put it in the back seat of her car. "Well, they get lots of practice, I'm thinking. At this point, we should be getting group rates."

"Yeah, first Granny and Grandad, and now Mom and Dad." She shook her head trying to let reality soak in.

"Put what you can in the back seat and we'll find a home for these when we get to the house," Kelly said to Don. He filled the car with more greenery. They got into their own cars and headed back to the house on Day Road.

"Not as comfy as the limo," Lee said as they drove away in Karen's Intrepid.

"Yeah, but not nearly as costly either." She stared out the window remembering yard sales she and her mom had visited as they passed through the familiar neighborhoods.

They pulled into Barb's driveway. The yard was packed with cars. "I haven't seen this many cars here since we threw Mom and Dad their 25th anniversary party," Karen said. She wasn't looking forward to walking in without her mom waiting for her at the door.

Instead of Barb, she saw people walking from room to room. It was a full house. "Wow." She took a deep breath, opened the storm door, and walked into the house that bulged with friends and family.

She grabbed a diet Pepsi from the kitchen counter. People were kind with words of support and comfort, although most of them were just as stunned as she was. She walked from the kitchen to the living room to find Darlene, the last of the original Tensies, recounting a story about Barb and Ellie crabbing down on the docks of Deale, Maryland. "Yeah, she came off the boat and took a step on the dock. The boat started floating backwards. She had one foot on the dock and the other on the edge of the boat and started doing the splits!"

Karen piped up to add her recollection. "She started hollering, 'Help me! Help me!'" Karen imitated Ellie trying to hang on, teetering back and forth. "A man came out of nowhere and pulled her over to the dock. He found the rope that had come loose from the dock and tied it up."

"Yeah, he was really nice," Darlene said. She was still as pretty as ever, despite her age. "Cute too. When he left, Ellie insisted he had the hots for her." "Did you see how he looked at me?'" Darlene imitated Ellie with her hands on her hips and head cocked to one side. The roomful of people giggled.

"I still got it!" Darlene shifted to the other foot and continued her Ellie imitation. "Too bad I'm married!" She held out her ring finger in typical Ellie fashion. The room busted out in laughter.

"I wonder what heaven is like with the two of 'em there?" Karen said.

"One thing's for sure, it'll never be the same." Darlene plopped down on the sofa and stared at her hands.

"Yeah, and neither will this place," Karen said. She looked around Barb's living room at all the folks that loved her mom. She wiped away a tear, kissed Darlene on the head, and walked away.

---

Ginger found Karen cornered in the kitchen by her Great Aunt Mary. She recognized the look of desperation, of her wanting to make the great escape, but couldn't. She walked over to Karen and linked her arm into hers. "Will you excuse us?" she asked Karen's great Aunt Mary.

"Well, I was just about to . . .," the older woman tried to object.

Ginger looked Karen in the eyes. "Dad wants to talk to you," Ginger lied. "Got a minute?"

Karen was visibly relieved. "Sure." She looked at her aunt and grabbed onto Kelly's arm as she walked by. She pulled her over. "Kelly can stand in for me, right Kel?"

Kelly looked at Karen not sure what was happening but played along and smiled. "Absolutely!" Karen left Kelly to dodge the skeletons on her own, feeling relieved and just a little bit guilty.

"Well, she just never forgave herself!" Aunt Mary said, never missing a beat.

"Forgave herself for what?" Kelly asked taking the bait. Karen and Ginger made their escape out of the kitchen.

"Thanks for the rescue. She cornered me and before I knew it, the family skeletons were falling out of the closet," Karen whispered in Ginger's ear as they walked out the door to the porch overlooking the pool.

"Yeah, you looked like you wanted out." They stood and looked over the backyard.

"You always could tell what I was thinking." Karen took a deep breath. She'd taken many of those today. "Wow, we had lots of good times in that pool," Karen said. "Nellie learned to swim in it." She buttoned up her sweater when the wind kicked up. "It sure is good to have you back."

"It's good to be back to the land of the living," Ginger said. "I'm sorry I didn't call you sooner." She figured she might as well get rid of the elephant on the porch.

"That's okay. I'm sure you had a lot to figure out."

"Yeah, well I started to call many times and then didn't. And then I meant to call," Ginger stuck her hands in her pockets, not sure of what to say. "Only I didn't call, but I guess you know that . . . " Ginger sighed and sat down on the picnic table. Karen joined her. "Sorry I cut you off like I did." Ginger stared at her feet. Why didn't she wear more comfortable shoes? It was too cold to kick these off.

Karen shook her head. "Enough, Ging." She leaned her head on the shoulder of her sister from another mother. "I did the same thing. I quit trying. I just got busy with life and there didn't seem to be a way to reach you anymore, so I stopped." Karen hadn't been sure what she would get from Ginger if she made the first move. She figured if Ginger didn't call her, she didn't want to talk, didn't want to resume their friendship. "But I never quit praying."

"Sometimes that's all you can do," Ginger said. "I think I've finally learned that."

The few times they'd been together had always been with someone else around. Will's birthday, the home movie party at Barb's, and now the funeral. The shadow that had followed them in and out of every room since Ginger got back, finally packed up and left.

"You don't owe me an explanation. Let's just be us with no apologies needed." Karen's knee nudged Ginger's. "You just saved me from Aunt Mary. That's a good start. I think we've got our groove back." Karen said. "How's it been since you got back? Culture shock?"

"You betcha. Lots of things have changed."

"I know it's gotta be weird for you dealing with Roberta," Karen said.

"Yeah, it's a definite buy one, get one free deal with Dad." Ginger nodded. "It was hard at first, but I learned in rehab, unless you can forgive, you can't move past what it was that really hurt you."

"Well, hats off to you, girl. It's cool you're building a relationship with your dad. Funny how he got nicer when I got older."

"He did, didn't he? Seems like he only hates kids." Ginger reached in her pocket and pulled out a pack of cigarettes. "Do you mind?" Ginger asked. Karen shook her head. She lit up the cigarette and took a long drag and blew it up into the air. "So, Kar, when are we gonna have that pajama party?"

"As soon as this house clears out, if it ever does. Can you stay?"

"Not tonight, I have to work in the morning. How about Friday night?"

"That's perfect. I have to stay to take care of some stuff, so Sue and I will still be here." She stood up and offered Ginger her hand and pulled her to her feet.

"Looks like it's a buy one, get one free deal with you and Sue too." Ginger shook her head.

"Always have been good at bargain hunting. We learned from the best!" Karen said.

"Nobody would argue that." Ginger said.

As they walked back through the kitchen, she could hear Aunt Mary talking. Kelly was still trapped.

"You know my father was this terrible alcoholic. Jewell, your grandmother, was the oldest and when Momma died delivering me. Jewell became like a mom to me and the rest of us." Kelly leaned against the wall ready to dodge the skeletons at any minute. "Well, she never forgave herself . . . "

Karen walked over to Kelly. "Hey, did you know that Mom's friend, Linda, is here? She was asking for you," Karen lied. Well, she knew Linda would want to see her, so was it really a lie? The last thing they needed was to deal with any skeleton secrets today. They were still trying to come to grips with the shock of losing their mom and dad.

"Oh really?" Kelly looked at her aunt. "I'm sorry, Aunt Mary. Can we finish our talk a little later?"

"Well," Aunt Mary hesitated. She wasn't finished unloading the family secrets just yet, but nodded anyway. Kelly reached over and grabbed a cupcake to take with her. "Where is Linda?" Kelly looked at Karen and followed her to the other room leaving Aunt Mary with her secret intact.

Karen made the rounds to greet everyone as best she could. She walked into the dining room to make a sandwich. Ginger's Dad, Will, walked up as she spread the mustard onto the rye bread. He had that familiar look of shock that stared back at her in the mirror every day since her mom was diagnosed. For 70 years old, he was still a handsome man.

"I still can't believe they're both gone," he said looking at her.

"I know," she said and hugged him.

She found it strange that she enjoyed Will's company so much as an adult. As a kid, she always felt so intimidated by him. As an adult, she'd come to realize that he just never knew how to relate to kids even though he had five of his own. He was an only child and had been her dad's closest friend for almost 50 years. As she got to know him, she understood why. Although the two men were so different in almost every way, she could now see why her dad had loved him as a brother.

He reached in his pocket and pulled out a small piece of paper and put it in her hand. "Someone gave me this when my mother died and it has helped me a lot. I've carried it in my wallet all these years. I want you to have it."

Karen looked at the crinkled white paper with the black typed words. It was taken from a church bulletin and was a quote of Henry Scott Holland, Canon of St. Paul's Cathedral (1847 – 1918). "Death is nothing at all. I have only slipped away into the next room . . . Call me by my old familiar name, speak to me in the easy way which you always used to. . . . Why should I be out of mind because I am out of sight? I am waiting for you, for an interval, somewhere very near, just around the corner. All is well."

Karen took yet another deep breath. "I know how much you loved them. They both loved you like a brother." He smiled. Ginger walked up and put her arm around his shoulder.

"Hi, Pops," she said and kissed him on the cheek. Karen thought it strange that Ginger and her dad would be so close. Strange but so very right.

"You remember the time we went crabbing and we almost burnt Dad's boat up?" Ginger sat Indian style on the couch of Barb's living room entertaining the mourners in a way only she could do.

"Yeah, we didn't have enough lanterns, so we lit a bunch of the old Christmas candles we'd made and were too ashamed to give away as presents. I don't think my mom ever burned another candle, . . . " Karen said as she sat down next to her. Darlene walked over.

"Yeah, Barb held that one over Ellie's head for a long time. I know for a fact that El had to bribe her more than once to keep her quiet," Darlene said.

"Those two were always blackmailing each other," Ginger said. "There was once when your mom wrecked her car." She looked at Karen. "My mom didn't buy her own Pepsi for six months." The guests watched intently as the three of them began to act out the scene on the boat for the living room crowd.

"I've got a big one!" Ginger said to Karen. She was pulling up one of the strings that were tied to the end of the planks on the pier. She could feel the crab chomping on the chicken wing bait that was tied to the end of the line. She pulled it up slowly so the crab wouldn't feel her tug. Karen held a flashlight in one hand and the net in her other. She shone the light on the line where it entered the water. Slowly, the crab appeared a few inches below the murky water's surface of the Chesapeake Bay.

Karen put the flashlight down and put two hands on the long broom length handle of the crab net. She positioned the end that held the net just under the crab and scooped him up like a spoon would pick up a floating noodle in a bowl of soup.

"Wow, I think he's the granddaddy! Look how big he is!" Karen held him up for all to see.

"Hey, what's that?" Barb pointed toward Will's boat one pier over from where they were crabbing. There was a golden glow brighter than before.

"Oh my god! The boat's on fire!" Darlene hollered.

Ginger let go of the line and she and Karen turned to look.

Ellie was closest and ran back over to the boat to see what was happening. Smoke slid out of the cabin as a curtain was turning into flames threatening to engulf the boat. "I need a bucket for water!" Ellie yelled.

"No time for that. Smother it with something if you can!" Barb hollered back at her.

"I have a bucket!" Darlene shouted. She and Barb ran down the pier toward the boat.

Ellie pulled her shirt up, covered her nose, and went into the boat. She looked around the cabin and picked up the first thing she saw, Will's favorite blue sweater. She wrapped her hand up in it and pushed up on the burning curtain until she could smush the flame out on the window.

By the time Barb and Darlene got to the boat, the flames were gone and the smell of Will's melted sweater lingered. They coughed from the smoke that tried to engulf the cabin, but filtered outside. Ellie grabbed the bucket of water from Darlene and threw it up against the burnt curtain and dashboard to make sure the fire was out.

"Uh oh, wasn't that Will's favorite sweater?" Barb asked.

"Used to be. He might not have a sweater, but at least he still has a boat and I can live to talk about it," Ellie said after they were sure all the flames were gone. "Can't let him know. He'll never let us come back down here again."

"What are we gonna do about the curtains and soot on the walls from the smoke?" Darlene pointed to the charbroiled curtain that used to provide privacy across the front dashboard. They stood silent for a few seconds.

"I guess I'll have to either buy some or make some, but it's gonna have to be fast. I'll come back in a few days and clean it up. Will is supposed to take the boys fishing next weekend."

Once they were sure the boat wasn't going to burn up, Ginger and Karen continued their crab catching. "And he thought he was gonna get away," Ginger snickered. Karen tapped the crab net on the edge of the wooden bushel basket. She stepped backwards only to find a hole in the pier with her foot. She stepped into the hole and fell backwards onto her back. Her leg was thigh deep in the hole and kept her from falling into the brackish water of the Chesapeake.

"Oh no!" Ginger called out. The others looked over to see Karen lying half on and half off the pier, her hair dangling in the water. Karen's arms flailed catching nothing but air.

"Help me up, help me up!" she cried. Thoughts of swimming with the crabs freaked her out. Ginger stood motionless for a second and started to laugh. "It's not funny!" Karen cried.

"Oh my god, she broke her leg!" Ellie yelled from the boat on the neighboring pier. "Oh my god, she broke her leg!"

Ginger gathered herself and reached down to grab Karen's hands, pulling her up to a sitting position. She continued to laugh. Ellie, Barb, and Darlene came running.

"Are you okay?" Barb asked. She knelt down next to Karen. Ginger covered her mouth and tried to stifle her giggles.

"I don't know," Karen cried. "I think so," she reached down to touch her calf and knee that was scratched from the rotted wood.

"I'll get some ice," Darlene headed for the cooler.

"Sorry for laughing, Kar," Ginger said. "It's just that you looked so funny," she started to giggle again. "And your eyes were this big!" She made large circles with her fingers. "Oh geez . . . " she looked down to see that she'd wet her pants.

Karen shook her head. "Now, *that's* what I call karma!" They helped Karen to her feet and walked her back to the boat. Darlene put a bag of ice on her leg and they propped it up on the cooler.

"Look at the lines!" Ellie pointed. The crab lines were pulled tight. The little buggers were biting.

"You okay for now?" Barb asked Karen.

"Yeah," Karen held the ice on her knee. "Go get 'em!" They headed back to the crab lines on the neighboring piers and started reeling and scooping up the hungry crabs. Within 45 minutes, word had gotten out. The crabs quit biting and they packed up to leave.

"We might as well get going," Barb said. They'd nearly filled up the basket and had to get home to cook them while they were still alive. "A dead crab is no good to us!"

Karen limped back to Betsy, Ellie's blue station wagon, as she leaned on Ginger's arm. "Pants still wet?"

"Nah, I found some old sweats in the boat."

"You still smell like pee," Karen giggled. "Between that and a bushel of smelly crabs, it should be a fun ride home."

"He'll never miss this sweater, right?" Ellie asked Darlene as they headed for the car. She picked up the lid of the trashcan at the end of the pier, held up the melted ball of yarn that used to be Will's favorite sweater, and dropped it in.

"Your secret's safe with me!" Darlene said.

"Do you think I left it on the boat?" Will asked Ellie as he got ready to leave for work. He couldn't find his sweater anywhere. She looked up from her sewing machine. She was working on replacement curtains for the boat. She hummed along with Ginger's radio as it played "Hey Jude," from her room.

"I'd say it's possible, but not probable," she looked back at her sewing to avoid his gaze. "I think there's a Red Dot sale at Hecht's on Saturday. Maybe I can find you another one." When one has a *real* reason to go to a Red Dot sale, life is good.

"Oh, you'd love that wouldn't you?" Will laughed. "You think I'm nuts? No way I'm giving the green light to a Red Dot sale!" He walked out the door.

Part of Ellie wished she had held onto the melted ball of yarn and shoved it up his nose.

---

"I always wondered what happened to that sweater!" Will said as he stood in the doorway of the living room after the three had finished their performance for the crowd. Darlene twirled around to see Will standing there while Ginger and Karen ducked behind her feeling like they were ten years old and in trouble yet again.

---

The day after the funeral, Karen sifted through Barb's papers. She was looking for bills that might need to be paid. Barb had a few manila envelopes next to her recliner where she would sit and write out her monthly checks. One envelope was marked "To be paid" and the other "Keep", which Karen supposed translated to "File." She chuckled. "Everyone hates that word, I'm thinking," she said to herself.

She emptied the contents of the "Keep" envelope onto the dining room table. Sue's evangelistic letter fell out among the receipts and bank statements. Barb had never said anything more about the letter except that it was "nice".

As she read Sue's letter, tears flowed down her cheeks. Barb was the same now as before, still preaching without saying a word. Leave it to Sue to take care of the talking part. "Evangelistic?" Karen said aloud. "Billy Graham would have a tough time keeping up with this!" She blinked herself back to the present and smiled at her mom's silent testimony.

———

Some days Karen felt like she'd been sucker punched. This was one of those days. First Dad, then Mom just six months later. She still reached for the phone to call Barb every day. She adopted Sugar, her mom's white German shepherd. They mourned the passing of both their parents together. She found comfort having Sugar around to love and was pretty sure the dog felt the same about her.

And, in the midst of everything, Ginger was back. Karen was beside herself happy about it. The idea of spending time with her again, just like the old days, gave her hope that a part of her that she thought was gone, might not be. Not that Lee and Nellie weren't enough, but it was as if God knew she needed her old friend now. It felt like the curtain that blocked those childhood memories had been lifted. Smiles and laughter followed any story that included Barb and Ellie.

But she found things were far from the same, although Karen tried to make them so. Ginger had left Jamaica in less than ideal conditions. She no longer enjoyed a singing career, and had burned her Jamaican bridges.

Karen didn't feel she had the right to probe as deeply as she would have fifteen years before. They'd grown apart and only time would define just how far that was and if the road back to being sisters was even passable.

Karen now understood what was meant to be in a fog. She checked off a dozen things from her "to do" list daily, but barely remembered doing any of them. She dealt with estate attorneys and realtors along with keeping up with emails until she went back to work. She pushed on knowing God would catch her if she fell. The busy-ness of it all kept her a little removed from the horrible reality of saying goodbye to her mom and dad one last time. That was okay. She was in no hurry.

She looked up from the pile of file folders from her parents' file cabinet. "Lee, did you realize how much my parents had in stocks?"

"Nope. Who would've believed it?" he said.

"Does that mean we're rich?" Nellie asked from the doorway. Karen looked up.

"You aren't, but we might be," Lee said.

"Let's just say your school loans won't be on the installment plan much longer," Karen said.

"Grandmother would approve," Lee said as he wrapped his arm across his little girl's shoulder and squeezed. Nellie leaned her head on his chest as she always did and put her hand on her eight-month pregnant tummy. Enter grandchildren.

## "INDEPENDENT WOMEN"
### Destiny's Child

Karen, Ginger, Kelly, and Sue met for the weekend at Barb's. They worked to clear out her house and get it ready to put on the market. Karen was in no hurry to sell it, but reminded herself the memories lived within her heart and not a house. Sometimes that thought process worked, sometimes not. The next morning, after a night of memories and laughs, they dragged themselves out of bed. After downing two pots of coffee, they started cleaning out closets and drawers.

"Okay, let's put this caffeine buzz to work," Karen said as she reached in and pulled Big Blue out of a cabinet in the living room. It was the squirt gun her mom used on the Ocean City boardwalk to covertly spray water on unsuspecting passersby. "Look at this!"

Ginger turned, smiled, and recognized it right away. "You're gonna have to hold onto that, I'm thinking." Karen pointed it at Ginger and pulled the trigger.

"Darn, he's empty," Karen said as she examined the toy. "But I can fix that later." Ginger walked away shaking her head. Karen reached into the back of the cabinet and pulled out a box. It was her mom's dream journals. They were in a red box just as Barb had described when she was in the hospital. Karen pulled one notebook out and flipped through the pages. It was full of memories, dreams, and wishes. "Priceless," she said to herself and put them in her box to take home along with Big Blue.

Ginger called from the living room, "Hey, what's this?" Karen and Sue walked in. Ginger held up what looked to be a joint. Karen took it from her and stared at the cigarette.

"I'll bet this is the one your dad gave my dad when he was taking chemo," Karen looked at Ginger. "Mom told me about it. Knowing Dad, he would never do anything that he knew was illegal, even if it would make him feel better."

"This is probably Hawaiian weed, I'm thinking," Ginger said as she sniffed the cigarette. Will was not the rule follower that Jake had been. "Dad's got a good connection there."

"Well, is anyone gonna light that thing up or what?" Sue asked as she reached over and snatched the joint from Ginger.

"We can't do that!" Karen said and reached for the joint, but grabbed only air. "Ginger's just outta rehab!"

"Don't let that stop ya," Ginger said and poured a vodka and cranberry juice. "I'm good. It's gotta be five o'clock somewhere." Sue lit the joint.

An hour later, the sun started to set and the February winter chill set in.

"Here," Karen handed Ginger a lighter. "Out of the three of us, you're the undeniable pyromaniac." Ginger's years in Jamaica cooking over an open fire, made her the obvious choice for fireplace stoking. She walked over and crouched down to start a fire. Before long, the fireplace glowed and they laid back on the sofa and started telling Barb and Ellie "who would've believed it" stories.

"Yeah, well you know what they say about two's company and three's a crowd, right?" Ginger joked about Sue joining her and Karen's best friend status.

"That was a TV show, right?" Sue asked. Her naiveté rivaled Suzanne Somers from the popular TV show most days.

"Don't think I'm still stoned, do ya?" Sue asked.

"Sue, you were born stoned," Ginger said. "You don't need to smoke any ting!" Sometimes Ginger's Jamaican roots and slang sneaked back into her words.

They cleaned up the dishes from their spaghetti dinner. "Aunt Barb would be happy we're eating her spaghetti sauce."

"Did she leave her recipe behind?" Sue asked.

"Nah, the only recipes mom ever had were printed on the side of a box." Karen dried her hands on a towel and they headed to the living room, a bottle of wine, and some glasses in tow.

"So, Ging, why in the world would you leave a place like Jamaica? Most people can't wait to get there for a week and you actually *lived* there," Sue asked. One glass of wine and all her filters, what few she had, left her.

"A life of crime didn't agree with me. I finally realized that I was too big a chicken to live that way. Once I got busted and off the drugs, I could see what I'd been doing, I knew I had to get outta there." She picked up a cigarette and lit it up. Smoke curled in the air between them. "But they busted me again before I could leave. The Jamaican police force is so corrupt, the only way out of it was to pay them all off. But I had to do one more run first so I would have enough cash."

"Wow, how did you know how much to pay them?" Sue asked.

Ginger and Karen looked at each other and then back at Sue. "Oh, they'll send you a bill." Sue looked from one to the other and paused.

"Nu uh! Quit messing with me," Sue said and grabbed the potato chip bag from Ginger.

"But it's so easy," Ginger said. "Where did you find her anyways?" She looked at Karen.

"She was married to a friend of Lee's and when they divorced, I decided to keep her around for comic relief."

"Well, I guess that serves me right for staying gone so long." Ginger said. Karen laughed, but Sue wasn't sure if it was funny. Sometimes she didn't get Ginger's humor, but then again, there were lots of things about Ginger and Karen's friendship she didn't "get."

Karen hoped that Sue and Ginger would learn to like each other. Two girls in a friendship. There was nothing better. A third one always seemed to make it a crowd.

"What about Ginger Star?" Karen asked. She had wanted to ask that question for a while.

"Ginger Star is gone to me." Ginger's happy face dissolved thinking about her lost refuge. "Donovan cleared out my stuff while I was in rehab."

The elephant named, "Donovan," had finally shown up. "Well, since you brought him up, how's he doing?" Karen asked.

"He's good." She leaned back on the sofa. "He came to the airport to see me off." Ginger wished she hadn't said that.

"Wow, how'd that go?" Karen asked.

Donovan stood over Ginger as she dug through her bag at the Kingston airport looking for her passport. He held his hand out and pulled her to her feet. She drew in a breath of surprise and relief; surprise that he was here and relief that she'd found her passport. "What are you doing here?"

"What kind of greeting is that?"

She ran her hand through her auburn hair, pushing it out of her eyes. "I'm surprised is all."

"I'm not really sure why I'm here except," he stared into her hazel eyes that always managed to hold his gaze. The ones he could never look away from. They both knew their relationship was over, but that didn't make saying goodbye easier. "I will always love you, Ginga." Tears spilled down his cheeks. He shook his head as if he couldn't believe he'd said it out loud.

"I'm so sorry, Don. I should never have," her voice trailed when he put his finger on her lips, asking her to hush.

"Nu go der," he said in patois and shook his head. "Sorry. Don't go there," he translated the patois phrase. "We've done enough apologizing. I love you, Ginga. That's all."

"Oh, Don, I don't wanna leave, but I have to."

"I know, babe." He pulled her to him and stroked her hair. She'd forgotten how much she loved his hugs. She breathed him in.

"Last boarding call for flight 1432 to Baltimore," the airline counter attendant announced.

"Besides, Bob say 'No woman, no cry,'" he said quoting the famous Bob Marley lyric and a slight grin grabbed his smile. Her heart jumped at the familiar smile that made her world light up.

"Donovan," he pulled back and looked at her. The gate attendant announced the last boarding call for her flight. She stood on her tiptoes, kissed his cheek, and turned and ran toward the attendant holding out her ticket and passport. She looked over her shoulder to see him once more, blew him a kiss, and walked down the jet way. Once on the plane, she stared out the window at the mountains of Jamaica remembering all the reasons why she didn't want to leave.

"Oh, it was fine. You know Donovan, always doing the right thing by coming to the airport to say goodbye."

"No talk of the future?"

"We already had our future. I screwed that up." Ginger looked down at her feet and sighed. "Doesn't really matter. He's there and I'm not."

"Love always matters," Karen said and leaned over to hug her. She decided it was time to change the subject.

"What happened to Byron?" Karen asked.

"Who's Byron?" Sue asked.

"He's kinda like the groundskeeper at Ginger Star and a good friend," Ginger said and looked back at Karen. "I'm thinking he's still there. He'll squat till they make him leave, I'm sure." Ginger downed the martini in her hand and poured another. She picked up her guitar. "Prayin' whoever buys it, keeps him on." She strummed the strings and tuned it a little and started to play.

"You are my sunshine, my only sunshine," she sang with her famous reggae beat. Karen and Sue chimed in. "You make me happy when skies are gray!" Ginger stopped playing after the first chorus and their voices trailed off. Karen's eyes teared up as she realized Ginger had finally found her way back.

"So, back to your story," Karen said looking at Ginger when she opened her eyes. "Why did you quit performing? Couldn't you do that here?"

"Well, there's a few reasons. First, the lifestyle feeds my addiction with late nights and strange hours. And when I came back here, I agreed to provide some evidence for the US government to shut Andrew down and keep him out of the States." Chills ran up Karen's spine at the sound of his name. Could that have been who was calling and hanging up at her house? She had thought it was an imaginary girlfriend of Lee's, but since that theory didn't prove to be true, maybe it was Andrew. She knew nothing good could come of that possibility.

Ginger stood up, walked to the refrigerator, and grabbed a bottle of water. She twisted off the cap and took a long drink. "They strongly suggested I get a low-key job and stay out of the limelight. When the government "strongly suggests" something, I've learned it might be a good idea to take the advice. So, I decided I wanted to come back and stay under the radar." Kelly handed her a few tissues to catch the runaway tears that slid down Ginger's cheeks.

"Bottom line is, I'm fine with being a recluse. Staying home is preferable these days. I've found what matters. Family and friends. Other than that, all I have is God and He's a part of me. The important part," Ginger said and just about believed it.

Ginger cleaned up the stainless-steel table after filleting croakers for a customer. Sometimes she wondered why she bothered cleaning at all since the customers just came one after another during a sale. A dark-haired man about her age walked up and rang the bell. She walked over to the showcase to take his order. He looked familiar and when their eyes met, each instantly knew who the other was.

"Mike?" Her hand automatically went to her hair. She forgot she had an old lady hairnet on, so no need to worry. She looked like crap. She flashed a smile hoping to keep his attention away from her old lady hairdo.

"Ginger!" Mike was an old boyfriend from high school. "How are you? It's been years." He looked much the same, just a few extra pounds and a trimmed beard, dark like his hair with a few flecks of gray here and there. Not bad for forty-something. They talked long enough to discover that the two of them were both single and agreed to meet for a drink on Thursday, her day off.

"Do you remember Mike Monroe?" Ginger asked Karen over the phone. She'd made the mistake of answering after a few martinis.

"Yeah, the guy you used to sneak out your window to see in the middle of the night?"

"That's the one. Well, I saw him at work the other day. He's still quite cute."

"Married?" It irked Ginger that Karen knew her well enough to ask that question.

"Nope, not any more. He used to be married to Norma Weatherford. Remember her?"

"Yeah, sure do." Norma had lived down the street from Ginger when they were kids.

"Well, we've starting seeing each other."

Karen was thrilled for Ginger and her new love interest. "That's awesome, Ging. I'm so happy you've met someone." She wished it were Donovan for a second, but shoved the thought aside.

"Yep, it's just one orgasm after another with that guy!" Ginger said. There she went, talking too much. That's what you get when you answer after two drinks.

"Whadya mean?" Karen asked.

"You know, *multis!*" Ginger said and stirred the pot of pizza sauce on the stove, her mom's old recipe.

"I thought the only way the word 'multi' was used was as in yard sales," Karen said with a straight face.

"Nope, you can drag them out." Ginger said.

"Are you really giving me sex advice?"

"Are you really in need of it after all these years?" Ginger took a sip of the sauce. Almost ready. "I would've thought Lee was a better coach."

Karen giggled. "He does alright."

"Well, next time, just don't give in. Drag it out."

"The only thing I'm gonna 'drag out' on a weeknight is the bowl of ice cream I'm gonna slurp down when we're done," she laughed. "I'll wait till the weekend to get mine, but I still think this multi thing is a myth." Ginger looked over at Spanky and rolled her eyes. He sighed and laid down, his big brown eyes staring back at her.

Mike would stop by for a conjugal visit once a week or so. Ginger never wanted to go out so he'd stop and pick up dinner and bring it over. Every month, Ginger would hope that her period wouldn't show up, but it always did. "Boy, I should be buying these things in bulk," she said as she pulled the pregnancy test kit out of the Rite Aid shopping bag. She'd have an extra martini or two on the nights when the pregnancy test turned up negative.

"My period is two weeks late. I think I'm pregnant!" Ginger announced when Karen called her on her way home from a late meeting. Theirs was a phone friendship more than in person with the three-hour drive between them.

"Really?" Karen knew there was nothing Ginger wanted more, but suspected it might be menopause more than pregnancy that delayed her period. She decided not to bust her bubble and let her hold onto her hope.

"Yeah, Mike's a pretty good candidate for a dad."

"Does *he* know that?"

"Nah, I doubt he'd be into the parent thing, but that's okay. I can handle it by myself."

Karen wasn't so sure about that either, but kept her opinion to herself. "Well, keep me posted. I need time to plan your baby shower." She felt bad encouraging her, but didn't have it in her to dash Ginger's dreams. Heck, she was still in recovery. A big disappointment could be disastrous. She was already drinking again. She shuddered when she thought of what else could happen.

"Where did I put the spoon?" Ginger asked herself and Karen when she went to stir the sauce again. "Oh, there it is." She picked it up from the kitchen table. "Geez, I'd probably lose a baby if I had one."

Karen laughed. "True, but he wouldn't let you for long. They have a great homing device. It's called 'crying.'"

Ginger had opened each box from Jamaica, reached in, pulled out what interested her, and left the rest inside. Before long, her house was nothing but boxes piled high with a path that wound from room to room. She just didn't have the desire to finish emptying them. She'd have to decide what to keep and what to toss. Too many decisions. When the urge to get it done would threaten to hit, she'd have a few drinks instead.

She managed to keep Karen from visiting by agreeing to meet for lunch every now and then when she was in town. Ginger didn't want her to see the mess she lived in. She was too tired after working all day to clean it up. The phone rang and she followed the sound, not able to find it at first. It sat under a McDonald's bag she'd picked up on her way home from work. She grabbed the cordless phone.

"Hello?" Ginger said.

"Hey there," Karen said from the other end of the line. "I'm gonna be in Annapolis this afternoon. You gonna be home?" They'd been talking on the phone a lot, but hadn't seen each other for several months. Annapolis was just a few miles away.

Ginger panicked and looked around her wreck of a house. She hadn't spent any time cleaning up in quite a while. Like ever. "Yeah, sure. You'll have to forgive the mess." She looked around the boxes and junk littered all over the place.

"I'm not coming to see your house, I'm coming to see you," Karen assured her. Ginger hung up the phone and did a quick assessment.

"Oh well, if she's coming to see me fine . . . the house, not so much." She scrambled through the living room and kitchen, gathering up pizza boxes, beer cans, and empty wine and vodka bottles. Ashtrays overflowed and she hadn't done dishes in . . . well, a long time. The way she figured it, she had about an hour until Karen arrived. By the time she heard the knock on the door, she'd at least been able to clean the bathroom and clear a path and some space for her to sit on the sofa.

"Hey, woman!" she opened the door and let Karen in. They hugged hello.

"Yeah, I didn't realize I'd have time to stop in. Sorry to be so last minute. I'm so happy to finally see your place!"

"Sorry about the mess, I'm still unpacking."

"Hey, I came to see you, not your mess." Unpacking? Hadn't she been back more than a year?

"Good thing. Come on in and have a seat. Want something to drink, beer, wine, vodka?"

"Nah, I can't. Have that darn three-hour drive home. How about some water?"

"Sure thing," Ginger said and disappeared into a path through the maze of boxes that led to the kitchen. Karen looked around and took in a deep breath. She'd never seen such a mess. Ginger had always been a meticulous housekeeper, on a hillside or in a plantation. Not so much in a townhouse.

"Here you go," Ginger handed her a bottle of water. Karen cracked it open and took a drink. She heard a dog bark. "That's Spanky in the back yard. Sit tight, I'll let him in." A minute later, the little black and white pug was jumping onto Karen's lap. "Spanky, get down!" Ginger said. "Sorry, we don't get much company."

"It's okay, he's fine." Karen stroked his back. Spanky sniffed her and jumped into her lap. Ginger's cat, Tiger, circled the two of them trying to get a fix on their visitor.

"Looks like you passed the test," Ginger said. "She didn't scratch you and Spanky didn't pee."

"So glad to hear it! Is today your day off?"

"Nah, I worked from 6 to 2. Just got home right before you called. Crappy day."

"What was 'crappy' about it?"

"Croakers were on sale." Karen cocked her head, not getting it. "Croakers are a pain in the butt to fillet, and after doing it all day it kills my arm." She stroked her forearm.

"Oh wow, I didn't know." Karen said.

"Yeah, I'm stuck in the onesies on this one. Once they found out I could fillet a fish with my eyes closed, it was all over. I was doomed."

"Doesn't your boss know better than to let you work with sharp knives?" Karen tried to lighten the mood.

"He'll figure it out."

Karen picked up a VCR tape of Forrest Gump. "Don't you just love this movie? We've watched it over and over in the camper with Nellie."

"Yeah. Did you know it was Hurricane Carmen that took out his shrimp boat?" Ginger asked.

"No kidding?"

"Yep, funny thing is, I remember the fishing industry on Jamaica's north coast boomed for a while after Carmen left the island, just like it did for him." She didn't talk about Jamaica with many people. It was strange to hear her own voice talk out loud about her life that was now long gone.

"Didn't that portrait used to hang in the living room at Ginger Star?" Karen asked. The woman in the long flowing dress, holding on to her hat, stared down at them.

"Yeah, it did. Donovan packed it up and sent it not knowing that I didn't mean to bring it here. There was a nail already above the mantle, so I figured I'd hang it up. Whadya think?"

"She's beautiful there. Seems strange to see her here instead of Jamaica, but good." Karen looked back at Ginger. "So where's the portrait of you that Sylvia did?"

"It's in the closet." Ginger pointed to the hallway.

"Why don't you hang it up? It's a beautiful likeness."

"Seems a little self-indulgent to me. Besides, it's creepy looking into your own eyes every day."

Karen moved on. "Okay, if you say so. So, when are you gonna tell me if you can go or not?" Karen asked and took a sip from her water bottle. She'd been trying to talk Ginger into taking a trip to Ft. Myers, Florida. "We can get the tickets in the morning and book a rental car for the airport at the same time. Kelly's invited us to stay with her at her new condo."

Ginger continued to make excuses as to why she couldn't go. Karen was starting to think she was agoraphobic. Other than going to work, it was hard to get her to leave the house.

"Kar, what is it about the word 'recluse' that you don't get?"

"Why do you wanna be a recluse?" Karen asked.

"It's not that I wanna be, I just am. Can't you tell?" Ginger's arm waved across the crowded living room.

"Looks like you're more of a hoarder than a recluse to me." Karen immediately wished she could rewind her words. She braced herself for a retort that didn't come.

"I've come to kinda like the boxes everywhere. Makes me feel like I just got back from Jamaica."

"Why do you wanna feel like that?"

"Less guilt in not cleaning it up, I guess!"

Karen suspected it was easier to just stay home and drink and think of what might have been or never will be, but didn't dare say it out loud. She still didn't know what would and wouldn't set Ginger off. She's momentarily stepped over the line with her hoarder quip, but didn't get a bad reaction. Their friendship was back, but the honesty between them, definitely on hold. Karen wondered if anything would ever be the same between them. She suspected things were the way Ginger wanted them and tried to just take whatever she could get.

"So, who you dating?" Karen asked.

"Nobody."

"Liar."

"Well, I wouldn't call it dating. Mike, I told you about him, right?" Karen nodded. "Well, we have fun and never leave the house." Ginger winked and walked over to the kitchen sink. "Yeah, for a couple weeks I thought I was pregnant. I was just about to call you and let you know you were gonna be an aunt, but I got my period." Karen bit her lip to keep from stating the obvious. She wondered if Ginger was going through menopause. Again, the honesty was on hold. All Ginger wanted was to get pregnant. After three abortions, Karen wondered if somehow that prevented her from conceiving, but never said it aloud. Each month, Ginger would let Karen know if the rabbit died, but it never did.

On her way home from Ginger's, Karen turned into the parking lot of the offices near the toll booth of the Chesapeake Bay Bridge. They confirmed the rumors she had heard. She got back into her van and picked up her cell to call Ginger.

"Okay, if you won't go to Florida, then let's go to Assateague," Karen said. "I just stopped at the offices by the bay bridge." She tried everything she could think of to lure her out of the house. She hoped this might help change her mind. "They have a service that will drive you across the bridge. It's only twenty bucks." Ginger's main objection to coming for a visit was driving across the bay bridge.

"Hmm . . . that just might work." Ginger said. For the first time in a long while, Karen had hoped that Ginger might actually make the trip to Ocean City.

Karen slowed down and paid the toll to drive across the bridge. She was grateful she didn't have the same fears Ginger did when it came to driving across. The cargo ships waited their turn to head up to Baltimore's harbor to unload and reload. She never tired of watching them come and go. Too bad she had to drive. She would have loved to just stare at the water.

As she drove, she thought about her visit with Ginger. She tried to understand the disappointment and fears that gripped her friend. Wanting something that would never happen and knowing deep down it may have been her own choices that dragged her into sadness had to be a hard world to live in.

⸻

Ginger felt like she'd made a jail break when she drove over the seven-mile-long, tall and curved, Chesapeake Bay Bridge on her own. She never thought she could do it, but she did. She'd decided at the last minute to drive across on her own rather than hire the service. Ginger was surprised she found it so exhilarating. She turned the radio up and settled in for the rest of the drive. Singing always calmed her down, even with no guitar in hand. After a few miles, she turned off the radio and picked up her cell phone.

"I made it over the bridge!" Ginger said to Karen over her cell phone as she drove down Route 50 East towards Ocean City.

"That's great! Did it take long for you to get them to drive you across?"

"Nope, I decided at the last minute to drive myself. I just paid the toll, closed my eyes, and drove like an Assateague pony headed for the barn, only he doesn't have a barn, I guess." Assateague ponies were wild and roamed the island just a few miles south of Ocean City. The ponies' only shelter were small thickets of trees. It was her and Karen's preferred beach. Assateague Island held lots of childhood memories camping and beaching it with their moms.

"Well, that's great except for the closing the eyes part." Karen continued making tuna and tomato sandwiches for their trip to the beach.

"That's okay, Spanky kept his eyes on the road for me." She looked over as Spanky sat in the passenger seat looking out the windows. His tongue hung out and she knew he was smiling. It dawned on her that the poor dog had never really been anywhere except to the vet. "Yeah, I'm stoked. Never thought I could do it!"

"Well, keep your eyes open and I'll see you in about two-hours. Just stay on Rt. 50 till you see Route 90 East. You'll be almost here at that point. Just keep your directions handy or call me back."

"There's still at least two bridges left, Cambridge being one." Ginger said.

"Yeah, but the Choptank's an easy one compared to the Chesapeake."

"Yeah, you're a fine one to talk about the ease of *that* bridge. As I recall, you brought Route 50 traffic to a virtual standstill the first time you drove it!" Karen chuckled and didn't argue. The old Choptank River bridge was narrow with no shoulder. A taller one had replaced it since then, but the old one remained. They had cut the draw bridge section out to allow the taller boats through and built the new one tall enough to let boats through.

"Ha ha, you're right. Lee thought twice before trying to give me another driving lesson. Hey, you'd better hang up and watch where you're going."

"Yeah, great way to change the subject, Kar." They hung up and she continued down Route 50. Ginger laughed out loud at the memory of the bridge incident and it spurred many more as she drove east toward Ocean City. She drove over the Choptank River Bridge and looked at the vaguely familiar shoreline that was Cambridge, the town where she was born.

She took a quick right as she came off the bridge and drove into the sleepy town. Memories of swimming in the river at the base of the bridge, eating French fries with her brothers at the luncheonette counter, and playing hide and seek in the cemetery across the road from their little house came rushing back. She recognized the little draw bridge that was almost in the middle of town. The sleepy little fishing village had given birth to racial unrest in the 1960s. It hadn't changed much from what she could remember.

She pulled up in front of the little white clapboard cottage they had called home. It was older, but well cared for and much smaller than she'd remembered. She put the car in park and stared at the house. She could almost hear their voices as she and her mom would sing while making dinner or hanging up laundry in the back yard.

"We might as well give you a bathroom break while we're here." She reached over and clipped Spanky's leash onto his collar. They got out of the car. Spanky sniffed his way up the lane and lifted his leg to pee on a bush. She stared at the cemetery remembering the scary stories her older brothers, Scott and Roger, would torture her with, the dirt clog wars they would fight when a freshly dug grave would leave red clay lumps everywhere, and how mad her mom would be when they'd come home covered in red clay dirt. Spanky made a deposit, but she'd forgotten to bring a plastic bag. She looked around and when she was confident no one was watching, they ducked back into her car. A few tears welled up in her eyes from the memories, but she wiped them away, put the car into drive, and headed back through town.

She turned back onto Route 50 East and headed for Ocean Pines. Ginger followed Karen's turn left, turn right, directions and slowed down when she saw the soft yellow house with brown shutters nestled in a forest of pine trees. She recognized Karen's van and pulled into the driveway.

The door opened. Lee jogged down the steps to greet her. They hugged hello. He reached in the trunk and grabbed her luggage. "Still traveling light I see." His hands were full of her things.

"Now wait a minute, Buster. Karen still has me beat. When you guys came to Jamaica, we almost didn't all fit in the car 'cause of her luggage! Remember?"

"Yeah, well in her defense, it was mostly stuff for you."

"Hmm . . . I think you got me on that one. It's so good to see you, Lee." Karen came to the top of the steps and stood aside as they walked past.

"You made it!" Karen wrapped her arms around Ginger. "I knew you could do it."

"Well, that made one of us, 'cause I wasn't so sure. I still don't know how I did it with my eyes looking at the boats and ships in the bay. That was the only way I could do it, just kept looking at the water instead of the road."

Karen and Lee looked at each other and then back to Ginger. "Well, I was praying for ya on this end, so between the two of us, it all worked out." Karen gave Ginger a quick tour of the house before they set out for Ocean City.

"Sorry I'm late, guys. I took a quick tour of Cambridge on the way."

"Not much has changed, has it?" Lee asked.

"Nope." She followed them through their home. "This is great, Kar," Ginger said as she walked into the sun room in the back of the house.

"Yeah, this started out as a deck. Lee screened it in and a few years later, we put in the windows and HVAC to make it a year-round space. It makes me feel like I'm outside when I'm not."

"I can see that. You guys have done an amazing job not only with the house, but managing to live on the Eastern Shore. I love being back in Crofton, but the traffic and amount of people on my side of the bridge is crazy sometimes."

"Yeah, for sure. Maybe you could transfer out here. They have your stores on the Shore."

"You have an answer for everything, don't ya?"

"You're just figuring that out?"

Lee offered to let Spanky stay home with him and their dog, Noel. "They'll have fun sniffing each other all afternoon," he assured Ginger. The girls said their goodbyes and took off for Ocean City. They decided to play tourist for the day at the beach and eat junk food at the boardwalk. The sandwiches Karen made would hold until tomorrow when they would head eleven miles south to the beach on Assateague Island.

"Thrashers, Dumsers, Carouso's, Trimpers, and Candy Kitchen all on the same block. I think I've died and gone to heaven," Ginger said as she looked up and down the boardwalk from the Ferris wheel. Their seat rocked back and forth as the ride stopped to let on more customers. The sun's rays danced on the Atlantic and the waves crashed one after another on the shoreline.

"Yeah, I can gain weight just smelling all that stuff from here," Karen's tug of war with her weight was real. Look the other way. That's the tip of Assateague across the inlet." Karen pointed toward the shoreline. "Hey, after we eat our way back to the beach, let's save some room and plan on dinner at Harborwatch. It's a great restaurant right at the end of the boards. They have a great view of Assateague," Karen said.

"I don't think I've been there before," Ginger said.

"Yeah, it's new since you were here. Sits on the inlet with a beautiful view of the island." Karen pointed toward the end of the boardwalk from the top of the Ferris wheel. "Great seafood too. You're gonna love it."

"What about crabs?" Ginger asked. They always had to have steamed crabs when they came to the beach.

"That's tomorrow night. Gonna take you to Hooper's, another new spot for you. Great view of OC and the crabs are off the hook."

"Just making sure. There's some crabs in this town just dying for me to eat them!"

The girls got off the Ferris wheel as the attendant opened the bar on their seat. They grabbed their beach bags and chairs they'd left leaning on a bench and headed down the steps from the pier to the beach. Once they'd staked out their waterfront spot, they planted their chairs and blankets and headed into the water. "It's a little rough today, but we should be able to stay upright." Karen said and jumped a wave. She turned around to see Ginger facing the shoreline.

"Wow, Ocean City sure has changed since I was here," Ginger said. There were new buildings up and down the boardwalk since she had been there last.

"Look out!" Karen hollered as she jumped the wave, but it was too late for Ginger. The wave smacked her on the backside and pushed her down. She rolled around in the surf, tried to stand up, but before she could, another wave pushed her back down. As she tried to get up, she wondered if this was how she was gonna die or at least break a hip.

"Did you forget that you should never to turn your back to a wave?" Karen reached her hands down and helped Ginger to her feet. They stood in the shallow water while Ginger put her bathing suit back in all the right places. She spit out sand and pushed her hair out of her eyes. "I know you didn't have to dodge 'em so much in Jamaica, but really?"

"And I thought it would be like riding a bike," Ginger said, "but it's more like falling off a log. I feel like such a rookie . . . "

"Stick with me till we get out past the breakers," Karen shouted and waved her arm telling Ginger to follow her. "Then we can hang in the water when we're behind the 'bust your butt' zone. It's this part where you can still jump the waves, but you'll get planted in the sand if you miss."

"Just don't turn your back on the waves. That's a sure way to get knocked down. Just duck under the wave when it's too high to jump. Waves 101." Karen said. A wave came at them, she ducked under and Ginger followed suit. They bobbed up unscathed, after it had passed. After a minute or so, they navigated their way behind the second set of waves and were able to stand and bob up and down in the water, jumping over an occasional swell. "Yeah, the Bust Your Butt Zone can be deadly if not taken seriously. You'll get your sea legs back. Just takes practice and falling down a time or two to remind you." They floated and enjoyed the cool salt water while the sun beat down.

"Yeah, those waves are ruthless. Guess this old girl had better pay closer attention. It was easier to get up the last time I was here," Ginger said.

"Everything was easier back then," Karen said.

"Yeah, and we couldn't wait to grow up, remember?"

"I know. What was it we were in a hurry for anyway?"

"Maybe our moms were just having so much fun; it looked like a good time?"

"Yeah, could be. They were pros at having a good time. Even having four or more kids in tow on any given day. We did learn from the best." Ginger said and Karen nodded.

"It was never dull, that's for sure. How to have fun on a shoe-string," Karen said. Something nibbled on Karen's toe. She jumped a few feet to the right. No way was she gonna tell Ginger a crab was on the loose. She'd be outta the water lickety-split. "My mom was so thrilled that you came back and we were connected again," Karen said. "She'd be really proud of you for driving over that bridge." Karen kept moving her foot around to be sure the critter had hit the road.

"Yeah?" Ginger stared at the rolling waves headed their way. They bobbed over top of each swell and touched down on the sandy bottom each time. Ginger remembered how to doggie paddle when needed, but mostly just floated in the salt water waves. The cool water kept the heat of the fierce summer sun at bay. She was grateful for sunscreen. They'd both suffered sunburns when they were growing up. Coppertone and baby oil were the only options back then. "You really think so?" They jumped a big swell and landed on their feet.

"Yeah, you would've been here a lot earlier had she been around to nag you. She wasn't as patient as me."

"So, you call that 'patient'?"

"Hey, be nice. I don't have to reach down and pull you up out of the waves next time!"

"I'd come back and haunt you if you didn't, you know."

"Yeah, for sure." Karen knew she would if she could. "Speaking of haunting, how's your ghost?"

"Oh, the duppy's fine. She came with me from Ginger Star you know."

"What makes you think so?"

"Oh, doors that shut, things that fall off counters all by themselves, stuff like that. At first I thought it was Mom, but now I know it's not."

"How do you know?"

"She has a gardenia scent. I used to smell it at Ginger Star. It didn't show up here right away. I figure Donovan packed the duppy by mistake in one of those darn boxes and eventually I unpacked it, but didn't know what it was."

"She won't try a new fragrance, huh?" Karen rolled her eyes behind Ginger's back as they jumped the next wave. She didn't believe in ghosts or duppies, no matter what anyone called them.

"Aren't you the standup comedian today?"

"Look out, here comes a big one!" Karen pointed to a swell that was going to turn into a wave before it reached them. "Duck!" They both went under the wave and came out the other side.

"It's kinda like life, if you ain't watching, it's gonna come and smack you upside the head," Ginger said when they resurfaced.

"Yeah, if you don't duck right in time," Karen said, "you'll get stuck in the salt water onesies!" She pushed her hair out of her eyes and jumped another little wave.

"Do you think we'll ever make it to the Tensies, Kar?" They jumped the oncoming wave in sync.

"Sometimes I think I already have." She immediately wished she could rewind the words. Having Lee, Nellie, and three grands was everything any woman could ever want. Nellie and Chris had been popping out babies the past few years and had two girls and a boy, ages five, three, and one. Karen and Lee embraced being grandparents. Lee was the consummate grampa: fun, energetic, and full of laughs. Karen was "Grandy" and she loved everything about her new name. She felt bad talking about her grandkids too much it in front of Ginger. She worried that all of her happiness could be a source of sadness and regret for her.

After all the years of feeling inferior to Ginger, being the over-weight tied-to-the-kitchen-stove friend instead of the one with the successful musical career living on a tropical island, it was odd to think that her life was now the one more coveted.

There had been times over the years when Karen thought there must be something wrong with her. It seemed as if she was the only one that wasn't divorced at least once. Was she that easy to please or just waking up too slowly? She and Lee had their challenges. She knew they'd married way too young and as a result, each had to wait for the other to grow up. Now she was glad they did. They were enjoying the results of love and loyalty. Lots of couples share love, but without a good dose of loyalty, it can too easily slip away. Sometimes, waking up slowly could be a good thing.

"Yeah, I'm thinking you have indeed made it to the Tensies," Ginger said. Karen didn't argue.

## "EVERY TIME YOU GO AWAY"
### Paul Young

*G*inger started out having a drink to unwind after work. She preferred to be at home alone with Spanky and Tiger to the company of anyone she knew with the exception of her brothers, but they were busy with jobs and families. She refused to drive even after just one drink because of what happened to her mom. She'd learned to live with lots of regrets, but knowing she could kill someone's mom or kid while drunk, was enough to keep her from leaving the house. Before long, she went just about nowhere except to work and back.

She thought a lot about Jamaica and missed Donovan every day. He called her every now and then from his cell phone, but the reception was poor in the mountains, so he had to wait until he went into town to get a good connection. He would tell her about the construction sites where he worked. Construction on Jamaica's north coast had gone into overdrive with new resorts being built along its stunning coastline, so he stayed busy.

They talked about everything except what really mattered. She should have told him about her dreams. The ones where he held her and kissed her neck. The dreams where they were one again, but she never did. She kept those memories to herself, too embarrassed to talk about what should have been. She kept them tucked away and would only let them out after a martini or two. Then there was the night Karen called after she'd passed the two martini mark. She picked up the phone. Big mistake. It was Karen. "So, did you think any more about going to Fort Myers on the 25th?" Karen asked.

"Yeah, let's do it. I gotta get out of this cold weather and croakers are gonna be on sale again that week," Ginger said. She reached for a cigarette, lit it, and took a deep drag. She knew she was gonna regret this, but did it anyway. "I'll put in for the time off when I get there tomorrow."

"That's so cool. Ft. Myers, here we come! I'll let Kelly know and get our flights booked. Don't worry about a thing." So she didn't. Ginger let Karen make all the arrangements.

"Let me know how much it is and I'll write you a check."

Ginger woke the next morning remembering bits and pieces of the conversation. "I think I said I'd go to Florida," she said to Spanky as she got dressed for work. "And I'm supposed to put in for a few days off. What were those dates anyway?" Spanky didn't answer.

---

Snow began to fall as Karen pulled out of her driveway to head west for the three-hour drive to Ginger's house. They were flying out of Baltimore to Ft. Myers in the morning.

She'd bought a new bathing suit for the trip. She was over a hundred pounds lighter, so the sizes went down, but she was still self-conscious about the loose skin that hung from her upper arms. "I think I need to invent a bathing suit with three-quarter length sleeves," she told Ginger over the phone. "I'd better get started. It's beginning to snow really hard."

The roads got worse as she drove. She hated driving in this mess, but at least West Virginia had given her skills for driving in bad weather. At least there weren't any hills on the Eastern Shore. It was a lot easier to navigate flat roads in the snow than mountainous ones. The drive took almost five hours and by the time she was at Ginger's there was eight inches of snow on the ground and it was still falling.

"I have Timmy lined up to drive us to the airport in the morning," Ginger said as Karen dragged her suitcase into the foyer.

"That's awesome, but he might need a plow just to get in the parking lot if this snow keeps up!" They set the alarm for 4:30 so they would be ready when Timmy got there at 5 a.m.

When they woke, a blanket of snow about fourteen inches deep covered everything outside. "Don't worry, Timmy will get us there," Ginger said as she patted Karen on the shoulder. At 5 a.m. sharp, Timmy pulled up in his pickup truck, blazing a trail into the parking lot. The truck did a few fishtails getting up the slight incline. He pulled up in front of the townhouse next to Ginger's car.

"Boy, it's a good thing I got that truck when I did," Timmy said as he stomped his boots trying to get the snow off before he came in the door. "You guys don't mind riding in the back, do ya? Could use the extra weight on the back wheels." He winked at Ginger. "Never mind," he said as he picked up Ginger's suitcase. "Between these two suitcases, I think they weigh enough to do the job. How long are you staying anyway? A month?"

"Hey, a girl's gotta have choices, you know?" Ginger laughed at him. "There's bathing suits, shoes, summer and winter clothes for coming and going, and of course, makeup and other unmentionables. And just for the record, I followed Karen's instructions and packing list."

"There you go again, throwing me under the bus. You'd think I'd get used to it by now," Karen said.

"Yeah, that bus knows the route even without a driver," Ginger grinned.

Timmy came to Karen's defense. "Good thing, 'cause we all know if you're driving, you'll get lost!"

Timmy drove slowly through the snow-covered roads to BWI airport. The normally fifteen-minute ride took almost an hour, but gave them time for some laughs along the way. "Remember when's" came easy for the three of them as they talked about their antics when they were kids.

"Yeah, Ginger and I would take you to Capital Plaza when you were still in a stroller," Karen said to Timmy. "You and the stroller provided a great way for us to hide the stuff we wanted, but couldn't afford to pay for."

"You guys shoplifted? Did you ever get caught?" Timmy asked, his eyes wide open in surprise.

"Not by the stores, but my mom figured it out," Karen said.

"Get in trouble?"

"Oh yeah, I don't think I saw freedom until I was a junior in high school. My dad made us take everything back to all the stores. No fun at all."

"Ever steal anything again?"

"Nope. Cured me for sure." Karen said. Ginger didn't respond.

"Why are you so quiet?" Timmy looked at Ginger.

"Who me?"

"I know when you're dodging a question. Ever shoplift again?"

"Only when I get pissed at Galore about something."

"Well, that narrows it down to daily. Let's get you outta Dodge before they come after you with handcuffs."

They flew into Ft. Myers and didn't waste any time. Kelly picked them up at the airport and they drove across town directly to Sanibel Island. The bridge leading to the island boasted a view of the Gulf of Mexico and the Caloosahatchee River at the same time. Folks were windsurfing, swimming, and boating. Once they reached Tarpon Beach, it was shell shopping along the shoreline. They walked and bent over to pick up one conch after another. Sanibel, the little barrier island just off the coast of Ft. Myers, was world renowned for the shells that washed up onto its shores. "How are we gonna get these back to Maryland?" Karen asked as she held up the bag of conch and scallop shells.

"You could stuff your bra with them," Kelly said but Ginger was the only one to see the humor. Since Karen had lost weight, most of her boobs had packed up and left. She could only wish her thighs would do the same.

They stopped to eat lunch at Gramma Dot's on Sanibel Island, an eclectic restaurant that offered something for each of them. They sat outside in the shade overlooking the marina. Ginger ordered a round of Bloody Marys and offered up a toast, "To stretching out every minute this weekend. So thankful for you two." Their glasses clinked and the girls drank up while they decided what to order.

"Why don't they have crab cakes?" Ginger asked.

"Oh, you wouldn't like them even if they did," Kelly said.

"Why not?"

"They don't appreciate crab like we do. Don't even know what Old Bay is." Old Bay spice was popular in the mid-Atlantic states. Chesapeake Bay crabs were considered the best in the world and they considered Old Bay its partner. It was crushed red pepper, celery salt, and paprika but hadn't made its way south. It's spicy red pepperish taste was unique and attention getting.

"Are you kidding me?" Ginger sat her menu down. "How do you serve crab with no Old Bay? In Maryland we practically snort the stuff!" Old Bay French fries, popcorn, and potato chips were big sellers in the D.C. and Delmarva marketplaces.

They hung out at the beach all weekend and when their toes weren't in the sand, they swam in the pool at Kelly's condo or went out for another meal.

"Let's go to Ford's Garage for dinner. It's a new place downtown," Kelly said. They walked the few blocks to the Fort Myers downtown area. Walking past Centennial Park, they stopped at a sculpture of Thomas Edison, Henry Ford, and Harvey Firestone, called "Uncommon Friends."

"That's the light bulb guy, right?" Ginger asked.

"Yep, and Ford's the car guy and Firestone made the tires." Kelly said.

"Says here they became friends and wintered in southwest Florida," Karen said as she read a description in a brochure she'd picked up earlier. "Evidently, they took camping trips with quite an entourage, inviting the press to cover their trips." Karen read. "Turned out to be good for business too."

"The press would've had more fun covering our camping escapades at Assateague," Kelly said. She was still traumatized by Timmy threatening to kill her frogs.

They walked on to the downtown area. Royal palms lined the streets and open-air cafes dotted the sidewalks. People ate, walked, and shopped while enjoying the live street music. The atmosphere was relaxed and fun.

"You know me, I never miss a meal," Karen said. "Even if I can only eat two bites I'm not gonna skip it." Karen had always enjoyed food and a gastric bypass didn't have the ability to take that away. "It's learning not to drink my calories, that's the tough part. Especially when we're on vacation." They laughed and clinked their glasses. Ginger ordered another round.

The restaurant, Ford's Garage, carried the automotive concept to the hilt. "I just love it when a restaurant has atmosphere." Karen held up a napkin that used a metal clamp for a napkin ring and a service rag for a napkin.

"I hope they washed the oil outta that rag," Ginger said as she came back from the ladies' room and sat down. "Did you see the bathroom sink? It was a car tire!" The restaurant was decorated in a way that would make Henry Ford smile. Transmissions, oil cans, license plates, and car parts lined the walls and ceilings, giving it a true garage feel. Their drinks arrived and Karen offered the toast this time. "To sisters and friends, the best of both that life has blessed me with."

Kelly reached under the table and pulled out a purple shopping bag. "Hey, I got you guys something you're gonna love." She reached in the bag and pulled out a blue sequined squirt gun. She reached with the other hand and pulled out a pink one. She handed the blue one to Karen.

"Wow! Where'd you get these?" She held the gun up and examined her handiwork.

"One trip to the Dollar Tree and Michaels. A hot glue gun can make anything shiny." "Nice and small, easy to hide on your lap under a sweater."

"Yep, you sure did get Mom's shiny gene," Karen said. Barb had always liked things that glittered: chandeliers, sequins, and slot machines.

Ginger held the pink gun up, blowing into the barrel. "Ladies, it looks like we're in for a good time."

"Okay, here's the deal," Ginger said holding her now loaded-with-water pink squirt gun. "Never shoot directly at someone. Arch it like this," she pointed the gun in the air at an angle. "Wait till their back is turned and give it a squirt." She demonstrated. "No laughing, or we'll get busted for sure."

After a few drinks, Karen turned into a marksman with the squirt gun at Ford's Garage. The next night, they visited Cabos just down the road from Ford's. They were standing on the corner waiting to cross the street. A young man with short black hair, wearing a white shirt, tie, and black pants, stopped and asked, "What am I, chopped liver?"

The girls looked at each other and then back at him. "Not chopped liver, but more like a burger maybe?" Ginger said. "Why do you ask?"

"You come into my restaurant and before the night is over, squirt every one of my servers and even manage to get a chef." Karen took a deep breath and looked over his shoulder for a cop that was sure to show up now that they were busted. "But you never shot at me. How come?"

"Well, I'm thinking we saved the best for last," Karen said and looked at Ginger and Kelly. They pulled out their guns and chased him back to his restaurant, soaking his shirt. "Careful what you ask for!" she laughed as he ducked back into Cabos.

───◆───

They laid on the beach and Karen opened another wine cooler. The wind had kicked up that morning and caused the water to develop waves worthy of Ocean City. Ginger was in the water jumping the swells. "Looks like Ginger's having a good time," Sue said. Karen looked up and laughed.

"Yeah, she's getting her exercise for sure," Karen said. But as she watched Ginger, it occurred to her that she couldn't get up. She was rolling in the waves and couldn't get her footing. Karen jumped up and headed into the waves. She held out her hand and hollered, "Grab my hand!" Ginger did and Karen pulled her to her feet. They held onto each other for balance and navigated their way back onto the shore.

"You saved my life again, Kar!" Ginger said as she plopped down on the blanket.

"What do you mean 'again'?" Kelly asked.

"Well, when we were kids we went to Great Falls for an Easter picnic. My brother, Scott, was goofing around and pretended to push me over a cliff. If Karen hadn't reached out and grabbed me, I would've been a goner."

"I'd forgotten about that. I was hanging onto a bush 'cause I'm such a sissy when it comes to heights. Guess that paid off," Karen said.

"You're always there when I need you, Kar," Ginger said. "Except you can't seem to keep me from eating and drinking too much." Ginger patted her belly. "I must've gained five pounds this weekend!"

"I'll be happy if that's all," Kelly said.

They returned from Florida to the cold wintry weather of the mid-Atlantic. Ginger went back to her daily routine of working and having a few drinks at home in the evenings. She didn't answer phone calls for the most part. Talking with coworkers and customers gave her more human contact than she wanted. Other than her dad and Timmy, and occasionally, Karen, she'd didn't have much contact with the outside world. Winter turned into spring and summer into fall. The leaves turned brilliant shades of red and gold in her backyard. She would sit in her living room with a fire burning in the fireplace and the patio curtain open to see the leaves drop. She saw no reason to leave her little oasis, so she didn't.

"Yeah, Beth is really worried about him," Karen said to Ginger about her elderly girlfriend's son. He'd been diagnosed with Hepatitis C. There was nothing but silence on the other end of the line. "Ging, are you there?" She continued to put away the groceries she'd brought in from the car, the phone cradled between her ear and shoulder.

"I think I do too," Ginger said.

"You think *what?*"

"I went to the ER last week to get my elbow checked when it flared up." Ginger's elbow had started to give her problems. "They did a blood test." She often had pain in her elbow, probably from the constant back and forth motion while filleting too many fish. Karen felt a lump in her throat. She knew with Ginger's past drug usage, it was a real possibility. One they'd never talked about and she'd hoped they never would.

"I went to my doctor and he took more blood. I go for the results on Thursday."

"Want company?" Karen asked. "I have to be on the western shore later this week for work anyway."

"Sure, Kar, that'd be great."

Karen's practical-self ran to the rescue. "Well, you've got great insurance through your job."

"Yeah, I'll be able to get the good meds. I'll be fine."

The rest of the conversation skirted around the "what ifs" that filled both their heads.

Karen pulled up in front of Ginger's townhouse. Tall weeds and dead petunias in the flower boxes begged to be cleaned up, but no one paid any attention. She walked up the steps, knocked on the door, and pushed it open.

"Hey, you ready?" she called and heard her answer from the top of the steps that went up to the bedrooms.

"Come on in, I'll be right down!" She found an open spot on the couch and sank into the cushions. Spanky twirled in circles, delighted at having a visitor. She reached over to pet him and he jumped up on the sofa next to her. "Did I take your seat?" She smiled at the dog. There was always a menagerie of stuff sitting on her coffee table from mostly full ashtrays to empty water bottles and beer cans, to a random selection of remote controls. Karen had learned to accept that Ginger's housekeeping habits would never change, but it still worried her. She wondered if it was a sign of Ginger's depression.

Ginger walked down the stairs wearing jeans and a dark green sweater. Her auburn hair fell across her shoulders. "You look great, Kiddo," Karen said.

"Thanks, wish I felt that way."

"It's gonna be fine. No matter what."

She looked at Karen and smiled that familiar not-so-sure smile and shrugged. "My past comes back to haunt me yet again."

"Yeah, but at least the ghosts took a hike." Karen stood up.

Ginger muttered something, but Karen couldn't hear. "Huh?" Karen asked.

"Never mind," Ginger said. She knew Karen thought she was nuts with the duppy stories and decided to keep its antics to herself. She locked the door behind them and slid into Karen's passenger seat.

"Sorry about the flowers," Ginger said. She knew it drove Karen nuts that she didn't take care of them. "I start out with good intentions, but that's about it." Karen didn't respond. She was lost in her own thoughts. She shook herself out of it and made small talk as they drove ten minutes to the appointment.

Why do all doctors' offices have to be cookie cutter experiences? A sliding window with a counter, chairs that line the walls, and a television set to a channel you wish you could change. You sign in. You wait. They call your name. You get all excited, but it's only to take your vitals. You sit and wait . . . again.

Only today was indeed vitally important. Ginger was facing the possibility of a life-threatening diagnosis. The thought of losing her again was one Karen relegated to the back of her mind. She knew she needed to tell her imagination to take a hike. The "what ifs" could drive her nuts if she let them.

They sat down in the waiting room and the nurse called Ginger's name. Karen stood up with her and they walked into the examination room. Neither of them said much, they just waited. Karen fiddled with her cell phone and checked for messages. The young handsome dark-haired doctor walked in. Ginger introduced her. "This is my friend, Karen. It's okay to share the results in front of her." He nodded and grinned at Karen. When did doctors start looking as young as Nellie? He looked at Ginger.

"Well, I don't know who told you that you have Hepatitis C, but you don't. The tests all came back negative and you're in good shape." Ginger and Karen looked at each other and back at the doctor in disbelief.

"But they took tests in the emergency room and they said I had it."

"How long were you there? Were they blood tests?" the doctor asked.

"Yeah, they did them while I waited. It was a couple of hours."

"Well, this test takes over eight hours to give an accurate answer. So whatever they were going by, I'm not sure, but I do know for sure that you don't have it."

"That's good enough for me. I'm not gonna argue with you!" Ginger said. She grabbed Karen's hand and squeezed. The doctor continued with the usual, "You should quit smoking, lose a little weight, and cut back on alcohol" speech. Ginger nodded in agreement and Karen grinned knowing that none of it would happen. The doctor made his exit and they stood and stared at each other.

"Well that's a new lease on life, if ever there was one!" Karen said and gave Ginger a hug. She wasn't sure who needed it more. She opened the door for Ginger and they walked out.

"No kidding," Ginger replied. They stood on the sidewalk. Ginger fished her cigarettes out of her purse and lit up before they were even close to Karen's van.

"You wanna go eat lunch and celebrate?" Karen asked as she unlocked the van. "You know I never miss a meal." Karen let her smoke in the car for once, figuring she needed to relieve the stress.

"Nah, I just wanna go home and get drunk."

So much for the doctor's advice. She was batting zero and they weren't even in the van yet. Karen didn't answer and knew better than to argue. She drove back to Ginger's townhouse. Ginger leaned over and gave Karen a hug. "Once again, you're a lifesaver, Kar." She slid out of the seat into the parking lot. "I love you, now get back to work!"

Karen watched her walk up the steps to her door. Ginger stood on the top step and turned to wave goodbye. Karen tooted the horn, backed out of the parking space, and waved. She put the van in drive and let out one of her heavy sighs of resignation. Her cell phone rang and the rest of the day reared its ugly head, keeping her busy till late. As she drove to her next meeting, she wondered why, even with the good news from the doctor today, Ginger kept slipping away.

***

Ginger thought she was doing pretty well. Yeah, she was having a few drinks now and then, but managing to be happy. Then her brother, Timmy, got sick. Really sick. He'd been diagnosed with pancreatic cancer. The black cloud was back. One thing she knew was that she couldn't change the weather.

Getting to know Timmy when she came back from Jamaica had given her hope and a source of happiness. She was able to be fun loving Aunt Ginger to his kids who were already in double digits and growing up fast. Now that part of her happiness was slipping away.

She spent as much time with him as she could once he got sick. She was no nurse, but hospice was involved which she knew meant he didn't have much time. She sat with him and did all she knew how to make him comfortable, but even with the pain meds, he was hurting and agitated. She picked up her guitar and began to sing "Somewhere Over the Rainbow." He drifted into a fitful sleep. She knew he needed something more and it occurred to her that she might be able to help him endure and get to the other side of his rainbow.

***

Ginger picked up the green receiver on her kitchen phone, dialed the international operator, and gave her Andrew's number. She pulled the phone cord as far as it would go from the wall and stood looking out her kitchen window seeing nothing. Her stomach tightened with dread at the sound of his voice. "Hello?"

"Andrew? It's Ginger." There were a few seconds of silence before he spoke.

"Yeah, why you call me? I no hear from you for years."

"I need a favor."

"A favor? Ha! What you want me to do for you? Your boy, Byron, nearly got me killed and I supposed to trust you?" She knew about his seaplane almost getting intercepted at Ginger Star not long after she left for rehab the last time. Andrew was collecting the last of his crop when Jamaican officials nearly nabbed him. He left out the part where Byron managed to divert their attention long enough for the plane to take off just in time.

"Look, my brother is dying of cancer and needs some really good weed. Can you tell me where I can score some here in the States that will help with his pain?" She'd heard Andrew brag that he grew a certain strain that was helpful to cancer patients. Timmy needed the best there was.

"You trying to set me up?"

"No! I would never do that. If that were the case, you'd already be locked up a long time ago, my man!"

Andrew laughed. They had never said a formal good bye. He never knew for sure whether or not she would turn evidence against him, and he still wasn't convinced. It had been several years with no hint of her retaliation, so he was inclined to believe her, but he also knew firsthand how cagey she could be.

"How I know you not setting me up?"

"Andrew, my brothers are all I have left in this world. Timmy's in so much pain. If you don't wanna help, forget it. Just forget it!" She slammed the phone receiver back on the wall. Tears that were always just a thought away these days, flowed and she cried out loud, plopped down into a kitchen chair and put her head on her crossed arms on the table. Spanky put his front paws in her lap, wondering what was wrong. "That creep. Some things never change! Why did I call him? I knew better!" She shook her head back and forth on her arms. The phone rang. She raised her head and stared at the wall. Could it be him calling back? She stood up, took a deep breath, and picked up the receiver.

"Hello?" It was.

"Ginga, I don't know why, but I'm gonna trust you to help your brudda. Take this number. Bruce will hook you up. He has the strain you need."

She pulled up to the curb in front of Timmy and Sharon's house. Her cell phone rang and she reached into her purse and pulled it out, but not in time. She recognized Doctor Burns' phone number on her cell. She listened to the voicemail from his nurse asking her to come in and see the doctor the next day at 9 AM. Something about some blood test results. She shrugged and made a mental note to go by on her way to work in the morning.

"So, where'd you get this?" Timmy asked as he held the joint up after he took a drag. He held in the smoke while she answered. She noticed his pale skin was even lighter today, a little grayer.

"Don't you worry about it. I got connections." No way she was telling him that Andrew was her source. Although it might just be enough to get him up out of his sick bed.

"Well, I guess I can't twist your arm for an answer this time." He took another drag and held it in. The weed made him less agitated and more willing to talk. It even seemed to increase his appetite a little.

"So, how are things at Galore?" Timmy asked. He closed his eyes to listen.

"Oh, pretty good if you like smelling like a fish. Actually, I could skip a shower and nobody would notice."

"Not true. I could tell." He managed a weak smile at his own joke.

"So, your nose is still in good shape, huh?" She reached behind him and propped up his pillows. She climbed up beside him and laid down on her side facing him and rested her hand on his arm. "I love you like a mom, you know," he said as he let the smoke escape his lungs.

She squeezed his arm a little and took a deep breath hoping she wouldn't cry. "I know. If I'd had a kid, I would've wanted him to be just like you. Sorry I wasn't a better mom."

"You were a great mom, Ging. And so good at getting under Roberta's skin."

"Yeah, all we had to do was start telling Mom stories and she'd exit stage right!" Ginger said.

He closed his eyes. "I'm just resting a little. Don't leave." She sat there looking at him remembering the little blonde-haired boy that loved to tease and make everyone laugh. He was the one in her life that would make her feel special on Mother's Day, even though she wasn't one. And on her birthday, even when she didn't want one, he was there to celebrate with her. His wife, Sharon, poked her head in the door. Ginger nodded at her that everything was fine. She grinned and quietly closed the door, leaving them alone.

"Remember when we went camping at Assateague and the storm knocked down all our tents?" Timmy asked.

<hr />

They crammed into Betsy, Ellie's station wagon, with the little and big kids whining at having to cut their day at the western theme park, Frontier Town, short. They'd had a great time watching mock gun fights between Wyatt Earp and the bad guys and can-can girls dancing in the saloon. The dark cloud that had been off in the distance for a while, showed up with sideways rain and wind. They piled back into the car and wrapped up in their already wet towels.

Ellie drove in short spurts, pulling over to the side of the road when it rained too hard to keep going. The trip took a half hour instead of the normal fifteen minutes to get to their campsite. As they crested the bridge to the island, the clouds began to clear and move off shore. They drove onto the island and through the gate to the campground.

Tents were down and some were ripped apart. People slowly got out of their cars and campers to investigate the damage. "I hope ours will be okay," Barb said. She no sooner got the words out of her mouth when hope took a hike. They drove around the corner to find Barb's tent leveled, but Ellie's tie-dyed tent stood leaning to the left.

Everything they owned was drenched. They all stood just looking with their mouths hanging open. Even the little kids had the good sense to keep quiet. Ellie broke the silence and rubbed it in that at least *her* tent was still standing.

Ellie ducked inside her tie-dyed tent to find a puddle of water had saturated all the bedding inside. "It's not that bad, we can just shore up this middle pole and pull out the sleeping bags," Ellie's muffled voice said from inside the tent. "Ginger, pull that outside pole in just a little" she said. Ginger tried to help, but as soon as she moved the pole an inch, the entire tent fell leaving Ellie as the sole support pole inside. She stood inside the green and orange canvas looking like the Statue of Liberty had made a guest appearance in hippie-like fashion.

"Oh my god! They're jumping all over me!" Ellie said from inside the tent. She started jumping around with the tie-dyed canvas covering her. Frogs came hopping out from Miss Liberty's soaking wet dress.

"Oh no, there goes Kermit!" Timmy jumped up from the picnic table bench and tried to round up his frog collection, but the frogs were too fast. He chased them into the bushes.

The sound of Ella's muffled cry for help made them laugh even harder. Timmy came running out of the bushes, swatting away mosquitoes. The insects followed him and helped themselves to the rest of the crowd. "Here!" Barb ran to the car and grabbed a few cans of Off and the spraying began.

"Aren't we a sight?" Barb said as she looked at the kids all covered in blotchy mosquito bites, wrinkled clothes, and beach hair. They had just returned from a few hours in the laundromat drying their clothes and bedding.

"Oh, how I long for the day when I get to listen to the waves through a real window and not the hole of a tent," Ellie said as they laid their heads on soggy pillows they'd wrapped in plastic bags for the night. They decided to all bunk together in Ellie's tent that night and wait until morning to put Barb's tent back together.

The kids fell asleep after a few sessions of whining and scratching. Barb and Ellie lay awake.

"There's nothing like a tent full of itchy kids to keep ya from sleeping!"

Barb felt something move. She picked up her flashlight and turned it on. "Don't look now, but Kermit's back!" Barb shrieked. A lone frog made his way out from under Ellie's sleeping bag.

"Timmy!" Ellie threw off her covers, jumped up and pointed at the frog. Timmy sat up and rubbed his eyes. Barb pointed her flashlight in Kermit's direction. "Get that thing outta here or we're having frog legs for breakfast!"

"That's one of the last memories I have of Mom." He tried to laugh, but it hurt too much. He flashed his mischievous smile at her one last time and closed his eyes. With him, went her resolve.

Karen and Lee made the two-and-a-half-hour trip to pick up Ginger and drive her to Timmy's funeral. Karen warned Lee about the state of disarray of Ginger's house as they pulled up in front of the brick townhouse. "It's always a mess, just ignore it," she said knowing it would be worse now that Timmy was gone. He had fussed at her about her lousy housekeeping. When he would come over, she'd tidy up some. Karen doubted she would clean up again anytime soon, if ever.

They sat in the car and stared at the house, not sure what they would find when Ginger answered the door. Karen half expected her to be drunk. Flower boxes hung on the railings still full of dead petunias. A bag of trash sat at the curbside waiting for the trash man. Karen could see an empty bottle of Stoli vodka through the white plastic trash bag as they walked across the sidewalk. "My silent competitor," she said and shook her head as she pointed to the bag. Lee didn't answer, but nodded in agreement. The December chill hung in the air and fallen leaves collected in the corners of the small yard and porch. Christmas wreaths hung on just about every townhouse door except Ginger's. Karen knew there was no need to encourage her to decorate this year. They walked up the steps, knocked on the door, and waited. Spanky barked a greeting from the other side.

Ginger opened the door, her hair still in hot curlers and a satin bathrobe that hung open over flannel pajamas. "Sorry, I'm running just a teensy bit behind." Her eyes were red and puffy. She didn't appear to be drunk, but the smell of weed lingered in the air. Spanky ran past Karen and jumped up on Lee's leg and he reached down to pet him. "Spanky, don't jump!"

"That's okay. Lee can handle him. Let's get you fixed up!" Karen said as she hugged Ginger in the doorway. Lee leaned over and kissed Ginger on the forehead as he walked by. He cocked his head to see her better and said, "I think Karen's got her work cut out for her!" They laughed. How is it laughter makes sadness a little easier to take? For an instant, the sadness disappears and happiness returns. Just for a second.

Ginger picked up the stack of magazines and old mail up from the dining room chair. She stacked it on top of the existing pile on the table. She shoved the pile further toward the middle to keep it from sliding off, using her elbow to keep the stack at bay as she sat in a chair. Karen pulled out the rollers and handed them to Ginger who cradled them in her lap.

"I always measure the bad days in my life up against the night we found out Mom died. Nothing ever came close, not even a Jamaican jail," Ginger said. Here she was, years later, remembering her grief yardstick. "Until now," she said to Karen as she removed the last of the curlers and brushed out her hair. "Not sure which is worse, the shock of losing someone quickly or watching them slowly die."

"I know. I think seeing them in so much pain makes it easier for us to let them go," Karen said remembering her parents' deaths. Funerals always opened the door and let her own sadness back in. Her dad was ill for a year, her mom, only a few weeks. She'd seen it both ways. "Maybe you should think about seeing a therapist or going to a meeting." She'd tried to suggest Alcoholics Anonymous before with no luck.

"I've had enough talking when I was in rehabs to last a lifetime, Kar. Nuh worry bout nuttin!" she slipped back into patois like she always did when she was upset. "I know you're just trying to help, but I'll be fine."

Ginger couldn't see his face as he walked toward her holding out his cell phone. She wasn't sure who he was. "Here, it's for you." She took the phone from his hand and recognized the ring he wore. It was Andrew.

Her spine tingled with dread, the kind you get when you know something bad has happened and you can't fix it. "How did you get?" her voice trailed. He raised his hand.

She woke. Her pillow was soaked in sweat. Her heart raced as she stared at the ceiling. Fear made its way through her body. Why was she dreaming about Andrew? Must be because she'd called him for the weed.

She threw off the covers and walked to the kitchen and reached for the vodka bottle under the sink. No problem rationalizing it since it would help her to go back to sleep. She had to get up early for work. She shook her head as the liquor made its way down her throat to her stomach. She headed back to bed with Spanky following close behind.

The winter months passed by her in a gray haze, mostly due to the self-induced kind thanks to lots of vodka. Ginger went through the motions of going to work and living her life. Mike was still around, but once she realized that menopause had shown up instead of pregnancy, her interest in hot sex diminished. She quit answering his calls and clung to the bottle instead.

Ginger found herself buying a large bottle of vodka a week. When she stopped to figure out how much it was costing her, she decided not to think about that any more. What choice did she have? Sobriety wasn't all it was cracked up to be.

Karen would call her weekly. Sometimes Ginger would pick up, but most times not. She tried to avoid anyone's calls when she was drinking and that was most of the time these days. She drank to stop the tears, escape the pain of losing Timmy, and the realization that she'd never have a family of her own other than Spanky and Tiger. She missed Timmy, her mom, and sometimes, the babies she'd sent back.

Ginger woke up on the couch as she did most mornings with the TV still on and Spanky curled up next to her. Tiger walked on her trying to get her up to open a can of cat food. Ginger gave in and sat up. She pushed her hair back out of her face and frowned. Little snippets of a conversation on the phone with Donovan the night before flashed in her mind. She couldn't remember too much of it except that she was crying and finished off the bottle of Stoli after they talked. She picked up the phone and called in sick for the day. She fed Tiger and Spanky and then let them out the back door. She joined them in the backyard for a cigarette and her first cup of coffee. She decided she didn't want to stay awake, so she dumped the coffee in the grass, went back upstairs and fell asleep listening to Robin Roberts and Good Morning America.

She watched bad movies, drank vodka, and smoked a little weed. She still had some of the strain she'd copped for Timmy. It was good, but didn't touch her kind of pain. Well, at least it wasn't cocaine, she reminded herself. That was one promise she was gonna keep.

# "ALONE AGAIN, NATURALLY"
### Gilbert O'Sullivan

Karen decided there was nothing like grandchildren to help her keep track of time.

She sensed Ginger tried to keep her at arm's length and after a while, she let her. She wondered if Ginger stiff-armed her because Karen had three grandkids. She tried not to talk about them too much, but found it hard to avoid. Karen would try to get her to agree to another girls' weekend here and there, but Ginger had no interest.

After a year or so of Ginger's cold shoulder, Karen acquiesced and let go. She came to realize that no matter how much she wanted to continue their friendship, she would have to take whatever Ginger was willing to give and that wasn't much. Perhaps her need for her old BFF had lessened with Nellie growing up. She and Karen had developed a close friendship in addition to their mother/daughter relationship.

On the rare occasions when she and Ginger were together, they stepped right back into their banter, but the closeness they had in the earlier years never returned. Too many blanks, too many things left unshared.

"She's changed and I guess I have too," Karen said to Lee. "Maybe I was trying to hang onto something I should've let go of a long time ago."

Karen eventually resigned herself to their telephone friendship and whatever else happened to come about. She had been elated when Ginger had made the trip over the Chesapeake Bay Bridge to Ocean City and they'd had such fun in Fort Myers, but years had passed since then. During a phone conversation with Ginger where it was obvious she'd had lots to drink, she had made it clear she was not going anywhere else. Her agoraphobia was real and so was her alcoholism.

Karen knew if she called Ginger after 7 p.m. there was a chance she wouldn't pick up. She could tell how much she'd had to drink by the slurring of her words. Who was she to judge Ginger's drinking? She'd been to rehab and made a promise with God not to do cocaine again and as far as Karen knew, she never did. An occasional joint and whatever alcohol in the evenings was her new norm.

After Timmy died, another part of Ginger slipped away, and it was hard to tell just what part had been left behind. It had been a few years since he passed and sometimes she thought part of Ginger had died with him.

She set a plate of lasagna in front of Lee. "I can't get ahold of Ginger."

"I tried calling her a few days ago and left a message, but haven't heard back."

"Still?" He reached for the pepper shaker.

"Yeah, been trying since last week. This usually means she's on a binge."

"When's the last time you talked to her?" He sprinkled on crushed red pepper.

"Don't come crying to me when you have indigestion and can't sleep, young man," she said. He loved spicy foods, but they didn't seem to like him back. She took the shaker and added some to her plate. "It's been a few weeks now. I tried to call her on my way home again today, but no luck."

He shook his head and shrugged. "I guess all you can do is wait for her to surface again."

"I wish we lived closer so I could go by and check on her."

"I thought you said you were gonna step back from all this," Lee said and looked at her from the corner of his eye to check her reaction. "Why do you think you always have to fix things for her?" He took a big bite of lasagna.

"Somebody has to."

***

A few days later, Karen sat down ready for the weekly staff meeting at the newspaper office. She reached for her legal pad, but remembered that she'd left her briefcase in the car. She ducked out of the meeting and went back to her car to get it.

As she walked to the parking lot, she flipped her cell phone open to see what caused the vibration a few minutes before. There was a message from Will O'Reilly, Ginger's dad. "I wonder what's up," she said aloud. She almost never heard from Will, but decided the message would have to wait until after the meeting.

When they finally ended the meeting, she pulled out her phone as she got into her car. She played the message from Will, "Karen, this is Will, Ginger's dad. I have some bad news. Please give me a call when you can." Karen's mouth went dry and she could feel her heart rate quicken.

Maybe he had finally convinced Ginger to go back to rehab, but that familiar punch-in-the-gut feeling stuck with her. She immediately hit the "call back" button on her phone. Will picked up on the third ring.

"Karen, thanks for calling back," he said.

"Sorry it took so long. I was in a meeting." She bit on a hang-nail, something she did when she was nervous or killing time.

"I have some awful news. Ginger died last night."

There it was, that punch-in-the-gut was for real. Just like that, she was back in the Onesies.

"What? What happened?" She stared out the car window see-ing nothing.

"She went on another binge last week."

"Yeah, I've been trying to call, but no luck. I figured she was underground for a while." She took a deep breath. "Was there an accident?

"She died in her sleep."

"Oh my God. What happened?"

Will had no answers to Karen's questions. How did she die? What happened? The sadness in his voice was palpable. "We're not exactly sure just yet. But she'd been on a binge and they said it appeared she died in her sleep."

"Will, I'm so sorry. I can't imagine," Karen said. Losing a child had to be the worst horror in life. Timmy just last year and now Ginger.

"I know how much you meant to her, Karen. You were the sister she never had," his voice cracked. Silence stretched out between them. Will gathered himself and they agreed to keep in touch regarding funeral arrangements. Karen hung up the phone and stared out the windshield of her car. Tears flowed down her cheeks.

"Why, God? Why did she have to be so unhappy? Why couldn't she figure it out? Why didn't I do something?" She cried out loud and stared at nothing through the van's windshield. She felt like a deflated balloon with hardly any air left. There was a deep sadness she could feel, but not touch. She hung her arms over the top of the steering wheel, laid her head down, and cried. She wept for Ginger, for her, for Will, and for the life Ginger was never able to live. She reached in the glove box of the van and found a stack of napkins. She wiped her tears, blew her nose, and took a deep breath. She put the car in drive and drove south to Assateague, her refuge where she would always go to figure things out. It was September, so the weather was still warm and the tourists mostly gone.

She drove over the two-lane Verrazano Bridge to the island from the mainland. Ocean City's boardwalk and Ferris wheel beckoned from the left. Ponies dotted the bayside shoreline grazing in the marshy grasses. The arthritic arch of the trees reached out to greet her as she drove onto the island. She turned right and headed to the National park. It was a two mile drive down the center of the narrow island. One side was dunes with campers dotting the sandy soil and the other was marshlands that hosted the bayside shoreline. Egrets perched in trees and seagulls soared through the air. Memories of camping with their moms tapped her on the shoulder. She showed her pass to the ranger in the ticket booth and drove toward her favorite spot on the beach.

Tired of hearing her voice cry out to God, she turned on the radio. "I can see clearly now, the rain is gone," Johnny Mathis crooned. Karen smiled through her tears. She recognized the song as it had played on the radio when they drove away from Ellie's funeral forty-years before. Ginger thought then, as Karen did now, that Ellie was telling her everything was good.

"Why didn't I *make* you go back to rehab?" she cried. "I didn't know it was this bad. I didn't know!" She cried until the tears would no longer come. Her sister from another mother was gone forever, at least on this side of the rainbow.

She pulled up to the beach, put the van in park, and got out. She trudged over the wooden sidewalk to the top of the dune. The wind was gentle and warm. She walked over, sat down, dug her toes in the sand, and stared at the water. The waves crashed on the shoreline, one after another. She and Ginger would never hang out in the waves together again. The place where they'd shared so many secrets as they stood dodging the oncoming waves and an occasional jelly fish still remained.

"So, what's it like on the other side of the rainbow?" Karen asked Ginger half expecting an answer. The lyrics of "Somewhere Over the Rainbow" played in the back of her mind. "Where the heck are you guys?" She dug her toes in the sand and covered her feet to her ankles. "It's so not fair, you know. You guys being together and I'm here." She picked up a shell and rubbed it between her fingers. "Not that I wanna come just yet, but I kinda know you're having fun without me. I can only imagine the jokes. Just not fair." Her tears flowed. She reached in her pocket, pulled out a tissue and blew her nose.

No one answered. The sound of the waves and an occasional seagull's cry lingered, soothing her, but no substitute for a close hug. She had the comfort of knowing she'd get that from Lee when she got home. That was something Ginger never had.

She cried for the loss of her parents. "I guess you've seen every-one by now," she said to Ginger. Again, no response. "Who looked older, your mom or mine? I know mine was worried about that." She smiled at the thought of Barb and Ellie teasing each other again, but along with that smile came a pang of envy.

Again, no answer. The past twenty years were not what she had hoped for when it came to Ginger's life, but the most recent ones were precious to her. She was grateful for every conversation, in person or on the phone. "Well, I guess I'll have to settle for one-sided conversations from now on." Karen smiled through her tears. "You're not here to set me straight, so I guess I'm gonna be right all the time." She grinned. "I suppose there's an upside to just about everything."

What she did know was that since Ginger had returned from Jamaica, she was back, but not totally. There were parts of Ginger that went to Jamaica, but didn't return. And there were parts that came back that were not there before she left. She'd given up the drugs, but traded them in for something else. Alcohol. Loneliness. Sadness. Karen's heart hurt knowing that Ginger had been lost to her and pretty much everyone else for a long time now.

After Jamaica, Ginger's ability to live in the world around her had diminished. She shrank back from people and there were times when Karen felt as if she might as well still be in Jamaica, thousands of miles away. It occurred to her that when someone had a substance abuse problem, it was in some ways as if they were already dead, checked out from the world everyone else lived in.

Karen sat in the sand and cried over the memories, for the lost times, and the ones they would never have. She'd never forgive herself for not dragging Ginger to yet another rehab.

She pulled her cell phone out of her pocket and called Lee to give him the bad news. "Oh my god, Kar. Where are you now?"

"I drove over to Assateague. I'm sitting on the beach."

"Do you want me to come home?"

She loved him more now than she did the minute before. Just the sound of his voice could calm her. "No, I'm okay. I'll see you when you get home." They hung up. She was never as grateful for him as she was right now. He always made her feel safe and secure, no matter what. He was truly her best friend. Why had she ever tried to find another one? The thought of ever losing him made her cry all over again. Losing Ginger was more than enough.

After talking with Lee, she had a chat with God. She cried, railed against the injustice of it all, and asked for strength. She took comfort knowing that He knew her sadness and would pull her through, but she still couldn't help the anger that kept bubbling up. "Why did I find her only to lose her again?" she cried. When she received no audible answer, she stood up, brushed off the sand, and headed back to the top of the dune. She could hear the rumbling of thunder and looked north toward Ocean City. A large black cloud was heading out to sea.

The wind picked up and along with it, came the chill of fall. She stopped at the top of the dune and turned to look at the shoreline again. The waves had dug a trench in the sand, creating a little river of saltwater running parallel to the shoreline. It was a sure sign that summer was ending and fall was on the way when the waves dug into the beach. This was a place that would always remind her of Ginger, but it was also her happy place. She'd be back with her memories and knew she'd make new ones. She let out a deep sigh, turned, and headed back to the car.

Karen opened the door to the van and slid onto the seat. As she drove back over the bridge to the mainland, tears slid down her cheeks. She'd lost people before and cried because she was sad, but being angry at the same time, was something new.

Ginger was gone, dead, and had officially given up on life. Why hadn't it been the fairy tale ending Karen always hoped it would be? "Why didn't you let me help you?" she shouted through her tears as she drove. She pushed in a cd. Phil Collins' voice soothed her immediately, "Just look over your shoulder, I'll be there," Karen wanted the lyrics to be true and looked at the empty seat beside her. She drove across the bridge to the mainland and looked in her rearview mirror to see a huge rainbow behind the black cloud that was now over the ocean. A sense of Ginger telling her that all was good flooded her. She pulled the van over to the shoulder and got out. The rainbow seemed to stretch into infinity. "Well, I guess you've finally made it." She stood for a minute soaking up the phenomenon of a rainbow that never failed to stop her in her tracks.

At first, she felt strange talking to Ginger out loud, but did it anyway. "Well, you weren't here when you *were* here, so how do I know for sure you're not here now?" She knew she wasn't making sense, but it didn't matter. "When I pulled you out of the waves in Ft. Myers, you said I'd saved your life twice, but it appears as if the third time, I struck out." She was disappointed that their sisterhood had not been enough to keep Ginger happy on this side of her rainbow. She counted on the love that met Ginger on the other side of her rainbow to bring a smile back to that beautiful face once and for all time.

Karen's phone rang. It was Scott, Ginger's brother. "Dad wanted to know if you would handle the service," he said to her over the phone. "Ginger wasn't a churchgoer, so we don't know what to do or who to ask. Dad's Catholic and he doesn't think Ginger would want that."

"Well, I suppose I could, . . . " Karen said. He wanted *her* to lead the funeral service? "I'm not a preacher and in this case, you will definitely get what you pay for."

Scott laughed. "You'll do fine. The family really appreciates it, Kar." She stared out her office window.

She hung up the phone and took a deep breath. Maybe she could take this pain and anger and turn it into something positive.

She packed up her briefcase, locked her office door, and headed for the car.

That night, she spent hours making notes and setting up a schedule for the service.

Lee hung up the phone after his conversation with Donovan. "He can't get here in time for the funeral. He's pretty broken up. Feels like he should have done something more to help her."

Karen looked up from the kitchen table. "I could tell from your side of the conversation. Poor guy," Karen said. She laid her papers down on the kitchen counter. "Maybe he could call in during the service. We could put him on speaker phone so he could listen and maybe even say a few words."

"Good idea. I'll call him later and see," Lee said. Karen sighed and walked away. Nobody wanted to think they were responsible for Ginger's death. Her included. When would she ever learn to quit beating herself up for other people's choices?

Karen, Lee, and Nellie walked into the funeral home. Memories of Ellie's funeral some thirty-seven years before in the same building greeted her. Karen pointed to a door, "That's the ladies' room where Mom almost flushed Roberta down the toilet!" They laughed. She'd told the story many times of how her mom and Roberta got into a fight during Ellie's funeral.

A man in a suit walked up to them in the lobby. "Are you Pastor Karen?" She looked from him to Lee and back again and laughed.

"Well, I've been called many things, and 'pastor' isn't one of them, but yes, I'm Karen!" The man, who turned out to be the funeral director, looked confused. "I asked my pastor if it was okay for me to lead the service and he said I needed a license to marry people, not bury them!" Her comment did nothing to change his confused look. "Yes, I will be speaking and running the service for Ginger O'Reilly."

"Oh, okay, that's great!" he said. He looked relieved and showed them into the room. Ginger's ashes stood on a pedestal in an aqua vase, the color of the Caribbean. Most appropriate.

Karen talked with him about the music that would be played before and after the service. She handed him a cassette tape. It was only one song, Ginger's latest favorite, "Somewhere Over the Rainbow." The ukulele played softly in the background as Ginger's friends and family arrived. Karen greeted those she knew and some she didn't. It was apparent that Ginger was loved much more than she'd ever realized. People lined the walls when all the seats were taken.

Karen signaled for the music to fade and began to speak to the crowd. She greeted everyone and started the service with a heartfelt prayer. When she finished, she opened her eyes and looked down at her notes.

"Let's welcome Donovan who is listening to us from Jamaica." She held up her cell phone for all to respond and they did. Donovan called out in response, "Greetings from Jamaica. Our hearts cry out with pain from losing Ginga." A rooster crowed in the background. "Even the roosta, he sad too."

The crowd laughed. "It's always good to laugh when we feel like crying," Karen said. She put the phone down on the podium and went on to talk about her childhood memories with Ginger. "We all grew up with the Wizard of Oz. Well, Ginger went nuts over the new Hawaiian version of "Somewhere Over the Rainbow" that came out a few years back. She played it all the time and you heard it as you walked in."

"Ginger was a lot like Dorothy. She wanted love, intellect, and courage. She went to Jamaica to look for it and while she found it for a while, she also lost it for several years. She was always trying to get to the other side of the rainbow, but she didn't realize you can't see a rainbow if you haven't had some rain first. She was always trying to avoid the darn rain.

"She rose to fame as a reggae star. I realize many of you didn't know that until recently. She wanted to start over and knew that her singing career had to take a back seat for her to get well and stay well.

"She came back to the States to try to start over, trying to live a normal life on this side of the rainbow." Karen took another deep breath and made eye contact with Lee. She pushed on.

"When's the last time you saw a rainbow and didn't pause to look at it?" She looked around the room. "Most of us do. I did some research and found out that the Bible says that a rainbow will be visible when it rains as a sign that God keeps his promises and faithfulness to His word. The day Ginger died, I drove to Assateague Island. When I left, I looked in my rearview mirror and you know what I saw? A huge rainbow. It was so big I had to pull over on the highway and get out. I like to believe that Ginger was trying to tell me something. Exactly what, I'm not sure, except to say that she was on the other side of her rainbow and finally found peace. The best of this side of her rainbow had been Assateague. I thank God for memories. How awful this life would be without them?

"We've all looked in our rear-view mirrors and seen things we didn't expect. Things we couldn't explain. The rainbow started to dissipate by the time I got back in my car. As I drove home, I listened to 'Somewhere Over the Rainbow' over and over again through my tears. Ginger, someday I'll wish upon a star and wake up where the clouds are far behind me too." Karen's voice shook. She took another deep breath and continued. "But until then, I'll check out all the chimney tops I see and look for melted lemon drops." She quoted the song.

"So, now it's time to bore you with some family history. Our childhoods were unique. Our two families were closer than most cousins. Our parents were best friends and Ginger and I carried on the tradition." Karen had worried about mentioning all this knowing Roberta would be there, but decided she would have to get over it. She continued. "Our friendship had its ups and downs over the years. We tended to be polar opposites on most things, politics, music . . . other than hers, of course! . . . , and friends. Had it not been for Ginger, I would never have finished my first novel as early as I did. She was always my biggest cheerleader. I wish I'd been better at being hers.

"We were apart for over ten years when she disappeared into the drug culture and were reunited after all those years. Years of only occasional contact until we reconnected at her dad's 70th birthday party. Our friendship was still there. She helped me through the loss of my parents. I was as convinced then as I am now that God brought her back to me right on time and when I needed her most.

"But right now, I'm feeling like I'm under the rainbow. I can't see the beauty on this side and I don't feel the joy of the other. But I know my sadness is not what she or God wants for me. I know the sadness will 'melt like lemon drops on the chimney tops,' if I let it.

"I miss her every day. I cried when I realized I'd heard her say, 'I love you, Kar,' for the last time. That's what she always said when we hung up the phone. What I'll miss the most is hanging out in the ocean waves with her sharing secrets. For those of you that love the ocean like I do, you know that the best conversations are those floating around in salt water." Heads nodded all across the room.

"We'll never 'make skies' from the clouds floating above and tourists are safe from our squirt guns on the boardwalk." The guests chuckled at Karen's raised eyebrows. "From the sound of things, I think a few of you have heard the stories or maybe even been a victim of our shenanigans!" She smiled and sighed. She would wait until later to cry. She was, after all, her mother's apprentice.

"When Ginger's dad called to tell me she had passed, the first song that played on my radio was 'I Can See Clearly Now', which turned out to be the same song that played when we drove out of this very parking lot thirty-seven years ago when Ginger buried her mom, Ellie. I don't know about you, but I'm not a believer in 'coincidence.' I prefer to think of them as Divine communications.

"Well, I like to think that not only are our moms, Barb and Ellie, now reunited, but Ginger is there with them along with her brother, Timmy. I can only imagine how that's working out. Might have to sharpen my writing skills, put my imagination to work, and start another book." The crowd laughed. She wasn't sure if it was about a new book or the sound of the rooster in the background on her cell phone.

"Donovan?" She picked up the phone and talked into the speaker.

"Yes, Karen. I'm here!" The phone was tinny in sound, but loud enough for all to hear when she held it up to the microphone.

"Everyone," she looked at the crowd. "Donovan Williams is on the line from Jamaica. Ginger's dear friend." She held the phone closer as she spoke. "Donovan, do you have something you wanted to share?"

"Yes, I do. I want to say that Ginger was a very special friend to many of us here in Jamaica. She also did many good things for the people of our island country. She had a heart for the girls of Windsor Home, an orphanage of sorts. I would like to introduce a young woman by the name of Pinky. Pinky was a friend of Ginga's and many years ago found herself a resident of Windsor Home. Pinky?" Karen remembered the fundraiser at Ginger Star to help the girls of Windsor and she remembered Pinky too.

"Yes, Brother Donovan. Tank you and greetings to those of you in the US," Pinky said. "I was a young runaway and ended up at Windsor Home. Ginga came to see me when my mudda couldn't come. She came back and spent time with us. She raise money to help us to have books to read, games to play, and find ways to smile. But more than any of that, she loved on us, taught us manners and how to love one another." Pinky choked up and couldn't talk for a few seconds.

"You okay?" Donovan asked her. Pinky took a deep breath.

"Yes, I'm good," Pinky said. "I just want to say 'tank you' to Ginga for loving me. For showing me and my friends what it meant to really love and help someone. Ginga was love."

"Yes she was," Donovan said. "Karen, we here in Jamaica know what a giving and sincere person Ginga was. She will be missed by all that knew her." His voice cracked and choked for a second. "She was the love of my life." Karen could hear him break down into sobs. Karen picked up where he left off.

"Yeah, Ginger loved you all so much," she took a needed deep breath to keep from breaking down too. "She missed Jamaica every day and wanted to go back someday." She looked around the room. There didn't seem to be anyone with dry eyes. She looked at the aqua vase that held Ginger's ashes. "And just maybe she will."

"She enjoyed those of you she worked with at Galore." She looked around the room and saw several Galore uniforms in the crowd. Many had come to the service on their way to work. "But, I'm sure you all knew she didn't like it when croakers were on sale. Her arm would hurt from all the fish filleting that she would have to do when the price was affordable." She could hear giggles and saw heads nodding across the room.

"Well, the good news is, croakers are no longer on sale, Ging. At least not on your side of the rainbow. You've finally made it to the Tensies." Karen folded up her notes and stepped aside from the podium. The ukulele tinkled and 'Somewhere Over the Rainbow', came on over the PA system again. Lee wrapped his arms around her. She buried her head in his shoulder.

"Spoken like a true friend." He hugged her hard. The service broke up. She shook hands and said goodbye to the guests as they left. She picked up her purse, grabbed Lee and Nelly's hand, and walked back to the car.

Finding a best friend in this life is a treasured experience. Keeping the same one for a lifetime can be tricky. The Kincaids and O'Reillys found a closeness that most families never share. They managed to remain friends through the toughest of times, divorce, death, and addictions. Karen and Ginger followed suit as best they could, but the remnants of addiction pulled them apart.

Karen tried to forgive herself for not being able to rescue Ginger. Life and choices had changed them both. Sometimes those changes were enough to leave gaps that couldn't be bridged. She missed Ginger every day, but realized that while Ginger had come back, she was only a shadow of her former self, unable to

## "STARTING OVER"
### John Lennon

Karen and Lee pulled into the parking lot of Ginger's attorney. They'd made the three-hour drive west to Baltimore and would head back home when the meeting was over. It was a sunny fall day. Leaves covered the parking lot from the latest burst of wind that helped to undress the trees. Lee put his blue Toyota Tundra in park and Karen sighed. "Not looking forward to this," Karen said. Lee nodded in agreement.

"Me too, but for whatever reason, we have to."

"There's Will," Karen said and pointed across the lot. Will stood outside of his blue SUV while his sons, Scott, William, and Roger climbed out of the front and back seats. Lee turned off the car and they took a collective deep breath. "Let's go."

Karen and Lee walked across the parking lot. Lee shook hands while Karen hugged everyone hello. "Not sure what this is all about, but I guess we'll soon find out," Karen said to Will.

"Well, evidently Ginger had enough foresight to write a will," he said and sighed. Karen thought it must be awful to have to say those words aloud when talking about his daughter, but kept it to herself. Will had lost two children, Ginger and Timmy, in the last two years. He looked smaller than he used to. His shoulders slumped more than the last time she'd seen him at the funeral. He put his hand on Karen's shoulder as they turned to walk inside. She was surprised that Roberta wasn't there, but thought better about bringing that up. Maybe Roberta had finally learned when to step back a little.

They made small talk to fill in the blanks as they rode the elevator up. The door opened into the law firm's offices. The reception area was typical, or at least Karen thought so. It was covered in wood paneling and leather sofas. Will walked over to the desk to let them know they were there while the rest sat down on the cool smooth sofas.

"So, how's the book coming along?" Scott asked. Karen noticed he had gray hair coming in to replace the red. Guess her old nickname of "Howdy Doody" for him wouldn't hold out much longer. She didn't have it in her to tease him about it today.

"Well, my new agent finally sold it to Holden House, a publisher in New York." Karen sat back in the sofa and leaned on Lee just a little in an effort to add a little distance between her and everyone else. She wasn't sure why she would be uncomfortable except that she wasn't used to being around the O'Reillys without Ginger. Ever since they were kids, it was always the girls against the boys. No longer. "We'll see what happens."

"Yeah, I'm thinking she just might be able to quit the day job soon," Lee said and kissed her on the head. "My girl's a bona fide author now."

Will walked back over and said, "I think they're ready for us." They stood up as a group just as a raven-haired young woman in a red dress showed up.

"Good morning. My name is Athena. I'm Ted's assistant." She reached around the circle and shook everyone's hand. "Please follow me." She smiled and turned on her heel. "Would anyone like a cup of coffee?" She opened a glass door that led to a conference room bordered with glass walls all the way around again, just like in the movies. Karen thought maybe it was a way for others in the office to keep an eye on what was happening inside the conference room. She assumed tempers could flare when the destiny of large amounts of money were involved. They all declined the coffee and opted for the water that was already poured in a glass in front of each chair. They made their way around the table and chose a seat. She noticed that boxes of Kleenex were strategically placed around the table.

A forty-something attractive man with a full head of premature gray hair walked in. "Good morning, everyone. I'm Ted Logan." He walked around and shook everyone's hand. Athena proceeded to place a folder in front of each of them, making sure she had their names right.

"I'm assuming you're Karen," Athena smiled and handed her a folder with her name on it. Karen smiled back and sat in a chair between Lee and Will. Ted pulled out the chair at the head of the table and sat.

"Ginger hired me to help her with her will and several other issues a few months back," Ted said as he looked around the table. "I'm sorry to hear that she's gone." Everyone nodded.

"Thanks," Will said.

"Well, let's get down to it," Ted said as he leaned on the conference table and opened the file that lay in front of him. "Ginger met with me about a year or so ago and drew up the will that is inside your folders. Once I go over the highlights, you can have your copies to peruse later. Your portion is highlighted on your copy in yellow to make it easy to spot, but let's go over all the highlights together first." Karen wondered what he meant about "your portion," but let it go and tried hard to listen. Ted proceeded to read the pertinent sections of the will. Ginger had left funds to cover college tuition for both William and Timmy's children. Her townhouse would go to her dad, Will. There was nothing unusual there. Karen wondered again why she and Lee were included in the meeting. Ginger couldn't have had that much more to leave behind.

"She said this would be a surprise to most of you. At the time of her death, she still owned Ginger Star, her home in Jamaica," Ted revealed. Gasps could be heard around the table. Karen was stunned. "We'll get to the distribution of the plantation in a moment."

"But she said the bank had taken it back," Karen said. She looked around the room to see everyone's head nod in agreement. Everyone except Will. This was obviously no surprise to him.

"Well, that wasn't the case. She paid it off several years ago not long after she returned to the States," Ted said. "And that's why I asked you here, Karen," he looked up at Karen and Lee who stared back at him. "Ginger wanted you and Lee and Donovan Williams of Maroontown, Jamaica to have the Ginger Star estate. It's a 51 percent share for you and Lee and 49 for Donovan."

Karen frowned and shook her head. She didn't understand. She looked at Lee who was as perplexed as she. Why didn't Ginger tell her she still had the house? "Does Donovan know yet?" were the first words out of Karen's mouth.

She looked at Ted. He nodded and replied, "I called him earlier this week and he called back just a few minutes before you arrived here this morning."

"I just can't believe . . . " Karen looked at Lee. He shrugged and shook his head.

Ted cleared his throat and continued. "I'm sure all of you remember how devoted Ginger was to the Windsor Girls Home in Jamaica." Heads nodded around the conference table. "Well, she started construction on a building about four months ago. It's located on the rear acreage of Ginger Star. Her vision was to build a halfway house for girls leaving Windsor at age eighteen. It would be a place for them to go to learn how to live on their own and become productive citizens. The home will house twenty women."

Karen looked around the table. "Did anyone know about this?" Heads shook in denial. Everyone except Will.

His head looked down at his hands. "Yes, I knew."

Ted tried to keep the meeting going in the right direction. "Karen, she left a letter for you to read in private after our meeting." He pulled an envelope out of his file folder. A few murmurs came from the others, but quickly quieted down when Ted slid the letter over the shiny conference table. Karen picked it up and recognized Ginger's handwriting on the front, "Karen Murphy, undisputed Queen of the Tensies (this side of the rainbow)" Lee pulled a tissue from a box and handed it to her. Every time she blinked, a tear betrayed her.

"I know this is a lot to take in. We can talk about details later after you've had time to let the news soak in." He picked up a large cardboard tube and pulled out a copy of a blueprint of Ginger Star and the halfway house and unrolled it across the conference table. He anchored the corners with paperweights. Ted motioned for the group to gather around him to take a look. "She already sectioned off the back twenty acres of the old Ginger Star estate, so you, the new owners of Ginger Star, will not have to worry about its care and operation." Ted pointed to a section that was portioned off with a sketch of a building. "There is a NGO, the Jamaican equivalent of our non-profit organization, in place to handle the management and expenses."

"Who is going to run the halfway house?" Lee asked.

"We have set up a trust that will help to find someone suitable," Ted answered. "Ginger was hoping to maybe hire someone that had lived in Windsor. Someone that will understand the mission, but we have plenty of time before that's needed. Nothing moves fast in Jamaica." Pinky's name came to mind for Karen, but she kept the idea to herself for now.

"Don't we know it!" Lee laughed and everyone chimed in.

"The road back to the house has already been dug out. The floor has been poured and the foundation is being laid this week."

"Wow, how long has this been in the works?" Karen asked.

"Construction began about four months ago. Again, not much moves fast down there," Ted said. They all sat back down. Karen took a long drink from her water glass. "By the way, Ginger already chose a name for the Windsor project; The Rainbow House."

Karen smiled and said, "I like that. It sounds like something she would think of."

"Well, Dad, I'm thinking none of this is a big surprise to you," Scott said what everyone else was thinking. "You've been handling her finances for years now."

"Yeah, I knew about Ginger Star. I tried to convince her to sell it more than once, but she just wouldn't let it go. Somehow, she was convinced she needed to hold onto a home she could never visit. Didn't make any sense to me." He cleared his throat and looked from Scott to Karen. "But as we all know, if you didn't let it go with Ginger, she'd let go of you. I didn't wanna risk losing her again," his voice cracked. He took a deep breath. "But I did anyway." A tear escaped and slid down his cheek. He wiped it away with the back of his hand.

Ted sat back in his chair making it obvious that he was out of surprises. They pushed back their chairs. Ted stood up and walked to the door. He shook everyone's hand as they left the room. "Call me when you have questions. I'm sure you will," he said to Karen and Lee as they walked out. They thanked him and walked through the reception area and waited for the elevator. No one spoke as they entered the elevator for the ride down to the first floor. Thoughts and questions swirled in Karen's mind. The elevator door closed in front of them.

"Wow, that was amazing. Who knew Ginger had it in her?" Scott asked. The elevator moved slowly toward the first floor.

"I knew she had it in her, but didn't know she still had so much left over from her savings or that her songwriting residuals were so lucrative," Karen said and they all turned and looked at Will who stood in the rear of the elevator in silence.

Will grinned and shook his head. "She didn't want the money she had. She felt like it was left over drug money although it really wasn't until just a few months ago." The elevator slowed to a stop on the second floor and the door opened. A couple with a toddler walked on and stood in the front facing the elevator door as it closed. The conversation stopped as the toddler squirmed to push the buttons as they moved downward again. The elevator slowed to a stop and the door opened. They exited one at a time.

"What did you mean by, 'until a few months ago'?" William asked his dad once they were standing in the marble tiled lobby.

"She received a chunk of money from a guy named Andrew Phillips. I guess he was her manager at one point," Will said. Karen felt her face flush at the sound of Andrew's name.

"Yeah, we know who he is," Karen said and looked at Lee who nodded. "He was a former crooked cop and more than a manager. I always thought it was him that led her down the path to addiction. He gave me the creeps." She unconsciously grabbed on to Lee's hand and remembered seeing Andrew's name pop up on Ginger's phone along with all the hang ups she'd received over the years, suspecting it was him. Her stomach tightened at the thought of dealing with him again.

"Yeah, well your suspicions were right, but he's evidently turned his life around. He got busted, went into a rehab called Teen Challenge, and found Jesus. He must've gone on a guilt trip he couldn't get off and decided he owed Ginger a bunch of money. He wired it to her. She didn't want anything to do with what she perceived to be drug money. That's when she decided to build the halfway house with it."

"Well, I know her heart broke for those girls. At least she was able to see one of her dreams come true before she checked out," Karen said. She couldn't bring herself to use the word "died," when it came to Ginger. She just couldn't.

"Well, I guess we need to call Donovan after this sinks in," Karen said. "Guess I'll read her letter first though." She looked at the unopened letter in her hand. "I'll be in touch when we figure this out. I have a feeling Ted's gonna become our new best friend," Karen said. She walked around and gave the O'Reilly's each a hug goodbye wondering when she would see any of them again.

―――

Karen and Lee had planned to drive straight home, but the envelope with Ginger's handwriting called her name. "We need to know what this says," Karen held the envelope up.

"Yeah, well I think you should read it in private and then tell me about it, if you want," Lee said. "Let's stop in Kent Island for an early dinner and you can read it there."

"You just want an excuse to stop at The Jetty," she said. It was their favorite restaurant on their way back east to Ocean Pines. It was just a wooden shack built on a pier next to a marina. Nothing fancy, but had great seafood, service and atmosphere.

"Not gonna deny that!" He reached over and took her hand. The warmth of his touch calmed her once again. She stared out the window at the sailboats scattered across the Chesapeake Bay on the unseasonably warm October afternoon.

"Looks like folks are taking advantage of one more Indian summer day," Karen remarked as she pointed at the boats, leaned back, and enjoyed the view as they drove over the bridge. She remembered Ginger's fear of bridges and was grateful she didn't share the phobia. She'd always loved crossing over the bay and the view the bridge provided. When she was a kid, crossing it meant she was headed toward the beach, Ocean City, and Assateague Island. As an adult, it meant she was headed home to Ocean Pines. Life was good even when it wasn't.

Lee pulled his pickup into the restaurant parking lot facing the water. There was nothing fancy about The Jetty, but that was one reason they liked it. The exterior was made to look like a shanty and had a pier that reached out into the waters of Kent Narrows that led into the Chesapeake Bay. The hostess sat them at a table overlooking the water.

"Tell you what," Lee said as they took their seats. "After we get our drinks, I'll leave you for a bit so you can read the letter. Tell me about it over dinner." As if on cue, the server delivered two beers. He picked his up and walked down the pier to admire the passing boats.

Karen pulled the envelope out of her purse and stared at it. She braced herself for the last one-sided conversation in the form of a letter. "Well, once again, you're getting the last word." Karen smiled and picked up a dinner knife, opened the letter, and pulled out the familiar air mail stationery. "How did she ever come up with this? They don't even make air mail stuff anymore," Karen said out loud to herself and chuckled. "I guess being a pack rat paid off one more time." She opened the letter that was several pages long and noticed the date, August 18, 2010, just six weeks earlier.

Hey, Woman?

I guess you have to endure one more letter from me and this time, I don't need a stamp, although Ted, my attorney, cost a heck of a lot more than air mail postage or a long-distance call from Jamaica.

If you're reading this, you are now officially the Queen of the Tensies on this side of the rainbow. You can bet our moms and I will have already had a throw down on the other side as to who gets top billing there . . . stay tuned. By the time you get there, we'll have seniority, so no Tensies throne for you on that side. Live with it. Something tells me as good as you've been, you'll have plenty other rewards to enjoy inside the gates of Heaven. I'll put in a good word for ya anyways.

I guess you're wondering why I never told you I still owned Ginger Star. I don't really know the answer to that question except to say that it was just too painful to talk about it, so, I didn't. I lied about the bank taking her back so you wouldn't ask again. And you didn't. Thanks for that.

I think part of me just didn't wanna think about it and the other part didn't have the guts to sell it. You know me, if I don't talk about it, I don't have to deal with it. I think I was afraid that if I talked and thought about Ginger Star too much, I'd go back and I knew I should never do that. I kept Ginger Star knowing that I could never live there again, but hoped maybe you and Lee could enjoy it one day.

By now, you know about the plans for the Rainbow House. Yeah, Andrew reared his ugly head once more, but this time it turned out different. At first, I didn't want the money, but realized that Rainbow House would be my chance to turn the dirty money into clean. Bad into good. Sad into happy.

I'm excited that my life will stand for something when I'm gone and give the girls of Windsor the second chance that everyone deserves. Lord knows I had enough of them and I'm grateful for this one last chance to make a difference. I remember Bob Marley said, "Live for yourself and you will live in vain. Live for others, and you will live again." While I won't live again on this side of the rainbow, maybe the love in me will live on through the Rainbow House.

Ginger Star has lots of acreage that's not being used and I've subdivided off twenty acres for Rainbow House. Remember the sugar cane field that backs up against the mountains? That's where it will be. Far enough away from the house at Ginger Star that you won't even know it's there. There's a non-government organization (NGO, Jamaica's version of a non-profit) in place, so it's ready to take off before the building is completed. Please know that this project will not land in your lap to manage. The NGO and Ted will handle all that.

Karen looked up from the letter and stared at the water that flowed past the pier. She remembered visiting Windsor with Ginger a few days before the fundraiser so many years ago. It was just as sad a place as Ginger had described. Karen realized had she personally landed in such a situation as a young girl, she would never have survived. She wasn't tough enough. So many weren't. Maybe they were the lucky ones. Who would want to survive not being loved? She sighed and continued reading.

My hope is that you and Lee will love spending time in Jamaica again. What I want the most is to see you write more books from your favorite writing perch at Ginger Star. Heck, maybe you'll write a book about your favorite former reggae star. Who knows?

Your wicker desk and IBM Selectric are still there waiting for you, although I suspect you will *retire the IBM and use your laptop this time around. Remember when you thought Willie had thrown out your manuscript? That was the only time I thought you might actually be capable of a criminal act. Poor Willie, I think she aged ten years until she found it at the bottom of the laundry basket? Enough with the memory sidebar . . .*

Karen chuckled when she remembered the scene and put the paper down on the table. She stared at the water. She could see Lee leaning on a pylon enjoying the view as bikini clad ladies passed by on a boat. She grinned. There was a time she would have been jealous. She wasn't sure if it was the result of losing over a hundred pounds that brought her confidence back, or if she'd ever really had much to begin with. Probably the latter. She woke up slowly to having confidence with anything other than being a mom and a reporter. She looked back at the letter and turned the page.

*So, I hope you're okay with sharing Ginger Star with Donovan. I figure you will need to have someone from Jamaica live there on the property to look after things while you're doing your whirlwind book tours across the States (I plan on pulling some strings from above, just so you know). If not, you guys can decide how you want to work things out. If you end up selling it, please know that's okay with me. I just couldn't bring myself to do it. Tag you're it, but if you do sell, please take care of our dear Byron for me.*

*Byron's still living at Ginger Star and has been looking after the place since I left. My desire is to have him live there until he wants to leave or dies, whichever comes first. I'm not sure how old he is. He doesn't even know for sure, but there's a good chance he'll outlive us all. I never could convince him to move into the main house, so he remains in his cottage overlooking the sea* remembering his Lydisha. He's been a great help getting the halfway house construction started and I'm sure, with Donovan's help, he will watch over it as long as he's able.

Kar, you've been the best friend anyone could ever have. Please don't beat yourself up over the choices I made throughout my life and death. I've reconciled my shortcomings with God and He's got my back. Of that I'm sure. It's just that some days I'm better at remembering that than others. The days I don't are the ones that I disappear from my reality and shut everyone out. I know it frustrated and hurt you and everyone else that I loved and loved me back. I'm so sorry about that.

The smartest thing I ever did was let Dad handle my finances. I started sending him half of everything I made when I hit it big. I didn't need it all, so I figured I'd let him deal with it and look what happened. Good old Dad was always tight with a buck and an expert at squirreling it away. How many times did I hear Mom fuss at him for being so tight? But it turned out he was a good investor. Who knew? You might wanna let him take a look at your portfolio. Haha. Also, how about you let him and Roberta come for a visit to Ginger Star? You can hit me when you get to Heaven for that one. But really, she's not so bad and takes good care of him. I guess they really do love each other.

I woke up slowly in so many ways. You used to say you were the late bloomer, but I don't think so. You always had a good sense of right and wrong. I did for a while, but quickly shoved that aside after Mom died. When I look back, I know I didn't deal with losing Mom as I should have. Moving back in with Dad and the boys made it impossible to grieve her as I could have somewhere else. I woke up slowly to that one and only did after years of rehabs and therapists, did I ever grasp the reality of it.

The abortions . . . I'm not so sure. I know it never seemed to be the right time and I didn't want to have a kid that I might have to leave behind one day. I didn't want that kind of pain or to give it to anyone else. Forget the career, forget the timing of the abortions, they were all excuses in an effort to hide more pain of my reality. Problem is, I let each one of them into my heart and once I did that, I could never get past the guilt of letting them go. Every boy or girl I would see that was the age of the one I let go, reminded me that I would never see them on this side of the rainbow. Each one has a place inside of me that will always love them. Maybe I'll see them on the other side of the rainbow, or maybe I'm just crazy for thinking that could happen, who knows?

Thanks for putting up with my crazy dream of getting pregnant once I came back to the US. I spiraled again when I realized it would never happen. I woke up way too late for that dream to stick. And losing Timmy . . . that was more than I care to write about at the moment. Poor Dad. I can't imagine what he's going through.

Okay, now it's time to come clean. Remember when we went to the doctor about Hepatitis C? Well, his office called me a few days later and said they had more test results and wanted me back in their office. Turned out I didn't have Hep C, but did have an advanced case of cirrhosis of the liver. By now, you've probably already figured that out. Dang alcohol. Should have stuck with just weed, although that's not good for my lungs, I'm thinking. Guess we all have to die from something.

That's the bad news. Ready for some good news? I was a wreck when I left Doc Burns' office after the diagnosis. I don't remember getting behind the wheel of my car. I do remember crying and driving down Route 450. I drove down the highway screaming to myself and God. "Why is this happening? I'm finally trying to do things the right way and now this?" A car honked its horn at me. I was leaning into the next lane. I wiped my eyes with the back of my hand, trying to see better. I was scared. Really scared. I had always been able to stay a step ahead of death, but I must've slowed down without realizing it and now I knew I was going to take that step to the other side of the rainbow. But I wasn't ready. Not yet. I pulled into a parking lot to keep from wrecking the car. I looked out the window to have my eyes land on a cross on the side of a building.

A young woman knocked on the window of my car. I lifted my head from the steering wheel, grabbed a napkin from the console, and rolled down the window. She was worried about me, but I assured her I was okay. I put my head down on the steering wheel, cried, and had a good old self-pity party.

When I couldn't cry any more, I turned off the ignition, got out of the car, and walked inside the church. It was different from the Catholic church I'd grown up in. There was a cross, but no Jesus hanging on it. I didn't see any candles to light, so I went to the front and knelt down. I leaned over and cried like I'd never cried before. I cried for forgiveness for all the bad things I'd done in my life. That alone took a long time. I don't know how long I was there, but when I was done, a calmness surrounded me that I can't come close to describing, but something like a spirit.

Remember the duppy? When I would hear her, it always kinda scared me. She was always looking for something. Kinda like me. Never satisfied. Never at home where she landed. Well this wasn't a duppy, but had a presence that invisibly wrapped its arms around me. I think it was the spirit of God's love. Nothing but love. I know you've tried to tell me all this before and I wouldn't listen. I wish I had, but now I know it's true. I'm always waking up slowly, aren't I?

*Why did I wait so long to find this? God says He was always there. It was me who walked away. I hope this feeling haunts me forever and carries me to the other side of the rainbow when it's time.*

Karen put the letter down. She could see the answered prayers written in Ginger's script. In the past few years, Karen had struggled with questions regarding her own trust in God when she didn't have the guts to quit her day job and make the move to writing full time. She'd also questioned her faith when Ginger died. Why didn't she insist she go to a rehab yet again? How did she let this happen?

Finally, after endless rabbit holes and sleepless nights, it occurred to her that Ginger had made her own choices and mistakes. Karen knew she had to quit owning Ginger's choices and now her friend had given her license to do just that. She continued reading.

*As I write this, I realize how inadequate this letter is. I can't come close to finding the right words to describe the change inside of me. But I knew immediately what it was. It was forgiveness. Forgiveness for being weak and fearful. I was afraid of having a baby. Mom wasn't around to walk me through it. Afraid I wouldn't measure up, afraid of not having my career, afraid of just about everything. Fear has cosigned most of the decisions in my life. Now it no longer does. I feel as if a thousand-pound weight has been lifted off my shoulders. I can't explain it. I have a calmness that follows me everywhere. It must be what you've been trying to tell me all these years.*

Karen looked up from the letter. She was stunned, elated, and still confused. "Why didn't you tell me before this?" She took a deep breath, let it out, and continued reading.

*I woke up slowly to what was true, that's for sure. Anyway, I didn't see the need to share the news with anyone. It was such an epiphany and hard to describe. So please don't beat yourself up because I didn't tell you. I can see you headed down that rabbit hole right now, so just turn around and climb back out!*

Karen laughed out loud and then looked around to see who might be close by. Ginger knew her better than just about anyone except Lee, that was for sure. She had certainly gone down several what-if rabbit holes over the past few weeks since Ginger checked out. "Thanks, my friend. You know me well." She felt as if a weight had been lifted from her shoulders too. Ginger was reaching her from the other side of her rainbow. She looked back down at the letter in her hand and continued reading.

*Well, Kar, I guess it's time to wrap this up and move on to the other side of my rainbow. I'm kinda looking forward to finally finding that pot of gold along with the catching up with our moms and Timmy.*

*But before I sign off, I want to say that I hope you keep writing. Tell my story if you can. Let folks know not to hide from their pain. Not to let the ghosts of their mistakes haunt them like they did me. Let them know that their journey is a part of what they have to offer this world we live in. Let them know there is a ghost that will give them the peace they're looking for, only it's not a ghost, it's God.*

*And if you do write a book about me, just make sure I'm really pretty, sexy, and funny. If not, you'll find out what a real ghost is like.*

*And one more thing . . . Can you spread my ashes at Ginger Star? That way, I will get to go back there one more time.*

*Please stay out of the rabbit holes and every time you see a rainbow, think of me. Just know if you try and catch it, you'll have to get rained* on first. That will be me with a golden squirt gun pointed right at you.

Love ya forever,
Ginger

Karen looked up from the words that gave her the peace she never thought she'd find. Healing tears flowed down her cheeks. "Thank you, God." She sniffed and blew her nose with a napkin. "Thank you, Ging." She wiped away the last of her tears along with what was left of her mascara.

Karen realized that she had worked hard to recreate the friendship she and Ginger once shared. She'd felt a responsibility to her mom to keep the traditions of the past going. As Lee walked toward her, it dawned on her that finally, she was ready to move on. She now understood while learning from the past was a good thing, living in it was not.

—Chapter 20—

2011

## "SOMEWHERE OVER THE RAINBOW"
### Israel Kamakawiwo'ole

Karen had wondered about seeing Ashton again. She remembered how attracted to him she'd been all those years ago. She'd come to know that while she loved Lee, she wasn't dead. Love and loyalty are what mattered and for her, that was and always would be Lee.

They pulled their luggage to the curb outside the Montego Bay airport. Ashton ran up to greet them. He had aged, but as she'd discovered, Jamaican folks handled the years better than most. "Miss Karen! So good to see you, mi lady!"

"Ashton, it's been way too long!" She hugged him and stepped back. "This is my husband, Lee." The two men shook hands.

"I've heard a lot about you. Thanks so much for picking us up," Lee said.

"My pleasure. It so nice to know you'll be coming back to Ginger Star more often. I'm so sorry about Miss Ginga." They threw the luggage in the trunk and headed down the coastal road to Ocho Rios.

As they drove the North Coast, Karen and Lee were amazed at all the new resorts that dotted the coastline. "So, what have you been doing all these years?" she asked Ashton.

"Well, taking care of Ginger Star and her guests, mostly." Ginger Star had proven to be self-supporting. They had rented the estate out to tourists and business organizations over the years. The cash flow had been enough to keep its staff on board and the estate had been maintained well.

Ashton drove the highway toward Ocho Rios while Karen and Lee enjoyed the scenery along the North Coast. He looked in the rear-view mirror and remembered how smitten he'd been with Karen all those years ago. She was even prettier now than twenty years before. He felt bad calling her many times only to get cold feet and hang up without saying hello. But then he met Marta. He'd been happily married now for almost twenty years with two children of his own and now a grandbaby on the way. He was quick to share pictures of his family when they stopped at the roadside jerk pit for lunch. He was relieved that his love for his family eclipsed any fantasy he may have had about Karen.

Ashton pulled the white Toyota taxi up to the front of Ginger Star. The half-moon steps stretched out like arms as if to say "welcome back." A dog ran out and barked, but calmed down when he recognized Ashton. They stepped out of the car. It had been over twenty years since Karen wrote her manuscript at Ginger Star. "Oh my, it hasn't changed a bit." Karen stared at the great house.

"This place looks like a resort!" Lee said as he gawked at the beauty of the estate.

The three walked up the steps. A woman hurried out the door to the top step to meet them. "Willie!" Karen recognized the housekeeper who had become her friend all those years ago. "It's wonderful to see you!" Willie's eyes teared up with memories at the sight of Karen. "You haven't changed a bit!" Karen said.

"Oh, Miss Karen, 'tis a happy day that you come back to Ginger Star!" They hugged and Karen introduced her to Lee. "We were all so sorry to hear about Miss Ginga's passing. I know you love her like a sista," Willie said turning back toward Karen.

"Yes, I do and thanks for saying that. She loved and missed all of you so much." Karen felt a little bad about the last sentence. Truth was, Ginger had rarely talked about Jamaica. It was as if she'd tried to forget she had ever lived there.

Willie stepped back and took a good look at Karen. "And it look like we lost half of you!"

"Yeah, well, I had it to spare, that's for sure." Karen looked at Lee. "This is my husband, Lee."

Willie nodded and did a tiny bit of a curtsy. Lee reached out his hand and she took it. "Willie, it's great to finally meet you. Karen's told me so much about you and Ginger Star."

"Your wife is a wonderful woman. She no kill me when I almost lose her book!" Willie flashed her memorable smile.

"Yeah, I've heard that story told more than once!" They all laughed.

"Well, at least I live to tell about it!" Willie turned and waved over her shoulder. "Come, I show you to your room. Tis the same one." They followed Willie around Ginger Star. It looked much the same to Karen. Willie opened the door to the room she had stayed in when she'd been here last. "Dis is your same room and will be where you stay," Willie said. "Unless, of course, you choose another one. It is your house, you know." Karen smiled when she saw the same wicker desk in front of the window with the shutters thrown open.

"This room is my favorite. It looks just like it did before," Karen said and smiled. Drops of rain clung to the palm leaves outside the window. The sun peeked out after the brief shower, lighting them up like diamonds. "It's like living in a jungle."

After Lee and Ashton dropped the luggage in the bedroom, Willie showed them through the living room to the front yard that overlooked the sea. "This view never ceases to take my breath away." They stood and stared at the Caribbean. Its technicolor blues and greens radiated in the sunbeams that shot down between the rain clouds.

Lee walked down to the edge of the lawn and turned to face her. "Wow, Babe. It's just as spectacular as you described."

"Your dinner is cooked and you can eat when you get hungry. Jes take your time and holler at me when you ready," Willie said and made a quick retreat to the kitchen.

"Oh my goodness!" Karen said and pointed into the bushes. "There's Paulie and Carmen!" Paulie squawked hello and flew over to land near her feet. Ashton walked up and took a few pieces of mango from the platter on the dining room table and handed them to Karen.

"Here, Paulie," she tossed a piece of fruit on the tile in front of the bird. Carmen flew down next to him waiting her turn. Karen flipped her a piece.

"I can't believe they're still here," Lee said as he walked up next to Karen.

"You can see where Paulie looks a bit older. His feathers aren't quite as smooth anymore."

"Awwk!" Paulie cried as if in protest.

"Sorry, Bud. I have a few crows' feet and gray hairs myself these days," Karen laughed. She looked up at Lee. "I need to go see Byron and let him know we're here." Karen pointed to the pathway in the bushes, "There's the path. I'll be back in a while," she said to Lee and Ashton.

Lee took a step towards her. "You sure you don't want me to come with you?"

"No, I'll be fine." She walked up to him, kissed him on the cheek, walked across the yard, and disappeared into the bushes to find Byron. Paulie followed her. "Besides, looks like I'll have some company," she hollered back over her shoulder. The bird took the pathway branch by branch. Carmen went back to her original perch and stayed behind. The closer she got to the cottage, the more it was like stepping back in time. Nothing much had changed. The bougainvillea's pink canopy still provided shade all the way down. It still reminded her of walking through a tunnel. The doctor birds flitted back and forth while the Caribbean twinkled in the distance. Ginger Star cast its spell on her yet again. She'd forgotten the feeling, but quickly remembered how much she loved it here. She stopped when she saw Byron's cottage. It was much the same as before. A new tin roof had replaced the thatched one, but other than that, it was the same.

The old black man walked slowly out of the door leaning on a hand carved cane. His dreads were tucked up in his yellow, black, and green crocheted hat. His shirt was too big and unbuttoned. He was shorter than she remembered. "Byron?" she asked.

He turned and looked her way, shielding his eyes. "Who der?" His cloudy eyes couldn't see well in the sunshine.

"It's Karen. Do you remember me, Byron?"

"Miss Karen!" His cloudy eyes lit up. "I know your lovely voice." He slowly walked over leaning heavily on the cane. He reached out and she put her hand in his. He lifted it and gently kissed the back of it. The old Rasta man living in the bush could still make her feel like a princess.

"This old man no see like he used to, but I know your lovely voice. I am sorry to hear about Miss Ginga," he sighed. "I know you love her very much."

"Yes, it was quite a shock, but I brought her with me." She held up a Hecht's shopping bag that contained a vase with Ginger's ashes. She'd chosen this bag in remembrance of her and Ginger's moms. They'd spent many an afternoon shopping Red Dot sales at Hecht's when she and Ginger were kids. She knew it was fitting and appreciated by the heavenly Tensies. "I was hoping you would help me say goodbye."

He stared at the bag and reached over to peek inside. "She get smaller?"

Karen laughed. "Yeah, we had her cremated. It was what she wanted." She slipped her arm around his shoulder and looked out at the sea. Age made him smaller than the last time she was here. "She wanted us to leave her here with you, out there." She pointed to the sea. His eyes grew bigger and he smiled an even more toothless grin than years before.

"It look like you get smaller too. You only half the lady you once were, Miss Karen." He stepped back and took a closer look. Seeing people that only knew her as overweight still took some getting used to. She had shed those pounds, but the memory of living in an oversized body stayed with her. It was still easy to forget she was just a shadow of her former self.

"Yeah, I suppose I am, Byron," she smiled. "I must say, I don't miss the other half!"

"I think Miss Adria will like that Miss Ginga is back too," he said.

"Who's Adria?"

"Adria be the duppy of Ginger Star." He pulled a piece of sugar cane from a plastic bag in his pocket and offered her one. She shook her head. "Adria go away when Miss Ginga leave us."

"Are you serious?" Goose bumps formed on her arms and she felt the chill.

"Oh yes," he nodded. "Miss Adria had been walking the cliff of Ginger Star for many years. I know when she leave."

"Why didn't you tell me when I was here before?"

"I no want to scare you."

"What did you say her name was? Adria? Why would leaving Ginger here make her happy?"

"Miss Ginga always tink Miss Adria after her. She have problem sleeping sometimes and say she see her. Sometimes she tink it was her mudda, but no."

"How did you know it wasn't her mother?"

"Miss Adria always wear the same gardenia scent." Goose bumps ran up Karen's back. She wrapped her arms together to get warm. She remembered rolling her eyes when Ginger had said the same thing.

"But why would she think she was *after* her?"

"Me not sure why. Jes know dat Miss Adria die many, many years ago right here at Ginger Star," he wiped his brow with his sleeve. "She wander the house and cliff ever since." Byron pointed toward the cotton tree where duppies were rumored to hang out as they walked back toward Ginger Star. The roots of the tree lived above the ground and were as tall as she was. Plenty of room for duppies to hang out. "Sometime, the duppy jes want company."

The sun was beginning to dip behind the mountains. "Well, I'd better get back up to the house. Can you walk up with me to meet my husband?" Byron nodded and slowly stood up, leaning on his cane.

"Yes, but wait. I get sometin' for you," he turned and walked back inside his cottage. She stepped under a tree to catch some shade while she waited. He came back out with his cane in one hand and a bowl in the other. He handed her the pottery. "Dis is yours."

She took the bowl from him not understanding at first and then she remembered. "This is the bowl I made all those years ago!" He nodded and smiled as only he could. It warmed her heart as she remembered his kindness then and now. She remembered how therapeutic the pottery wheel had been. She wrapped her arms around him and squeezed.

"I bake it and save it for you. I pray one day you come back, and you did."

She ran her fingers over the pottery and turned it upside down. She saw her initials and the date, 1983, twenty-eight years earlier. "You saved it all these years." She looked at him and smiled. "You are a true friend, Byron. Thank you." He grinned, nodded, and looked down at the ground.

"Well, let's go. Lee's going to be wondering where I am." They turned and walked slowly up the pathway back toward Ginger Star. The island's beauty wrapped itself around her. The sun shined through the green of the vegetation with colorful flowers peeking around every corner. "So, Byron, how have you been?" She could see the years were beginning to take their toll on him.

"Oh, dis old man feeling pretty good for an old one."

"Well, you look great to me. The years are working on all of us." They walked back up the hill to the opening of Ginger Star's lawn that overlooked the sea. She waved at Lee and Ashton who were sitting in the large wicker chairs on the veranda waiting for her. They stood and walked down to greet her and Byron.

"Lee, this is my old friend, Byron." The men shook hands. Lee towered over Byron who seemed even smaller to her now.

"Karen said you were a great friend to her when she was here. Thanks for looking after her," Lee said to the old man.

"Miss Karen a great lady. You a lucky mon!"

Lee and Ashton laughed. "Yes, I am for sure. What's that?" Lee asked reaching for the bowl in her hand."

"This is a bowl that Byron showed me how to make on his wife, Lydisha's pottery wheel when I was here before." She handed the bowl to him. "He fired it after I left and saved it for me all this time."

"That's incredible. You are just as special as Karen always told me." Lee patted Byron on the back. "Thanks for looking after her like you did." The older man beamed and nodded.

"Hey, Byron, remember this painting?" Karen walked up the steps into the living room that faced the lawn. She pointed to the portrait of the woman in the blue dress leaning against the wall. She'd taken it down from Ginger's fireplace and brought it back to Jamaica, where it belonged.

The old man walked closer and stopped short. He stooped and put his hands on his knees squinting through his cloudy eyes. "Dat Miss Adria." He didn't move. "Da duppy. I told you she back!" He stood, turned, and looked at Karen. The scent of gardenias wafted through the area. Karen and Lee looked at each other reading the other's mind. If you didn't believe in something, it couldn't be real, right?

"Well, maybe we can put all this to rest once and for all," Karen said feeling less confident than she sounded. "Do you think you could help us?" The old man smiled again.

"Yes. If we put her ashes in the sea, Miss Ginga, she will no more be a duppy."

"Really?"

"Yes, Miss Karen. Duppies no like salt." The old man winked.

The river water followed the path created over thousands of years from the top of the mountains in the center of Jamaica to the sea. It twisted through the green Jamaican forests. The river turned itself into waterfalls and creeks as it traveled through towns and villages down the face of the mountains. Its sound went from gurgling to splashing, to a constant rush of soothing whispers until its ultimate merging with the Caribbean Sea.

They stood at the bottom of the river where the waterfall met the sea. Despite the ninety-five-degree temperature, the mist from the fresh water falling into the salt water in front of them, kept them cool.

It was a diverse group that gathered to pay tribute to Ginger. Karen, Lee, Donovan, Donna, Pinky, Byron, Judy Ann, Matthew, Arlene, Willie, and Ashton each loved her in his or her own way. The roar of the falling water forced them to holler to one another to be heard.

"Somewhere over the rainbow," Karen started to sing as loud as she could and the others joined in. The crashing water of the falls did little to drown out their resolve. They finished the song.

"Ginga, we love you," Donovan said as he opened the aqua vase. He turned the vase upside down and Ginger's ashes floated down to the swirling water. Some were captured in the floating mist. "Jamaica love you and so do we."

Matthew, their neighbor from the days living on the hillside, stepped up next to Donovan. "Yeah, she loved Jamaica and it love her back. The now grownup kids of Steer Town still talk about her," Matthew said with his arm around Arlene, his wife. Arlene stood next to Pinky who held a baby on her hip. They had all met earlier that morning to sprinkle some of Ginger's ashes on the pathway up to their old hillside home before meeting again at Ginger Star.

Karen knew this would bring a smile to Ginger's face. She was here in spirit, that much Karen knew. It was a good feeling to know she was finally at peace.

"I don't know about you, but this feels so right to me," she said to them. Karen opened her Bible and read Romans 8:28, "And we know that in all things God works for the good of those who love him, who have been called according to His purpose." She looked at the eclectic group that had gathered to honor Ginger. "Our friend struggled throughout most of her life, trying to come to grips with grief that went unresolved. When she found Windsor, she found her reason for being here. She found her purpose and a way to reach out to others with their own unresolved issues." She closed the Bible, tucked it under her arm, and they joined hands. "May many lives be blessed and benefited from the love she is showing from the other side of her rainbow."

They turned and walked as a group down the shoreline to the steps that would take them back up to Ginger Star. Donovan carried the urn that had held her ashes. Byron handed him the lid and when he did, he stopped, grabbed hold of Donovan's hand and wouldn't let go. Everyone gathered close to see why. Bryon's eyes opened wide as looked at the heart-shaped birthmark on Donovan's hand. "You have the heart?"

"Yeah? It's my birthmark." Donovan stepped back a bit and looked at the older man. "My daughter have it too." He nodded toward Donna.

"It the same mark as Miss Adria had," Byron brought up the duppy again.

"Adria, the Ginger Star duppy?" Donovan asked. Karen was amazed that Donovan knew about her.

"Yeah," Bryon let go of Donovan's hand. "She jes come back."

"How did you know about the Ginger Star duppy?" Karen asked Donovan.

"Here in Jamaica, tales of duppies float all around us," Donovan said. "Adria is a famous duppy."

"Well, we brought her back it seems," Karen said not believing her own words. "Remember that painting you sent to the States when you boxed up Ginger's stuff?" Donovan nodded. "That was Adria. We brought it back. Come on, I'll show you."

They walked back up the cliff side steps and back to Ginger Star. Karen walked over to the portrait where Lee had left it propped against the living room wall. She stooped down to take a closer look at the painting. Adria's left hand held onto her wide brimmed hat and on her right hand that held onto her blue dress, was the same heart shaped birthmark.

"Wow, Donovan, it looks just the same as yours and Donna's," Karen said and stood back up. She took his hand in hers. "It's *exactly* the same."

Karen woke with a start. That sometimes happened when an idea popped into her head for an article, novel, or just a task to write down for the next day. She grabbed the notepad and pen she kept on the nightstand, even in Jamaica, for her middle of the night ideas. "EM Sam. Pitch MMA." She'd been sleeping soundly before she woke. The cool Jamaican breeze found its way through the windows. She lay back down, rolled over, draped her arm over Lee, and drifted back to sleep.

"It seems strange that this is really our place. Ours and Donovan's," Karen said to Lee as they ate lunch on the veranda.

"I know. I feel like we're on vacation in some resort instead of our own place. I could get used to this." Lee reached over and grabbed the pepper. They coexisted quite well during her novel writing short term sabbatical. She rose when he got up to head out for a morning of golf or fishing and she stayed behind to write. He would get back by early afternoon and they had the rest of the day to spend together.

"I think I remember waking up in the middle of the night with a good idea for a new project. I'll be right back," she jumped up and headed to the bedroom, returning with her bedside notebook in hand. She was almost done with the novel she was working on and always thinking about the next project.

"Well? What is it?" He looked up from his salad.

"Can't tell you yet. Don't wanna jinx it. I'll send an email to my agent's office for an appointment when I'm done with lunch."

"Guess I'll just have to peek at that notepad when you're not looking." He grinned and looked at her out of the corner of his eye. Yep, he got the reaction he was looking for. Her eyes flew open.

"It's written in my personal shorthand. You'll never figure it out," she said as she closed the notebook. He let her believe that, but made a bet with himself that he already knew what it was she would write.

A few weeks later, Karen walked into Samantha's office. The agency had just moved and there were still boxes sitting in the corner waiting to be unpacked. She stood and stared out the window that looked onto a brick courtyard.

She'd gone through several agents before she figured out they weren't all created equal. It took years, but she finally found the right one. It had been a painfully slow and disappointing process with years of hoping, waiting, and rewriting, but now she was truly confident she'd made the right choice by settling on Samantha.

She heard the door open and turned to see Samantha standing there. She was a tall attractive thirty-something with long black hair that was pulled back into her signature ponytail. She wore a white blouse tucked into a pair of fitted black slacks. "Sam! I love your new office. Looks like you're moving on up." The two women hugged instead of shaking hands. While they weren't best friends, they had always liked each other and enjoyed their business relationship.

"Yeah, except it's the first floor, but hey, I do have a window." Samantha motioned for Karen to sit down as she went around to the other side of her desk. She pulled out her chair and sat with her arms crossed in front of her on the desk. "So, what's new in your world? I was sorry to hear about Ginger." The newspapers had carried the story of Ginger's death and made a big deal about it when they discovered she was Ginger Starling, the former reggae star and not just Ginger O'Reilly. She knew Karen and Ginger had a history.

"Yeah, we'd been friends since we were five years old." Karen didn't think she would ever get used to referring to Ginger in the past tense. "I wrote the draft of my first manuscript while at her plantation in Jamaica."

"I think I remember you telling me that once." She reached for her coffee cup on the edge of the desk and took a drink. "Allie said you wanted to talk about a new project. What do you have in mind?" Samantha leaned on her desk with her elbows, put her head in her hands, ready to listen. Karen was a talented writer and Samantha had just sold and released her first book a few months earlier. Sales were good, not great, but promising for a first-time author.

Karen pulled out the printed manuscript. "It's a very rough first draft. I've been working on it for a little while now. I'll email you an electronic copy, but I know you prefer to read it on paper." She took a deep breath and tried to remember the pitch she'd rehearsed. Her memory left her stranded, so she started from scratch. "Well, Ginger's story is part of what I want to tell." Karen proceeded to fill Samantha in on the past thirty years, Ginger living in Jamaica, getting involved with the wrong people, and eventually losing her life to alcohol and addiction. "I'll never forgive myself for not at least trying to do an intervention. She's gone now and I have to live with that reality every day. I know this might just be my way of coping, by writing it all down, but I think there's a pretty good story here too. I'm sure you'll let me know."

"Well, yeah. I sure will," Samantha thought Karen might just be on to something good. "Do you want to do it as a biography? With Ginger being a former rock star, it could be quite timely."

"I'm not sure, but I could talk to her family to see what they think." Karen shifted in her chair and let out a sigh of relief that Sam thought the book might be a good idea.

"Okay, I'll take a look at the draft and you check with them. I think you might have something here."

"What's your working title?" Samantha flipped through the pages to see if it was noted.

"My Mother's Apprentice."

# Epilogue

When I wrote *Stuck in the Onesies (SITO)* I didn't know there would be a sequel. It wasn't until SITO's readers wanted more of the characters, that I put down the other novel I was working on and started on *My Mother's Apprentice*. The "other novel" will now be the third in the *Stuck in the Onesies* trilogy.

*Stuck in the Onesies* had stuck me back in the onesies because of the way I'd written the ending (not knowing there would be a sequel) where SITO was loosely based on a true story. *Stuck in the Onesies* had already told some of Ginger and Karen's story, so I had to start out with the truth, at least some of it. I decided to make it mostly fictional with the exception of a thread in Ginger's life. The "real" Ginger was not a rock star in Jamaica, but did struggle with addiction. She and I talked about my writing a book that included her and she picked out the name of Ginger. It was a throwback to Gilligan's Island and the pretty redhead on the old sitcom. Our Ginger was even better looking, just so you know.

When I was writing *My Mother's Apprentice*, I toyed with the idea of giving Ginger a "happy ending," thinking that if I didn't, my readers would complain that I killed off my main characters every time. Besides, Ginger deserved a happy ending even if she didn't get one in real life. But then again, why was I telling her story anyway? Just to have a sequel? No, it was more than that.

While going through this time of decision making with regards to the ending, I attended a luncheon in honor of author, Lisa Scottoline. During her talk she said, "Because it doesn't connect if it's not true." That was good enough for me.

Writing has always been a therapeutic exercise for me. It helps me to process things when I write down what's happening. It started with letter writing many years ago when we moved away to West Virginia (sound familiar?). Evidently, novel writing can do the same. I decided to make some sense out of what had happened to her. I needed to deal with the regrets that I had. I needed to show her struggle.

They tell you to "write what you know." Well, I've spent a lot of time in Jamaica over the years doing mission work and vacationing. Setting *My Mother's Apprentice* there enabled me to write about a place that lives in my heart. The third part of the trilogy will also be set in Jamaica, but back in the 1700s. I suppose I'll have to go back to Jamaica and do some research. Any excuse will do.

Not long after Ginger died, my husband, Jeff, and I had an RV permanently parked on Chincoteague Island, Virginia (remember, I said it was "mostly fictional"). Our neighbor next door was a few years older than us, but had Ginger lived, she would have looked just like Lottie. A slender red head that tanned great, smoked cigarettes, and loved to fish. Lottie left out every morning on her golf cart for the pier to go fishing. I would look at Jeff and say, "There goes Ginger!" It saddened me to think of all the fun we would have had as old ladies riding around on golf carts and beaching it every day in our retirement. Now it's just my laptop and me. No Ginger or Jeff. But don't feel sorry for me. I'll be that old lady on the golf cart heading for the beach and if it's raining, I'll be home writing, pretending to be in Jamaica.

I hope I have done Ginger's story justice. If *My Mother's Apprentice* has encouraged just one person to take that step toward an intervention for a loved one, then I've accomplished my goal. And so has Ginger.

If you have someone in your life that struggles with addiction, please don't ignore it. Step up and talk to him or her about it. Don't worry about them being mad at you. I was and you saw how that turned out. At least you will know you tried. It's their journey, not yours. Prayer helps and handing them over to God isn't easy, but is often our only choice. Let Him handle the rest.

# Acknowledgments

First of all, I want to thank the fans of *Stuck in the Onesies*. You asked for a sequel and birthed *My Mother's Apprentice*. There are too many to list here, but you know who you are.

I could not have gotten through without the honest feedback from my beta reader, Susan Konow Walker. Also, a huge thank you to my critique group and fellow authors, Kari Alice and Frank Hopkins who were faithful to the last word. Thanks for keeping me focused.

My Jamaican friends have been a wealth of information for me. There are too many of you to list here, but Susan Allen, Elet Brown, and Judy Ann MacMillan are of special note. Susan helped me so much with the patois interpretations. Elet (my dear BB) helped with many details, and Judy Ann graciously allowed me to share her lifetime's work of art with my readers (check her out on Google!).

I'll always be grateful to Kevin McGrath for coming up with the title of *My Mother's Apprentice*. He knows me well and as a result, knows my mom too. I am and always will be her apprentice.

Over thirty people volunteered to join the *My Mother's Apprentice* Launch Team, too many to list here, but I love each one of you for stepping up to help. All of you pushed out social media posts as the book was released and collaborated on everything from the book's cover to how to hold a launch party on-line and in person. A huge thanks to those that took part in *My Mother's Apprentice* Review Team; Deb Lyman, Sheryl Poplstein, Karen Thompson, Wendy Walker, and Mary Buso. I appreciate your dedication to perfection and willingness to jump in at the last minute.

Thank you, my dear friend, Lynn (aka, Ginger) who was always my biggest fan. She was constantly encouraging me to write. She understood that while I might write some truth, I had to mix in a little fiction to fill in the gaps. She crossed over to the other side of the rainbow way too soon, but left behind love and smiles that will carry me until I join her. I'll miss you always and thank you for allowing me to share some of your story. You live on in my heart as do those who have crossed over to your side of the rainbow. Please give them all a hug from me.

Thanking my family seems trite, but they are always there for me. They support my passion for writing. (even when they find themselves in a blog). You are, and always will be, my heartbeat.

Most of all, I thank God for constant encouragement and correction. Without You, I am nothing.

# About the Author

Diana McDonough wrote her first novel, *Stuck in the Onesies,* over the course of ten years while pursuing her career with Ecolab. She retired after 26 years to pursue writing full time in 2016 publishing *Stuck in the Onesies* in January 2017.

*My Mother's Apprentice* is her second novel and is again, creative non-fiction. Her next book, *Ginger Star* (working title), will be the third in the *Stuck in the Onesies* series.

Visit Diana's website at www.DianaMcDonough.com and on her Facebook pages for both *Stuck in the Onesies* and *My Mother's Apprentice.*

# My Mother's Apprentice

## BOOK CLUB DISCUSSION QUESTIONS
## — SPOILER ALERT! —

1. What was your initial reaction to the book? Did it hook you right away, or take some time?

2. What do you think of the setting? Could the book have been set anywhere else and been as effective?

3. Was the book plot based or character driven?

4. What was your favorite quote or passage?

5. Did you pick out any themes throughout the book?

6. Which character did you relate to the most? What was it that made you feel connected?

7. How did you feel about the ending? What did you like and what do you wish had been different?

8. How did the end of the book leave you feeling?

9. Did the book change your perspective about anything?

10. How did you feel about the communication between Karen and Ginger?

11. What would have made the biggest difference for Ginger? Where was her ghost?

12. Who influences who?

13. What deception do you perceive in the story?

14. What feelings did *MMA* evoke for you?

15. If you could ask one question of the author, what would it be?

16. What do you think of the book's title, *My Mother's Apprentice?*

17. Was the story believable? If not, why?

# Thank you!

I trust you enjoyed this small peek into my world and I would love to hear from you. If you enjoyed reading this novel, please consider leaving a review and share the joy of reading. For those of you who are not comfortable using your given name, you can use "Avid Reader" instead.

It's simple to leave a review. Go to your favorite online book store listed below and type in *"My Mother's Apprentice"* in the search bar.

Click on book icon, then "customer reviews" or scroll to "write a review".

Amazon: https://www.amazon.com

Barnes & Noble: https://www.barnesandnoble.com/

Goodreads: https://www.goodreads.com/author/
show/16304780.Diana_McDonough

## Do you want even more?

To receive updates on Diana's next novel, sign up for her blog at www.dianamcdonough.com/about.

diana.
mcdonough1

dianamcdonough

diana-
mcdonough-
826a89121/

dianamcdonough

CPSIA information can be obtained
at www.ICGtesting.com
Printed in the USA
JSHW030245230322
24154JS00003B/10